WALKING ON AIR

WALKING ON AIR

Christina Jones

WINDSOR
PARAGON

First published 2000
by HarperCollins*Publishers*
This Large Print edition published 2013
by AudioGO Ltd
by arrangement with
HarperCollins*Publishers*

Hardcover   ISBN: 978 1 4713 1234 2
Softcover   ISBN: 978 1 4713 1235 9

British Library Cataloguing in Publication Data available

Printed and bound in Great Britain by
MPG Books Group Limited

For Rob and Laura, with all my love.

Thank you both for always managing to keep my
head in the clouds and my feet on the ground.

acknowledgements

Thank you—

To everyone at Harper Collins, especially Susan Watt, Fiona McIntosh, Jane Harris, Martin Palmer and Yvette Cowles, for all their hard work, patience, and their wonderful friendship.

To Sarah Molloy, my agent and a very brave lady. I owe her one or two . . .

To The Utterly Butterly Barnstormers—the most intrepid and incredible wingwalking outfit in the world. To Helen Tempest, Rachel Huxford, Sara Mozayeni, and Juliette Pendleton, the stunningly glamorous wingwalkers; Vic Norman and Mike Dentith, the no-less-glamorous pilots; Helen Holness in the Engine Shed office and Tony and Andy the engineers (also all glamorous—of course!). Thank you all a million times for trusting me in the Boeing Stearman, for giving up so much of your precious time to make sure I got everything right, for the amazing hospitality at Rendcomb Airfield, and for becoming my friends.

To Michael Owen (no, not *that* one), ace aviator at Jersey Aero Club, who was fearless enough to take me up in a two-seater plane and teach me the technical bits.

To all the additional people who helped with the wing-walking information, especially Marilyn

Fountain, Katrina Hocking and John Johnson.

To the *Essex Belle*—the most beautiful Shorts in the air—and her crew, who flew me backwards and forwards across the English Channel and gave me some of the most unforgettable experiences of my life.

To Chris, the KLM pilot, who taught me so much about happy landings.

To Faith and Stan Hardy, my friends since childhood, who allowed me to nick them and borrow their perfect lives.

To Clare Cooper and Gaynor Davies for their unstinting support and friendship, and for being such good sports.

summer

chapter one

'Whiteacres Industrial Estate, please, dear.' The taxi's rear door was yanked open by a plumpish figure wearing khaki shorts: 'You do know where it is, dear, don't you?'

Billie Pascoe, jolted from some serious daydreaming in the driving seat, did her customary customer eye-meet—which was slightly hampered on this occasion by sunglasses through the rear-view mirror. 'Yes, of course. Oh, would you like me to put your luggage in the boot?'

'No thanks, dear. It's only a few bits and bobs, and anyway you really don't look strong enough to be humping baggage.'

The woman, who could have been anywhere between forty and seventy, was accompanied by various carrier bags, a shocking pink sombrero, and a small vanity case. After an indecisive tussle with the sombrero, she rammed it on her head and thumped heavily on to the rear seat.

She beamed kindly at Billie through the driving mirror. 'I always like to get a cab with a female driver because you can't be too careful, if you know what I mean, dear, but to be honest, I thought you were someone's *child*. You simply don't look old enough to be driving a taxi ...'

Billie grinned as she moved the Granada smoothly away from the Spicer Centre taxi rank and into Amberley Hill's mid-morning traffic. She'd heard the same remarks at least three times a week, every week, for the year and a half that she'd been driving for Reuben's Cabs. Being a smidgen over five feet tall, weighing a smidgen over seven stones, and with layers of short blonde hair, she'd probably pass for Zoë Ball on an off-day.

She'd never felt it necessary to reassure her passengers that she was all of twenty-six and a half, and having been brought up on a farm she'd been shifting sacks of sheep feed and hay bales since she was old enough to walk, and therefore stowing the average weekly shop or holiday suitcase in the Granada's boot would pose her no problems whatsoever.

Leaving the town, and heading for the bypass which linked Amberley Hill to Whiteacres, Billie glanced again in the mirror. Her passenger was now nursing the sombrero, gazing out of the window and showing no inclination to chat, which suited Billie fine. There were things she needed to think about. Things that needed mulling over . . . Things like changing direction, taking stock, getting a grip; things like jacking in the taxi-driving and being in control of her own destiny. Again.

'Lovely day, isn't it?' The lady suddenly loomed forward, interrupting Billie's mental letter of resignation to Reuben Wainwright, proprietor of Reuben's Cabs, slimeball, and long-term bane of her life. 'Flaming June with a vengeance. It always makes one yearn for silver sands and transparent turquoise seas on days like these, doesn't it?'

Billie nodded as she overtook a string of lorries heading for the retail village and inhaled vast quantities of toxic fumes through the open window. 'Not much chance of that round here, though. We're totally land-locked.'

Away from Amberley Hill, with its gently undulating roads and quiet crescents of greystone

4

houses, the countryside had quickly become flat and barren. It was a grimly desolate area, commandeered in the sixties for London overspill housing and providing just that. Whiteacres, with its industrial estate, retail village, and scrubby airfield, was as far removed from bucolic bliss as it was possible to get.

Her passenger beamed. 'Physically, yes—but I'm a great believer in dreams, dear. In wish-fulfilment. If we want something badly enough I believe we all have the power to achieve it.'

Billie wasn't sure. She was pretty convinced that however much her passenger may long for seaside splendours, all the wishing in the world wasn't going to bring coastal erosion galloping across the county to engulf the urban wasteland of Whiteacres.

Anyway, she'd had the sea, and the sand, and the glorious countryside at home in Devon, and she'd left it, because—well, because, among other reasons, at twenty-five she'd thought that by moving away from the cosiness of the farm, and her undemanding post as the most junior reporter on the *Devon Argus*, she could prove that she was a person in her own right, and could stand or fall alone. Oh, and because of Kieran Squires, of course, but she'd rather not think about that . . . No, she'd thought that London was going to provide everything she'd ever wanted. London had lasted for four short, amazing, exciting, heart-breaking weeks.

She shook her head sadly at the foolishness of that long-ago innocence as she indicated to turn the Granada onto the Whiteacres slip road. There had been so many dreams—most of them, she admitted miserably, connected with Kieran Squires—and they'd all turned spectacularly to dust.

Still, at least now, with the small inheritance left by Granny Pascoe, and the careful stashing away of her cab tips and her overtime payments, she had a reasonable sum of money to invest in her future, which was, she thought, a big step forward from last time. Last time she'd left London with nothing but the clothes she was wearing; last time she'd arrived in Amberley Hill without even the price of a hot meal or a cup of tea; last time she'd made every mistake it was possible to make. This time there would be no mistakes; this time she'd do things properly—

'Oh, my God!'

A tiny plane had suddenly slithered low overhead, dipping its wings, it seemed, almost onto the Granada's bonnet as it skimmed the slip road. The sun burnished it with dazzling silver stars as it tipped sideways and made its approach to Whiteacres airfield. Billie, her hands damp on the steering wheel, instinctively waited for the crash.

'Made you jump, did it?' Her passenger scrabbled her way free of the sombrero. 'You get used to them round here. Such pretty little things, aren't they? I love to watch them and imagine where they're going. I do so envy people who can fly away, don't you?'

Billie didn't. Flying, as far as Billie was concerned, if it had to be undertaken at all, should be done in semiconscious comfort with at least four hundred other passengers, a nail-biting Nicholas Cage film, intravenous gin and tonics, and a scorching resort waiting at the end of the terror. Flying had absolutely nothing to do with

6

these flimsy airborne sofas enclosed in Perspex and fuelled by Calor gas.

'Um—I'm a bit of an aerophobe, actually,' Billie smiled shakily into the mirror. 'I think if I was going to make my escape it would have to be on foot.'

Settling the Granada into the tailback of traffic heading for the industrial estate, Billie sighed. What exactly had she got to show for nearly two years' independence? The London disaster, followed by humiliation—and now a job she disliked, a boss she disliked even more, and a share in an Amberley Hill basement flat with Miranda the man-eater. She also had predicable social life—yo-yoing as she did with the rest of the girls between Mulligan's Genuine Irish Ale House and Bazooka's Nite Spot—and no man, which was understandable after the débâcle with Kieran Squires, and no prospects of anything happening to change the pattern.

Even if she gave up driving for Reuben's Cabs, what on earth was she going to do? She was hardly qualified for anything. Driving, at least, gave her some freedom. Maybe she'd start up her own minicab firm if Reuben's reference wasn't too damning . . . She'd employ lady drivers to take children to school, and OAPs to out-patients, and harassed mothers to Tesco. Or maybe—just maybe—she'd become a proper chauffeur . . . hired by the rich and famous to sweep up to the palatial porticoes of the Savoy or the Dorchester . . .

Her passenger slid forward again. 'Turn in here, dear. Just through those gates on the airfield's perimeter fence. It's the back way into the units and much quicker. Just drive on past Arrivals and Departures and follow the road round.'

Billie turned, sweeping beneath the archway that proclaimed they were now entering Whiteacres Airport—a grand misnomer, she felt, for the small airfield with two tarmacked runways, a couple of grass landing strips, and the sort of ramshackle outbuildings that should have Kenneth More stomping about with a white scarf. Not even the perfect blue sky and spiralling June sunshine could quite relieve the look of neglect. Notice boards slapped dismally backwards and forwards against flaking paintwork; the light bulbs illuminating the signs had gone out; the buildings were all decorated in sepia shades; and everything had an air of desperate desolation as small clumps of whey-faced people clutched hand luggage and looked understandably apprehensive. The various planes dotted around on the scrubby grass appeared to belong to the post-war era, and probably seated two people at a push. Who, Billie wondered as she drove past, issued the passengers with their helmets and goggles?

'Just here, dear. Stop anywhere. I want the second one along from the far end.'

The industrial units were in a towering row behind the airfield's perimeter lights. Each one was the size of a large aeroplane hangar, and built uncompromisingly from grey breeze blocks with sky-high corrugated iron roofs. There were six in all, and they cast massive sombre shadows across the brilliance of the morning. Billie pulled the Granada to a halt on the parking area of unevenly slabbed concrete, just managing to avoid the carcasses of two burned-out hatchbacks which seemed to provide the only spot of light artistic relief.

'Lovely, dear. Thank you so much.' The plump lady started to scramble from the back of the taxi, collecting her scattered belongings as she did so. 'Now, how much do I owe you?'

Billie told her, gazing at the surrounding ugliness. How could anyone bear to work here? 'Oh, no—' she looked down at the wodge of notes in her hand—'I can't take this much.'

'Of course you can,' her passenger beamed. 'You've given me a lovely ride—and to be honest, if I hadn't seen you sitting there on the rank, I might not have had the courage to do this.'

'Sorry?' Billie furrowed her brow. 'I don't understand—Oh, not again!'

Another two-seater plane suddenly spurted into life on one of the runways, bounced a bit, then hurled itself into the sky at a suicidal angle. Billie held her breath, waiting for it to plummet earthwards, but with a sputtering roar it vanished into the steely grey clouds. Her palms were sweating with second-hand terror.

'Goodness—you really don't like aeroplanes, do you?' Her passenger laughed kindly. 'Look, dear, unless you have to dash off, why don't you come in and have a cup of tea? You look like your nerves could do with calming . . . I'm Sylvia, by the way.'

There were strict rules that Reuben's Cabs' drivers never, ever, on pain of death, accepted hospitality from customers . . . Oh, sod Reuben and his rules. 'I'm Billie Pascoe. And a cup of tea would be lovely. I'll just radio into the office and tell them where I am . . .'

She did, speaking to Veronica, Reuben's radio operator, explaining that she'd just dropped off at Whiteacres and would be available to pick up a return fare at the airport or the retail village in about half an hour.

'All sorted?' Sylvia, wearing the sombrero and a pair of Chloe diamante sunglasses, tugged her double doors open. 'Good-oh. Welcome to paradise.'

Billie stepped through the doors. Although it was scorchingly hot outside, inside Sylvia's unit the temperature was throbbing at equatorial. Verdant palm trees fronded into plastic pools of ludicrous blue, a fountain trickled into a turquoise waterfall, and every inch of the warehouse was vibrating with spicy colour. Vivid pinks and oranges, scalding yellow and searing red: every inch of the walls was awash with tropical splendour. Two plastic parrots and an evilly grinning monkey swung listlessly from a tangle of vines. Billie wouldn't have been at all surprised to spot David Attenborough.

Totally bemused, she smiled warily. 'I—um— seem to have wandered into a parallel universe . . .'

'Bit of a stunner, isn't it?' Sylvia picked her way through a maze of polythene-wrapped bundles and lodged the sombrero on a raffia-roofed cocktail bar. 'Watch where you step, dear. I'm a bit overcrowded. I could do with more space, really.' She waved at a full display of highly coloured bottles behind the bar. 'Piña colada? Small chartreuse? No? I suppose not if you're driving. We'd better stick with a cuppa . . .'

As Sylvia rattled through a multicoloured bead curtain, Billie had to make an effort not to pinch herself. She'd probably wake up in a moment in the flat, with her Winnie-the-Pooh pyjamas all of a tangle, and find Miranda with her early morning bug-eyes raiding her dressing table in search of a

10

stale Marlboro Light.

'There now,' Sylvia said, her head on one side through the beads like an inquisitive budgie. 'That's got the kettle on. Now let me explain, dear . . . I'd had a bit of a row with Douglas, my husband. I'd flounced out of the house all full of burning indignation, like you do, saying that I was going to work and not to wait up.' She indicated the vanity case. 'I'd even made a big show of packing a few things to make him think I was leaving. But my courage had almost deserted me by the time I'd reached the taxi rank. And, you see, if you'd been a man, I wouldn't have got into the cab, and I'd have slunk home again, and Douglas would have won. But it was you, and I'm here, and I haven't lost face. So, it was fate, don't you think?'

'Er—well—yes, maybe . . . So, have you? Left him, I mean?'

Sylvia shook her head. 'I haven't got the guts, dear, sadly. No, I'll just hang on here for a while and hope that when there's no meal on the table this evening he might miss me. Then I'll go home and we'll spend three days not speaking . . . It's all a bit of a bugger, to be honest.'

Billie, feeling nothing but sympathy, squeezed herself between the packages, staring at huge posters for Goa and the Maldives and the Florida Keys. 'What exactly do you do here? Are you some sort of travel agent?'

'Only in my fevered imagination.' Sylvia smiled ruefully. 'But I do so like playing the part. No, my dear, it's far more mundane. I'm a sorter, packer, and distributor of dreams for the travel industry.' She looked at the bewilderment on Billie's face. 'I send out the brochures to the shops, dear.'

11

Billie followed Sylvia to a revolving dais in the centre of the room. Stacks of brochures were piled on the floor, and, expertly, Sylvia flipped up half a dozen from each to make a complete set as the rotunda revolved.

'Simple,' she said, 'and deadly dull. So—I spice things up a bit. I'll never go to any of the places I see in these little beauties—' she tapped the highly coloured glossy brochures 'so I made my own resort here. The guys who do the deliveries and collections all think I'm bonkers—but who cares, eh?'

Billie shook her head in admiration. 'So the brochures come from the printers, and you sort them and bag them into mixed lots and then—'

'They go off to the travel agents. About ten from each tour company in every batch. I even do my own shrink-wrapping. These travel shops don't have storage facilities or the hundreds of brochures that are issued, so it's nonstop work for me. All year round. It was a gap in the market, you see. They pensioned me off from the civil service and I was out of my mind with boredom. My Douglas told me he'd divorce me if I wasted my endowment—but I thought balls, Douglas, it's my money. So I approached all the big holiday companies and put myself forward as a brochure co-ordinator—and well, here we are. He's never forgiven me for being successful. Oh, that sounds like the kettle. Excuse me a sec . . .'

Sylvia's scheme was so simple—and dead clever. Billie stared at the tropical splendour in admiration. If only she could do something half so inventive. If only she had the nous to tell Reuben that she was definitely leaving the taxis, and plunge

12

Granny Pascoe's few thousand into a similar plan . . . A plan that would bring independence and some self-respect . . . She sat down next to the waterfall. *Could* she do something like this? Obviously, yes— as long as she had the premises, the idea, and a ton of courage. Billie knew she didn't have the first, definitely didn't have the second, and was feeling rather doubtful about the third.

'There we are.' Sylvia handed her a mug and sat beside her. 'Nothing like a cup of tea, even on the hottest day, is there?'

Sylvia suddenly sounded so much like Billie's mother that she felt desperately homesick. Next weekend she was going home to Devon for a special family party. She wished fervently that it was now, that she could hijack the Granada and belt off down the A303 and never have to make another decision as long as she lived.

She sipped her tea, trying to wipe out images of the farm, and her parents, and her brothers, and how uncomplicated life had been before she'd attempted to be grown-up. 'Er—and all these warehouses? They're all owned by small businesses like you, are they?'

'God, no!' Sylvia looked shocked. 'Not owned, dear. Leased. From Maynard and Pollock in Amberley Hill. Five-year leases, with fairly stringent clauses attached, but worth it in the long run. If you had more time I'd introduce you to the others. A nice little crowd we've got here now. Chummy, you know?'

Billie could imagine. Chummy had been sadly lacking in her life in the last couple of years. Oh, Miranda had become good friend, and Miranda's friends had become hers, and most of the

13

taxi-drivers were OK—but she had no sense of belonging to Amberley Hill. No identity. No roots.

'So,' Sylvia swallowed her tea with an appreciative murmur, 'you know all about me. What about you? I mean, you don't look like a cabby, dear. In those navy trousers and the Aertex shirt you look like a schoolgirl. What made you want to do this for a living?'

Billie stared into her mug, playing for time. The real reason was appalling; the often-repeated fictional version somehow no longer rang true. She shrugged. 'Oh, you know. It was something I just drifted into . . . It's not what I really want to do with the rest of my life . . . Actually, I'm just planning a change of direction . . .'

'Good for you. Any particular direction?'

'Not really. Maybe running my own car-hire firm or chauffeuring.'

'Go for it then,' Sylvia beamed. 'You've got so many advantages, dear. Being young, free and single—oh, I mean, you are single, I suppose?'

'Very single.' Billie finished her tea and stood up, smiling at Sylvia. 'Thanks so much for showing me your unit. I really admire you for doing this—and, you'll be all right, will you? With your husband and everything?'

Sylvia stood up, straightened her T-shirt, and shrugged as she followed Billie to the door. 'God knows, dear. Douglas is a man. Who knows where the hell you stand with men? I'm damn sure I don't.'

And neither, Billie thought, blinking outside in the searing sunshine, do I.

chapter two

Having collected a rather bilious-looking family from Whiteacres Airport and deposited them at the Four Pillars Hotel in Amberley Hill, Billie pulled the Granada back onto the taxi rank outside the Spicer Centre, still unable to shake the ingenuity of Sylvia's tropical paradise from her mind.

The sun spiralled down across the tops of the grimy advertising hoardings, hitting the ground, sparkling on rainbow pools of oil and glinting from shards of broken glass in the gutter. Billie stared at the beauty springing unbidden from the detritus. That was exactly how it had been at the industrial estate. Huge grey buildings, looking dank and cold and uninviting, and yet hiding all manner of dreams.

Several of Reuben's drivers, in front of her on the Spicer Centre rank, ambled over and leaned companionably against the Granada in the sun. The talk was idle, like the day. Soporific and sleepy, Amberley Hill dozed in the midday heat. An Elizabethan market town, it had clung on to most of its half-timbered buildings, glorious small churches, and the touristy things like the crumbling Guild Hall. The Spicer Centre, therefore, with its chrome and glass shops, fibre-optic fountains, Mulligan's Genuine Irish Ale House and Bazooka's Nite Spot, having been built slap bang in the middle of all this historical splendour, was considered something of a carbuncle by the older residents. Billie, who had never known Amberley Hill any other way, rather liked it.

Only half listening to the salacious gossip going on around her, her head still filled with dreams, Billie leaned back in the sun-hot driving seat and gazed up at the advertising hoardings. Most of them seemed to have buxom women in jacked-up bras. No wonder Reuben Wainwright had picked this spot for his taxis. One of the elevated chests had a 'For Lease' notice slapped across the cleavage. Billie grinned, imagining Reuben taking up squatter's rights.

For lease. . . property . . . Whiteacres . . . industrial units with office space . . . parking . . . contact Maynard and Pollock . . .

Billie frowned. Where had she heard the name before . . . ? Of course! They were the leasing agents for Sylvia's unit, weren't they? So were these the same units? The same chummy community that had saved Sylvia from the boorish Douglas and given birth to her Utopia?

She reached for her mobile phone. OK, so it was crazy, but if she didn't try, she'd never know . . . and of course it was horrifically close to the airfield, but she wasn't going to be involved with the planes, was she? She could afford to rent a similar building to Sylvia's with her savings, surely? And then . . . She paused in punching out the number. Ah, yes. First stumbling block. And do what, exactly? Still, there was plenty of time to think about that later. It wasn't as if she was actually going to lease the unit today, was it? She wasn't that impulsive. She was only going to look.

The voice that answered at Maynard and Pollock was totally noncommittal. It immediately put her on hold and played 'Greensleeves'. Billie, trying to keep calm, drummed out the rhythm on the

16

steering wheel.

Greensleeves came to an abrupt halt. 'Simon Maynard. And how may I be of assistance?'

Pulling shut the door on the gaggle of taxi-drivers, Billie explained about seeing the premises for lease at Whiteacres and asked if she could make an appointment to view.

Simon Maynard only barely kept the boredom out of his voice. 'I have a window available in my schedule for later this afternoon. Four thirty? Of course the vacant lots have been empty for some time so you may not see the units at their best. Do you want to meet at my office, or shall we touch base at Whiteacres?'

Having agreed on Whiteacres, Billie rolled down her window and smiled at her fellow cabbies. 'Doesn't look as though there's much going on here. I think I'll pop back to the office and see if Vee needs a hand.'

As a man they unpeeled themselves from the Granada and moved in a clump to the next cab along. Billie, still wearing an ear-to-ear grin of delight because she'd actually done something, switched on the engine and headed for the office.

*   *   *

Reuben Wainwright was knocking back antihistamines and looking suicidal. 'You habbn't fidished?'

Billie shook her head, trying not to beam. 'Just having a breather. The rank's full. You look terrible, by the way, and the pollen count forecast is way up. Why don't you go home?'

'And hab you lot skive the middit my back's

17

turd? Dot a bloody chance.'

Veronica herumphed loudly over her radio. Billie perched on the edge of Reuben's desk. 'Reuben, can we talk? Well, can I talk and can you listen without shouting? You know I said a couple of weeks ago that I wanted to leave, well—'

'You're dot leabing.' Reuben wiped his nose and his eyes. 'If you dink you're leabing you're mad. What do you dink you're going to do?' He sneezed violently. 'Oh, bugger. Cad we talk about dis later? Wed I feel better?'

'Sure.' Billie felt almost sorry for him. After all, unpleasant or not, he lived alone in a rather dismal bedsit. It was pretty sad to think that, when he felt ill, Reuben could find more comfort at work than in staying at home. 'But I am going to leave, and,' she leaned perilously close to him, considering the power of his sneezes, 'there's nothing you can do to make me change my mind.'

'We'll see about dat.' Reuben snuffled. 'Dote count your chickens—or your centre forwards.'

Billie winced. Still, later this afternoon she'd know whether or not Whiteacres was an option. And if it was, then she'd be able to tell Reuben that his hold over her was finished.

*   *   *

Until she pulled onto the cracked concrete for the second time that day, and parked behind the burned-out hatchbacks, Billie had hoped that she'd be able to have a quick word with Sylvia, but the desert island unit's double doors were closed. Maybe her Douglas had arrived, beating his manly chest, and carried Sylvia, kicking and screaming,

18

back to suburbia. Billie sincerely hoped not.

Simon Maynard was waiting for her and looked even more depressing than his warehouses. Also bunged up with the seasonal malaise, he was tall and thin and his glasses were lopsided.

'Going like hot cakes, these premises,' Simon Maynard said, wrestling with the keys at number three, immediately contradicting what he'd said earlier about the units being empty for a while. 'Very popular venue, of course. And ideal for export. Are you intending to export?'

Billie presumed he meant via the airstrip. Did the planes really make huge cargo runs to Düsseldorf and Bruges, then? They looked as though they'd be lucky to get to Southampton.

'Er, no . . . well, not immediately . . . In fact, this is just a first step. I mean, I'm not seriously intending to sign up for one of these today or anything. I just wanted to have a look.'

Simon had managed to get the key to turn and was ineffectually tugging at the door. Billie, feeling sorry for him, helped. It scraped open suddenly, catapulting them both inside.

'Christ!' Billie clapped her hands to her nose in the darkness. 'What's that smell?'

'I can't smell anything.' Simon Maynard fumbled for the light switches. 'But then I have got a touch of hayfever.' The lights all faltered into candleglow brightness. Simon looked hopefully at her. 'There! Now what do you think?'

Billie's first thought was that Granny Pascoe would be hovering overhead urging her only granddaughter to take the money and run to the nearest car dealership and buy herself something sporty, or have a good holiday, or update her

19

wardrobe, or all three.

She gazed around the acres of cold, damp space with a sinking heart. Girders soared away into the dark unknown and despite the heat of the day a piercing wind whistled through the gaps in the door frame. 'Um—well—it's difficult to say—but, oh God. Could we just find out what the smell is, please?'

Simon referred to his clipboard. 'You've got full services. Still all connected. A kitchenette and lavatorial facilities. It may be something from there . . .'

Great, Billie thought, snuggling deeper into her uniform Aertex shirt. The thought of staying at Reuben's seemed really quite attractive. She trotted behind Simon's gaunt figure in the shadowy light. She kept bumping into things and somewhere she could hear water dripping.

'The facilities—' Simon threw open a peeling cream door and stood back to let her through in what Billie considered to be an act of total cowardice.

Kitchenette and lavatorial facilities really should have Maynard and Pollock sued under the Trade Descriptions Act, she thought, as the bile rose in her throat. There were probably rats. No, on second thoughts, any self-respecting rat would have deserted this particular sinking vessel many moons ago.

'There is a bit of a whiff,' Simon acknowledged, pulling a handkerchief from the recesses of his Daks and wrapping it protectively round the lower part of his face. 'Nothing that a good clean-up couldn't cure though, I'm sure. Our other lessees have worked wonders. Now, would you like to see

20

the office?'

The office looked as though it had been recently hit by a Scud missile.

'Plenty of room for all your hardware,' Simon said briskly. 'Be lovely after a lick of paint. Now are there any questions?'

Can I go home, please? was top of the list. Billie shivered. Still, being reasonable, this had to be it at its absolute worst, didn't it? She rattled off the few things she'd decided she ought to ask. Simon Maynard had obviously been asked them all before by the way he churned out the answers. Just the sneezing and nose-blowing added variation.

A five-year lease, non-negotiable. No livestock, no cooking, no subletting. OK, so far? Billie nodded. He continued with no HGV vehicles without prior permission from the airfield authority, no high-frequency radio ditto, no fumes, gases or noxious substances. Still OK? Billie nodded dutifully for the second time.

She cleared her throat. 'And the money?'

Simon Maynard muttered into the hanky. Billie, sure she hadn't heard him right, asked again. She had. God Almighty! Still, the alternative was staying as a taxi-driver. There was no contest. And Sylvia had turned her place into a little goldmine— and the other units probably housed competitors to Richard Branson—and it would mean she was her own boss . . . Oh, God . . . Should she . . . ? Was she brave enough . . . ? She'd been impetuous before and it had ended in disaster . . .

'Um—could I leave it for a couple of days? Think it over . . . speak to someone?'

Simon Maynard sneezed explosively. 'Not if you want to secure this unit, no. I've got someone else

21

interested—saw it this morning—and, of course, you won't find anything of this size for miles around for anywhere near the same price.'

Billie closed her eyes. Then she opened them. 'OK...'

Simon paused in blowing his nose and straightened his glasses. 'Is that an affirmative to purchase the lease?'

Slowly, Billie nodded. For the third time that afternoon. Like a traitor's kiss.

'Lovely.' Simon practically broke into a canter as he headed towards the door. 'I'm sure you won't regret it. Shall we go back to the office and finalise things?'

Billie looked doubtfully around the rancid mausoleum and agreed.

*   *   *

'You've done *what*?' Miranda, Billie's flatmate, peered at her th'ough a veil of pungent scented steam. 'What the hell possessed you?'

'Reuben being a git and the fact that I'm nearly twenty seven.' Billie perched on the bathroom stool. 'And I don't want to be a wage slave any more.'

'You know Reuben will go ballistic when you tell him.' Miranda, head down in the wash basin, made a sort of superior snorting noise. 'And I don't blame him. You must be barking. I'm all for striking out on your own, doll, but you have to think about income and expenditure and stuff. You have to have a business plan. You can't just lease millions of square feet of empty space without plans.'

'I can and I have. I've written the cheque and I

22

take over at the end of the month.'

Miranda's voice was still censorious, if a little echoey. 'Christ! But I thought you liked being a taxi-driver.'

'I did.' Well, she had. When Reuben had offered her the lifeline she'd clutched it with both hands. But she'd stopped drowning in guilt a long time ago. 'I don't any more. It's just time to move on. Don't worry, I won't miss out on paying the rent.'

'That's not my main concern,' Miranda muttered. 'I mean, doll, what exactly are you going to do with this unit now that you've got it?'

Billie shrugged. 'I'm not exactly sure . . . But I've got a whole three weeks to come up with an idea. I've only got to give Reuben seven days' notice, but I'll stay until the end of the month anyway.' She watched Miranda ooze red slime through the length of her hair, and thought it might be politic to change the subject. 'What on earth are you doing?'

'Dyeing organically. Plum and bilberry. It's new. I thought I'd better try it out on myself before I depilate the customers. I could give you a freebie if you came to the salon.'

Miranda ran Follicles and Cuticles in Amberley Hill's Spicer Centre. It had started off as Wendy's, a wash-and-set hairdressers for ladies of a certain age, but Miranda had developed it into a full-blown beauty salon and aromatherapy parlour in the time that Billie had been sharing her flat.

'No thanks. I'm happy with bimbette blonde.'

'Suit yourself.' Miranda's voice was still muffled. 'Personally, I think you're completely crazy. You've got a nice steady little job—and you're going to chuck it up for a massive old shed full of nothing! Anyway, why are you so keen to ditch Reuben?

23

He's a bit of all right.'

'Bloody hell!' Billie nearly tumbled from the stool 'Reuben? He looks like a pirate—which is probably being unfair to pirates. And he's as old as the hills and nasty with it.'

Miranda wrapped her dripping scarlet hair expertly in a towel. 'He's the right side of forty and a dead ringer for Pierce Brosnan. I wouldn't kick him out from under the duvet.'

Billie grinned. Miranda, who had married at sixteen and divorced at eighteen, had spent the twelve years since feverishly searching for the Right Man, and had never turned down anything. As long as it shaved and had a pulse, Miranda considered it worth the effort. But *Reuben*? Holy Moses!

'Yeah, well, apart from getting shot of Slimeball Wainwright, I just want to do something different with my life. I've really had enough of ferrying people about and being insulted.'

'Oh, come on,' Miranda blinked a scarlet rivulet from the corner of her eye. 'You've always said most of your passengers were sweeties. You're becoming very bitter and twisted. You want to find yourself a man to take your mind off things. It's bloody murder sharing my house with a nun. That Damon has a lot to answer for.'

Miranda knew nothing about the Kieran Squires and London segment of Billie's past. Billie had explained away her sudden appearance in Amberley Mill and her subsequent self-imposed celibacy as having been hurt badly by her boyfriend back home and never trusting another man. Sadly, because of Miranda's own unfortunate experience of disastrous youthful relationships, she'd become particularly tenacious on the subject. Billie had had

24

to give this mythical teen heart-breaker a name and a personality. Now even she'd begun to believe that Damon from Newton Abbot had once existed.

Billie stood up before they could get into some embarrassing conversation about Damon's sister, whom she'd had to invent as her best friend at school. Miranda could never understand why Billie didn't contact Denise and ask her to mediate with her sibling. And it got worse. They had a dog called Jasper and took their family holidays in Babbacombe.

Billie could see trouble looming again. 'Do you want a drink? I got a stonking tip this morning from a lovely lady called Sylvia who is really responsible for me deciding to rent a warehouse, and I picked up a couple of bottles of plonk on my way home.'

At the mention of alcohol, Miranda perked up. She nodded, spraying scarlet streaks across the tiles. The bathroom looked like something from *Psycho*. 'OK. But we'll have to make it a quick one or three. Keith's taking me to Bazooka's tonight.'

'Keith? This would be Keith from the bank? Keith from the insurance office? Keith the postman? Keith who just happened to be delivering the charity envelopes? Keith the geriatric gardener from the old people's home? Keith the—'

'Keith from the garage. He MOT'd my car, remember? He's pretty good on rubbing down bodywork. He's certainly got husband potential. I've asked him to stay over next weekend—when we have the booze-up for Kitty's birthday . . .' Miranda paused in the bathroom doorway, her face now streaked with crimson. 'You hadn't forgotten, had you?'

Billie pulled a face. Oh God! Next weekend

25

she was going home to Devon. 'I won't be here. I'm going to my brother's wedding reception— remember?'

Billie's youngest brother, Ben, and his girlfriend, Maria, had married secretly on some Caribbean island the previous month. Billie's parents had been determined to give them a proper Pascoe party on their return.

'Oh, bugger, doll! It won't be the same without you! And Kitty'll be really mad . . .'

Billie sighed. 'I'll have to apologise to Kitty. And you'll be so wrapped up in—er—Keith that you won't even notice I'm missing. I really want to go home, anyway. I'll have to pick my moment in the festivities to tell Mum and Dad that I've spent Granny Pascoe's money on a warehouse—oh, and that I've left my job.'

'Don't be silly.' Miranda wrapped Billie in a vermilion hug. 'It's all pie in the sky. Anyway, your parents'll make you see sense and get your money back.' She dripped a few more scarlet drops onto Billie's white uniform shirt. 'And I'll bet a million quid that you won't leave Reuben. He'll never let you go. You wait and see.'

chapter three

'Dot a bloody chance! Doe way! Over by dead body!' Reuben Wainwright swivelled in his chair and glared at Billie across a wodge of Kleenex. 'It's the height of subber and we're rud off our feet and—'

The rest of the invective was lost in a sneeze.

Billie flinched. 'But I've been telling you for ages that I wanted to leave.'

Reuben raised black eyebrows above bloodshot eyes. 'And I'be beed telling you you can't leabe. You owe me, Billie. Big time.'

'Yes I can, and no I don't.'

Billie glowered at her employer across the crowded taxi office. As Reuben didn't have a room of his own, the conversation was being carried out over the crackling of the radio and Veronica's squawked directions. Several cabbies were savouring a late lunch-time cup of tea and a cigarette, and listening avidly.

Reuben blew his nose vigorously. 'Ah, that's better. I can breathe—not that you care.' He leaned closer to Billie. 'Are you having bother with the punters? Trying it on, are they? I told you to let me know if they gave you a hard time.'

'They don't.' Well, they didn't. Not really. The more laddish of her passengers seemed to find having a diminutive blonde driving their taxi something of a challenge, but it was nothing she couldn't handle. She'd coped with drunks every weekend for two years, and once she'd had a couple Kama Sutra'ing all the way to Bognor. Then there had been that woman in the final stages of labour whose body-pierced birth partner had tried to Feng Shui the Granada in between the roars of agony. But she'd always coped. 'That's not why I'm going. And you can't stop me—I just have to hand in my notice. I don't owe you anything. Not any more.'

Reuben started swivelling again. Maybe, Billie thought, it helped to clear his nasal passages. His eyebrows arched even more dramatically. 'Short memory, sweetheart. And, just supposing you did

27

leave here, just what exactly do you intend to do?'

'I've already done it,' Billie said triumphantly. 'I've taken a lease on a warehouse because I want to be my own boss. I want—'

'A warehouse? Your own boss?' Reuben's eyebrows disappeared. 'With your track record? God Almighty! You can't just set up in business, you know. And,' he swivelled towards her again, 'people check things. You start up in business, and there'll be all sorts of investigations into your past.'

'So?' Billie hoped that the bravado in her voice was also evident on her face. Somehow she doubted it. 'I haven't got anything to hide.'

'Stone me! Do you want me to tell them why exactly you've been working for me? How you came to be a cab-driver?'

Trickles of age-old fear spiked down her spine. 'That was ages ago. Anyway, who are these people? I've signed the lease, paid my money, and I pick up the keys to the unit next week. I certainly won't need a reference from you, so I don't think anyone will be bothering you with questions about me.'

'Oh, don't you? You'd better hope not, because I've got a very long memory, sweetheart.'

Billie glared at the dark features. She'd never liked Reuben; now she almost hated him. He couldn't hold that over her, could he? It had been foolish, yes, but not illegal.

'So, you're on the run again . . .' Reuben twirled a ballpoint between his fingers and laughed nastily. 'You were running away from London when we met, weren't you? Listen, babe, I could have made a fortune out of that story. I could have retired on the profits from the tabloids. But did I? No. Out of the kindness of my heart, I gave you a job, set you on your feet, and kept my mouth shut. No, like I said, you owe me one.'

But she didn't. She'd worked off her debt a thousandfold. And it was ancient history now, anyway. Surely, there wasn't a newspaper in the land that would be remotely interested.

OK, Kieran Squires was still famous: he still played in the Premiership, he appeared on television sports quizzes, and had even had a short run of adverts for toothpaste, but he and Fenella and the children were rarely featured in *Hello!* these days.

'Hiya, Billie.' Veronica suddenly removed her headset and looked up from her microphone. 'I didn't know you were here. Ooh, your hair looks nice. You been to Follicles?'

'Follicles! Bollocks!' Reuben swivelled wildly, obviously angry at the diversion. 'Your daft mate with the pink hair been at you, has she?'

Billie nodded. 'Miranda thinks very highly of you, too. In fact, she quite fancies you.'

'Sad cow,' Veronica muttered under her breath before reclamping her earphones.

Reuben chuckled. 'Yeah, well she's got a fairish pair of pins on her. No knockers to speak of, though. And she's a bit of an old slapper, by all accounts.'

Jesus. Billie glared at him. 'She is not. She's just exercising her right to sexual freedom.'

'Which you'd know all about . . .' Reuben rocked backwards and forwards, his eyes travelling up and down her body. 'Still, I'll say one thing, Kieran certainly had good taste.'

'Shut up!' Billie nodded towards Veronica, who had stopped directing four cabs through the

Amberley Hill town centre snarl-up, pushed back the headset once more, and was listening with interest. 'You promised!'

Reuben tilted his chair back. 'So I did. But I also remember some promises from you too. And jacking in the job wasn't one of them.'

'I never promised I'd stay for ever. I was very grateful. I still am. I just want to move on.'

Her fellow cabbies were sitting back, watching the exchange with unashamed amusement. This clearly was a far more entertaining lunch-time diversion than the *Sun* crossword. Billie knew that rumours had been rife when she'd arrived. The drivers had all thought she was Reuben's bit of totty. A year and a half later and it was very apparent that she wasn't, but they were still all convinced that Reuben, King of the Misogynists, had the hots for her.

Billie, fortunately, knew differently. Or maybe it wasn't so fortunate. Wouldn't it have been preferable to have Reuben Wainwright loving her truly, madly, deeply, rather than the unpleasant reality? Just how long did he think he could carry on with the emotional blackmail? She stood up and moved across to Veronica's desk. 'Do you want me to do the shoppers this afternoon, Vee? I don't mind tootling about in the centre or popping out to Whiteacres even. It would free up some of the guys for the longer runs. After all, I'm finishing at five today.'

'Ta. Nice one.' Veronica didn't bother to remove her cigarette from the corner of her mouth. 'If you've finished bawling Reuben out, you could start at the Spicer Centre and pick up on the rank, an' then call in later.'

30

'Fine.' Billie looked back at Reuben. He was blowing his nose and she dived in while he was off guard. 'OK, then—I'm going back to work now, and I don't care what you say—you'll have my notice in writing on your desk first thing in the morning, and I'll be out of here by the end of the month.'

It was gratifying that she slammed the door to a rousing round of applause from her fellow drivers.

* * *

Two hours later, Billie pulled up outside her unit. Her unit . . . She smiled, acknowledging that she already thought of it as hers. Switching off the Granada's radio and hoping that Vee wouldn't have an apoplexy trying to contact her, she leaned back against the sticky seat and gazed at the breeze-block mountain shimmering in the scorching sun. It was all hers—almost—and this time, whatever happened, she'd succeed or fail alone. This time, if it all went pear-shaped, there'd be no one to blame but herself.

Sylvia's doors were again closed, with a huge neon notice pinned to them and a message scrawled in marker pen saying, 'Run away to sea! Back in the morning! Any deliveries—drop at unit one!' Billie laughed. At least the grim-sounding Douglas hadn't dampened her sense of humour. She was really looking forward to having Sylvia as a neighbour. She couldn't wait to see Sylvia's face when she realised who'd taken unit three.

Through the windscreen, Billie watched a tiny speck in the deep blue sky grow larger and larger as it approached the crisscross of runways. That was something else she'd have to cope with. She'd never make a go of the business—whatever it turned out to be—if she had a panic attack every time she heard the whine of something airborne hammering overhead.

She continued to watch the plane as it circled for landing. As it came closer, she could just see the pilot and his passenger looking cramped inside the transparent body, and gave an involuntary shudder. A private plane, she guessed, belonging to the Aeroclub, whose logo was dotted about Whiteacres with jaunty 1920s-type pictures of brightly coloured machines doing nose dives through fluffy white clouds. She followed it with her eye as it circled over one of airport's buildings and disappeared from view.

The name Sullivanair was emblazoned in huge silver, purple and emerald-green lettering across two of the largest hangars in the distance, the word quivering in the heat. Billie, who had always flown on holiday with British Airways, had never heard of Sullivanair. Not that she'd expected to, of course—for years she'd thought Virgin Atlantic was Richard Branson's answer to the Stax label.

Still, perhaps next week, when she came back from Devon, she'd start her aeroplane therapy. She might even walk across to the airport and actually touch a plane. At the end of the month she'd be able to collect the keys and unlock her own door. She unpeeled the Aertex shirt from the leatherette seat. She'd have to think about getting business cards printed, and headed notepaper. Then she'd be free of Reuben for ever . . .

The night when they'd met would burn for ever in her memory. It had been four months into her relationship with Kieran Squires, just before

Christmas, she had been hopelessly in love with Kieran's looks and his gentleness and his total lack of arrogance, despite his status. God—she shivered—it was all so horribly, embarrassingly real again.

They'd come giggling out of that country club, she and Kieran, slightly squiffy and very happy, and decided that neither of them was remotely fit to drive. It had been cold, with the wind howling down from the north, threatening snow, and they'd snuggled together and she'd thought about how lovely it would be to sleep with him later, curled against his muscular strength, listening to the gale outside in the darkness.

'We'll get a taxi back to London,' Kieran had said. 'I can get someone to collect my car in the morning. Let's not go back to your flat. We'll go to a hotel, shall we?'

And she, foolishly besotted, had shivered in her little strappy dress and her stupid spindly sandals and said what a great idea that was. She'd never been to Kieran's home—but that was because he was famous and he said that his manager said the paparazzi would pounce on them, so they always stayed at the flat he'd found for her, or in hotels. She'd so quickly got used to Kieran's wealth; hotel rooms and car-collectors were available at the drop of a hat to people in Kieran's position, after all.

She'd giggled—God help her—that her bag and her jacket were still in his car, and Kieran had said leave them, they could be sorted out in the morning too. They'd got his plastic and their love to keep them warm . . . She groaned at the memory. He'd actually said that, and then she'd thought it was so sweet . . .

So Kieran had dashed back into the club and phoned for a cab picked at random from a selection of cards on the wall, and they'd waited, shivering and laughing, until the illuminated roof light that heralded Reuben's Cabs glimmered through the darkness. She'd been pleased to see the taxi—delighted—had leaped in to the back seat, Kieran close beside her, and carelessly told the dark, saturnine driver that they wanted to go all the way to London.

It had all turned sour then. The driver, looking in his rear-view mirror, had said yes, he supposed they did, and had driven off very slowly . . . and he'd kept looking. And—Billie shook her head—she and Kieran were messing around in the back seat and her dress was all rucked up and she thought the driver was a bit of a peeping tom . . . and she'd glared at him. Then he'd stopped the cab, leaving the engine running, and she'd seen the Amberley Hill signs in the distance and thought he was going to mug them.

But of course, he hadn't. He'd just turned round, dismissing her with a pitying stare, and then calmly told Kieran that he'd be better off getting home to his wife and children.

God! The horror shot through her again. The shame. She'd wanted to laugh—Kieran wasn't married! Children? God, no! Kieran had sworn to her that he didn't even have time for regular girlfriends, what with the training schedules and the matches and everything . . . and she'd been so stupidly delighted that he saw her as often as he could. She'd even felt privileged. And now he was faffing and prevaricating and trying to bluff his way out of answering what the taxi-driver had just said . . .

Billie shook her head at her own naivety. She'd believed Kieran was single because he'd told her so. She had only asked once, although he told her often.

She'd turned on him in the taxi, demanding that he tell her the truth, praying that he wouldn't . . . And then the taxi-driver—bloody Reuben—had said that every football fan in the country knew about Fenella, Kieran's Page Three wife, but Billie hadn't . . . She'd sat there in that stupid skinny dress, looking and feeling like a cheap tart—and hurting. She still felt the hurt. She'd loved him and trusted him. There was a wealth of difference between having an affair with a married man when you knew, and being hopelessly in love with a man who had sworn he was single . . .

And then suddenly Kieran was throwing open the door and leaping out into the darkness and disappearing.

'Looks like he's changed his mind,' Reuben had said laconically over his shoulder. 'Probably be at home with the wife and kids before daybreak. So? Where do you want to go?'

And Billie hadn't known. Because there was nowhere to go. She didn't even know where she was. Everything she owned was in the little flat in Notting Hill—and that belonged to Kieran. She'd never go there again . . . And because she was crying for being a fool . . .

'OK then.' Reuben had started the cab again. 'Bit of a nasty night to be hanging around. I'll drop you off at the Four Pillars for tonight until you get yourself sorted out.

And he had, and then she'd still sat there in the

back of that cab outside the hotel because all her money was in Kieran's car . . . and Reuben had given her a fifty-pound note which she'd thrown back at him in disgust because she thought he was paying for her to spend the night with him. He'd laughed, nastily, and stomped out of the cab and into the hotel and came back saying he'd paid for a single room and full board for two days and he'd be back to see her in the morning.

She hadn't slept. She hadn't even undressed. She had no clothes. No toothbrush. No self-respect.

She hadn't even eaten the breakfast that Reuben had paid for because she felt so sick. Then Reuben had turned up, and, convinced that he was going to be in charge of a call-girl racket or something equally squalid, she'd refused to see him.

So he'd come up to her room, with a pair of jeans and an oversized sweater and a pair of trainers which were too small, and said if she'd like to work off her debt—and if she had a driving licence—he was short of cabbies . . .

Billie sniffed at the memory. She'd been so bloody grateful. And scared. It was just before Christmas, and she'd already told her parents she'd be working and staying in London—she'd simply imagined she and Kieran would be spending it together . . . She couldn't go home . . . Not to her parents, or Devon, or the *Argus*. She'd chucked that up simply to be with Kieran, telling everyone that she'd decided to be a nanny for a few months, just for a change . . . Her parents had been sorry to see her go, but proud of her for striking out in a different direction in London . . .

She simply couldn't live with herself, couldn't accept what she'd become. What an idiot she'd

36

been.

So she'd agreed to work for Reuben until after Christmas, and he'd agreed to pay her bill at the Four Pillars, which would be deducted from her wages, until she'd sorted out what she wanted to do. Then days into the new year she'd seen Miranda's advert for a flat-share and Amberley Hill had become her home and Reuben her employer and tormentor, because he knew.

'Here!' There was a sharp rap on the Granada's window. 'This isn't a car park, right?'

Startled, Billie opened the window. 'Sorry?'

'I said it isn't a car park. Or are you a customer?'

Billie blinked at the couple standing threateningly beside the Granada. Very New Age, with matching noserings and tattooed Celtic bands on their wedding fingers, they burrowed deep into the necks of their hand-crocheted ponchos and stared at her with suspicion. She opened the door and scrabbled out onto the sizzling concrete. The air rushed hotly into her throat. 'Neither. That is, I'm not parking and I'm not a customer. I'm Billie Pascoe—I've just taken over this unit.'

The male half of the couple blew a gap in a matching set of wispy moustache and beard, and parted his straggly hair. 'Cool! We'd heard it'd been let—Sylv said—but we didn't know who to.' He grinned suddenly through the hair and held out his hand. 'I'm Zia. Short for Zachariah, only it's pretty run-of-the-mill to be Zach these days, so don't make the mistake, right?'

'Yes. No. Er—right.' Billie shook hands. Zia seemed to emanate patchouli from his pores.

'And this is Isla, my wife. It's cool to be married, right?'

37

Billie nodded again. 'Right.'

'Right. Well, we're from number four, and Sylv says she'd heard from Fred'n'Dick at unit one that you're into fashion. And if that's right then we want you to stop, right? We don't want no competition just next door, right?'

'Right—er—no, wrong.' Billie leaned against the door then leaped away again before the metal welded to her skin. 'Look, it's really nice to meet you—but I'm not into anything, least of all fashion. I promise I won't be competition at all. I'm probably going to be doing something with cars.'

'Not resprays?' Isla had emerged from her layers, looking scandalised. 'Nothing that would taint our stock?'

'No. More—um—luxury limousines. Nothing even remotely to do with fashion. Or anything smelly.'

'That's cool then,' Zia grinned. 'You just having a look?'

'Yes—I haven't got the keys yet. But I'm really looking forward to moving in and painting and, well, just getting started. It's all a bit of a mess in there.'

'They all are to start with. It's the worst time,' Isla agreed. 'You'll be fine when you're up and running. Do you want to come and see our place?'

Billie didn't particularly. She had the feeling that it would probably be a little goldmine like Sylvia's. She was going to be a thorn between two ferociously flourishing floribundas. Zia and Isla, however, proved very persuasive, and following them into their warehouse, Billie found herself completely bedazzled by ingenuity for the second time.

Zi-Zi's—'Our initials, right?' Zia explained proudly—was stacked practically to the ceiling with clothes. Not any old clothes, though. Oh, no. Zi-Zi's was no jumble sale. Zia and Isla, they told her, travelled the country, buying unwanted clothes at house clearance sales, at charity bazaars in villages, from second-hand clothes shops, in fact from anywhere where anyone might once have worn something unusual or original.

They got very good leads, right, Zia said, from the obituary columns in the broadsheets. Not like they were grave-robbing or nothing, right? But usually you found the grieving relatives were only too pleased to have the job taken away from them. Sad business, sorting out the clothes and that.

They always went for genuine period stuff, Isla said quickly, apparently not as comfortable as her husband with this particular source of material. As old as they could get if possible, but they never turned down anything. Today is tomorrow's yesterday, right?

'Then,' Zia explained, 'we clean them ourselves—real delicate work, no solvents, right— and repair them, right—Isla is magic with a needle—and sort them into decades. See . . .'

Billie saw. There were outfits from Victorian times, roaring twenties Charleston dresses, forties austerity, fifties New Look, sixties hippy, and then on to more familiar recent fashions.

Isla indicated a massive pile of cardboard containers stacked practically to the ceiling. 'This is our overspill area. We're terribly overcrowded because we're hanging on to all the eighties power suits and the nineties stuff for a while. It won't be long before there's a revival, though.'

Billie blinked at the row upon row of clothes; at the sumptuous array of colours and fabrics. It was a shopaholic's nirvana. 'And then, what? Do you sell them? Open up the shed and have like a huge rummage sale or something?'

They smiled gently at such naivety.

'Well, yes, some we sell. But not from here. The ambience wouldn't be right. We've got stalls in a couple of the London antique markets, but no, the bulk of our business comes from hiring to wardrobe departments. Television, theatre—there's a nonstop demand and a huge purse, especially from the independent television companies. Costume drama, period pieces—we dress 'em all. We just saw the niche and went for it, right?'

Billie sighed heavily. Sylvia had found a gap in the market: Zia and Isla had slotted into a niche. And what the hell was she going to do? Wait for the right moment, the right opportunity, to come along? She might as well be waiting for the entrepreneurial equivalent of Godot.

chapter four

Profit and loss. Not enough of the former and far too much of the latter. Yawning, Jonah Sullivan switched off his computer in the empty office and pushed his chair away from the desk. The letters from the bank, all unanswered from the beginning of the month and neatly stacked to make them look less intimidating, kept drawing his eye. He scooped them up and thrust them out of sight at the bottom of the in-tray. It didn't make him feel any better.

Reaching over the mountain of paperwork he removed the latest stern missive and, making half a dozen neat creases, launched the vellum Concorde across the office.

It landed with a satisfying clunk against the radiator. Grinning, Jonah went to retrieve it and gave it a second flight. This time it nose-dived into the waste-paper bin.

Jonah regarded the crash-landing cynically, then fishing the paper plane from the bin, smoothed out the creases and added it to the pile on the desk. Estelle, Sullivanair's secretary, PA and resident lifesaver, would deal with it when she came in later. She had a fudging answer held on file, especially for the bank. She only ever needed to alter the date.

Two years he'd been running the business; two years in which, according to the bank's latest letter, he should be showing a healthy return on their investment. Two years in which, allowing for the massive rent and overheads and his first mad splurge on stock, Sullivanair should at least be breaking even.

Jonah walked to the window and leaned his hands on the sill. Whiteacres Airport spread mistily in front of him, a mass of dying grass and cracked concrete in the pearly light of a late June morning. He loved it. All of it. True, it had been allowed to run to seed a bit, and the row of towering warehouses on the perimeter gave it a bit of a slum-clearance air, but it had given him his break; and he'd fondly imagined it would make him his fortune. It looked more likely now, unless the bank gave him more time, that it would bankrupt him.

Long gone were the days when he'd thought he'd rival Ryanair—and any mention of easyjet made him laugh at the irony. It was fine for Stelios Haji-Ioannou to buy thirty million pounds' worth of planes at a time—he'd no doubt been blessed with the Greek equivalent of silver spoons and golden handshakes. Not for Stelios the RAF redundancy payoff, the remortgage on the family home, and a bank loan loaded with interest.

Not, Jonah acknowledged sadly, that Sullivanair was ever likely to be in the same league as easyjet: A single fifteen-year-old Shorts 330 doing private hire flights to small British airfields, and a Slingsby T67 Firefly, which went nowhere, were hardly comparable . . . But if this new scheme got underway, if the bank would just give him a few more months to realise Sullivanair's potential, then it may well be a different story.

Peeling off a handful of Post-it notes, he scribbled enigmatic messages and dabbed them in a yellow rash round the outside of the computer screen.

'Thanks for doing a couple of extra hours today. Much appreciated—as always. Hope you had a great weekend. Mine was best forgotten so don't ask.'

'If the bank ring while I'm flying tell them I'm lost in space. That should please them. They seem to think I've got the same budget as NASA.'

'I probably won't be back in today. Once I've dropped off in Norwich, I'll fly straight back, and meet up with Barnaby.'

*　　　*　　　*

And buy the Stearman . . . maybe? Jonah laughed at the self-delusion. He knew there was no maybe about it. Even if Barnaby told him that the Boeing Stearman biplane was a heap of mouldering scrap he knew he'd buy it. It was the plane he'd always wanted. They didn't become available very often—and never in England. Barnaby had apparently tracked down this one in the depths of Kentucky. Sod it. He'd always taken risks. His lifeblood was stirred by danger, by the excitement of uncertainties. He wouldn't be a pilot, would he, if he didn't thrive on thrills?

And there was the old adage about speculating and accumulating—one had to come before the other. If the bank would just get off his back for five minutes, he could buy a second Shorts, and with two planes doing short-hauls he was pretty sure that the Sullivanair charter flights would be making a healthy profit by the end of the year. All he needed was to get the Slingsby operational and have it up and running as a pilot-trainer—then he'd have two strings to his bow. It was just that the money he'd salted away for a partial repayment of the bank loan, the purchase of another passenger plane, and the Slingsby repairs would be what he'd be using to buy the Stearman . . .

He scribbled a final note. 'If Claire should ring—tell her I'm orbiting in the stratosphere for the next six weeks at least.' He grinned. Estelle would enjoy that bit. There was absolutely no love lost between the two women. 'And don't mention a word about Barnaby or the Stearman.'

Pretty certain that he'd covered all eventualities, Jonah carefully checked in the mirror that his navy-blue uniform was relatively wrinkle-free, wishing, not for the first time, that he could just take the controls in his jeans and flying jacket.

Ramming his peaked cap on to his head, he inspected his reflection again and winced. It was hardly Brian Trubshaw.

The airfield was practically deserted at this hour. The small single-engined planes belonging to the Aeroclub were still covered with their waterproofs, and nothing larger was due in until later in the morning. Jonah, with his fifteen passengers all one-way bound for Norfolk, was the only pilot crossing the tarmac towards the air-traffic control tower. Still, it was only June, not yet peak holiday time, hardly the busiest time of the year at Whiteacres . . .

He shivered, a mixture of elation and anticipation, as he filed his flight plan with the controllers in the tower. The Stearman—his dream plane—was almost a reality. He could see it, restored in all its glory, its silver, purple and emerald-green livery matching that of the Shorts and the Slingsby. God—it would almost be a Sullivanair fleet!

Jonah knew he was grinning inanely and stopped, concentrating on the more mundane but essential tasks of informing the ATC of his intended destination and route, estimated time of arrival in Norwich, and the Shorts' SOB—aerospeak for souls on board: passengers and crew needed to be accounted for in case of an emergency. Then he leaped down the stairs three at a time and out of the building.

The Shorts had been hauled from the hangar and Jonah spent a proud moment just staring. True, it wasn't the prettiest plane in the world, being stubby-bodied and pointy-nosed, and its twin turboprops gave it a somewhat dated appearance.

44

But it was steady, reliable, flew like a bird—and had Sullivanair emblazoned all over it.

'Christ!' Vinny, Jonah's copilot, paused in his exterior checks and raised his eyebrows at Jonah as he walked towards the plane. 'Something's made you happy. Who is she?'

Jonah again reined in his ear-to-ear beam. Vinny was unbelievably indiscreet and would immediately tell the entire aviation world about the Stearman via the shortwave radio. 'It's not a she. I'm just totally ecstatic about having to fly to East Anglia.'

'Bollocks.' Vinny resumed his walk round, making sure that there was nothing hanging off the Shorts, nothing loose, nothing dripping, no sinister puddles developing on the tarmac. 'A half-empty planeload on a one-way ticket doesn't usually make you smile. I'll put money on it being a woman.' The prospect of the Stearman was a million times better than any woman, Jonah thought as hauled himself up the half-dozen steps and into the plane. Steady, reliable—and faithful. Claire, his ex-wife, had been none of those things. Give him a plane any day. Planes didn't break your heart.

The empty Shorts, with its silver interior, offered thirty passengers seats in pairs on one side of the offset aisle, with a single row on the other, all immaculately upholstered in green and purple. When there were no passengers, Jonah and Vinny unbolted the seats and turned the plane into a cargo carrier. It had paid a lot of bills.

Pam, the stewardess, was bent double in the minuscule galley, unpacking cardboard boxes. There was no on-board catering as such—the Sullivanair flights were far too brief—but Jonah had always made sure that his passengers enjoyed a

45

gratis drink and some sort of prepacked snack. Pam continually grumbled that she felt a marked affinity with cinema usherettes when she swayed between the seats doling out miniature bottles and cans and little Cellophane packages.

'We've got a hell of a lot of peanuts in this load,' Pam straightened up. 'I thought we were going back to boiled sweets and gingernuts? Jesus, Jonah,' she pulled a face, 'you've done a deal on them, haven't you?'

'A bit,' Jonah didn't meet her eye. 'Well, they were practically on their sell-by date. I got them for a song. And anyway, people got a bit sniffy about half a pint of gin accompanied by two ginger biscuits, as I remember.'

'People'll get a hell of a lot sniffier about stale peanuts,' Pam chucked a dozen packets into a basket, 'not to mention salmonella or listeria. And who exactly am I catering for today, then? Please tell me it's something exciting.'

'Fifteen middle-management trainees wasting their summer break on going to Norfolk for a bonding session. One of those paint-throwing things . . .' Jonah shrugged. 'And we're flying back empty. I'm collecting them in five days. Pretty mundane, I'm afraid. But Estelle took a booking from some Elvis Presley impersonators for later in the year—they might cheer you up.'

'I hope so. At my age I don't get that many offers'.

Jonah laughed as he headed for the front of the plane. Old enough to be his mother, Pam had been a stewardess for over thirty years, having been rigorously trained in the good old days of BOAC. She'd fitted into Sullivanair's far more relaxed

46

regime with ease.

Lobbing his cap out of sight in the cockpit, Jonah shrugged out of his jacket and sat down. The pre-flight check routine was as automatic as breathing: getting out the charts, setting both the normal and back-up radio frequencies, followed by the altimeter. He was just completing the flight controls check for free movement when Vinny plonked himself into the copilot's chair.

'All OK out there.' Vinny, like Jonah, clapped on his headset. 'Might as well get 'em loaded. Anything for the hold, or is it hand luggage only?'

'Just cabin bags.' Jonah spoke into the radio, informing the terminal that the passengers could start boarding. 'Apparently part of their initiative. Dress up in combat gear all day and have one set of civvies only. Minimal comfort—and a hell of a way to be spending the week, poor sods. Who'd be desk bound, eh?'

Vinny joined him in looking back across the tarmac, as their fifteen middle managers filed out through the pale blue morning, heading for the boarding steps, and gave a wry chuckle. 'Put like that, maybe this old crate has her appeal.'

'Please!' Jonah raised his eyebrows. 'You'll hurt her feelings! What?' He spoke into his mouthpiece to the ground handler on the tarmac. 'Oh, yeah— sorry, Kev. No, I was talking to Vinny . . . Yeah, I've got ATC clearance to start the engines. OK with you?'

Kev, twelve feet below them, gave the thumbs up and unplugged the auxiliary power unit just as Pam popped her head into the cockpit. 'All on board, seated and strapped. Miserable-looking bunch.'

Jonah laughed and started both engines, the

47

propellers whirring rhythmically as he checked the fuel gauge, oil pressure and temperature on the console in front of him, while Vinny confirmed with Kev that the chocks were removed.

It was all as routine to Jonah as brushing his teeth, he thought as he radioed again to air-traffic control that everything was AOK and he was ready to taxi.

'Received Golf Hotel Charlie Foxtrot,' the air-traffic controller said merrily. 'Cleared to left taxi way. Taxi out to holding point Bravo Two.'

'Charlie Foxtrot received and understood.'

Once at the holding point Jonah turned the Shorts into the wind, running the engine up to full power and then letting it fade down again. Sweet music. He flicked the radio switch.

'Good morning, ladies and gentlemen. My name is Jonah Sullivan and I am your captain.' He always loved that bit. 'My copilot today is Vinny Taylor, and your stewardess is Pam. The weather is calm and clear all the way to East Anglia and we will be climbing to a cruising height of eight thousand feet on our short journey to Norwich. We expect to arrive in approximately forty-five minutes. I hope you'll enjoy your trip and thank you for travelling with Sullivanair.'

Vinny chuckled as they gained speed and taxied towards the runway. 'You always make it sound like you've got a stand-by crew of thousands.'

'One day, Vin. One day.'

Jonah could hear Pam doing the safety and emergency drill behind him and was pretty sure that none of the passengers would be listening. They never did.

'Charlie Foxtrot,' the air-traffic controller

crackled in his headset, 'cleared for takeoff.'

With a quick word to Pam to strap herself in, Jonah noted the traffic controller's air pressure setting—the wind direction and speed—as he set the flaps and taxied to the end of the runway. Again turning into the wind, he put the brakes on, ran the engine up to ninety per cent power, released the brakes and immediately increased the engine thrust to full.

This moment of supreme roaring power, of speed, never failed to exhilarate him, and as the Shorts belted down the runway Jonah felt the thrill prickle his spine. Vinny, counting the airspeed to 130 knots, was grinning too. God, they were like kids!

'Rotate!' Vinny said sharply.

Jonah, exultant as always, pulled back on the stick and felt the Shorts slide smoothly away from the ground and glide upwards. Climbing quickly away from Whiteacres, Jonah passed the controls to Vinny while he turned on to his heading and put the flaps back.

'Brilliant, though I say so myself,' Jonah grinned.

'I've seen better takeoffs in the babies' class at the aeroclub.' Vinny relaxed back in his seat as they reached their allotted altitude and reduced the engine power. 'Now switch on to auto so we can have a cup of tea—I didn't have time before I left home . . . Heavy weekend. I met her on Friday night. We didn't get out of bed until this morning.'

'Really? What a surprise.' Jonah flicked on the autopilot. 'Anyone I know?'

'Out of your league, mate.'

Jonah radioed Whiteacres control tower to confirm the Sullivanair's destination, then set the second radio to Norwich ATC for their estimated time of arrival. He wasn't sure he wanted to spend the forty-five minutes of the flight discussing Vinny's love life, fascinating though it was. It always reminded him of the might-have-beens with Claire . . .

'Two teas, well sugared for the nerves.' Pam pushed her way into the cabin. 'I didn't bother with the peanuts.'

*   *   *

Four hours later, Jonah sealed his fate. Having safely dispatched his middle managers in Norwich and flown the return trip with no hitches, he'd driven home to his Whiteacres flat and kept his date with Barnaby Molton-Kusak.

'The transportation's a gift,' Barnaby, sleek-haired, elegant and looking every inch the country squire, said as they shook hands in Jonah's functional living room. 'I'll stand you the cost of the containerage and shipping and temporary storage, as long as I can have a go with the old paintbrush—oh, and be up there on the inaugural flight.'

'Anything,' Jonah said fervently, staring at the array of photographs of the Boeing Stearman fanned out amongst the junk on his coffee table. 'I just can't believe it. It's in amazingly good nick—although I'd have said yes even if I needed to reshape every rivet by hand. I'll never be able to thank you enough.'

'Crap.' Barnaby's cut-glass accent failed to hide the emotion. 'I owe you one, Jo. I owe you a hell of a big one.'

Jonah shook his head. Reference to the way

they'd met always embarrassed him. He'd only been doing his job. It could have been any pilot in charge of the Hercules carrier that flew the first released prisoners of war away from the Gulf. The Stearman, scruffy but in excellent condition, was Barnaby's way of saying thank you.

'If there's ever anything you want,' he'd said all those years ago, 'anything I can do for you, Jonah, you only have to name it . . .'

Jonah had shrugged. He and Claire had been happy then. There had been only one thing that he'd really wanted. 'Find me a Boeing Stearman to buy and I'll be your friend for life.'

It had been a joke. True, of course, but a joke nevertheless. He hadn't expected to ever hear from Barnaby again. They'd kept in touch occasionally, but the phone call last month had been out of the blue. Barnaby, now in his forties and out of the RAF, had inherited the Molton-Kusak family fortune plus a minor stately home. He'd ploughed most of his money into breeding racehorses and had been on a bloodstock visit to the Kentucky Bluegrass country when he'd just happened to come across a retired Boeing Stearman which had been used as a crop-duster. He remembered the promise. Was Jonah still interested . . . ?

And the rest, Jonah thought with only a fleeting moment of panic about the size of the cheque he'd just given Barnaby, would be aviation history.

'I wish I could stand the whole cost,' Barnaby said. 'Purchase price and all that. Sadly, being a racehorse owner and trying to maintain a house the size of Wembley Stadium that has galloping rot and no mod cons has rather eaten away the finances. Still, she was a good price, considering she's still

51

airworthy, wasn't she?'

'It was a brilliant price. And I still feel guilty about you paying for dismantling and crating it in the States, and shipping it over here.'

'The least I could do. I'll ring my boys in the States and get things moving. As soon as you've found a home for her she could be docking at Southampton as soon as you like . . . and then you'll have all the hard work of rebuilding and painting, won't you?'

'Yeah.' Jonah's eyes gleamed pleasurably at the prospect. 'And the absolute bliss of flying her. So, have you got to belt off back to Derbyshire and the stately pile—or can I persuade you to stay overnight with me in squalor, and celebrate properly?'

'Oh, I'm easily persuaded—and after all, there's no one waiting for me at home, is there?' Barnaby gave a fruity laugh. 'And all this has given me a hell of an appetite. Is there anywhere in this neck of the woods that does a good lunch?'

Jonah flinched a bit, thinking of Whiteacres restricted culinary delights. Then he brightened. 'The Dil Raj in Amberley Hill does food to die for—but if you're looking for pub grub we could try Mulligan's. It gets crowded, but it has a good menu and it's pretty reasonable.'

'Lead on, then.' Barnaby slapped him chummily on the back. 'I'd like to find a nice local pub. Somewhere I can flirt with the barmaids and bore people rigid with stories about flying and racehorses. After all, once you've got digs for the Boeing, I'll probably be spending a lot of time round here, won't I?'

chapter five

'Billie—you're cheating! That was a foul!'

'It was not! It was a fair tackle. It was a—Ouch!'

'It was a bloody foul! Under FIFA rules you'd have been sent off for that. Now what are you doing?'

'Taking my ball and going home.' Picking up the football, Billie brushed down the straw clinging to her knees and poked out her tongue. She wrinkled her nose. 'And I'm telling Mum of you!'

Jon, her oldest brother, sat on the iron-hard rutted ground and shrugged. 'See if I care. I'd got fed up with playing, anyhow. You've lost your edge—I reckon townie life is making you soft. You could tackle harder than Stuart Pearce before you went away.'

Grinning, Billie hauled him to his feet. Like all her brothers, he towered above her, was fair-haired, broad-shouldered, his face permanently tanned. And like all her brothers, he worked on the farm because he had never wanted to do anything else. Billie had never been treated by any of them as anything other than a younger, if slightly more dainty, male sibling.

Jon and Alex, both in their thirties, lived with their wives and assorted children in granite cottages across the yard: Ben and Tom, in their late twenties, still lived in the parental farmhouse. Well, at least Ben had, until he and Maria had whizzed off to the Caribbean to plight their troth. Now they'd be living in the stable flat. Another branch of the Pascoe dynasty well and truly established.

After being back in Devon for twenty-four hours, it was as if the years had been peeled away. Billie's nails had broken off on the sacks of sheep feed; the carefully constructed wedding party hairdo had been reduced to a tufty knot on top of her head, and her silky smooth waxed legs had been permanently bared in a pair of ancient denim cut-offs.

Only two more days of this bliss and she'd be trekking back to Amberley Hill and a very uncertain future. She tried not to think about it.

'You two get in here now!' Faith Pascoe hurled open the kitchen window. 'I'm not spending all day in this dratted kitchen cooking for half of Devon without any help. If you want to be having a party tonight, don't you think you should be making some sort of input? And don't you think you're both a bit old for football?'

'Yes, Mum. No, Mum.'

Jon and Billie exchanged guilty looks and then exploded with laughter. Mrs Pascoe shut the window with a crash.

'Come on, then.' Jon ruffled Billie's hair. 'We'd better pull our weight or we'll be in the dog house all night. And you've been treated like Lady Muck for long enough.'

'Crap.' Billie eased off her trainers in the porch. 'As the Prodigal, I expected nothing less.'

Since her arrival the previous day, and in between eating and drinking, helping out with the animals, and playing wild games of Subbuteo and Scalextric, Billie had endured hefty bouts of parental cross-questioning. She'd managed to avoid anything too embarrassing, and had made her deciding to leave Reuben's Cabs and lease a warehouse sound like she was now on a par with Nicola Horlick. It was obviously, she'd told them, the next sensible step to be thinking of setting up on her own. Her family, still not at all sure why she'd wanted to alienate herself from the West Country in the first place, couldn't quite see the logic in the argument. Her mum had even looked anxious and had tried to ask Billie all about her new setup, and her reasons for leaving the taxi-driving, but Billie had said she didn't want to think about work this weekend, and had refused to be drawn.

The farmhouse kitchen was in chaos. Every available surface was covered with food in some stage of preparation, and the various dogs and cats were hovering expectantly with wide eyes and lolling tongues. The Pascoes' parties were legendary; and people were expected to start making their way across Dartmoor by mid-afternoon. Faith always seemed to cater for about a hundred more guests than necessary, and Billie, closely followed by Jon, swooped on a pile of freshly baked and still-steaming crusty rolls.

'They're for later.' Faith slapped at their hands as she straightened up, puffing, from the bottom oven of the Aga, a proper solid-fuel battered cream monster which radiated constant warmth and delicious smells. 'There are plenty of yesterday's batch still in the bread crock.'

'It's not the same.' Billie watched a dollop of thick yellow butter melt into the bread. 'Oh, don't be cruel, Mum. In forty-eight hours I'll be back to prepackaged white sliced.'

'You don't have to be.' Faith checked a hock of gammon simmering on the top plate, adding to the breathless heat. 'You could stay here and have freshly baked rolls every day.' She threw a gimlet glance at her son. 'And where do you think you're sloping off to?'

'Home,' Jon spluttered through a hastily crammed mouthful of hot roll. 'Ann will want to be getting ready for the party. She'll have my guts for garters if I leave the hens to her again.'

'I thought you were going to stay and help?'

'Nah. Billie can do that. I reckon she ought to get some practice in the kitchen. She's no great shakes at football any more, so she really should learn to cook. She might, just might, even capture a man if she can offer him more than takeaway pizza. See you later.'

Typical, Billie thought, as her brother disappeared across the yard. Getting out while the going was good. She wandered to the window, clutching a second bread roll, savouring the smell. The view was as it had always been: two tractors in the corner, the Dutch barn piled with hay for the winter feeding, the stables, the hens and ducks skittering around amongst the remains of pigsties, which were now overgrown with Russian vine. Somewhere, Stan, her father, was yelling at the dogs as the heat haze rolled down from the moors, and the tors towered like benevolent grey ghosts on the skyline. It was all so lovely. So familiar.

She turned and looked hopefully at her mother. 'Do you think Maria will wear her wedding dress for the party?'

Faith was surveying a mountain of cheese. 'I think I might do a fondue. They always go down well, don't you reckon? What? No, I shouldn't think so. It looked like half a bikini and a net curtain in the video. Probably wonderful for the wedding—

56

not so hot in Newton Abbot.'

Ben and Maria were due to arrive at the farm at any time. They'd been off doing the placating rounds of Maria's relatives, who apparently hadn't quite had the Pascoes' equanimity about not being invited to the nuptials. Billie continued to gaze from the window and sighed happily, contented and secure. Right now, in the middle of all this wonderfully familiar family bustle, she felt she could stay here for ever. But she knew before long the claustrophobia would set in, as it had before, and she'd be missing the lights and noise of Amberley Hill, and her no-holds-barred conversations with Miranda. And, yes, oddly, even the challenge of doing something with the warehouse . . .

Billie watched her mother clanking about in the cavernous larder cupboard for the fondue paraphernalia. 'I suppose Jon's right. Oh—not about the husband-baiting, but I ought to earn my keep. What shall I do?'

'You could knock up a few salads, green, tomato and herb, mixed, pasta, whatever you fancy. Oh, and open that bottle of Baileys. We might as well have a drink while we work. No, don't fuss with the little glasses—get the schooners. It's only like milkshake, after all.'

Three milkshakes later, they were giggling immoderately.

'Go on then.' Faith leaned towards her daughter across the cluttered table. 'Then what happened?'

'Oh, um, nothing much . . .' Billie back-pedalled. She'd been regaling her mother with graphic tales of Miranda's varied love life and had just remembered how this particular encounter had

57

ended. There were still some things far too racy for her mother's ears. 'Er—is that enough garlic in this one, do you reckon?'

'Ample. It'll keep the vampires away right up to the Tamar. Now, tell me to mind my own business, but while your friend is having all this fun, what about you? You always talk about Miranda's men when you ring, but you never say anything about your own love life. Still no man on the horizon?'

'None at all. Which suits me fine. Honest. Come on, Mum. Why do you want me to settle down? You've just acquired another daughter-in-law—and you certainly can't want more grandchildren. Alex and Jon seem to be going for the world record.'

It was true. Ann and Katy, her established sisters-in-law, each had two children and were again both pregnant. Billie had picked her way through the chaos of their cottages, which already seemed awash with Pampers and toddler-meal cartons and discarded toys and surely far more mess than four children could possibly create, and was absolutely delighted to be single.

'I don't want you to marry, necessarily, or to have babies. Ann and Katy are joyously maternal— perhaps you'll never be. I just want you to be happy with your life.' Faith squinted at the depleted bottle of Baileys in surprise. 'I've never understood why you left that nice job you had on the paper—and after you'd studied so hard. It all seemed a terrible waste to just throw it in and move to London for such a brief time. And then end up miles away driving a taxi. Your dad and I never really understood what went awry . . . I thought maybe it was a man when you left, but I was obviously wrong.'

58

'One hundred and ten per cent wrong,' Billie lied, hating herself.

She would have loved to explain, but she'd left it far too late; and anyway, she'd always felt so protective of her mother. The more lurid storylines in EastEnders made Faith practically apoplectic about declining morals and hussies who stole other women's husbands. The reality about her only daughter and Kieran Squires would probably finish her off.

'And I've been happy driving a taxi. And now I'll be happy doing—well—something else. And if the something else doesn't involve bouncing down the aisle in a fondant fancy wedding dress, then I'll still be happy.' She had been about to add that no one should marry before they were thirty anyway, and look what had happened to Miranda, but remembered just in time that her parents had been married at eighteen. 'Er—shall I mummify these salads with clingfilm?'

'Yes, please. Oh, and while you're putting those dishes in the fridge, get the other bottle of Baileys out, there's a love.'

*　　　*　　　*

Really, Billie thought hazily about two hours later, this was even more inebriated than one of her sessions with Miranda. She'd remained just sober enough to steer her mother away from any dangerous topics, and instead had concentrated on the local gossip. It was odd how all the girls in her sixth-form class were now married or partnered and had produced at least one child apiece. It occurred to her that she must be quite a let-down for her mother on the jumble-sale and coffee-morning chitchat circuit—no man, no baby, no career to brag about, and no prospects of any of the three in the foreseeable future.

If she'd stayed on the *Devon Argus*, it would have been different. If she'd stayed on the *Devon Argus* and stuck with covering council meetings and court cases, and not pestered the editor to be sent to interview Kieran Squires about his plans to open a farmhouse restaurant near Bideford, then she'd have probably had her own column by now. It would have been called Billie's Blabber or something similar, and she'd have been able to write it from home because, of course, she'd have married a neighbouring farmer's son and produced the regulation baby every year.

She pushed her chair away and stood up. The room swam slightly. God, she'd be comatose by midnight if she wasn't careful. 'I'll go and have a bath and get glammed up if we've finished here. I'll be out of the bathroom then in time for Dad to have a soak.'

'Good idea.' Faith stared at the Everest of cubed cheese on the table with apparent surprise. 'Heavens. I hope everyone's got a good appetite. I seem to have done a bit too much. Still, never mind. There'll be dozens of the boys' friends here tonight. You know, from the football club and what have you. They're bound to be as hungry as hunters.'

Billie groaned as she galloped upstairs. Unsubtle as ever! Her mother had probably been through the Torquay telephone book, surreptitiously inviting every lone bachelor under sixty.

*   *   *

The night was sweet-scented and velvety warm, and the midsummer sky was diamond-dotted with constellations. Billie pressed her burning forehead against the leaded window and wished she had half as much energy as her parents.

The party had been roaring for more than four hours—and there were still thirty minutes to go until midnight. Outside, the farmyard was thrown into elongated shapes of black and silver, with an occasional golden beam as people suffering from heat exhaustion piled out of the back door. Billie had danced and chatted, eaten enough fondue to sustain a calcium famine, and drunk at least eight of Faith's killer-mix gin and tonics.

The eating and the drinking had been relatively painless. The chatting and the dancing had both posed more of a problem. God, she was becoming so adept at inventing false lives. Of course, down here, Damon from Newton Abbot was a no-no, so she'd fended off any sort of chat-up lines by vague references to a man waiting patiently back in Amberley Hill. No, he hadn't been able to make it down to Devon to meet everyone . . . an ailing mother, you understand? Sadly, everyone seemed to, and said he sounded like a really decent bloke.

The men her mother had invited—the football clubbers, the Young Farmers, the lifeguards, the fishermen—were mostly classmates from primary school, as homely to her as her brothers. They held no attraction for her whatsoever. But she, having been away and having resurrected Follicles and Cuticles knock-'em-dead party hairstyle, and wearing a dress from Joseph, which was the only other thing she'd spent her grandmother's money

61

on and which would have to see her through every festive occasion until the end of time, seemed to be able to pull them in like iron filings to a magnet. Miranda would have loved it.

She'd spent the evening slipping from one to the other, interspersing the escapes with brief gossips with childhood neighbours, and reminiscences with old girlfriends. The house buzzed with happiness and every face was dearly familiar. This was her security; her rock. She could come back here, and just pick up the threads, and it would be like the last two years had never existed.

'I wondered where you'd got to.' Stan Pascoe's voice cut through the musing. 'I thought some young man had whisked you off into the night.'

Billie swung round and grinned at her father. 'No such luck. I'm just having a breather. I'm not used to all this. Can't take the pace. I'd forgotten how manic your parties are.'

Stan, big, burly, and comfortable, with a glass of whisky in one hand and a cigar in the other, nodded ruefully. 'I blame your mother's HRT. She gets worse.' He lodged himself on the edge of the windowseat. 'You'll be back in the fray for the midnight conga, though, won't you?'

'Of course,' Billie sat beside her father and linked her arm through his. 'I want to do the whole traditional Pascoe party bit. Singing the silly songs out in the yard, like we always do so that the animals can join in, and all the dancing, and making the wedding wishes . . .'

She trailed away. What would she be wishing for? What did she really want? Her own successful business on the perimeter of Whiteacres? Was that it? Was that the extent of her ambition? Not

62

perpetual happiness? Or untold wealth? Or even a home of her own? Or, how about a man? Someone to share the rest of her life with? Wouldn't that be the most sensible thing to be wishing for?

'Dad, what did you really think when I told you that I'd spent Granny Pascoe's inheritance on a monstrous breeze-block shed?'

Stan swigged his whisky and tapped the ash from his cigar into a rather shrivelled geranium. 'My first thought was that Granny Pascoe would come and rattle her chains at you for the rest of your life.' He took another mouthful of whisky. 'To be honest, love, my main concern was the situation, on the edge of an airfield. You know what you're like about flying . . .'

Billie smiled. 'It was one of Miranda's main concerns too. But it won't be a problem—I won't be involved with the airfield at all. The industrial estate is quite separate.'

'That's a relief.' Stan flicked more ash into the geranium pot.

Billie, imagining Faith's wrath in the morning, leaned across and poked the ash deep into the soil. 'You don't think I should have used the money for the deposit on a house, then? I know Mum does.'

'Your mother would like to see you married and settled in cosy suburbia, whatever she may say to the contrary, but it's your money—and it's not a fortune, just a few thousand, love, and if the warehouse is what you want, then I'm certainly not going to chuck in any objections.'

Billie hugged him. 'And when I get into a right muddle over invoicing and tax and VAT, I'll be able to ring you in a blind panic, won't I?'

'Course you will, love. Whether I'll be able to

help or not is another matter, but I'll give it my best shot, you know that.' Stan glanced at his watch. 'Hey it's nearly midnight. Time we were getting outside to dance with the happy couple. Look, when we've all recovered from our hangovers tomorrow, we'll talk about it some more, OK?'

'OK. Thanks, Dad.' Billie stood up and hugged her father again. She knew what she wanted. The house, the wealth, even the man would have to wait. Tonight her wedding wish was going to be for the success of the Whiteacres warehouse.

chapter six

Miranda and Reuben were of the same opinion: that Billie had lost not only her marbles, but also the bag she kept them in.

'It's a dump,' Miranda said cheerfully, the day Billie officially started her own business. 'A condemned shit tip. And how much did you pay for it?'

'More than I'd expected to,' Billie admitted, not wanting to be barracked this early in the morning. 'There were all sorts of things on top of the lease: insurances and deposits and stuff . . . Anyway don't criticise it yet. You haven't even seen it.'

'I don't have to. I can smell it on you when you come in. It's all cold and cabbagey.'

Billie was beginning to feel the first stirrings of doubt. Not to mention anticlimax. The previous day had been her last as a taxi-driver. She'd walked into the office prepared to do battle with Reuben—but he hadn't been there. The hayfever had worsened and had laid him very low. Bronchitis now, Veronica had said, with a hint of malicious pleasure. He'd phoned in early and said he still wasn't well enough to come into the office. Her fellow cabbies had said it was more like he couldn't admit when he was beaten, and that he didn't want to be there to see her go.

Billie doubted this. She had an unpleasant feeling that Reuben was planning something nasty.

'You should take Reuben a bottle of whisky as a gesture of goodwill and offer to rub his chest,' Miranda said, still sitting on Billie's bed. 'I know I would.'

'Well, go on, then. But don't blame me if he bites you. Oh—pul-lease! Take that look off your face! You're so disgusting! Reuben Wainwright is the pits.'

In Reuben's absence, Billie's leaving party had been pretty tame. Veronica had made a cake in the shape of a taxi with only three wheels because she'd run out of sponge mix, and the other drivers had clubbed together to buy her an electronic organiser, and then they'd all gone to Mulligan's and got fairly drunk and sang 'The Rose of Tralee' with the bar staff on the karaoke.

And now it was the first day of her self-employment and she had the premises, the keys, less than two thousand pounds of her capital left, and still, despite racking her brains until the small hours, absolutely no idea what she was going to do. So far, her venture into big business had been completely unedifying. Miranda had said she'd be welcome to shampoo the blue-rinse brigade and sweep up at Follicles and Cuticles in lieu of rent if things got desperate. Billie had a feeling it might

65

just come to that.

'Shift.' She kicked away the duvet. 'I've got an empire to create, and I'm sure you should have been tarting up the population of Amberley Hill hours ago.'

Miranda reluctantly got to her feet and slouched towards the doorway. 'You're a whizz on understatement, aren't you? Tell you what then, when you've created your empire and I've beautified the masses, I'll see you in Mulligan's. We'll have a beer or ten to celebrate, OK?'

'Sure,' Billie nodded. 'Anita Roddick probably only took a morning to create the Body Shop. It should give me the whole afternoon free.'

'Being sarky is no defence over stupidity.' Miranda twirled a plait which had now faded to a dull mauve. 'Oh—and did I tell you that the salon's going unisex? Starting next week. I mean we've always done haircuts for men, of course, but we thought we'd start offering facials and massages and manicures—and well, hey! Whatever they want...'

Billie paused in searching for a matching sock. 'And would this have more to do with you trawling through the population for the ideal husband, than dragging the men of the area into the twenty-first century?'

'As if! How could you even think such a thing?' Miranda giggled. 'But I've told Kim to give me first refusal on all the muscular six-footers who want body oiling ...'

*　　*　　*

Billie gazed around the warehouse with mounting

66

despair. Even allowing for the input of proper lighting, and electric heaters to dry out the damp, and every spare minute she'd had in the past week being spent hefting and sweeping and washing and cleaning, it still looked appalling. If only it weren't so empty. If only it was filled with something. Anything. But what?

Wandering around the vastness, her canvas boots echoing on the cold concrete, she took stock. Granny Pascoe appeared to have funded a few hundred million square feet of nothing which soared to cobwebby heights of improbable proportions. Simon Maynard's kitchenette and lavatorial areas, despite having been bleached and scoured, still reeked; and the office must have been constructed from ice blocks.

Billie had written a scarily huge cheque at a second-hand office furniture warehouse, and now had a desk, two chairs, and one lop-sided filing cabinet. Her hardware, to which Simon Maynard had referred in such an off-hand manner, so far consisted of a portable radio, her mobile phone, the new personal organiser—which would no doubt be a real boon as soon as she had something to organise—a very basic mail-order computer, a printer and an optimistically huge box of paper. Billie reckoned the computer would probably be repossessed long before she got the hang of using it.

B & Q's sale had provided several industrial-sized tins of remaindered paint. This was today's task: to decorate anything that didn't fall apart at the flick of a roller. The shade strips on the paint tins would have had Laurence Llewelyn-Bowen capering with glee. No two colours were the same.

By lunch time she'd got a rather splodgy red, white, and blue kitchen, and a candyfloss-pink lavatory. The rest of the paint would probably stretch to covering the office walls in various shades of sludge and daffodil. The grey breeze blocks of the shed itself would have to stay in their native plumage—well, at least until she had some more money. Paint-streaked and exhausted, Billie picked up a can of Diet Coke and wandered to the doorway.

She hadn't seen Zia and Isla or Sylvia again. Zi-Zi's, she guessed, were out on a clothes-buying mission, and possibly Sylvia had taken some time off—either that or the unpleasant Douglas had got his way and forced her to abandon her project. Billie hoped fervently that it was the former.

Despite the heat, every one of the double doors was closed, and although there were cars parked on the weedy concrete at the back when she arrived, so far this morning she had seen no one. Fred 'n' Dick at number one, she knew, did replacement doors and windows, because she'd read the sign; two belonged to Sylvia; three was hers; and four was leased by Zia and Isla. Unit six, on the far end, was still empty. And likely to stay that way, according to Simon Maynard. It wasn't, he'd said with understandable embarrassment, quite up to standard. So, that still left number five to be investigated.

Anything, absolutely anything, could be going on behind those shuttered doors. And presumably as long as it didn't involve fumes or high-frequency radio, and Maynard and Pollock got their money, no one really cared.

Sheltering beneath the porch from the scorching

68

sun, Billie surveyed her surroundings as she finished her Coke. The airstrip looked even more unprepossessing from behind the perimeter fence; like a war-torn no-go zone on the news. In the glaring heat, the colourless stubby grass merged into the dazzling sky, the wind sock hung listlessly like wet washing, and the radio control tower had all the charm of an offshore oil refinery. Sporadic small planes dithered along the runway and eventually coughed their way into the ether.

There were several medium-sized planes sort of parked at haphazard angles, and a clutch of smaller ones sheltering from the glare of the sun with tarpaulins pulled over them. A couple of trucks meandered across the tarmac square in no apparent hurry, and the occasional figure in neon safety clothing dashed between the planes, only to duck out of sight beneath the wings.

As she couldn't see the departures and arrivals area from the perimeter fence, there wasn't even the joy of people-watching to pass the time. Not that she'd envy them their journeys anyway: they'd probably be businessmen going somewhere boring, or cut-pricers taking a chance on a cheap trip across the Channel.

'Jesus!'

The overhead roar made her duck her head. She dropped the Coke can. The plane was merely feet above her; the pulse of its engines punching into her stomach. Her heart beating a tattoo of terror, her mouth dry, Billie watched as it turned sharply towards the runway. The propellers were whirling twin circles of transparency. The fat black wheels appeared to be stretching themselves towards the ground and the scream of the brakes made her clench her teeth. Hitting the runway at what seemed a ludicrous speed, the plane bounced and twitched, then subsided into an elegant break-neck glide. Just as it appeared destined to plough off into the grass, it turned sharply, and, with the propellers slowing, almost jauntily cruised towards the glass-plated buildings.

Billie realised she'd stopped breathing. It had never been like this at Gatwick.

The plane was silver, purple and emerald-green, and could probably seat about thirty people as long as they were on good terms. The Sullivanair logo brashly inscribed across the side seemed vaguely familiar. Oh, yes, of course . . . the name splashed vibrantly across the hangars in the distance . . . Obviously Whiteacres was Sullivanair's home base.

Billie gave herself a good mental talking-to. She really was going to have to get used to the comings and goings if she was to stay here for five years. She simply couldn't jump into catatonic shock every time anything larger than a hang glider appeared in the sky.

The trucks and neon-jacketed men were all hurrying towards the new arrival, but anything interesting was happening behind the buildings, out of her line of vision. Wiping her damp hands on her jeans, she turned back into the shed.

It was seriously time to take stock. Billie sat at her new desk and, still not confident about the computer, reached for a Biro and a notepad. Wimpish, she knew. She'd done computer studies at school, but as the teacher had looked an awful lot like Ruud Gullit she hadn't concentrated much. And on the *Devon Argus*, she'd filed her copy on to the regulation AppleMac without having a clue how

70

it worked. She really should have listened . . .

Reduced to basics, she drew up two columns on the first page of the notepad: 'What I Can Do' and 'What I Can Afford'. The second would probably remain blank.

So—what were her skills? Small-time journalist. Driver. She wrote them down. She could cook, but nowhere near as well as her mother, and anyway, Simon Maynard had said no food, so there was no point in writing that down. What else? She chewed the end of the pen. Well, she could play football, but that didn't seem to have much potential. Oh God . . . she stared at the sadly brief list. Was that really all she had to offer the world?

It looked like it would have to be the driving, then.

The double doors would slide back and were plenty big enough to get vehicles through, and the shed itself could house half a dozen large cars in comfort. So, limousine hire—or executive chauffeuring—was a definite possibility.

OK then, so, what would she need? Well, cars would be a help. Or one at least. Any more than one and she'd need to employ staff—which would mean paying wages . . . So, one car. Which, of course, posed a new problem. She looked despairingly at the 'What I Can Afford' column. She couldn't afford to buy one. There simply wasn't enough money left. Not even if she traded in the Nova and hocked the Joseph dress—which was the most valuable possession she had—could she even think about buying a respectable Mercedes or a BMW, which was what she was going to need.

Of course, on the other hand, she could tinker with the Nova and offer her services as a taxi at

71

the airport. But Reuben's Cabs had always had Whiteacres' franchise—and she somehow couldn't see being able to fight off Reuben in a takeover battle, even if he'd let her enter the fray. Which of course he wouldn't, because Reuben held the joker. The truth card.

'Bloody hell.' She closed the notepad and slumped forward across the desk. It was at moments like these that she wished she hadn't been stupid enough to give up smoking. 'What on earth do other people do?'

Pushing aside the thought that other people, like Sylvia and Zi-Zi's, probably had really thriving businesses going in their back bedrooms before they even approached leasing agents for massive premises, Billie knew there were two courses of action. One would involve going cap in hand to the bank for a loan, and the other—far less frightening—was literally on her doorstep. She could always visit her as yet unseen neighbours at number five, and pick their brains.

Of course, if this was fiction, her neighbours would all have arrived on her first morning, bearing home-made cakes and jugs of scalding coffee, and offered to roll up their sleeves and help her decorate the shed. In fiction, there would have been half a dozen cheery neighbours with half a dozen brilliant ideas on how she could make her fortune on a shoestring and with no expertise in any field whatsoever. In fiction, she'd be knocking up baskets of dried flowers to sell to the well-heeled in next to no time, or making seashell mirrors, or suddenly discovering that she had hidden talents—and with the help of the neighbours—turn the shed into a theatre and put on shows to save local orphanages

72

from closure . . .

Billie, in the real world, tucked her vest into her jeans and set off to see if she could stave off insolvency.

As there was no bell at number five, she thumped on the door. A plate simply said *Guspers*. No one answered. The sun was scorching her neck. She thumped again. A sliding peephole opened in the flaking woodwork. A pair of androgynous eyes peered out suspiciously.

'Hi! I'm Billie Pascoe, and I've just moved into number three, and I wondered—'

The eyes disappeared and the peephole slammed shut. Oh, great. So much for the myth of shiny happy people. Billie turned away. Maybe they had good reason for not wanting her interference. Maybe they were a drugs cartel, or money launderers, or makers of pornographic videos . . .

'Hello, sweet.' The door opened behind her. The androgynous eyes belonged to a frankly matching face and body. 'Sorry. Can't stop right now. We're in the middle of shooting.'

Billie blinked. Number five housed *hit men*? Were debts settled and scores evened at point-blank range? Did the airfield perimeter industrial units house Whiteacres' answer to the Corleones? Surely, it wouldn't be allowed? On the other hand, Simon Maynard hadn't mentioned no firearms . . .

Surely, though, this pale, wispy person couldn't be right up there with Desperate Dan McIver or Nick The Knife Borsino or whatever Quentin Tarantino called them, could it?

'OK. Fine. Sorry.' Billie backed away. Best not antagonise them. 'I'll—um—come back later when you've—er—finished.'

'Okey-doke. Give us about an hour. We should have got everything wrapped up by then.'

'Oh, right—super . . . See you later . . .'

Not. Billie was still smiling maniacally as the pale wispy one closed the door. Wrapped up? Christ. What did they do then? Mummify the bodies in black sacks and wait until nightfall for disposal? Oh God—if it wasn't human disposal, it might possibly be animals . . . She exhaled slowly. Could this be one of those secret Government-funded research places that she and Miranda had campaigned against so vigorously, marching through the Spicer Centre, waving banners, and standing shivering in the sleet outside Woolworths, collecting signatures on petitions?

A rather shabby brown Mini was bouncing across the cracked concrete from the direction of the airfield. Shading her eyes from the sun, Billie watched its erratic progress until it juddered to a halt outside unit two. Tough, she thought, if it was someone delivering or collecting brochures for Sylvia. She walked towards the car, prepared to tell them that Sylvia's island was deserted at the moment but that she'd be happy to take in any packages.

'Billie?' The Mini's driver hurled open the door. 'Billie? It is you, dear, isn't it?'

'Sylvia!'

Sylvia, still in shorts, shades and T-shirt, extricated herself from the Mini's tight confines. Her smile was ear to ear as she bounded across the concrete. 'Billie! What on earth are you doing here?'

It took five minutes of stereo babbling to

74

establish that Billie now leased unit three, and that Sylvia had splashed out the last of her invested pension fund on the Mini—although brown wouldn't of course have been her first choice for a colour, dear—so drab—so that she could get away from Douglas without having to rely on taxis. There was a lot of hugging and exclamations and excitement.

Sylvia, reeking of Ambre Solaire, eventually held Billie at arm's length and surveyed her delightedly. 'Oh, this is going to be wonderful! Another chum to add to our little family! So, dear, what brilliant scheme have you come up with, then?'

Billie scuffed the concrete. Even in the towering shadows of the row of warehouses, the humidity was stifling. Sweat was snaking between her breasts. She didn't want to admit that she didn't have a clue. Not to Sylvia. 'Well, um—'

Suddenly, remembering Sylvia's teetering boxes taking up all the floor space in the tropical paradise, and the fact that she'd been going to offer to take in a brochure delivery, and the lack of space in Zi-Zi's unit, and all the firms in the overcrowded retail village, not to mention the airport, she took a deep breath. 'Actually I'm—er—thinking of warehousing.'

Billie clutched at the words as they grew—like the idea—from nowhere. 'Using my space for other people's storage—' She had to bite back the triumphant grin. That really was it. It was exactly what she could do. 'I'm—um—going to be developing the business locally and—um—before long—er—be rivalling Pickfords . . .'

'Super!' Sylvia hugged her. 'Just what we could do with. I'll certainly be your first customer, and

75

Zia and Isla—you'll love them, dear—will be ecstatic. We can make use of your premises and expand our own at the same time! And it'll be so easy for you, dear! Now, let me pop in and get my rotunda stocked, then I'll come over to you and we'll run through a check list, shall we?'

Still beaming from the beautiful simplicity of the scheme, and actually wanting to rush off and start canvassing people, Billie was practically jigging up and down on the spot.

'Oh, yes please. I suppose I'll need cards and flyers—and a slogan—and maybe an advert on local radio . . .'

She stopped. There was one problem that could halt this corporate extravaganza dead in its tracks. 'Sylvia, the people at number five . . . are they into something iffy?'

Sylvia, who had bent double inside the Mini to remove a clutch of carrier bags, straightened up. 'The Gusper boys? Have you seen them?'

'Briefly.'

'And you don't approve?'

'Not if they're doing what I think they are.'

Sylvia shook her head. 'Then that might cause a few stumbling blocks. Look, dear, let me get myself sorted, and I'll come in and tell you all about them.'

chapter seven

Billie's peculiar feeling of unreality stayed with her as she wandered back into the unit. She had an instant business—well, almost. She'd discovered, albeit accidentally, her own niche, her own gap in

76

the market. Maybe it wasn't exactly what she would have chosen; there wasn't much excitement or glamour in running a storage warehouse, after all, but who cared?

Her feet echoed empty drumbeats on the floor as she crossed the vastness. But at least warehousing was something, and it was something positive, and it could possibly lead to something else. And, more importantly, it was all hers. She drifted into the office and sat behind her desk. The business would flounder or flourish because of her. She would never be beholden to Reuben again.

Although the computer was switched off, Billie ran her fingers over the keyboard. It gave her a feeling of continuity. Of achievement. She was sitting, behind her own desk, at her own computer, in her own office, at the inception of her own business. Pascoe's Warehousing . . . Wow— Pascoe's Warehousing . . . She played with the dead keys a bit more, feeling increasingly like the businesswoman of the year.

So, to business. Well, Sylvia would be a certain customer, and Zia and Isla were definite probables, which meant she could kick off the venture with the excess holiday brochures, and the boxes of eighties and nineties fashion. Naturally, she'd give Sylvia and Zi-Zi's special rates, and also Fred 'n' Dick at number one, who might want somewhere to store surplus sheets of glass. And there were bound to be other avenues just waiting to be explored . . .

She hadn't had a clue how much she should charge for storage, but decided to phone other warehousing companies that afternoon, pretending to be a potential customer, and ask for their literature. As soon as it arrived she would undercut them all. So far so good.

Next step . . . ? Billie pulled a face—oh God, it had to be done—and surely the best time was now while the confidence was still bubbling? With only a moment's hesitation, she switched on the computer, and slowly opened the *Instructions for Idiots handbook.*

By the time she heard Sylvia click-clacking across the concrete floor, Billie had plucked up enough courage to produce an optimistic twenty files on the computer, one for each would-be customer, with a column for the goods they were depositing, where in the warehouse they were to be kept, and the rate she would be charging them. Of course, the blank columns could be filled in later when she'd worked out all the details.

Not wanting Sylvia to know what a techno-novice she was, she hid the handbook and reluctantly closed the files, totally convinced that if she ever tried to open them again they'd be gone. Then, holding her breath, just to check, she moved the mouse tentatively and clicked again on the appropriate icons. There was a lot of whirring and a few bleeps and then . . . Hallelujah! There they were! Magically, the files appeared exactly where she'd hoped they would be.

'Oooh! Paint! What a pong! Lingers like blazes on a hot day, doesn't it?' Sylvia bustled through to the office, carrying a tray of tall glasses overbrimming with pink liquid, lime segments and ice cubes. 'Lovely colours, though, dear. I do like the patriotic kitchen. I had a little squint on my way through . . . Now, I'll take eight shelves to start with. How much are you going to charge?'

'Er—I actually don't know.' Billie sat back from

78

the computer, 'It was something I was just thinking about. Do you want to hold off on a decision to use me until I've worked things through?'

'No, I do not!' Sylvia set down the tray with a clatter. 'I'm just desperate to get rid of my overspill and take on more work. And I'm sure Zia and Isla will feel the same.' She pulled up the second chair. 'You just name a price and I'll cough up and then we can straighten things out at the end of the month. Now, I took the liberty of ringing the Gusper boys from my place, and they'd love to see you at lunch time. They could be really good customers, dear.'

Billie sucked in her breath. 'Not if they want me to store murdered animals.'

'What?'

'Not if they're into anything to do with vivisection or—'

'Dear God!' Sylvia hooted with laughter. 'If they were, dear, do you think they'd still be living and breathing? I'd have killed them—not to mention Zia and Isla, who are vegans and who'd have none of that sort of thing! Goodness me! Whatever gave you that idea? No, the Guspers are sweeties!' Sylvia handed Billie one of the tall glasses. 'Real loves. Frantically busy, of course, which is why we never see much of them, but super people.'

'But what do they actually do in there?' Billie asked, savouring what she thought was possibly a strawberry daiquiri, and feeling mightily relieved. 'Is it something to do with films?'

'Spot on!' Sylvia chortled.

'Not mucky vids?'

'That's what I love about you young people! You act like you've invented sex—behave as if there's

79

nothing that will shock you—then you turn into Mary Whitehouse at the drop of a *double entendre*.'

'Not at all. I just don't want to be stocking someone else's hard-core pornography and be raided by the vice squad before I've even got started, that's all.'

Sylvia chuckled. 'Understandable—but business is business. You can't really afford to be choosy—or prudish.'

'No, I realise that. But there's a lot of difference between entertaining smut and downright exploitation. I'd never condone anything that degraded women.'

Sylvia chuckled again. 'I'm sure you wouldn't, dear, and neither would I, so stop looking so outraged. I've just found that as one grows older, one's mind becomes broader in direct proportion to one's waistline. Despite my Douglas getting a tad po-faced, I'm not averse to a bit of late-night raunch on Channel 4—and if the boys at Guspers are into titillation, then it's fine by me.'

Billie shut up then. She felt vaguely uncomfortable, discussing things like this with Sylvia anyway. It was like talking about sex with her mother. Completely unthinkable. She smiled. Miranda discussed sex with her mum all the time. Billie had been shocked rigid when she'd first moved into the flat to find them poring over a 'you too can have twelve orgasms a night' article in *Cosmo*. Faith never took anything more outrageous than the *Farmers Weekly*.

Sylvia rattled her ice cubes. 'So, dear, to get up and running you need to let people know that you're here and what you do. Advertising is a must. You'll need business cards, of course—there are

80

some nice little printers in Amberley Hill who can sort them out for you—and leaflets . . .'

'Can I get those done at the same time? Will they take ages?'

'Well, not really, but if you want to have an early blitz why don't we knock up some flimsies on your PC, dear? You could have them printed in half an hour and be distributing them straight after lunch. Striking while the iron's hot, so to speak . . .'

'Er . . .' Billie spent a lot of time twizzling her drink, 'actually, I'm not too sure how the computer works on—um—that sort of thing . . .'

'Good Lord—piece of cake.' Sylvia drained her glass.' Tell you what, you scribble down what you want to say, and I'll play about with the layout and artwork and stuff while you're seeing the Gusper boys. OK?'

'More than OK . . .' Billie looked at her with admiration. 'You're so surprising—I mean, I didn't think—'

'That someone of my advanced years would be *au fait* with the World Wide Web? Well, to be honest, dear, I only started taking computer studies at evening class because it totally pissed Douglas off. He's such a Luddite that he wears wellington boots and Marigolds to change a lightbulb. Now, you write down what you want to say and leave the rest to me . . .'

Half an hour later, Billie looked at her watch. Five to one. Lunch time in anyone's language. Time to visit the porn merchants. Leaving Sylvia skimming merrily across the keyboard, she walked outside into the stifling July heat.

She didn't care how prudish she appeared to Sylvia, she thought as she hurried across the broken concrete, she really didn't want to do business with the Guspers if they were into sleaze. She didn't want to offer a home to reels of grainy grime—but she was also well aware that to turn them down completely would be folly at this early stage in her career. Maybe she could just offer them shelf space for their dirty raincoats?

Several medium-sized planes were revving up on the airfield's concrete strip, taxiing towards their takeoff slots, and a couple of smaller ones were beetling about, zigzagging across the grass. Billie watched them for a moment. What the heck: she might as well drop some of Sylvia's leaflets off at the airport too. There must be companies inside the perimeter fence who might make use of storage space. Being an aerophobe really shouldn't make her picky about her potential customers.

Her customers . . . She felt a buzz of real excitement. This must be exactly how all the early industrial revolution pioneers had felt when an inventive glimmer suddenly ignited into a spark of reality. She stopped and looked back lovingly at number three.

The sun spiralled relentlessly over the sepia tones of Whiteacres and the greyness of the units, the glaring dazzle exaggerating every defect of the warehouse: the grubby windows, the streaky, flaking paintwork, and all the dust and grime which she thought she'd managed to clear. It looked appallingly shabby. She grinned. If she was going to invite potential customers to see the premises, maybe she'd have to arrange the viewing days during stormy weather.

Oh God. She couldn't put it off any longer. Knocking at number five, she instinctively took a step backwards when the peephole opened.

The same pair of asexual eyes peered at her. 'Yes? Oh right, yes! It's you! Lovely to have a chance to get to know you at last! Hang on a mo while I get the doors unstuck . . .'

There was a scuffling and a high-pitched curse, then the door creaked open to allow a six-inch gap of darkness. Billie held her breath as the door juddered, then swung open.

'There! That's got the bastard,' the pale wispy person she'd seen on her first visit said with some pleasure. 'It can be a right bugger sometimes.'

It was very hot inside. And dark. There were no overhead lights, just dimly glowing red bulbs in wall holders. Billie followed the skinny shadow along a corridor.

'I'm Mike, love. Director, producer, sandwich maker and general factotum. I know you're Billie— Sylvia said—pretty name.' With a lot of huffing and puffing he tugged at a sliding door. 'We really ought to get these buggers oiled. Ah! There we go, love. It's a bit cooler in here.'

It was. Thanks to a rank of cold-air blowers the shed was deliciously air-conditioned. It was also brilliantly lit by a dozen huge spotlights dangling from overhead gantries. Billie hardly dared to look at the lighted set. Expecting to see pneumatic peroxide blondes in see-through scarlet, and men looking like Engelbert Humperdinck in wing collars and bulging thongs, she gazed at the scene in front of her in amazement.

Two middle-aged men in sober suits sat sweating under the halogen brightness, holding a sheaf of insurance documents and looking extremely nervous. A harassed sound man was tinkering with a boom microphone while the cameraman, totally ignoring the signs, had obviously taken advantage of the break and sloped off to a darkened corner for a crafty cigarette. It was as far from pornography as you could get and Billie laughed, immediately disguising it as a sneeze.

'Bless you.' Mike raised pale eyebrows. 'Oh, it's all right, love. You can make a noise. We're not running.'

'You make *proper films*!' She gazed around at the cameras, the microphones, the lights. 'I'll murder Sylvia! She *knew.*'

'And you thought we peddled porn,' Mike chuckled. 'I know that too! Sylvia said she'd wind you up. She's a bit of a one for a tease, is our Sylv. Right now, if I explain what we need, maybe you can say whether you can help?'

Guspers, it turned out, made mainly television commercials for small companies. They also did promotional videos. They employed six people and had an editing suite, a cutting room, a make-up area and a greenroom of sorts. They didn't, it seemed, have enough space to store all their props, backdrops, spare bulbs, rolls of cable, and a host of other vital bits of equipment without which sixty seconds of instructive selling would never flash onto millions of screens each evening.

Billie, being careful not to step on the myriad writhing cables, followed Mike around, said hi to the other employees, who were all eating Pot Noodles in the greenroom, which wasn't green at all but Billie didn't like to say anything—and said there was absolutely no worries—she'd be able to solve their storage problem at a stroke.

They then shook hands and Mike said he'd start

shifting stuff this afternoon if that was OK. Billie, having explained about the planned leaflet drop, said she should be back by four and she'd look forward to seeing him then.

Standing outside again on the weed-infested concrete, and now knowing what was going on inside each of the units, gave her a sudden rush of belonging. This time the smile came from deep within. For the first time in two years she felt free—and truly happy. Before the bubble burst, she belted back into her warehouse.

Sylvia had worked wonders. There were five hundred A4 flyers in a neat pile on the desk, with a note saying, 'Hope these are OK. They'll certainly do the bizz for now. I'm going back to my desert island for a spot of lunch—good luck, dear. See you later. PS—hope you enjoyed your close encounter with the porn merchants!!!'

Billie laughed and ran her fingers over the brightly coloured illustrated flyers.

'Pascoe's Warehousing. Safe and Secure Storage. Reasonable Rates.' She'd run out of alliteration then and tried waxing lyrical. 'Items large or small? We'll take them all!' OK, so that might not be exactly true, but she had tons of space and would try not to have to turn anyone away at least to start with. The flyers added the Whiteacre address and her mobile phone number and she reckoned that if she could shift all the leaflets, and if even twenty people replied, then she'd be more than satisfied.

Humping the flyers into the back of the Nova, she paused outside Sylvia's door. Steel band music was limboing from beneath the shutters and Billie could visualise Sylvia, probably wearing a sarong, sitting under the infrared lamp, lunching on pineapple and mango and sticking voodoo pins in a little wax effigy of her Douglas. She grinned. She wouldn't disturb her now—but later she'd buy her the biggest box of chocolates in the world to say thank you.

She leaped into the Nova and almost leaped out again. If the temperature was going to remain in the eighties she'd really have to remember to park her car in the shade. Getting in again, this time more gingerly, she turned the key in the ignition and headed away from the warehouses on her first business trip.

*   *   *

It was four thirty by the time she returned. Her feet were screaming from tramping up and down various paths and driveways, and her knuckles were raw after having been trapped by various aggressive letter boxes. Billie now felt total solidarity with postmen. Still, she'd shifted almost all the flyers. Targeting every little trading estate within a five-mile radius, plus the Whiteacres Retail Village, and making a last haphazard dash round the housing estate too, she felt she'd covered a fairly wide field. The last half a dozen or so leaflets she'd pushed into several likely-looking reception areas on the airfield.

Mike and the Guspers crew were waiting for her and made an immediate start on stacking their surplus gear.

'You're OK for insurance, aren't you?' Mike paused in the middle of off-loading what looked like battered leatherette hat boxes. 'Only some of this stuff is irreplaceable. We've got our own insurance, of course, but we'll need to know if you're covered.'

Billie, making a frantic mental note to contact Maynard and Pollock first thing in the morning, nodded confidently. She certainly had insurance cover for the premises—but she couldn't remember anything about stock. And would there be extremely hefty premiums to pay to safeguard other people's property? Oh God, maybe running a warehouse wasn't going to be as easy-peasy as she'd thought.

What on earth would happen if a fire swept through the shed overnight? Sylvia's brochures wouldn't be too much of a problem, she supposed. After all, they could simply be reprinted; but the stuff from the film company was probably unique— and Zi-Zi's clothes certainly would be.

She shuddered, thinking of Zia and Isla's rage if anything should happen to their costumes. She'd definitely get insurance sorted out tomorrow. And security. Relying on an elderly mortise lock and sticky hinges probably wasn't the best form of protection she could offer potential clients. There would no doubt be further pitfalls along the way— hazards she hadn't even contemplated yet. But somehow, it didn't feel daunting. It was a challenge, like the computer: something to get organised so that the business would run efficiently. Maybe, by the end of August when she'd collected her first payments from her neighbours, she might even be able to afford headed notepaper and a proper telephone system.

'Your phone's ringing,' Mike said, shouldering past her with rolls of cable.

Spooky! He must read minds. 'Can't be. I haven't

87

got a phone. Oh, you mean the mobile . . .'

Where had she left it? Hell—how bloody inefficient. It might be a customer. Mind you, it was more likely to be Miranda organising her social life, or her mother with news of the arrival of one of her sisters-in-law's impending babies. Still, you never knew . . .

She rushed into the office. The phone was still chirping away, and Billie had to hurl aside the remaining flyers and various piles of paper before she discovered it.

'Hello . . . Hello . . .' Nothing. Just silence. But the crackle indicated that the caller was still there. 'Hello—Miranda? Mum?'

'Oh, excuse me,' the voice was female, husky, and definitely didn't belong to Miranda or Faith. 'I think I may have got a wrong number. This is obviously a personal line. I was trying to contact Pascoe's Warehousing.'

'Sorry. This is my mobile—I'm afraid . . . What?' Oh, bugger . . . 'Actually, yes, this is Pascoe's Warehousing. I'm—er—still waiting to have my BT line connected. Can I help you?'

The husky voice hesitated a bit, sounding almost as if, after that introduction, it very much doubted it. 'Well, I hope so. Someone from your company left a flyer this afternoon. We may be interested . . . I wondered if I could come and see the premises. If they're suitable it may be just what we're looking for. What time do you close?'

'Never,' Billie said faintly. 'I mean, well, if you want to see them today I'll be here until—oh, seven at least.'

'Christ,' the husky voice sighed, 'I'll be halfway down a bottle of Chardonnay by then. I could be with you in fifteen minutes.'

'Fifteen minutes would be great. I'll look forward to seeing you.'

Billie switched off the phone and collapsed into her chair. A customer! Well, almost. Just like that. And within a couple of hours of delivering the leaflets!

Seventeen and a half minutes later and no one had arrived. Guspers had finished unloading their stock, a hastily hand written invoice had been signed, and Billie, having walked round the shed—which looked far more impressive now that some of the emptiness was occupied—felt very let down.

What was it her mother used to say? Everything worth having is worth waiting for? The best things are left unhurried? Fine, if you're six and three-quarters and longing to be seven and there's all the time in the world—not so hot if you're twenty-six and a half and trying to justify your existence.

The buzzer on the double doors suddenly wheezed into life.

'Calm down,' Billie told herself, scrubbing away at any stray mascara smudges beneath her eyes and pushing her hair into its layers as she rushed across the shed. 'It's bound to be Mike or someone else from Guspers with a piece of equipment they've forgotten, or Sylvia, or Zia and Isla just popping in for a chat . . .'

'Pascoe's?' The husky voice echoed from the other side of the door. 'Either I'm blind or someone has stolen your nameplate.'

What nameplate? She'd have to get a nameplate. 'It's—um—being refurbished. You're at the right place. Just coming. Won't keep you—it's—

89

just—a—bit—stuck—ah!' Billie tugged the door open and froze.

The owner of the husky voice looked like a living, breathing Barbie doll.

'So sorry I'm late.' She didn't sound it. 'I had an awful job finding you. The numbers aren't very clear, are they? I got someone with bad teeth doing double glazing first.'

Billie snapped her mouth shut. She eased it open again, hopefully into a smile. 'You must have started at the wrong end of the row. Please, come in.'

She couldn't help staring: the woman had a waist-length waterfall of silver-blonde hair, catwalk make-up, and an impossible figure encased in a black leather jump suit. Billie, in jeans, canvas boots, and one of her brother's tatty Steve Tyler vests nicked after the wedding party, wanted to scuttle away into a dim corner.

Instead, she threw her arms open wide in an expansive gesture, praying that it didn't make her look too much like Julie Andrews cresting that bloody mountain. 'Well, here we are! I've only just started, but as you can see I've already got customers. I haven't actually got my rates printed yet, but I can offer weekly or monthly. Or I can work out daily if you'd prefer. And we'll have plenty of shelf space round here and—'

'Do you have fork-lift trucks?' The blonde woman tossed back her hair. Her expression remained impassive. The make-up was very thick. 'And qualified warehouse personnel? And twenty-four-hour access?'

'Er—no.'

She pouted and thrust out a leather-encased hip.

'What about bonding?'

'Oh, yes. No problem. I mean it was a bit strange at first—I've only just moved in—but everyone is really friendly and—'

'Security bonding.'

Jesus. Not having a clue, Billie added it to her mental list for Maynard and Pollock and crossed her fingers. 'Oh, yes. Of course. And—er—I'm sure the rest won't be too much of a problem. I mean the fork-lift and everything. Fred 'n' Dick—I think you met Fred, you said?—well they've got one, and we'll all muck in to carry things and if you want access at strange times I only live in Amberley Hill and—'

'I want space.' The woman started jack-booting up and down the shed, muttering measurements under her breath. Then she turned and repeated the operation widthways. Eventually she stopped and nodded. 'Your space is fine. I want first refusal on all of this.'

Billie, still slightly overcome by the marching, reeled. 'What? You want to—um—rent the *floor* . . .? *All* of it?'

'Yes.' She smiled then, her fuchsia lips peeling away from perfect porcelain teeth. 'Well, my boss does. He's tied up at the moment but, of course, he trusts my judgement implicitly. I'm here in my capacity as his personal assistant.'

Billie felt there was a smidgen too much emphasis on the personal.

'Here.' She fished inside a breast pocket of the jump suit and handed Billie a card. 'I'll go back and tell him this looks OK. You work out some monthly rates on square meterage and e-mail me in the morning. The address and phone numbers are

91

all on the card. Hold the space for me until then—OK?'

'OK.' Billie decided now was not the best time to mention she'd never actually got as far as e-mail. 'And what exactly will you be wanting to store, Ms—um . . . ?' She looked down at the card and almost hooted with laughter, only just managing to turn it into another useful sneeze at the last moment. *Estelle Rainbow*! Never on your life! She quickly bit her lip. 'Er, Ms—um—Rainbow?'

'What do you think?' Estelle Rainbow tapped the card dismissively with a long fuchsia talon. 'I would have thought it was abundantly clear from the card.'

Billie, who hadn't got past the outlandish name, skimmed through the rest. 'Estelle Rainbow. Sullivanair. Whiteacres Airport.'

Sullivanair? Holy shit!

Estelle, fluttering flirty eyelashes and dropping her voice even lower, made the huskiness hugely sexy. 'I'm Mr Sullivan's secretary and PA.' She caressed the *Mr Sullivan* with her tongue. 'And what Mr Sullivan wants is somewhere to store a plane.'

chapter eight

Life, Miranda reckoned, fell into two parts: the expectation and the reality. And so far the reality had truly kicked the expectation in the teeth. She wished that she could just have something in her days—and nights—that would make her leap out of bed in the morning, like Billie did, singing along to the *Breakfast Show* and actually looking forward to the new day.

She had Follicles and Cuticles, of course, which was doing very nicely, and the expansion of the unisex side of the salon into beauty therapies for men had gone incredibly well. But there was still something missing. A huge chunk of nothingness in her life. Miranda sighed heavily. She was very nearly thirty. She wanted a secure, stable relationship. She wanted a baby. Miranda, the good-time girl, felt it was time to settle down.

It was something she'd have to keep well hidden beneath her trendy *fcuk* pull-on.

Still, even if work and her social life were a bit downbeat, at least it wasn't all gloom in the flat. Billie was positively blooming; zinging with energy, constantly waxing lyrical over her damned warehouse, and now getting ecstatic about the arrival of a *plane*!

Miranda, alone in Follicles and Cuticles, shook her head as she peered through the lavender slat blinds at the bustling Spicer Centre. Billie and planes simply didn't go together. Billie and planes were like . . . well, pilchards and custard. Mind you, she didn't begrudge Billie her happiness. Far from it. After her awful experience with the dodgy Damon from Newton Abbot, Billie really deserved a break. It just seemed strange that she should find it in a breeze-block shed and with something aeronautical . . .

Looking on the bright side, at least Billie's infatuation with Whiteacres meant that she'd be staying on in Amberley Hill. Miranda wasn't sure she could stand it if Billie suddenly upped sticks and went back to the bosom of her family. Billie coming to live in Amberley Hill had been the best thing that ever happened to her. Billie moving into the flat had probably saved her from sliding down a very slippery slope.

Watching the crowds sluggishly toil through the August heat in the precinct, Miranda wondered if any of them would have enough energy left to hurl themselves through Follicles and Cuticles' lilac doors for an impromptu cut and blow-dry. Throughout the scorching summer she'd closed the salon at lunchtimes to allow Kitty, Pixie and the other girls the chance to sit in the municipal park and bare as much as possible. She always stayed in herself, just in case.

Just in case, Miranda thought sadly, would probably be engraved on her headstone. It was probably why she was still intermittently dating the rather dour Keith from the garage, just in case nothing better turned up. She let the blinds drop and looked around the salon. Everything was neat and tidy, and had been for the last hour. There were only so many times she could straighten magazines, wipe round basins, and rearrange hairbrushes. She caught a glimpse of herself in one of the vaudeville mirrors and groaned. Hell, she looked terrible! The plum and bilberry dye was beginning to fade and there were bags under her eyes. God, were there bags!

She peered more closely. Surely those weren't wrinkles? And the start of *jowls*? Miranda bunched the skin round her chin. She ought to give herself a bit of serious tender loving care, not to mention a facial and a change of make-up. Well, why not? In fact she could probably do with a complete rethink.

Tall and angular, with the sort of face people

would probably refer to as interesting if they referred to it at all, Miranda knew that her eyes were her best feature. If she were her own customer, she'd definitely suggest she should make more of them by ditching the thick black eyeliner and bat-wing false eyelashes and simply highlight them with smoky smudgy emphasis. She swivelled round in front of the mirror. Oh yes, and maybe she should tell herself to stop wearing the freaky hairstyles and the all-black outfits.

Maybe she should just stop thinking about it and bloody well get on and do it.

She took a deep breath. Or should she? It didn't do to be too drastic, she always told her customers that. Change one thing at a time. Perhaps, then, she'd leave the hair for a while. She actually quite liked it. But—as for the rest of it—there was no time like the present. An empty salon, and all the time in the world—not to mention a mouthwatering array of goodies to experiment with. Miranda pulled on a lilac overall and headed through Follicles' lavender archway for Cuticles' make-over city.

*   *   *

'Any chance of a haircut?'

Bugger. Miranda, in the middle of massaging cucumber cream into her throat, peered towards the doorway. Should she say they were shut for the rest of the day? That she was simply stocktaking? She'd never turned away a customer yet, but with a strawberry mask drying fragrantly on her face, her plaits clipped on top of her head like a springer spaniel's ears at meal times, and all her eye

95

make-up scraped off to give her a blank canvas, she probably looked the epitome of heroin chic.

'Sorry!' She shouted towards the door as loud as the face pack would allow. 'I—um—I'm just the cleaner. We're closed for lunch. Could you come back in an hour?'

'No you're not and no I couldn't, you daft bat.' Reuben Wainwright loomed in the archway. 'I've got less than half an hour, my hair looks like Worzel Gummidge, my hayfever's driving me mad, and I want to talk to you.'

Shit. Shit. Shit. She scrubbed at the face pack, and scraped some of the green slime from her neck. She'd been cutting Reuben's hair for several months now, and always, always, made sure that she looked perfect. Now he'd seen her at her absolute worst. Sod it.

'OK. Give me a couple of minutes to get this lot off. Take a seat. Anywhere will do.'

Quickly mascaraing and slapping on some lipstick, and releasing her plaits from their anchorage, she snatched off the overall.

Reuben Wainwright was, as she'd kept telling Billie, a total dream. OK, he was definitely a laddish bloke of the first water, but she blamed that on the fact that he probably used *Loaded* and *GQ* as his bibles. Underneath it all, Miranda was convinced, was a lonely man who threw up antagonism as a defence against being hurt. She recognised the symptoms, and wondered if there had been a Mrs Wainwright in the dim and distant past who had taken the house, the kids, and the hatchback, and left Reuben heartbroken and railing against the rest of the female gender.

Billie had said, no chance: Reuben was just

96

a pig. Billie, who got on so well with everyone, really seemed to dislike him—and for the life of her Miranda couldn't understand why. Might it be a case of Billie protesting too much? Was their hidden passion going to be veiled in fights and sniping until they realised that they couldn't live without each other? Miranda sincerely hoped not.

Checking that her black T-shirt was firmly anchored into her black jeans and that her hair wasn't too spiky, she fixed her professional smile and sauntered back into Follicles.

'Sorry about that. I thought I'd just try out some of the new products.' She tucked a towel round Reuben's shoulders, trying not to take too long, trying not to touch his skin. 'I never like to use anything on my clients that I wouldn't use on myself.'

Reuben eyed Miranda's green neck suspiciously through the mirror. 'You look like you've escaped from Sellafield. And before you ask, no I don't want any of that poncy stuff—no shampoo, no conditioner, no nothing. Just a trim, OK?'

Miranda spritzed Reuben's hair from the squeezy water bottle and flicked a comb through it. Blue-black and glossy, it fell into perfect layers. It was the sort of hair that you could roll naked in. Lifting each section with the comb, and concentrating on snipping the ends level, she smiled at him in the mirror. 'Been on your holidays yet?'

'I don't take holidays. You?'

'Much the same.' She tried again. 'You must be busy at the moment. The taxis, I mean. All these hot days and sultry nights. Everyone wanting to go out and get drunk.'

'Yeah.'

Hell, this was more difficult than usual. Working in silence for a while, she flicked Reuben's hair back from his forehead, hotly aware that most of her was pressed against him. She stepped back a fraction but the heat was still there. 'Er—doing anything special at the weekend?'

'Trying to shake off this sodding hayfever.'

Miranda snipped and clipped. 'Have you tried aromatherapy? We do a really good infusion of—'

'I'll stick with antihistamines and inhalers and the doors and windows tightly closed, thanks.'

'Whatever. Still, you'll be able to watch the telly with your feet up, won't you? Plenty of sport on over the weekend. Football and that.' She stood back and lifted the layers. They melted coldly through her fingers like liquid. She swallowed. 'Er, do you like football?'

Reuben shifted a bit in his chair. 'Yeah. But not as much as Billie does.'

'Billie? No, you've got that wrong. Billie *hates* football. Apparently she had to play it all the time with her brothers when she was a kid. She walks out of the room when it's on. There? OK?'

'Fine. Thanks.' Reuben stared at her through the mirror.

'Funny, that. I could have sworn Billie was a football fan. You should ask her . . . Still, she's good at keeping secrets, isn't she?'

'Do you want me to blow it dry?'

Reuben shook his head. 'No. It's not wet. Don't muck it about. And don't change the subject.'

'I wasn't. I just thought that if you weren't feeling too good then it mightn't be a great idea to go out with damp hair.'

'You sound like my bloody mother! So how's

98

Billie doing? Did she say I didn't want to accept her resignation?'

Flicking at Reuben's shoulders with the clothes brush, Miranda bit her lip. Clever. That's what he wanted to talk about. Billie leaving. She'd known he wouldn't let her go easily. She'd warned Billie. Tricky one. What should she say here, then? Just how much had Billie told Reuben about her new business? Miranda decided to opt for caution.

'She hasn't said very much, honestly. I think she's very happy at Whiteacres—and that it's all working out well . . .'

Reuben stood up. He was taller than she, and didn't move away. 'She hasn't confided in you?'

'About what? The business? Nothing much to confide, as far as I can see. She's warehousing and it's working out nicely—although it's early days, of course. I suppose as long as she didn't set up a taxi firm in opposition to you, you don't have to worry.'

She moved away first. If Reuben thought he was using his height to intimidate her, then he was very much mistaken. The sensations his closeness aroused were miles away from fear.

'Oh, I'm not. I don't have to worry about anything.' Reuben pulled his wallet from his back pocket. 'Billie's the one who should be worrying. She's taking a hell of a risk.'

'Why on earth should she worry?' Miranda again opted for prudence as she punched the cost of the trim into the till and took Reuben's Visa card. 'She seems to have stumbled on a lucrative idea that's taking shape nicely, and she's certainly happier than she's been for years—' She bit her lip. Sod it. Possibly not the brightest remark to have made under the circumstances. 'That is—'

'I'm sure she is. But I still think she'll find that leaving me was a huge mistake.' Reuben smiled, taking the edge from the words. 'She's a good little driver, but she's got an awful lot to learn about business. It's not an easy ride.'

Bless him! Miranda thought, handing him his receipt. Billie had got him all wrong. He wasn't going to make things difficult for her at all. It was just that he was concerned about her future welfare.

She stopped and frowned. Oh, sod it. That must definitely mean that Reuben fancied Billie, mustn't it?

Reuben pocketed the receipt and reached for his jacket. 'To be honest, although you've been sharing a flat with her for the last two years, it strikes me that you don't know much about Billie at all. Exactly how much do you know about her past? Has she ever told you just why she came to Amberley Hill in the first place and why she was working for me?'

Miranda beamed. The broken romance with Damon was much safer ground.

'Oh yes, of course she has! She was escaping from Devon because her ex-boyfriend, Damon, had dumped her. She wanted to make a fresh start and she thought that driving a cab was a really good way to get to know people in a new town and . . .'

Now what had she said? Reuben's eyes were crinkled with laughter. He was practically chewing his lips to prevent the merriment escaping.

'I've got to give her a gold star for imagination.' Still laughing, he headed for the door. 'And you deserve ten out of ten for gullibility, sweetheart.

'Oh, get away, doll! You mean Billie's got a

secret past? Never!'

'Ask her.'

'Yeah, I might just do that.'

Miranda wanted to laugh out loud. Billie? With skeletons? Well, there might be something a bit iffy about Damon, of course, but who these days didn't have past relationships they'd rather not talk about?

It had taken Miranda a very long time to recover from her husband, Noel's, duplicity in running off as he had, only a year into their marriage, with her elder sister, Lexie. The cure for the heartbreak— far too much to drink and far too many men—had become something of a habit. With rock-bottom self-esteem, before Billie came along, Miranda knew that she'd pressed the self-destruct button. It had been an excruciatingly lonely time. And if Billie, like she had, had tried to assuage the loneliness and a broken heart with dozens of wine glasses and numerous strange bedrooms, why the hell should it bother anyone else, least of all Reuben?

Reuben suddenly sneezed violently. Miranda handed him a tissue from the box on the desk. 'You want to get yourself home to bed, doll.'

'Is that an offer?'

Laughing, she shook her head. 'I'll be sweating it out on Bazooka's dance floor tonight—like mostly every other night.'

'Enjoy clubbing, do you?'

To be honest, the nightly fiasco of wearing something new, and dolling herself up to the nines, and pretending to be having a ball, was becoming a chore rather than a pleasure. All she really wanted to do after a shattering day at work was curl up on the sofa with the telly, a takeaway, and the man of her dreams.

'It's OK. Better than being alone . . .'

Reuben nodded sympathetically. 'Tell me about it. Maybe you and me and Billie should get together and form some sort of sad saps' club, huh? Oh, well—I'd better get back to the joys of keeping the shoppers and boozers of the town mobile. See you—oh, and be sure to give Billie my love, won't you?'

Miranda watched Reuben's departing back view as he strode jauntily out into the Spicer Centre. He *was* lonely. She knew it! And gorgeous. And he very obviously had the hots for Billie.

Slowly, she began to wipe round the basin and sweep up the blue-black shiny snippets of Reuben's hair on the floor. She bent down and picked up a handful. The strands were cool, like silk. Unable to help it, she twisted them into a knot and slipped it into the pocket of her jeans.

autumn

chapter nine

Miranda peered at the pan bubbling on top of the stove. 'This doesn't look quite right, does it? D'you think there's too much paprika? Oh, sorry, doll, what were you saying?'

Billie, who hadn't slept much, was practically bursting out of her Eeyore pyjamas with impatience. 'Haven't you been listening at all? You *know* this Boeing thing's arriving from Southampton docks this morning!'

After weeks of argy-bargying with Maynard and Pollock, and meaningful discussions over the phone—e-mail hadn't yet materialised—with Estelle at Sullivanair, Billie had leased nearly all of her floor space.

'And it'll be there for ages—well, a month at least while they renovate and paint it, and maybe longer if they can't find anywhere else to keep it— which will keep me solvent, and—' She stopped and squinted at Miranda. 'What exactly are you doing?'

'I'm making a sort of goulash. Lovely colour, isn't it? I wonder if I could dye my hair with paprika . . . ? Oh, sorry, yeah, that's great, but isn't a jumbo jet going to be a bit of a squeeze in your shed?'

'According to Estelle Rainbow, who's the only contact I've got, it's in bits. They're going to build it up inside, so hopefully they'll be able to get it out again, and then—Goulash? Why the hell are you cooking goulash at seven o'clock on a Saturday morning?'

'Yeah, well, I sort of thought with both of us working all day and you saying you didn't think you'd be home from Whiteacres until late and—um . . .' Miranda stopped and blew her fringe away from her eyes. 'Actually, doll, I've invited Keith to dinner.'

'I thought you and Keith were on the skids?'

Miranda sighed. 'I think we are. I just thought I'd give it one last go. You know, the way to a man's heart and all that . . .'

Billie, who hadn't thought about anything but her warehouse for ages, forgot all her impatience and hugged Miranda through the goulash haze. 'I'm so sorry. Still, cheer up. Even if Keith isn't the one, you're bound to meet the right man—probably when you least expect it.'

Miranda hugged her back, then wriggled free and sprinkled more paprika into the already terracotta-coloured saucepan. 'Yeah, maybe I will. Maybe I already have—who knows? Hey, what do you reckon would happen if I added some saffron to jazz it up a bit? D'you reckon it'd look too much like an abscess?'

Billie shuddered at the image and, with a final horrified look at the suppurating saucepan, back-tracked to her bedroom. She was just closing the door when Miranda's voice echoed through from the kitchen.

'Oh, yeah. Tell me to mind my own business, doll—but why, when Sullivanair has already got planes at the airfield, do they want your shed for this one? They must have hangars everywhere.'

Pretending not to hear, Billie slammed the bedroom door. It was actually something she'd asked several times. Estelle Rainbow had been very vague and said that their current hangarage and service contract with the airfield didn't cover the

106

Boeing. Billie sincerely hoped it wasn't some sort of aeronautical tax fiddle. She had a feeling that Maynard and Pollock may just turn nasty at the idea.

*   *   *

Sylvia, Zia and Isla, Fred 'n' Dick, and most of Guspers were milling around outside the units as Billie parked the Nova. She smiled to herself. The other residents of the Whiteacres units had rapidly become her friends. United by their odd ball splurge into self-employment, they were a little community set aside from the rest of the world. For Billie, parking the car on the cracked and dirty concrete each morning was almost as good as coming home.

They'd all been delighted for her when she'd told them about the Sullivanair deal—with the exception of Zia, who'd worried about explosions and fumes, but she'd eventually won him over—and it was really sweet of them to turn out at the weekend to help with the unloading. Especially when it was so cold. September had roared in with wicked north winds ripping the leaves from the trees and rattling through Whiteacres' spiky grass in bleached blond waves.

She'd buy all the warehousers a huge drink later to say thank you. Of course, it would probably have to be on tick in Mulligan's, but who cared? If this went well, Sullivanair May put other work her way, or spread the word through the aviation industry. She might even be able to afford to lease the unoccupied not-quite-up-to-scratch unit at the end of the row and expand . . .

Sylvia, who was paying lip service to the unexpected autumnal chill by wearing a duffel coat over her Bermudas, was standing a little way apart from the rest of the crowd. Billie hurried towards her. 'Hi. I didn't expect to see you here—thanks so much. It's really exciting, isn't it? No one's arrived from Sullivanair yet, have they? I was petrified that I'd be late and miss the arrival and—goodness, Sylv, what's up?'

'Bloody everything, dear.' Sylvia heaved a huge sigh. 'Absolutely bloody everything. My Douglas is going to kill me.'

Panic started to punch its way under Billie's ribs, each punch cancelling out a bit of happiness. Had there been a fire? She glanced quickly at the breeze-block terrace. The units looked OK. A break-in, then? Vandalism?

Before she could put any of the horrors into words, Isla shimmied out from her hiding place behind the dual bulk of Fred 'n' Dick. She looked as if she'd been crying. So, now she looked carefully, did Zia. Billie exhaled. God, had someone broken into her shed and nicked all Zi-Zi's costumes overnight? Was she going to be faced with an insurance claim of gargantuan proportions?

'Is someone going to tell me what's happened? It's not the plane, is it? Sullivanair haven't bottled out? Don't tell me we're all here for nothing.'

'I know it sounds rude, but we're not actually here for your plane at all,' Isla said apologetically, sniffing into a musk-scented tissue. 'Although of course now we're here we'll help out if you need us. And no, as far as I know, they're still on their way from the docks. We really only came in because Sylvia phoned us. . .'

108

Billie now felt the earlier euphoria slipping almost beyond reach. 'What the hell has happened?'

'Bollocks has happened,' Zia said morosely, chewing the ends of his Zapata moustache. 'Bloody bollocks, right?'

Sylvia's face was pale beneath the tan. She tutted at Zia. 'Not very nice language to use in front of your wife, but possibly apposite. Before you get too thrilled about making your fortune from housing this aeroplane, you want to read your post, Billie, dear.'

Post? Billie blinked stupidly. 'What post?'

'Today's post.' Sylvia jangled her bangles in the direction of the units. 'You know I like to come in of a Saturday morning to get away from Douglas polishing the cat, and load up the rotunda ready for Monday? Well, I arrived at about the same time as the postman, gave him a cup of coffee as usual. Didn't take any notice of the letters until he'd gone . . . We've all had one.'

'One what?'

'Notice of sale.' Zia slouched into his poncho. 'Capitalist bastards.'

Billie rocked slightly. Sale? Who was selling what?

'Maynard and Pollock have had an offer to buy all the units.' Isla shook her head. 'The original owner was some mad old bird who lived in Madeira. She died recently, and her family don't want the hassle of the warehouses—so they've sold them. We'll have a new landlord—who'll probably push the rents sky-high—always supposing we're even allowed to stay here . . .'

Mike and the Guspers boys were looking

109

collectively suicidal.

'They won't let us stay,' Mike sighed. 'You can bet your sweet life on that. They'll be wanting to add this on to the airfield, you mark my words. It'll be the airfield buying us out—using the sheds for hangars or something.'

'No it won't,' Zia snorted. 'Not the airfield. It'll be Tesco or someone, right? Or a big multinational wanting to make this into a shoppers' paradise. Paradise—bollocks.'

Billie groaned. This couldn't happen. Not now. Not when things were just starting to take shape. Not when Sullivanair's money was going to make her warehouse viable. Not when something she really wanted to do was just taking off . . .

Leaving the others still speculating, and fumbling with cold fingers and fear, she unlocked her door and scooped up the depressing pile of buff envelopes. It never ceased to amaze her how quickly the bills started to come in. She riffled through them until she found the white envelope with the Maynard and Pollock logo.

The letter was, as Isla had said, pretty ambiguous. It didn't say that the units were definitely going to be sold off; it wasn't a notice to quit or anything. It merely said that an interested party had approached Maynard and Pollock with a view to buying up the leases—on both the land and the buildings. It also said that the units' incumbents had statutory rights, and that in all probability it would only mean—supposing the sale should go ahead—that they would be paying their ground rent to a different landlord. There may, of course, be new criteria. It added that Simon Maynard would inform them all of any further developments.

110

Lot of fuss about nothing then, Billie reckoned, switching on lights, gazing round the shed, and wondering for the hundredth time if Estelle Rainbow had jack-booted accurately and whether the plane would fit. Probably someone just wanting to make a fast buck on pocketing the rents. It surely couldn't be anything else, could it? Not redevelopment, or anything? Not slap bang up against the airfield? There simply wasn't room. For God's sake, who in their right mind would want to try to turn their dingy row of breeze blocks into the new Lakeside?

No, it would all be OK. She was sure of it. And anyway there were far more pressing things to worry about. Like the jumbo jet arriving in kit form at any moment now.

'Billie!' Zia poked his head round the door. 'I think it's here, right!'

Fizzing with excitement, Billie tugged the sliding double doors open and then stood with the rest of the Whiteacres contingent—Maynard and Pollock's letter forgotten—and watched open-mouthed as the very flash chromium-plated American container lorry purred to a halt.

Estelle Rainbow, looking very fetching in second-skin jeans and boots and a denim jacket, slithered sinuously from the cab. Tossing the long white-blonde hair away from her face, she shimmied across to Billie, obviously aware that Zia, Fred 'n' Dick, Mike and the heterosexual side of Guspers were gazing at her with ill-concealed lust.

Billie groaned. Estelle instantly made her feel titchy and boyish and scruffy—again. But she smiled. 'You're right on time. Good journey?'

'Apparently so,' Estelle yawned. She could even

111

do that sexily. 'I only joined them for the last bit. Mr Sullivan has been waiting at Southampton docks all night. He's absolutely shattered and certainly doesn't want any further delays. Now—are you ready?'

'Of course.' Billie wasn't sure why she disliked Estelle. It probably had something to do with her having a perfect body and face and hair and all that, and being intelligent and efficient to boot. 'Fred 'n' Dick have said we can borrow their fork-lift and—'

'We'll need more than a fork-lift,' Estelle said, looking dismissively at the clustered Whiteacres contingent. 'And a lot more muscle power than this lot seem able to muster. Have you assembled the winch?'

'Winch? No one had mentioned a winch, had they?

'We don't need a winch, my dear.' A milk chocolate- covered voice melted across the tension. 'The container lorry is extremely well-equipped with all the gear we need for unloading. And I'm sure all those good people outside will make themselves extremely useful. Oh, and good morning. You must be Miss Pascoe.'

Billie smiled gratefully into a pair of rather wicked grey eyes, and found herself shaking hands with the middle-aged man whose nails were far better manicured than her own.

'Billie, please. And it's wonderful to meet you at last.'

Mr Sullivan was exactly how she'd pictured him. No wonder Estelle purred when she mentioned his name. Obviously well heeled and educated, he was immaculately groomed, and showed no signs of having been up all night. Billie had long since forgiven him for being involved in aviation—what did it matter that she disliked anything that took off? Mr Sullivan and his kit-plane had saved her bacon. She couldn't wait to tell her mother and Miranda about the debonair tycoon.

'Come along.' Estelle obviously thought that the handshaking had lasted quite long enough. 'There's tons to do!'

Billie exchanged grins with Mr Sullivan and hurried outside.

Boxes, and crates, and massive things like huge wooden toast-racks containing flimsy fabric-covered structures, had already been disgorged, and the Whiteacres crew were buzzing happily amongst them.

'Probably just what we need, dear,' Sylvia said, 'to take our minds off the other business. I shall just spit if Douglas is proved right and my little venture goes belly up.'

Billie patted her well-padded arm. 'I think everyone's worrying unnecessarily. I honestly don't think it'll make a jot of difference whoever buys the units. We'll be OK—I'm sure we will.' She surveyed the industry hiving around the outside of her shed. 'And this doesn't look anything like I'd expected . . .'

It didn't, actually, look like a plane at all. Billie had imagined huge engines and a massive fuselage, and wings and seats for five hundred. This crisscross mass of delicate wooden frames and small unpleasantly beige metal bits all peppered with rivet holes looked like the end-of-day clearing up in the handicraft class at school.

'Most of the plane is still in the lorry,' Sylvia said, having spotted the erudite Mr Sullivan and looking

113

slightly more perky. 'I heard them saying that it was lucky they'd been able to ship it over with its engine attached. I actually went and had a little peek. It's rather daring.'

'What? The plane? God, Sylv—they're all the same, aren't they? Sort of silver and tubular, except this one's fawn at the moment, of course. And I suppose all these material and twig bits are vital somewhere along the way. At least this one will be a proper airliner—not like that archaic thing that Sullivanair flies over here every day with its pre-war propellers and—'

'This one's got a propeller,' Sylvia interrupted. 'Just the one.'

'It can't have! This is a Boeing. I know. I've seen the paperwork.'

'So it might be, Billie, dear. But it must be Boeing's equivalent of the Model T Ford. I think you ought to take a look.'

Noticing that Estelle was scrambling very dexterously amongst the giant toast-rack things, Billie picked her way through the crates, and peered in at the winch end of the container.

Jesus! Billie blinked. The inside of the wagon looked like a war zone. A First World War zone at that. The body of the Boeing was cradled like a beached whale, its single pock-marked propeller, as Sylvia had said, standing proud in front of an elderly engine-casing that had all the technical finesse of an oversized electric fan.

'It's an *old* plane!' She gazed up at the urbane Mr Sullivan, who was busily undoing the supporting straps. 'A museum piece!'

'Yes, it is. Fifty years old at least.' He patted the domed nose lovingly. 'But fortunately this one

114

won't be consigned to spending the rest of her days in a static display. By the summer, this old girl will be back in the skies where she belongs.'

Billie shook her head in some dismay. Up in the skies—some hope! More like nose-diving straight into the tarmac. The thing probably wasn't even airworthy. Still, what did it matter? It may not be glamorous, but it certainly solved the problem of whether she could squeeze a 747 into the warehouse; and what Sullivanair did with it after it had left her shed was really of no interest, was it?

Everyone was still frantically busy, hefting and heaving, and, determined not to be outdone by Estelle, Billie pulled up the sleeves of her fleece and dived into the fray.

'Billie! Not all haphazard—pul-ease! Grab that one there, right?' Zia ordered, his poncho discarded, his hair tied back in a businesslike fashion. 'The Sullivanair guys have got it all under control. They know what they want where. Everything is to be stored numerically in your unit, before we can pull the body out of the wagon, right?'

Billie raised her eyebrows but grabbed the box Zia had pushed towards her. She hated bossy men. And whose show was this anyway? Zia had grizzled for ages when she'd first told him about the plane, complaining that his precious outfits could become tainted. It had taken all her powers of fabrication to convince him otherwise, and now here he was playing foreman and loving every damn minute of it.

Fred 'n' Dick were trundling backwards and forwards rather redundantly with their fork-lift and several of Guspers seemed to have sloped off into

115

Billie's warehouse to inspect the bits. Isla, taking advantage of Zia's involved managerial role, was flirting with the lorry driver.

Billie lodged the box under her chin, still glaring at Zia.

'Anywhere particular you want this to go? In my shed?'

'Ask the boss.' Zia inclined his tendrilly head towards the back of the container lorry. 'He's directing operations.'

Mr Sullivan waved a Barboured arm and beamed down at Billie from the back of the lorry. 'What is it? Ah—electricals . . . Oh, absolutely anywhere will be fine. As long as it's not on the floor until we get everything in.'

Billie staggered into her unit and immediately shivered. It was still colder inside than out. And gloomy despite the lighting. Estelle was stacking boxes onto the shelves, helped by the slavering film crew who were making sure that they we in numerical order, and someone in the shadows was heaving at one of the giant toast-racks.

'Sodding thing! Why the hell no one thought to put it on sodding castors is beyond me! And I thought Vinny was going to be here to help with this! No doubt he's too busy humping some bimbo to remember he's supposed to be humping the Boeing!' There was a pause in the invective, followed by a nasty jagging sound. 'Shit! What's that?'

'This, I think . . .' Billie picked up a splintered piece of wood. 'Is it important?'

'Probably vital. It's always the important bits that snap off. Let's have a look . . .'

The voice emerged from the shadows along with

its owner. Billie's first thought was that she couldn't believe she hadn't noticed him before. Her second, hot on its heels, was that he looked very, very disgruntled and dishevelled. Like he hadn't slept for days.

'Thanks . . .' He took the piece of wood and nodded. 'Bit of wing structure. Have to glue it back on. What else have you got there?'

'Electricals.' Billie glanced down at the box she had tucked under one arm, then handed it to Estelle. 'Or so Mr Sullivan said.'

'Did I?' The man swept floppy dark hair away from his eyes and peered at her. 'Christ, I must be more knackered than I thought.'

Billie shook her head and grinned. 'No, you didn't. Mr Sullivan did. You know, Sullivanair's owner —the rather gorgeous elegant man out in the lorry . . .'

Estelle was giggling. The dark-haired man looked like he wanted to join in. 'I think you're a bit confused. Or maybe it's me . . . Perhaps I've forgotten who I am. Do you know who you are?'

'She's Billie Pascoe,' Estelle said, stretching up to put Billie's box on the shelf and managing to expose an expanse of perfectly flat golden midriff. 'She owns the warehouse.'

'Really?' The dark-haired man squinted at her. 'You look like you should still be at school. Estelle gave me the impression that you belonged to the bib-and-brace and hobnailed boot brigade—er . . .' he glanced at Billie's dungarees and Timberlands, 'that is . . .'

'Don't bother,' Billie narrowed her eyes. 'I get the picture. I just think it's a pity that Mr Sullivan can't employ people with his own class and brain power.'

'So do I,' the dark-haired man sighed. 'I've said it a million times. It's something I've always planned to do. And before we compound this rather confusing situation into something that is irretrievable, can I introduce myself. I'm Jonah Sullivan. The gorgeously elegant man in the lorry—who will no doubt be delighted to hear of your high opinion—is my friend Barnaby.'

Bugger, bugger, bugger . . . Billie glared murderously at Estelle, who had climbed the stepladder and was now innocently stacking boxes with her perfect rear view towards them. A million thoughts skittered their way through Billie's embarrassment. Jonah, in his faded Levis and grubby rugby shirt, looked nothing at all like an aeroplane magnate. He was possibly the most understatedly sexy man she'd ever clapped eyes on—which, naturally, explained bloody Estelle's hormonally charged purr when she'd mentioned his name. No doubt Estelle and Jonah were joined at the hip—and all points south . . . And if Jonah owned Sullivanair, then that meant he was a *pilot,* for God's sake! She'd always imagined pilots to be very posh and have slicked-back hair and be about the same age as her dad—exactly like Barnaby, in fact.

'Sorry if we've misled you.' Jonah was still grinning. 'Anyway, it's really nice to meet you at last. And I apologise for being so rude . . .'

'Me too.' Billie flicked idly at one of the cartons, itching to peep inside, and trying to look disinterested. 'And I'm looking forward to having you around and watching the plane take shape and—'

'Goodness!' Estelle stepped snakily down from

118

her perch and shook out her hair. 'Jonah won't have time to be here during the day. He'll be far too busy flying. He'll probably only be here when you've finished work and gone home. That's why we established if we could have keys cut as part of the criteria. I doubt if you'll be seeing anything of Jonah at all.'

Whereas, Billie thought, fighting the sudden irrational urge to remove Estelle's eyes from their sockets, you'll no doubt be seeing absolutely every damn beautiful inch of him—and more.

She smiled sweetly. 'Really? Oh, then that's just ideal. Because much as I'm delighted to be making money by offering you storage for your dilapidated monstrosity, I actually dislike aircraft intensely. And the little contact that I've had with avionics nerds has merely reinforced my opinion that people connected with planes are a bunch of sad anoraks. So, the less we all see of each other the better, as far as I'm concerned.'

chapter ten

Faith Pascoe was bored. No, it was more than that. Boredom could always be dealt with by making a cake, or reading to one of her grandchildren, or striding out across the moors with the dogs. This feeling of discontent not only niggled at the edges of her sleep, but also insisted on invading her busiest moments. She rarely experienced dissatisfaction with her life, and when she did it was only over short-term things like bank statements that were too red, or one of the tractors being out

119

of action, or the hens not laying; but this time the feeling had clung on for weeks. Ever since Ben and Maria's wedding party. Ever since Billie's last visit home.

She hung the dish cloth on the Aga, managing not to disturb the dogs, cats, or the fine array of steaming muddy boots, and stared out of the kitchen window. The morning rain veiled the yard in mist, making it impossible to see moors or the barns or even Jon and Alex's cottages. Everything was shrouded in a wet, dank curtain. It had been a relentlessly dour start to the autumn, but the weather never usually affected her moods.

And, she reminded herself, there were so many things to look forward to: two more grandchildren imminent, and that new contract Stan had picked up at the market for free-range eggs and goat's cheese meant that she'd have three extra mornings with her stall, and Billie was at last doing something with her life . . . Or was she?

Faith sighed. Even the background cheerfulness of Radio Two couldn't lift the gloom today. It *was* Billie that bothered her. If she was honest, she'd worried herself sick over Billie on and off for the last two years. It had been lovely having her back for the wedding party, and ever since she'd gone, Faith had missed her very much. Strange, really. She adored Ann, Katy and Maria, and was pretty sure they adored her back. She'd always prided herself on being the ideal mother-in-law—friendly, available, but not intrusive. But wonderful as her daughters-in-law were, the relationship simply wasn't the same as it was with Billie.

She and Billie had been real *chums*, if that wasn't too Angela Brazil for words! They'd shared jokes

120

and confidences for as long as she could remember. There had never been any secrets. Billie, she was well-aware, tended to protect Faith from things that she considered to be far too risqué for her mother's ears, and Faith had decided never to enlighten her. She rather liked the fact that Billie thought she was still shockable.

She'd been an old-fashioned stay-at-home mother, but, she hoped, not a clingy one, probably because she'd never had to be. The boys were all entrenched in the land and she'd never had the slightest doubts that they'd stay living locally simply because they wanted to. She'd always assumed Billie would do the same.

It had been such a jolt when Billie had left the *Devon Argus* and moved away to London so suddenly. There had been all manner of speculation at the time. The gossip had been rife in the village, putting it down to fingers in the till or an unsuitable liaison with a married man or an unwanted pregnancy or all three.

Faith had been loud in her condemnation of the rumour-mongers, knowing that if there had been a baby involved Billie would have had no qualms about telling her family, being a single mother, rearing the child happily with its multitude of cousins. Of course there was absolutely no question of any dishonesty. Billie had often said that the only freebies she could lift from the paper were cheap ballpoints or the occasional notepad. And Billie, she knew, would have had far more sense and scruples than to become involved with a man who belonged to someone else.

No, there had to be more to it than that. More even than Billie's explanation of wanting to be a nanny in London just to try something different. But despite her best motherly interrogation techniques over the last two years, both during her weekly telephone calls and on Billie's occasional visits home, Faith had been unable to discover the truth. Billie had stuck resolutely to the story of just needing to get away, to do something different. But to end up *taxi-driving*? In Amberley Hill? Faith, who had been secretly relieved that London had lasted only briefly, had never actually visited Amberley Hill but she always thought it sounded pretty dreadful.

Having been born in Devon and never ventured further north than Somerset for holidays because running the smallholding made distant travelling an impossibility, anywhere geographically up from Bournemouth might as well be Mars. And it didn't matter how many times Billie told her that Amberley Hill was old and beautiful, it was still a town—almost a city—and as far as Faith was concerned, anything even remotely urban was bound to be rife with violence and drug-dealing and unpleasantness. Goodness, she wasn't that insular! She knew what went on. Just look at what had happened to Torquay.

And now, the news that Billie had used her small inheritance to start her own business should have cheered her—but it hadn't. Oh, she didn't want Billie to be like her daughters-in-law and produce babies if that wasn't what she wanted to do, nor did she ache to have her only daughter married off— she just felt that this new half-cocked venture, like the flight from London to Amberley Hill, and the erstwhile nannying and taxi-driving, was as a result of something that had happened here before she left, and that until that something was uncovered and faced up to and dealt with, Billie would be unsettled for ever.

Dealing with a problem head-on was the only way, Faith thought. She'd spent her life dealing with minor troubles, dispersing them before they erupted into catastrophes, and this business with Billie had bothered her for far too long. It had to be sorted and there was no time like the present. It made sense, she justified to herself, as she pulled on her boots and buttoned herself into her raincoat, that as she was here, on the spot, and Billie was miles away, it really fell to her, as a responsible parent, to lay the ghosts on Billie's behalf.

She closed the kitchen door and shuddered in the torrential onslaught. She had no intention of telling the men in her family what she was doing. They would insist that she was interfering. But she wasn't. If she could get to the bottom of this, and understand it, then she'd be able to sleep at night— and, she hoped, Billie would be able to get on with her life without these demons driving her.

Faith sloshed across the yard and slithered into the driving seat of the Land Rover. Fortunately, Stan was out mending fences with Tom and Ben, and Jon and Alex were occupied in the fields out of sight of the house. None of them would return until lunch time. And as Maria was at work in Teignmouth, and both Katy and Ann were at the playgroup in the village and wouldn't be back for ages, it gave Faith plenty of time to start digging.

Also, she thought, as she slid the Land Rover out through the gate, if what she uncovered was nasty, then the fewer people who knew about it the better. Especially Billie. Changing up a gear as she

123

hit firmer ground, Faith pushed to the back of her mind that maybe Billie wouldn't want the horrors uncovered. Still, this wasn't just to do with Billie any more, was it? It was to do with Faith herself and her peace of mind.

Anyway, she thought, she hadn't been the only one to notice that there was something—well, odd, about Billie. After the wedding party, several of her friends had commented on the fact that Billie's stories about what she was doing all seemed to differ slightly. Faith had laughed and said they'd all been pie-eyed anyway and how on earth could they remember *anything*? But it had disturbed her far more than she'd been prepared to admit at the time.

Even more unsettling was the fact that Billie seemed to have told lots of people at the party' about a boyfriend in Amberley Hill who was unable to make the journey to Devon because of his sick mother. Whatever else she did or didn't know, Faith was absolutely positive that this man—this paragon of filial virtue—didn't exist. Billie had said she was still resolutely single—so why had she lied? And, even more worryingly, if she'd lied about that, what else had she lied about?

Stan had told Faith not to fret about it: that Billie was probably just fending off unwanted advances. But Stan had always been dotty about Billie and would have defended her to the hilt whatever the crime. Stan had said that Billie was just testing out her wings, like a fledgling, teetering on the edge of the growing-up branch. It was best that they just stood back and let her jump, but that they should make sure they were around if she fell.

That was typical of Stan's gentle homilies, Faith

admitted. And he was usually right. It was his ability to see the good in people that had made her fall in love with him over thirty years earlier; and his ability to soothe and protect and be totally rational in the face of the most appalling crises that made her love him even more today.

Sitting together late at night, reflecting on the past, she and Stan often said that they really hadn't changed from the seventeen-year-old student nurse and the battered and bruised eighteen-year-old motorcyclist who had met in the casualty department of Honiton General. Faith knew that they'd been lucky to have shared so much happiness. That happiness was the one thing she wanted to pass on to all her children.

Switching on both the radio and the windscreen wipers to full bore, Faith sailed through the village, waving to friends who were huddled beneath umbrellas gossiping outside the post office. Damn! It would have to be Pat and Miriam. Their daughters had both been at school with Billie, and had gone on to university, and made good marriages, and now combined their careers successfully with their babies. Pat and Miriam always spoke of Billie's defection in hushed tones as if it was a bereavement, and would now no doubt buttonhole Faith next time they met, and ask just where she was belting off to on a Tuesday morning. It was the main problem with the village—people not only asked questions, but they assumed they had every right to the answers.

Faith knew Pat and Miriam were still watching as she slowed at the crossroads and turned the Land Rover towards Willowbridge and the *Devon Argus*. It was the only place to start. Everything had been

125

fine until Billie had left the paper. If there was anything to discover, she was sure the *Argus* was at the root of it.

*   *   *

The *Devon Argus*, established in 1876, was still housed in its original granite and slate three-storey building on Willowbridge's curving main road. Faith, unable to park outside because of double yellow lines, had had to run from the municipal car park, and subsequently dripped into reception.

'Yes?' A severe-suited woman glared through the glass screen. 'Can I help? Whom do you wish to see?'

Faith wasn't sure. The editor during Billie's time on the paper had since retired, and she hadn't a clue whether any of Billie's friends still worked there. She exhaled. She really hadn't thought this through at all. Could she remember any of their names? Oh, yes . . .

'Um—Craigie MacGowan?' He'd been Billie's features editor. Billie had always seemed very fond of him. 'Does he still work here?'

'And if he does, then he certainly doesn't see anyone without an appointment.' The woman moved fractionally closer to the screen. 'I take it you do have an appointment?'

Faith really itched to say that if she had an appointment then she'd know he worked there, wouldn't she?, but she merely shook her head. Raindrops sprayed on to the reception desk. She wondered why on earth the *Devon Argus* would have bullet-proof glass on reception. Still, the woman behind it looked pretty unpleasant, so was probably to prevent her from beating up the visitors.

'Not a chance today, then, I'm afraid. Mr MacGowan is a very busy man.' The receptionist gave a ghastly grin. Her mouth stretched wide as if she'd swallowed a bicycle and the handlebars had got caught in her cheeks. 'Shall I tell him you called—er—Mrs . . . ?'

'No,' Faith straightened her shoulders. She wasn't going to be fobbed off like that. Anyway, she might never get another chance. 'Tell him I'm here now. In reception. I'll sit and wait.'

'I'm afraid you can't do that.'

'And I'm afraid I can.' Faith plonked herself on to a shiny leather bench. It made a rude squelching noise. 'Tell him it's Faith Pascoe. Billie's mother.'

A mature student of feminine thought processes, Faith watched the receptionist's cogs turning and coming up with 'paternity suit'. She wanted to laugh, and instead studied the 1953 Coronation edition of the *Argus*, which was gilt-framed on the wall. With a lot of huffing and puffing and flexing of shoulder pads, the receptionist punched at the telephone.

'Mr MacGowan? There's a Faith Pascoe wanting to see you. I've told her . . . Excuse me? . . . Yes—she's here. Now. I've told her—What? That's not what I've been instructed to—Well, I must say—What? . . . Oh, very well!' The phone was replaced with a crash. 'Mr MacGowan will apparently see you. He's had a cancellation.'

It made him sound like a dentist, Faith reckoned. She also reckoned that everyone in the staff rest room would be told by lunch time that Craigie MacGowan was playing away.

She smiled her thanks. 'Really? Isn't that nice of him to fit me in?'

The receptionist snorted and turned her back.

Five minutes later, Craigie MacGowan powered into reception. Probably not much older than Jon or Alex, he was very overweight and looked incredibly unfit. Still, Faith liked his grin—which was a proper one that crinkled the corners of his eyes.

'Mrs Pascoe? Billie's mum?' Craigie was pumping her hand. 'This is great! Just great! Please tell me you're here to say that Billie's coming back.'

Faith stood up, still shaking hands. 'I'm afraid not—but it's Billie that I'd like to talk to you about, only,' she shot a look towards the receptionist, 'not here.'

'No. Of course not. Come on up to the office. I'm only on the next floor.'

Which was probably just as well, Faith concluded, having listened to Craigie wheeze his way up a mere ten stairs and stagger into a glass-sided office. And if the nameplate was anything to go by, he'd been elevated too. No wonder the receptionist had been so protective. Craigie MacGowan was now the *Argus*'s editor-in-chief.

'Congratulations.'

'Ta. It'll probably kill me—if the fags and booze don't get there first. Oh, please sit down and ignore the noise.'

Outside in the big open-plan office, it seemed like a million phones were ringing and a million computer screens were flickering.

Faith sat. 'Look, I'm sorry to bother you. You must be incredibly busy. It was probably stupid of

128

me to come, but I need to ask you some questions.'

'Fire away then. I thought the world of Billie— she was a great kid, bloody hard worker, and she had a nice little future here. She's all right? Not in any trouble?'

'Not as far as I'm aware.' Oh Lord! This all sounded so pathetic now. 'It's just that this has been bothering me ever since she left the *Argus* . . .'

Craigie listened and smoked and ate a Mars bar and smoked some more. Faith watched his face as she talked. There wasn't any point in the monologue where Craigie looked as though he'd interrupt with an explanation. Her spirits sank.

When she'd finished, Craigie leaned forward. 'Let me assure you of one thing. Billie left here under no cloud at all. Everyone was shattered that she chose to go—and as quickly as she did. I know she said she was going to be a nursemaid or something, but we all assumed she'd been head-hunted by one of the nationals—although we were never asked for references. We tried everything we could to get her to stay, but she was adamant.'

'Oh, damn.' Faith sank back into her chair. It was all so futile. Billie had told the truth. She'd simply fancied a change of direction. 'Maybe she didn't like the assignments she was getting or something?'

Craigie lit another cigarette and wreathed the office in smoke. 'That's the funny thing. At the start, she was over the moon with her last-but-one job. She said it was a hell of a lot better than council meetings and school plays. She must have told you . . .'

Had she? Faith tried to remember. 'Ah, yes . . . Something to do with restaurants, wasn't it? I

129

remember the boys all teasing her about turning into Michael Winner.'

'Hardly! Billie was always a bit of a knockout!' Craigie spluttered into a hacking cough. 'We were planning to run a series on various foreign food fads in the South-West. She'd gone off to report for the first piece on the new faux French farmhouse restaurant which was being opened near Bideford.'

Faith nodded. She'd seen the place advertised. Rustique or Rustica or something . . .

Craigie shrugged. 'She came back and said she didn't think it was quite her and asked if she could do something else. Something not quite so local. So we gave her the Willowbridge expats column, which meant she was out and about all over the country following up people who had once lived here. She filed the lives of a couple of pieces and then—'

'And then she left, what, only a couple of months later?' Faith stood up. 'It just doesn't make sense, does it? Thanks for your time. I'm sorry to have bothered you. I'll give Billie your best, shall I?' Which of course she would—only not just yet. She had no intention of letting Billie know what she was up to.

'Please do. And tell her there's a job here for her if ever she wants it. Look, I'm so sorry I haven't been any help.'

Oh, but you have, Faith thought, as she smiled blithely at the receptionist on her way out. It may well be another blind alley, but it was somewhere to start. Something might have happened at that restaurant . . . Something that had made Billie want to get as far away from Devon as possible.

As soon as possible, she thought as she hurried through the rain, she'd pay a visit to Bideford.

chapter eleven

'Just try to get both wheels on the ground at the same time,' Vinny yelled across the twin-engined roar in the Shorts' cockpit. 'I don't know about the passengers, but you scare the shit out of me every time we land. I just close my eyes and hang on.'

'That's why I'm the pilot and you're only the tea-boy,' Jonah grinned as the runway lights and rooftops of Whiteacres swept towards him. 'Bloody concentrate on your own job and leave the tricky stuff to me. Just read the dials, try giving me the speed and height in a volume that I can hear, oh and, yeah, keeping your eyes open might help both of us . . .'

The Sullivanair Shorts 330, cruising along its allotted glide path, was coming in to land. Coming home, Jonah thought, with a touch of irony. There had been so many homes in the last few years— and he somehow doubted that Whiteacres would be the last. Still, it was fine at the moment. His flat was close by and functional, the airfield was perfect for his business, and the Boeing Stearman was taking beautiful, perfect shape in the privacy of the industrial unit.

'Golf Hotel Charlie Foxtrot. Clear to land.' The air-traffic control tower was already crackling in his headset as the Shorts' fat wheels touched the runway, bounced, skimmed, and touched again.

'Christ Almighty!' Vinny pulled an agonised face. 'You're not in the bloody Stearman yet! What was that supposed to be? Waldo Pepper's death dive?'

'Piss off,' Jonah said good-naturedly, braking

hard and slowing at the end of the runway with cool expertise, before swirling into a gentle turn. 'That was as smooth as silk. Inch perfect.'

'Charlie Foxtrot,' the air-traffic controller interrupted bossily, 'proceed to taxi way Alpha One. Stand Five for passenger disembarkation. Received?'

'Golf Hotel Charlie Foxtrot received.' Jonah taxied the 58 feet of plane into its allocated bay, and proceeded to shut down both engines.

As the throb subsided, Pam popped her head into the cabin. 'Nicely done, boys. Only two seizures and a panic attack. Forgot ourselves for a moment, did we?'

'Don't you start.' Jonah removed his headset and stretched. 'I have enough trouble with Boy Wonder here. He's got nerves of Kleenex. Seriously, the passengers are OK?'

Pam leaned across and kissed his cheek. 'The passengers are fine, sweetie. They didn't feel a thing—even if the descent was a tad rapid. You made up for it with a peach of a landing. As always. Some of them actually clapped. I'll just get 'em unbuckled and unloaded and head for my first vodka and tonic of the evening. What about you?'

'He's off to play in his shed,' Vinny struggled into his jacket. 'Unlike some of us who are off to play with things that breathe and giggle and don't make your hands dirty—unless, of course, you get very lucky . . .'

Pam raised her etched eyebrows into her bleached hairline and disappeared to sort out her passengers. Below, Kev was manhandling the chocks into place, untangling the leads of the auxiliary power unit, going through the routine

132

procedures necessary before the Shorts could be towed into its hangar for the night. Outside, the late afternoon was closing in.

Jonah collected his charts together. Slowly. Delaying for as long as possible the moment when the bliss of flying was replaced by the dross of being earthbound. Once back on the ground, the reality started to seep in pretty quickly. He'd like to stay flying for ever. Especially on days like this. Especially tonight.

Pam was going home to her live-in lover, a meal, and a bottle of vodka; Vinny to his latest doe-eyed conquest with probably a takeaway curry at half-time; while he was going home to—what? Jonah sighed heavily. Yeah, Vinny was right: he'd be checking on the Stearman tonight as he did every night—but not immediately. First he had to face Claire.

His ex-wife's phone calls to the flat that he'd been ignoring, and the more strident ones to the Sullivanair office that Estelle had been fielding, had culminated in a letter. Not a solicitor's one—they'd been down that road before, during and after the divorce. This was one of Claire's specials. It should have been written in green ink, or blood, or both, the way the vitriol streamed from the pages. Claire was coming to visit. Claire wanted something. Again.

She knew, the words screamed, what time he'd be home. She'd checked the schedules, so there was no point in him lying. She'd be there, at the flat, half an hour after he'd landed. Half an hour to drive half a mile. She hoped that he'd manage it.

He wished that Barnaby was around this week, but he'd returned to Derbyshire to deal with a

133

structural emergency at the stately home and wouldn't be back until the weekend. If Barnaby had been staying with him, he could have simply told Claire it wasn't convenient. He had company. Well, hell, he could say that anyway, of course. But it wouldn't be true. And he'd never lied to Claire. Never.

He also knew that he could easily avoid her by spending the night with Vinny, or Pam, or even locked in the shed with the Stearman, but what was the point? It would only be delaying the inevitable.

Wearily, he picked up the charts and his jacket and cap and stood up. The cockpit smelled warm and safe, and closed in around him in cosy familiarity. Protecting him. He groaned. For God's sake, get a grip! She can't eat you! But she could, and did, still hurt him . . .

Grabbing his flight bag, Jonah followed Vinny into the now-empty plane, checking on the way through that the overhead lockers were cleared, that the seats were back, that everything was in place.

'You on for a drink, then?' Vinny asked, jumping down steps ahead of Jonah. 'Or are you going straight over to pet your Boeing baby?'

Jonah shook his head. 'Can't stop tonight, Vin. Sorry. Previous pressing engagement.'

'Really?' Vinny grinned as they crossed the runway towards the terminal buildings. 'And I thought you weren't interested.'

'Interested in who?'

'The bird at the warehouse.'

'I'm not and she isn't. Either a bird or my pressing engagement for tonight.'

'Great—so am I in with a chance, then? Is it

worth me coming to give her the once-over? That is, if she's going be there this time. Why isn't she ever there when I've been there?'

'Bloody hell—first, not a dog's chance. She doesn't like planes, flying, or flyers. Secondly, even if she did, she's not your type at all—she can even do joined-up writing. And lastly, I expect she's got better things to do with her evenings.'

'Sounds right up my street. I love a challenge,' Vinny said happily. 'Is she married?'

'How the hell would I know? And more importantly, why would I care? We only speak in passing—and most times I'm not there when she is. And vice versa. She's making money hiring me her warehouse, and I'm renovating the Stearman in peace. That's as far as it goes. I reckon you'd have more chance of pulling Estelle than you would Billie Pascoe.'

'Ooh no! Not Estelle!' Vinny pulled a face of mock shock horror. 'Even I don't invite that sort of trouble. She's yours, mate. All yours—you lucky bastard.'

They'd reached the foot of the steps to the air-traffic control tower. Jonah took a deep breath. 'Vin, before you go—you haven't mentioned anything about the Stearman to Claire, have you?'

'Me?' Vinny's eyes were wide-innocent. 'You told me not to mention the Stearman to anyone, and I haven't. Not that it's the best kept secret or anything. I mean there's about twenty million people on the airfield alone that know about it. But I haven't seen Claire or spoken to her for months. Why?'

Jonah shrugged. 'Because you've got a rollaway mouth. And because somebody has told her

135

something. I think she's after money.'

'Tough tit, then. You haven't got any money.'

'Not now I haven't. Not now I've bought the Stearman. She'll probably try and make me sell it.'

'Why should she? Isn't Aerobatic Archie keeping her in recreational drugs any more? Tell her to get stuffed, mate. I would. See ya in the morning.'

'Yeah, sure. And take it easy on the booze tonight—we're airborne again at lunch time. No alcohol for twelve hours before.'

'Christ, you are such a nag!' Vinny grinned. 'No wonder Claire left you.'

Thanks a bunch, chum, Jonah thought, pushing open the ATC door. That's just what I wanted to hear.

*   *   *

Claire was late. He'd straightened cushions, shoved newspapers and takeaway cartons in the bin, squirted air-freshener, and switched the kettle on and off for the last half an hour. He'd showered and shaved and dressed in clean jeans and one of his less disreputable sweatshirts. He'd even used a splash of Boss and then washed it off again.

The doorbell rang. Jonah counted to twenty before crossing the hall, and another ten before opening the door.

'You're late.' As always, seeing her caused a physical pain. When they were apart he could convince himself that what she had become was everything he despised and detested. He could turn her into some sort of demon inside his head—as long as she wasn't there. 'I thought maybe you'd changed your mind.'

136

'The traffic was lousy. And sorry to dash your hopes. So? Aren't you going to invite me in?'

He hesitated for a moment. He'd really like to keep her on the doorstep. It was always safer that way. 'Yeah, sure. We don't want the neighbours hearing the fight, do we?'

'Jo . . .' she spoke reproachfully, stepping past him, 'there doesn't have to be a fight. Oh, you've decorated . . . It looks nice.'

He hadn't and it didn't. The flat was still basic beige, as it had always been. She'd probably been too stoned to notice the décor on her last visit. Jonah watched her as she drifted round the room, touching things with those long, probing fingers. Things that had belonged to neither of them. Things that had come with the fundamental furnishings; things that were included on the pathetic rental inventory. Ornaments and books— all supplied with the fixtures and fittings by the yard. No individuality. No taste. No life . . .

Claire stopped, and picked up a tiny china candlestick. 'You haven't got a drink, I suppose?'

'The kettle's on.'

'A proper drink, Jo. A real drink. No one can do a whisky sour like you can.'

'And no one can drink them like you. And you're driving. Tea or coffee?'

'Coffee, then.' She pouted and tossed the candlestick into the air. It fell, smashing against the fireplace's fawn surround. 'Oh dear. What a pity . . .'

He stared at the fragments and then at her. 'Yeah, isn't it?'

She didn't follow him into the kitchen. Even as he boiled water and spooned granules, he could

137

hear her moving around, could picture her usual wry amusement at the starkness of his home: a four-walled shell with no woman's touch and no soul.

He tried to concentrate on everything he disliked about her, and not to think about her body. The good bits from the past kept inveigling their way in . . . Claire's hair had always looked like she'd just tumbled out of bed, but these days it looked that way by design rather than reality. Her make-up was just the other side of tasteful, and probably applied under the watchful eye of a professional cosmetician. Her clothes, designer now rather than RAF base thrift shop, were pulled just that touch too tight on the statuesque body.

Jonah added milk. Claire had been on a perpetual diet all through their marriage. Weight Watchers had been fine until she'd discovered amphetamines. She was singing now. Oh God. He'd loved her voice. He'd loved the way she moved, the way she looked, the way she spoke. He didn't love her any more, he knew he didn't, but not loving didn't mean an end to lusting. He still fancied her like mad.

'Bollocks. Bollocks. Bollocks.' He snatched up the two mugs and headed back to the living room.

Claire was sitting on the sofa, legs tucked under her, like a child. She dangled a cigarette from her fingers. There was already a sprinkling of ash on the floor. 'Sorry, sweetheart—I couldn't find an ashtray.'

'There aren't any. I gave up. Here—use this . . .' Putting both mugs on the table, he picked up the largest piece of broken candlestick from the hearth. 'I never liked them much anyway. Do you want to smash the other one?'

'No thanks.' She smiled at him. 'It *was* an accident.'

'Yeah, sure.' He sat down on the other side of the room, nursing his coffee, almost using it as a shield. 'So, why the visit?'

'Because you won't answer my calls. I needed to talk to you. You're so mean—'

Mean? Jesus! She'd had everything—bled him dry. 'I can't afford to give you any more money.'

'Antony says—'

'Fuck Antony!'

'Oooh. Temper, temper.' She stubbed out the cigarette and leaned forward. 'I was just going to say that I wasn't actually asking for money. I was going to say that Antony says he's heard on the circuit that you're expanding your business. And he said that I should remind you that our solicitors came to the agreement that fifty per cent of your assets were mine.'

'*Were!* Yes—at the time of the divorce,' Jonah nodded, gritting his teeth, willing himself not to shout this time. 'You left me, remember? You swanned off with poxy Antony and left me, OK? You chose to go. I didn't have to give you anything—other than half the house, half my redundancy, half my RAF pension, half my bloody life. Don't you dare come round here two years on and demand more!'

Claire stared at him for a disconcertingly long time, then she laughed. 'You are so gorgeous, Jo. So bloody dead sexy. Antony isn't half as good in bed as you were—still are, I suppose ...'

Jonah closed his eyes for a second. He wished he could close his ears and switch off the memories as easily. 'Claire, sodding shut up. If you don't want money, what the hell do you want?'

'Your body, of course.' She laughed. 'I wish. No, don't look so scared. I know we're over. I blew it. And don't think I haven't regretted it.'

'It was your choice. Antony, as I recall, was a grown-up who could offer you so much more—of everything.'

'Don't remind me.' Claire lit another cigarette and exhaled the smoke. 'Oh, we still have a good time. The tours are fun, and glamorous, and it's so nice being stinking rich.'

'Which is what you wanted to be. Obviously what you still want to be—but if Antony's running out of dosh, you're wasting your time. I haven't got any money. Nothing. So don't try screwing anything extra out of me.'

She slid from the sofa, cigarette in one hand, coffee in the other, and crossing the room, eased herself onto the arm of his chair. God! He wanted her so much! Holding himself rigid so that they shouldn't touch, he tried not to breathe in her scent.

She leaned towards him. 'Jo, darling, try listening. I said I don't want money from you.'

'That wasn't how the letter sounded.'

'Which letter? Oh, *that* letter!' Claire shrieked with laughter, leaning even closer, her body touching his. 'I was on a real downer when I wrote that. Permanent resident in Misery Street. I'd've killed as soon as smiled that day. You know me and my moods.'

He did. He tried really hard to dislike her for her moods at that moment and not want her for her body. 'OK, but there were about a million phone

140

calls as well.'

'Yeah, right. Because I wanted to talk to you. I still miss you, and when Antony said he'd heard that you were not only planning to expand the short-hauls but also do something even more spectacular—oh, I don't know. It's just such a turn-on, darling. Since we split you've become this dashing flyer again, with your own plane, and now, apparently, planes. Maybe I should have stuck around.'

Jonah edged himself away. Claire had left him because he was boring, she'd said so a thousand times. He thought of nothing but flying twenty-four hours a day. A run-of-the-mill RAF pilot in dung-coloured overalls, with no excitement. About as much of a career thrill as a bus driver . . . Christ, piloting the Shorts on charter flights in the UK was hardly space shuttle celebrity status, was it? That's what she'd said, sod her. And sod bloody Antony with his ear-to-the-ground chums. He was damned if they were going to get their hands on the Stearman.

'OK, then. You don't want money—which is great because I haven't got any. And you can tell Antony that he's got it all wrong. I'm not expanding. I haven't even been able to afford to do any work on the Slingsby since we split. And as I'm not going to be rivalling Antony in pilot-thrill stakes, I guess this visit has been a waste of time.'

Claire shook her head. The cloudy curls brushed his face, arousing and disturbing.

'Nothing's ever a waste of time with you, Jo.' She squirmed round on the arm of the chair and leaned provocatively across him to stub out her cigarette and put her coffee mug on the floor. 'You're a

141

bloody bad liar. I think Antony's grapevine buddies have got it dead right. I think there's more to Sullivanair than meets the eye. And if there is, then Antony wants to know about it.'

'Forget it.' He stood up abruptly, almost tipping her to the floor. 'You're not entitled to anything in my life any more. And why the hell should Antony have any interest?'

Claire shook her hair away from her face. 'Because he's giving up the team next year. He'll have completed his five years and he's looking to invest his platinum handshake in something else. He thinks there's money to be made from owning your own airfield. You know, big business in running a flying school, offering corporate hospitality, that sort of thing. Maybe an aviation museum with a bit of virtual reality. Classic wing flights. Perhaps a nice little sideline in charter trips ... And Whiteacres is so central, isn't it?'

Jesus Christ! Antony couldn't do it—could he? How much of Whiteacres was privately owned? Was there a board of doddering old farts just waiting for someone to present them with a stonking cheque so that they could go off and spend their twilight years grazing in Hastings? Could Antony Bastard Archibald buy out the ground from beneath his feet?

Claire was heading for the door. 'Look, Jo, you probably don't believe me, but I just wanted to warn you, that's all. Antony is very determined. And very rich. If he wants something he gets it. It might be a good idea for you to run now while the going is good.'

142

chapter twelve

Strobes pulsed in time with the bass, splintering intermittent explosions of light into the darkness. A hundred or so packed-together bodies gyrated happily. The bar staff looked like they were going for the world record on Pernod and blacks.

Billie, in the Joseph dress, shrank away into a corner of a blue banquette and nursed her gin and tonic. Electric blue was Bazooka's predominant colour; well, in the dark anyway. Billie, who had once inadvertently seen the club in daylight, knew that the lights and the glitz hid a million tawdry secrets, most of them magnolia.

Miranda and the rest of the girls—Debs, Anna, Sally and Kitty—were all somewhere on the tiny dance floor, baring their oiled shoulders and flicking back their scented hair. Billie, who despite an hour in the bath still felt grubby, had excused herself on the grounds of exhaustion. Which wasn't far off the truth. It had been a pretty shitty day.

True, the Stearman seemed to be taking shape quite nicely, with Jonah Sullivan and his henchmen obviously beavering away in her shed under cover of darkness like the Tailor of Gloucester's mice, so that each morning there was a significant transformation. She'd skirted the beige bodywork, picked her way round the fretwork ribs, and been careful not to move anything. Two new customers, having kept her flyers, had telephoned and asked if she'd take their attic overspill, and she'd happily agreed and added them to her list of customers on the computer.

Feeling rather smug, she'd sat back in the wonky armchair and sipped her coffee, and watched the rain mist across the airfield. Sylvia's arrival, complete with dripping pakamac and squelchy jelly shoes, had damped the euphoria in more ways than one.

'Can't stop, dear. Worst day of the month, eh?'

Billie, wondering if maybe Sylvia was on HRT and therefore still experiencing the joys of the menstrual cycle, had nodded in feminine solidarity. 'Poor you—I do sympathise. Can't you go and put your feet up with a cup of hot chocolate and a couple of paracetamol?'

Sylvia had looked bewildered. 'Well, yes, I could—but I don't see how that would help, dear, honestly. The damn things have got to be filled in for Simon Maynard to collect at five o'clock prompt. Zia had his done by first light and Fred 'n' Dick always get their wives to do theirs. I'm not sure how the Gusper boys manage . . .'

Billie, sitting upright and putting down her coffee mug, had realised she'd been on completely the wrong track. 'Er, sorry, Sylv—what are we talking about here?'

'Maynard and Pollock's quarterly returns. You sign for the damn things with the lease and like VAT you always put them off until the last minute, don't you?'

Not having a clue, Billie had nodded, panic shivering through her veins. What quarterly returns? Which of the brown envelopes stacked in her pending tray contained the sinister paperwork? Oh God! How would she ever make a go of this business when she didn't have a clue about being an entrepreneur? Why hadn't she listened in her

144

business studies classes? Why hadn't she opened her bloody post? She spent nearly all day, every day, just trying to get to grips with the computer. The post didn't get a look in.

Sylvia had oozed damply towards the door again. 'I'll leave you to it, then, dear. Just needed a breath of air to clear away the cobwebs. The plane's coming along nicely, isn't it?'

Billie, still staring at the pile of envelopes and wishing Sylvia would go away so that she could rip them open in private and have a good cry over the contents, had nodded wildly. 'It seems to change every morning—although God knows what they're going to do with it when it's finished. It'll never get off the ground.'

'Maybe it won't matter,' Sylvia had said morosely. 'Maybe we'll have been bought out and evicted long before then.'

With that happy thought hanging over her, Billie had waited until she'd heard the plastic shoes squirting across the broken concrete outside, and had feverishly torn open the first envelope.

Four hours later, with Maynard and Pollock's quarterly return still only half done, Billie had screamed in frustration and hurled yet another set of calculations at the office wall. They'd bounced off and rolled under the desk. It was while she'd been bending down to retrieve them, that she'd heard the outer doors pulled open and someone step inside.

'Sorry, won't keep you a moment—oh, ouch! Shit!' Emerging from beneath the desk, rubbing her head, Billie looked up into the immaculately made-up face of Estelle Rainbow.

She'd sat on the floor, her dungarees and fleece

145

dusty, her hair haywire, and a million years of grime on her hands. Estelle, her hair smoothed into a chignon, and wearing a workmanlike set of overalls and still managing to look like Jodie Kidd on a Chanel shoot, had stared back disdainfully. 'Am I disturbing you?'

'No, no . . .' Billie had scrambled up, banging her head again and wanting to cry. 'I was—um—just doing some paperwork. Can I help you?'

Estelle had looked as though that was a definite impossibility. 'I've got a couple of hours free. Jonah asked me to start on the rivets and check the prop.'

Billie had whimpered. The woman was not only stunningly gorgeous and secretarially brilliant, she was a damned engineer to boot. 'Oh, right . . . yes, sure. I don't think we'll be in each other's way.'

Estelle had wandered to the desk and was scanning the quarterly return. 'This looks like a census. And you've filled that column in wrongly—oh, and that one—and if that's right there then you'd already be bankrupt.'

Billie, fighting back a second whimper, had shrugged. 'It's my first attempt. I—er—I've left it to the last minute. I'd—um—forgotten all about it . . . We have to complete them every three months to show how trading is going, apparently.'

Estelle had pulled up the second of the wonky chairs. 'You should always deal with these things as they come in. Jonah's just the same. Leaves everything until zero hour and expects me to sort out the chaos. It's the first rule of business—a clear desk means a clear head. Look, you go and put the kettle on while I get to grips here, otherwise you'll be out of business and the Stearman will be out on the runway long before we're ready.'

146

And Billie, humiliated, had stomped into the kitchen and made coffee, while Estelle had made short work of the quarterly return, several final demands, two red bills, filed a mountain of invoices and dispatched a clutch of statements.

'There,' Estelle had sat back in the chair, 'all organised. Now I've written you a check list for the future. Deal with them all in the order that I've written down here. Keep everything up to date— oh, and your computer system needs constantly upgrading. I've sorted out a game plan.' She'd looked Billie up and down. 'I don't want to sound unkind, but don't you think you're a bit out of your depth here? Running this warehouse isn't just storing other people's belongings. It's like every business—each transaction brings at least five sets of paperwork. You really need to be more organised . . . and I can't see any business cards or up-to-date literature at all.'

Billie had squirmed and admitted that she'd actually got as far as ordering things from the printers, but hadn't collected them yet, but it was in hand and she'd do it immediately. And then Estelle had risen from the chair, still looking as immaculate and unflustered as when she'd arrived, and Billie had had to emulate Uriah Heep and squeeze unctuousness and gratitude through clenched teeth. And then, to top it all, when Simon Maynard had arrived at five and snatched the damned quarterly return without even saying thank you, he'd ignored Billie and slavered all over Estelle and the Stearman and asked pertinent questions about horsepower and gravitational pull and velocity.

Billie had waited for him to leave, and then with reluctant admiration, had stood in the shadows, watching as Estelle, a professional toolbox lodged on a set of stepladders, fiddled with the mass of wiring looms, sank rivets, and replaced minute engine parts—all without the help of the *I-Spy Book of build Your Own Aircraft*—and still without a hair out of place, or one slightly chipped fingernail.

Feeling completely inadequate, Billie had made her exit pretty sharpish then, and driven the Nova back to Amberley Hill in a cloud of despondency. The last thing she'd wanted after that had been one of Miranda's fabled girls' nights out, involving drinking up to the point of visual impairment in Mulligan's, followed by dehydration and deafness in Bazooka's.

*   *   *

'Woo!' Sally collapsed onto the banquette. 'I'm shattered. Kitty, Debs and Anna are still hard at it—' she indicated the dance floor—'but I had to do something about my feet.'

Billie stared at Sally's dainty size four feet complete with delicate pearly toenails encased in strips of laced pink leather. To someone with the feet of a width indicative of a childhood spent in wellingtons, they looked fine. 'What about Miranda?'

Sally giggled. 'Oh, yeah—you'll never guess! Miranda's pulled! Pretty tasty too. Well, from the back at least. Dark hair. Nice bum. I didn't see his face.'

'Are you sure it's not Keith?' Billie knew Keith, despite Miranda's misgivings, was still somewhere on the scene. 'He's got dark hair.'

Sally was scathing. 'Keith's having a breakdown

148

in Winchester.'

'Don't you mean Keith's out on a—' Billie stopped, remembering the goulash, and Miranda's more recent mantrap experiment with a civet body scrub and two loofas. 'No, on second thoughts maybe you're right. So, what's he like? Mr Dark Hair and Nice Bum?'

'I said, I didn't see his face—Ooh, look! They're at the bar now. Tell you what,' Sally stood up and flexed her toes, 'I'll give my feet a bit of a workout and report back, shall I? G and T?'

'Just the T, please. I'm practically comatose as it is. My sight was blurred early on.'

'Poor old you. I'm so glad I'm just an office prisoner,' Sally said happily. 'I'd hate to work for myself. Think of the disadvantages. You'll never be able to skive a day off again, will you?'

Billie watched Sally swing her way expertly through the throng. The bar area was shadowy and packed so she couldn't see any sign of Miranda. Not that it mattered. She'd hear all about her conquest soon enough. She'd seen Keith's nondescript stubbled face sloping out of the bathroom in the mornings very rarely lately. He wasn't, according to Miranda, anywhere near being Husband Number Two. Maybe this one—dark hair, nice bum—might be a better bet.

Maybe she should shake off her lethargy and join the hunt. Now that she'd got rid of the mythical Damon, there was no reason why she couldn't meet a man. She stared at the sea of half-handsome male faces with their uniform trendy gelled hair and their uniform trendy logo'd shirts and their laddish drunken grins, and knew it was futile. Here, at least. That was the problem: falling in love with Kieran so

149

early had spoiled the game. Despite turning out to be a grade-one bastard, he really had been a pretty class act: certainly one with whom the Daves and Kevs and Andys—however nice—of Amberley Hill were going to be unable to compete.

Pathetic. Billie shook her head. Pre-Kieran, she'd have been head over heels if someone stocky and monosyllabic from the Newton Abbot Young Farmers had asked her to go to the cinema. Now she'd joined the ranks of the cynical: searching, like Miranda, for a follow-on substitute that simply didn't exist.

Sally returned then with the drinks and pulled a face. 'Miranda and the man—they've disappeared. My guess is that Miranda has taken him home. You'll have to be very discreet when you get in, won't you?'

Billie nodded, groaning inwardly. She only hoped Miranda would be test-driving Mr Dark Hair and Nice Bum in the privacy of her bedroom—and wouldn't be writhing on the sofa. It had happened several times before, and Billie had always felt so gauche, caught in mid-tiptoe and exchanging pleasantries with a naked stranger while Miranda made angry piss-off jerking motions with her head.

She poured the tonic into her glass and swirled it about with the piece of lemon rind. Her eyelids itched with tiredness and the drum'n'bass was beginning to set her teeth on edge. Sally had taken one sip from her glass then, with obviously revived feet, flown back to the dance floor. Billie felt like an interloper. If you weren't in the mood, then clubbing was a nightmare. And she definitely wasn't in the mood. Anyway, clubs still reminded her of Kieran.

150

Oh, not Bazooka's, of course. But Kieran had been a member of some pretty hot places all over the country, where discretion was guaranteed for famous faces, and they'd danced energetically and drunk for England and then staggered out to the nearest taxi rank and gone back to their hotel room, and it had all been absolutely blissful.

And all the time, in those early days before London, her parents had thought she was away on Willowbridge expats assignments for the *Devon Argus*, and sadly the *Devon Argus* thought the same, and if her expenses claims didn't quite tally with the paucity of her copy, then mercifully no one said anything, and she was convinced that this was It. Love. For ever and ever.

Feeling utterly wiped out, Billie stood up. She couldn't think about it any more. It was over. She'd lived through it and survived. She looked at her watch. Nearly two o'clock. She'd be able to call one of Reuben's Cabs for the journey home without any danger. Reuben rarely drove and certainly never did the nightshift these days.

Waving goodbye to Kitty, Debs, Anna and Sally, she fought her way through Bazooka's merriment, collected her coat, and headed for the all-night neon brightness of the Spicer Centre.

*   *   *

The driver who dropped her outside the flat was a stranger. Probably her replacement. Fortunately he hadn't talked at all, and Billie had slumped on the back seat, desperately trying not to fall asleep in the drowsy warmth.

'Please, oh, please,' she prayed quietly, sliding

151

her key into the lock, 'let Miranda be in bed. Please let me be able to go to the loo and brush my teeth and fall into bed without having to avert my eyes from *The Good Sex Guide*.'

The living room was in darkness. And silence. Not switching on the lights, and making the briefest of detours to the bathroom, Billie struggled into a Piglet and Tigger nightshirt—it was slightly depressing to think that her brothers all assumed that button-to-the-neck A. A. Milne winceyette was an appropriate gift each year—and setting the alarm clock for seven, wearily clambered beneath the duvet.

Half an hour later she was punched awake from a dream where she was having sand shovelled into her mouth by Estelle Rainbow, who then buried her beneath a mountain of paperwork. Gagging with thirst, she groped about on the bedside table for a glass of water. Bugger. She'd washed the glass up the previous day and not replaced it. There was no way on earth that she could be bothered to pull her exhaustion out of bed and trek to the kitchen. Oh well, all she had to do was close her eyes and go back to sleep. Easy to say—impossible to accomplish. Her tongue had congealed to the roof of her mouth. Her brain was full of images of tumbling waterfalls and ice cubes clinking in tall glasses . . . With a sigh of resignation, she pushed back the duck down and staggered to the kitchen.

The first glass of water was orgiastic; the second almost as good. She was just wondering whether a third would mean what was left of the night being spent trailing to the loo, when the front door opened.

Christ! No wonder Miranda had been quiet. She

and Mr Dark Hair and Nice Bum hadn't even made it home yet! Tugging down Piglet and Tigger to at least cover the tops of her thighs, Billie made a dash towards the living-room door.

Too late.

'Hiya, doll.' Miranda swayed into the kitchen. 'Great timing. I'm so glad you're still up. I've brought you a visitor.'

Caught in mid-yawn, Billie blinked sleep from her eyes. 'No you haven't. You're drunk. Sally said you'd met someone in Bazooka's and—'

'Oh, I did! And we've been for a meal at the Dij Raj. Absolutely scrummy. Chicken pasanda and aloo palak and tarka dall and—' Miranda clutched at the draining board for support. 'And now we've come back with some brilliant news.'

'Well, great. But I don't think it involves me, does it, so I'll just go back to bed and—'

'Oh, but it does involve you, doll. Believe me. It wasn't a cop-off, more's the pity. And if you don't mind me saying, I think you ought to do something with your hair. You look like you've just got out of bed.'

'I *have* just got out of bed!' Billie hissed. 'And I'm just going back there because it's the middle of the night and I don't want to meet anyone right now. I expect I'll see him when our paths cross to the bathroom in the morning.'

Miranda leaned heavily against the fridge. 'God, yes, I wish! And if I had my way—but, no, honest, Billie, he really wants to talk to you. Sadly, he doesn't fancy me at all.'

'Then why the hell did he take you for a meal?' Billie snapped. 'I'm wrecked. Just go and seduce him for God's sake and let me get some sleep.'

153

She pushed past Miranda and stumbled into the living room.

The dream about Estelle was heaven compared to the nightmare sitting on the sofa.

'Billie!' Reuben Wainwright gave a lip-service smile. 'So glad we've caught you. Miranda said you'd probably still be awake. No, don't try to hide yourself—there's absolutely no need. I've seen you scantily dressed before, remember?'

Billie remembered. She was bitingly angry. 'What the hell are you doing? You have no right to be here. It's—it's stalking, that's what it is! For God's sake—'

'It's not stalking and it's not harassment so stop twitching. Or is it the fact that I've just spent a few hours with your best friend that scares you? Worried that I might just blow the whistle on your fabricated fantasy past, are you?'

'No, I'm not! Of course I'm not! You tried that weeks ago—Miranda told me. She just thought you were confused. I know exactly what you're doing. You're trying to intimidate me into driving for you again, aren't you?'

'Don't flatter yourself.' Reuben stretched himself comfortably on the sofa. 'I wanted to talk to you, that's all. I was in Bazooka's for business, not pleasure, and Miranda kindly offered to buy me a drink. I didn't even know you were there.'

'Crap.'

Miranda poked pink pigtails out of the kitchen. 'No, honest. That's how it happened. We just bumped into each other and got talking, and Reuben told me his exciting news and I said you'd be dead interested, and then we had another dance and after that we couldn't find you and Sally said

154

you'd pooped, and we went to the Dil Raj and talked some more, and here we are. Coffees all round?'

Reuben nodded. Billie shook her head. It was a nightmare. Reuben never went near nightclubs.

'Come and sit down.' Reuben patted the sofa. 'I want to suggest something.'

'I bet you do.' Billie stayed resolutely put, wishing Piglet and Tigger would scamper down to her ankles. She wasn't at all happy with the way Reuben was eyeing her legs. 'But I don't want to listen. I've got work to go to in the morning and I don't want you within a hundred miles of me. And don't,' she glared at him, 'think you can trap me with that old rubbish about knowing my darkest secrets. No one will be in the slightest bit interested now.'

Reuben shrugged. 'Possibly not. I just think that you're being a little bit hasty. And it's your—er—career that I want to talk to you about.'

Jesus. Billie closed her eyes. Far too many gin and tonics were thundering inside her skull. So he *did* intend to scupper her plans. The bastard. What the hell was Miranda thinking of, bringing him back here to torment her?

'It's none of your business.'

'No, but it might be. From what Miranda said over dinner, I thought I might be able to help. You see I'm thinking of expanding. You'd obviously had enough of being a taxi-driver, so I thought I'd give you first refusal of a new job.'

'I've got a new job!' Billie ran her hand through her hair. Miranda was right. It was all tufty and standing on end. And he had to be joking! She'd rather die of starvation than ever work for him

155

again. 'And you? Expanding? Come off it! You run a two-bit taxi firm with clapped-out Granadas—and you live in a bedsit! Exactly when did you turn into Richard Branson?'

Reuben smiled. 'Sarcasm doesn't suit you, sweetheart. I run my life on a shoestring—unlike some—because I've been carefully saving to make further investment in my future. I figure the time is right with Bazooka's coming on the market—'

'You're going to *buy* Bazooka's? Dear God! What the hell do you know about clubbing? Until tonight you probably hadn't been near a club since they stopped having comics with flat caps and a magic turn after the bingo!'

'Exactly. Which is why I was hoping you, with your intimate knowledge of the club scene, might be interested in managing it for me.'

What? Billie closed her eyes, then opened them. He was still there.

'Sleep on it, sweetheart. Give me your answer in the morning.'

'I'll give you my answer right now. No. No way. No bloody way on earth. OK?'

Miranda crashed in at that moment with three coffee mugs and a bag of cheese and onion crisps on a tray. 'I couldn't remember who said what, so I've made us all one.' She beamed at Billie. 'See, doll—what did I tell you? Great news, huh? And brilliant for Bazooka's as well. It's about time it had a face-lift. And much more fun for you than hanging around in that musty old shed.'

Reuben was nodding maliciously. Miranda simply looked cross-eyed. Billie itched to slap them both. How dare they interfere in her life? How bloody dare they?

'Actually I couldn't consider it even if I wanted to. My own business, despite both of you obviously having no faith in me whatsoever, is doing very nicely, thank you. I've already got a lot of customers and plenty more on the way.'

Reuben looked mocking. 'Really?' He gave the word about twelve syllables.

Miranda was less ingenuous. 'Christ, doll! I thought that plane took up most of your space.'

Billie gritted her teeth. 'Only the floor. I signed up two new customers today and I'm starting a new advertising campaign, so sorry, but you see, running a shabby little nightclub for some seedy little get-rich-quick merchant would definitely be second best.'

Still beaming with triumph she almost missed Reuben's killer smile.

'What a pity,' he drawled as he refused Miranda's coffee and stood up. 'I automatically thought of you for the club, Billie, sweetheart, because I'm going to completely refurbish it. I thought it would suit you down to the ground. I'm intending to make it a footballing theme club and call it Caught Offside.'

chapter thirteen

As she unravelled another sausage-shaped curl from its roller, Miranda gazed out of the window. The Spicer Centre's shops were already revving up for Christmas despite the fact that it was still only the beginning of October. Sadly the weather over the last week hadn't implied with the seasonal snow scenes and leaping log fire and stripy stocking window displays: it had scorched into a glorious Indian summer.

She bent forward over the owner of the iron-grey sausages. 'Go anywhere nice for your holidays, Mrs Bowden?'

'You've already asked me that. I said what with our Wilf passing on last year, my heart wasn't in Skegness.'

Bugger. 'Oh, yes. So you did. Sorry. Um—maybe you'll enjoy Skegness again next year? Have a bit of a laugh over the memories?'

'I doubt it. Not with our Wilf passing away in his deck chair on the sands right by the ice-cream kiosk and me having only slipped off for a Mivvi.'

Double bugger. Miranda released a further clutch of curls. Roll on this afternoon, when she would be working the men-only bit of Cuticles. She'd got two appointments for facials and one for a stress-buster lavender oil massage.

As all the appointments had been made over the phone, and all three were new customers, she had no idea what they'd look like and had allocated them randomly between herself, Debs and Kitty. Naturally, she'd warned both of them that if any of the customers had even a hint of David Ginola about them then she got first pick. Boss's perks.

She brushed Mrs Bowden's curls into a smooth helmet and used enough hairspray to destroy the ozone layer. Nearly lunch time. Maybe she'd ring Billie at Whiteacres and see if she wanted to meet up somewhere for a glass of wine and a sandwich. Somehow she doubted if Billie would. Billie had been acting mighty oddly ever since the night that Reuben had come back to the flat.

Well, OK, Miranda admitted, it probably had

158

been a bit of a shock, but he hadn't been there to nag Billie into driving a cab or anything, had he? He hadn't been threatening or bullying, or behaved in any of the other diabolical ways Billie had said he would. He'd simply made her an absolutely brilliant offer and Billie had turned him down.

Miranda shook her head. Honestly, she really couldn't see why Billie would want to run a boring damp and dingy warehouse in the middle of nowhere if she had the opportunity to be in charge of Bazooka's. It would be like partying every night *and* getting paid for it. Except, of course, it wouldn't be Bazooka's any more, would it?

She took Mrs Bowden's money. There was no tip.

Over the meal in the Dil Raj, Reuben had explained that Caught Offside would appeal to everyone: with the decor being in the colours of all the Premiership teams, and signed posters of the latest star players on the walls, and the cocktails were to be named after famous footballers, past and present. Miranda had silent but nonetheless grave doubts about the success of the Bobby Charlton Slammer.

But Reuben hadn't finished; apparently he intended to install a Starvision screen to show nonstop matches as a backdrop to the dancing and drinking, and possibly introduce a bistro area which he thought he'd call The Penalty Spot.

It would certainly be a money-spinner, Miranda had said, and she could see that even if Billie couldn't. If she hadn't been doing so well with Follicles and Cuticles then she'd have been first in the queue for the manager's job without a doubt.

Billie had told Miranda, pretty huffily, that she

159

was more than welcome to it, and that she'd go and live somewhere else if Miranda ever brought Reuben back to the flat again—and that she would never, ever, set foot in Caught Offside, so there. She had also said that the whole subject—nightclub, Reuben and football—was taboo. Miranda had tried to dig a bit deeper, but Billie had just said that as far as she was concerned there was nothing remotely beautiful about the game—or the men who played it—and that most women were sick to the back teeth with football—and that the only good thing about it was that Reuben would go bust within a year.

Now Miranda shouted to Kitty that she was off to lunch and not to touch the massage oil until she got back. Oh, and if Billie should ring, to tell her to call on her mobile or meet up in Mulligan's. Still, she thought, as she pushed her way through the Spicer Centre's crowds, bringing Billie and Reuben face to face that night had proved one thing: Billie hated football. Whatever else Reuben might have got right, he'd got that very, very wrong indeed. Mind you, the evening had had its advantages. Reuben had telephoned occasionally since, and a couple of nights ago they'd met for a drink in Mulligan's. It was nothing datey or personal, but—given the fact that Keith's appearances were becoming even more sporadic than Michael Jackson's—Miranda had relished every moment.

Her phone started ringing just past Woolworths, and Miranda joined the crowd of mobile-users huddled beneath the Abbey National's awning. It was the only place in the whole precinct where you didn't get feedback.

'Hi.' Billie's voice echoed somewhere between

that of a girl to Miranda's right who was having a flaming row with her boyfriend, and a man on her left who was trying to explain unsuccessfully to his bank manager why he was still overdrawn. 'Where are you?'

Miranda poked a finger into her free ear. 'On my way to Mulligan's, doll. Where are you?'

'At the printers in the High Street. Are you meeting anyone?'

'No, just grabbing a pie and a pint. Why? Do you fancy it?'

'Make it a tuna mayo baguette and a spritzer and I might agree.'

'OK. Done. See you there in a bit.'

Brilliant! Billie sounded right on form again. Maybe she'd forgiven Miranda for the Reuben incident after all. Miranda snapped off her mobile and bounced towards the pub, feeling a lot more spry.

Mulligan's was crowded with its usual midday office-escapees and Miranda had to fight her way to the bar. Eventually being served, she looked around hopelessly for somewhere to sit. Not a chance; there wasn't even enough space to put her plate and glass of lager down on the edge of someone else's table, let alone Billie's wine and roll.

Balancing one on top of the other, she sidled her way towards the wall. It would mean craning her neck towards the door so that she'd spot Billie, but at least if she could lean on something solid she may well be able to eat and drink without spilling everything.

Lodging both glasses precariously on the dado rail, and trying to steady the baguette on top of her own chicken korma and chip butty, Miranda

161

looked around for signs of someone leaving a table. Everyone looked entrenched for the duration. Rosemary Clooney and Val Doonican always replaced The Corrs during Mulligan's lunch-time sessions, and the gentle crooning and the doors thrown open to the unseasonable warmth were obviously infinitely preferable to returning to stuffy offices and shops.

'Excuse me. Would you like a seat?'

Miranda cricked her neck back from staring at the door and blinked down at the table beside her. 'Sorry? Are you talking to me?'

The elder of the two men at the corner table nodded. 'We're just going. Let me help you.'

He was probably the same age as her father, handsome, expensively Aquascutum-shirted, with well-cut dark hair going grey at the temples, and nice hands. He stood up and off-loaded the glasses from the dado rail. He then took the plates from her and set them on the table. He was charming, urbane and courteous. Miranda ignored him completely. His companion, the man still sitting at the table, was simply sex on a stick.

Miranda stood transfixed, then belatedly remembered her manners. 'Er—thanks . . . Oh, I mean, thank you. Really. It's very kind'

'No problem. You're more than welcome.'

Her knight in shining pale blue herringbone was beaming, but she couldn't concentrate. Not when the younger man had stood up, displaying a lot of long leg in denim, and smiled at her. He was sensationally, wondrously, glorious. Definitely just the most beautiful man she had ever seen. And he was about to walk out of Mulligan's and her life for ever. Miranda nearly cried with the unfairness of it

162

all. All those nights doing herself up and strutting it about on dance floors and only meeting people like Keith, and now looking scruffy and frazzled and totally moronic, she'd met Him. The man of her dreams. The only man who could possibly be in the running for Husband Number Two. Well, the only man who came anywhere near holding a candle to Reuben—and as Reuben was in love with Billie, whether he admitted it or not, that put him way off limits.

Both men were turning away, still smiling. Oh God. She had to do something. Chucking her handbag across the two chairs so that no one else would leap into them, she hurtled her way through the crowd. She caught up with them just as they reached the door.

'Excuse me, look, I know this probably sounds daft but I'd like to say thank you.' She pushed two of her Follicles and Cuticles cards into their hands. 'I run the salon. If you ever need a haircut or, well, anything, I'd be more than happy to . . . to . . .'

They took the cards, both smiled, albeit rather distantly, and left.

Shit. Miranda trailed back to the table. No doubt they'd get outside and dump the cards in the nearest bin. How sad had that looked? Shit again. She sat down in Mr Wonderful's seat. It was still warm. It was most disconcerting.

The remains of the men's lunch was still on the table. Pasta and red wine, and egg and chips and a glass of lager. Miranda prayed the pasta and red had belonged to Mr Funky Hunky. She was still gazing at the plates, completely moonstruck, when Billie arrived.

'Brilliant—you managed to get a seat. I thought

we'd have to stand. I'm starving,' Billie wriggled into her chair and took a bite out of the baguette at the same time. 'I've been busy all morning getting things organised. I've collected leaflets and business cards from the printers and I've been to the library and got *The Idiot's Guide to Office Management*—never again will that bloody Estelle Rainbow make me feel like my IQ's in minus figures—and—what the hell is wrong with you?'

Miranda picked up a flaccid chip. 'I'm in love. Honest. I've just met the man I want to spend the rest of my life with.'

'Apart from Keith, the whole Arsenal football squad, that dodgy Italian you picked up at the cinema, and Reuben Wainwright, you mean?' Billie choked on her baguette. 'Tell me something new.'

'No, seriously. This is different. He was here—at this table. He was totally fabulous. And now he's gone—and I look such a freak, I'm not surprised. Oh, bugger it! Why couldn't I have had one pair of false eyelashes at least!'

Miranda still bitterly regretted toning down her eye make-up. She'd abandoned the vermilion lipstick too, and her hair, now the colour of desiccated sloes, needed washing and so consequently was scraped back in an elastic band. She looked like she'd just been exhumed. No wonder Mr Drop-Dead Gorgeous had done a bunk.

Billie licked mayonnaise from the corner of her mouth. You'll probably see him in here again. Or in the club. Unless, of course, he was just passing through on business.'

'Don't! I couldn't bear it!'

'Why didn't you sit with him, then? Plonk yourself down and start chatting him up? You usually do.'

'He was with someone. Another man. Older.'

Billie swigged at the spritzer. 'Could be gay, then.'

'Bugger off!' Miranda howled. 'I really, really hate you sometimes, doll, do you know that?'

Miranda decided to err on the side of caution and not mention to Billie that she'd handed the Follicles card to a complete stranger. Billie would misinterpret it entirely as some sort of pick-up attempt, and nothing at all to do with promoting the salon's business. Miranda didn't feel she was prepared for that much censure.

She got it anyway. Billie launched into her usual routine of: seriously though, you go about things all the wrong way, and you shouldn't judge a book by its cover, and maybe, even if he is local and straight and available, which is pretty unlikely, granted, then probably he's a complete nerd—or boring or arrogant or vicious or . . .

'Shut up.' Miranda drained her lager glass. 'I don't want to hear all that. I hear it from inside my head all the time. I want you to say, this is it. He's the one for you, Miranda. It was kismet, fate, preordained, sent by the gods . . .'

'Crap,' Billie said cheerfully, dabbing up the last flakes of tuna. 'He's more than likely a gay anorak on his way through Amberley Hill to sell fishing tackle in Birmingham. Anyway, I thought you were devoted to Reuben. You still sleep with a lock of his hair under your pillow.'

Miranda was sorry for giving Billie this information one night after too many glasses of red. 'I know—and I am. But he's obviously devoted to you. And I thought you weren't ever going to

165

mention him again.'

'I'm not and—for the millionth time—he is not after me!'

Miranda sighed, chewed the chicken korma and chip sandwich, and only half listened, her mind full of long lean thighs, floppy dark hair, and a smile that would win gold in the Olympic Turn-On event.

How could she possibly explain to Billie that the man in the leather jacket had had the same devastatingly arousing effect on her as Reuben, or even a Leonardo diCaprio video after two bottles of wine? It sounded a bit tacky, even to her.

Lunch over, the girls parted in the sunshine outside Mulligan's. Billie was shooting off back to her dismal dungeon, apparently to canvass more customers. All Miranda had to look forward to were two facials and a massage.

She pinged her way into Follicles and Cuticles. The pile of gowns was depleted and all the basins were occupied. There was a satisfying hum of conversation above the burr of the radio, and Kitty was on the telephone saying she was terribly sorry but there were no free appointments for three days. Business was picking up nicely. It was a pity, Miranda thought, her love life couldn't do the same.

'Mr Franklin and Mr Duxbury have arrived for their facials. Debs is doing their hot towels,' Kitty said, putting the phone down. 'Neither of them look in the slightest scrummy, so we've left you the oiler because he isn't due for another half-hour. OK?'

'Fine.'

'Oh, and there was a telephone call for you. Personal. Wants you to ring him tonight. Said it was important. Didn't leave a name. He said you'd

166

know who he was. I wrote the number down here somewhere . . .'

As Kitty scrabbled through the heap of cards and Post-it notes on the desk, Miranda bit back her smile of delight. It had to be Him! See, Billie was wrong. It had been fate after all.

She gazed at the number which Kitty had scrawled on the back of one of Follicles and Cuticles' lavender cards. It was Reuben's bedsit. And gorgeous through Reuben was, what was the point of harbouring desires for him when he so obviously had the hots for her best friend? She'd ring him tonight and he'd only want to talk about Billie and whether Miranda had managed to make her change her mind about Caught Offside.

Sighing at the unfairness of life, Miranda pulled on her mauve overall and walked briskly through the archway into Cuticles. Bugger. Sod. Bugger. Sod. Her footsteps groaned along with her. All she could hope for now was that Mr Greenaway, the lavender oil massage, was totally divine. She deserved that much, surely?

Kitty and Debs were doing very nicely with the facials, and Kitty had been dead right—neither of the men sprawled backwards in the purple leather chairs was anything to write home about. Miranda smiled encouragingly at them.

'Randa, your body massage has arrived early.' Pixie, Follicles' punk trainee, stood on one tartan DMed foot in the archway. 'Shall I tell him to wait, or do you want him now?'

Miranda closed her eyes for a second. Please, please, please, let this be pure pink and fluffy romantic fiction. Please, please, please let Mr Greenaway be the stranger from Mulligan's. Please,

please, please ...

'Randa? You OK?' Pixie peered through her vivid green fringe.

'What? Yeah, of course. No—I'll come through and get him.'

She followed Pixie through the archway. Please, please, please—oh, bugger.

Miranda grinned inanely. 'Mr Greenaway! Good afternoon. We're all ready for you. If you'd like to come with me ...'

Mr Greenaway, fat, florid and fifty plus, was, Miranda noticed, already salivating.

chapter fourteen

It was quite a relief, Billie felt, to be able to park the Nova in the darkness, unlock the shed and savour the pleasure of being alone. There were quite a few things that she wanted to mull over, and somehow the privacy of the warehouse late at night was better than the flat, with its distractions of television and food and drink, and Miranda getting ready to go out with Reuben.

Miranda, she knew, thought that Billie had no idea at all about the previous Reuben-outing, and certainly not about this, the second. Billie on the other hand, had sensed the shift in the relationship from the night of the revelations about Caught Offside. Nearly every one of Miranda's conversations since that evening had had a sprinkling of 'Reuben says' or 'Reuben thinks'. Billie still reckoned that as long as none of Reuben's words or thoughts involved her and

Kieran Squires, then she really didn't give tuppenny toss.

She edged her way round the wings of the Boeing Stearman and stepped carefully over the attendant paraphernalia, which seemed to stretch further across the floor every day. Anyway, she thought, heading for the office, all Miranda's subterfuge must mean that she was pretty serious about Reuben Wainwright. Which was a very scary prospect, especially as he now seemed to be the lone contender for Husband Number Two. Billie had given up all hope that last week's man of Miranda's dreams from Mulligan's would ever surface again, and Keith, it seemed, had finally bitten the dust.

Billie unloaded onto her desk the file of paperwork that she'd taken home. Estelle's words had hit home and she'd cleaned up her businesswoman act since that embarrassing day. She'd organised the computer, answered letters straight away, and asked the other warehousers whenever there were forms to fill in which she didn't understand. Much as she disliked Estelle, you had to hand it to her, she was red-hot at absolutely everything. And beautiful. And Jonah's partner. It was decidedly unfair . . .

Despite October's continued warm spell, it was now bitingly cold in the warehouse and Billie snuffled into a tissue as she zipped around turning on the hot-air blowers. All she needed now was intravenous coffee, and she could spend the night here if necessary. She knew that no one from Sullivanair was due in this evening, so the shed, for once, was all hers. Which was quite a blessing. Watching Estelle's stunning elegance, not to mention three miles of legs, shimmying around with not a hair out of place while she put bits of plane together with the ease of an astrophysicist tackling an Airfix kit, was daunting enough. The thought of working with the gloriousness of Jonah Sullivan in close proximity was even worse.

She hadn't bothered with make-up and her hair had gone all tufty again, and as she passed the darkened windows of the office she almost made herself jump. God—her reflection was pretty scary; the eco-warrior look was set off to perfection by her face being pinched and rheumy-eyed and red-nosed from the cold. It was just as well Jonah wasn't going to be there. He probably disliked her; she didn't want him feeling sorry for her as well.

She hadn't meant to be so dismissive about his plane—or his hobby—on that first day. It had been sheer insecurity in the company of so much brain-boggling beauty. And how the hell was she supposed to have known what the fêted Mr Sullivan looked like, anyway? It was a mistake anyone could have made, wasn't it?

They'd kind of sorted it out afterwards with much embarrassed laughter on her side and who-cares shrugs on his. Billie hoped she had managed to claw things back on to a business footing because, after all, it was Sullivanair that could make or break her venture, and telling your biggest client he was an anorak was probably not the best way to go.

They'd all carried on unloading the bits of plane and Jonah, immersed in the Boeing, had more or less ignored her for the rest of the afternoon apart from muttering words like tail-fin and ribs when she'd asked what things were. Then eventually,

170

when everything was down the ramps from the container lorry and organised, and everyone was dropping with exhaustion, they had all crowded into the shed and toasted the unpacked plane with a selection of multicoloured drinks from Sylvia's tropical cocktail bar. Estelle had glued herself to Jonah, and Billie had tried to look very grown up and disinterested.

She poured some coffee and flicked the computer files to 'Custs Estab' and 'Custs Prospect'. Still, her two subsequent meetings with Jonah Sullivan had, she hoped, restored some sort of status quo. They had been brief and decorous and very, very Cool Britannia. Over the past few weeks they'd passed a couple of times in the doorway, both being very English and saying 'Hello' and 'How's business?' and making some innocuous remarks about the weather, and then Jonah would beetle into her shed and she'd beetle out of it and into the Nova and that had been the end of that.

The blowers were roaring on full bore now. 'Custs Estab' and 'Custs Prospect' scrolled down the screen. It was, she decided, tucking her Timberlands under the chair and pulling the sleeves of her brother's jumper over the tips of her icy fingers, really quite cosy—if just a little spooky. Every so often a plane zoomed overhead, the roar more felt than heard, stirring the ground beneath her feet like a host of Amityville incumbents. She hadn't realised just how deserted the industrial units were, or how much the iron girders creaked and whispered in the wind that rattled across the airfield. To add to the gothic atmosphere, the breeze blocks all seemed to have developed gaps that emitted keening whistles. And had the doors always made that sort of groaning noise?

It took two cups of coffee for the nerves and three trips across the warehouse to check the doors before she was satisfied. Bloody hell, it was probably the start of obsessive compulsive behaviour syndrome. Everything was so quiet—except of course for the scary noises that weren't. It took her all her time to persuade herself to stay in the office, pour another coffee, and not skulk about in the shed looking for ghouls in the shadows. Eventually notching up a Richter scale volume for Radio One's hip-hop dance party, and wishing she hadn't sat up the night before watching a Wes Craven movie, Billie started to work on 'Custs Estab'.

More than an hour later, having transferred facts and figures from their scribbled origins on the backs of envelopes and Visa receipts to the computer, and feeling as proud as if she'd just performed a single-handed triple-by-pass operation, she took stock.

She now had Zi-Zi's, Sylvia, Guspers, Fred 'n' Dick and Sullivanair as regular customers; the flyers and business cards had brought in about a dozen more clients whose goods—ranging from heavily padlocked suitcases containing God knows what, through cardboard cartons of attic overspill, to an entire houseful of furniture awaiting transit to a retirement home in Swindon—now reposed on and under and around her shelves. She also had done as-and-when deals with several small Whiteacres firms who seemed to prefer the security of her warehouse to their own lock-up premises in what must be the petty crime capital of Southern England.

172

It all added up to a nice, regular income. Not millionaire-making, or anything exciting like that—and not yet as much as she'd have made on the taxis—but giving room to other people's property was already showing a profit, and she was getting new enquiries every day. The 'What I Can Afford' column, which had been moved daringly, thanks to Estelle, from her notepad to the PC, was now growing. A proper telephone system and a modem were top of the list—Estelle Rainbow's constant gibes about the lack of e-mail facilities were beginning to strike home—followed by a second-hand van so that she could offer to collect bulkier items, and a fork-lift truck of her own because Fred 'n' Dick seemed to need theirs most of the time.

She printed off a copy of 'What I Can Afford' and placed it proudly on top of her Pascoe's Warehousing leaflets. So, what if it wasn't a glamorous business? It was hers and it was working. The only flies in the ointment were the persistent letters from Maynard and Pollock reminding her that it looked increasingly as if there was going to be a buy-out. Tomorrow she'd ring Simon Maynard and find out exactly what was happening.

A plane whooshed in overhead, flying low as it came in to land, the drone of the engines as it headed for the runway reverberating against the doors. Billie glanced at the clock. God—it was nearly eleven. High time for sensible businesswomen to be heading for the delights of Horlicks and a soporific dollop of *The Late Book*. Billie stood up, stretched, poured another cup of coffee, and, filled with caffeine bravado, skittered out into the shed. With the worst of the groans and creaks being drowned out by the heavy rapping of Radio One's special tribute to Fizz Flanagan and the Jamaican All-stars, and the air blowers having reached meltdown, it was almost pleasant.

Clutching her coffee, she tiptoed round the outer limits of the Stearman. In the dim light it resembled a huge moth, captured in flight and pinned powerlessly by its tail against its concrete background. The two pairs of massive parallel wings were outstretched, the transverse wires taut between them like sutured arteries, the exposed bodywork looking like the cross-section of a helpless laboratory specimen.

Billie perched on one of the painting trestles. It was a kind plane, she decided. Robust and cheerful. Its two fixed legs with their fat-tyred wheels were like little chunky limbs in ankle boots—spats, Jonah had called them—reaching for the floor. The open cockpit, with the deep leather seats, one behind the other, looked as though the Stearman could withstand any onslaught and still envelope you with a hug. She decided that it wasn't the sort of plane you could be frightened of—not even if you were the biggest aerophobe in the world. It sort of looked as though it would always take care of you in a rather bossy and jaunty way. A bit like her mother, really.

Jonah, Barnaby, Estelle and their unseen helpers had worked miracles, not only in putting all the pieces together, but also in the painting. The main bodywork and wings were now silver, but not just any old bog-standard aeroplane silver. This silver was iridescent, like a dragonfly's wings on a scorching day, with vivid zigzag tongues of purple and green licking from every angle. Sullivanair

174

was inscribed in massive curlicued amethyst and emerald letters along the whole of the bodywork on both sides, and also on the top and bottom of each of the wings. She presumed that when the plane was flying—if it ever did, of course—the tricolour decoration would be visible from any position. Even upside down.

Billie was just wondering whether the caffeine kick had given her enough of a high to risk scrambling up on to the stepladder and peering into the Stearman's interior, when the doors reverberated. The wind must be getting up. The metallic rattle shuddered again across the concrete floor, through the breeze blocks, and up into the rafters. Fizz Flanagan was rapping with feeling from the radio, but even the joyous West Indian beat couldn't compete with the double doors' timpani.

Billie slid from the trestle and, picking her way round the Boeing's spare boxes and crates and wiring looms, crept across the shed. She'd used the Yale lock, but not the bolts, so she knew it wasn't anyone from Sullivanair deciding to burn the midnight oil, because they'd be able to let themselves in. It might just be the airfield security men, checking that she wasn't being burgled by the yoof of Whiteacres. It might even be the yoof of Whiteacres themselves, eager to indulge in the ever-popular local pastime of petty pilfering. But it was, she decided, far more likely to be something straight out of Wes Craven, intent on decapitation ...

'Yes ... ?'

'Billie? It's me, dear. Sylvia. Open the door, there's a love.'

Billie did. Sylvia, muffled in a duffel coat and headscarf, was crying. Without a word of explanation, she hurtled past Billie and the Boeing and into the office. Billie closed the doors, switched off Fizz Flanagan, sighed, and headed for the kettle.

'It's my Douglas,' Sylvia sniffed once she'd got her gloved hands wrapped round the mug of black coffee. 'We've had a row.'

Billie murmured placatingly and started stacking various bits of paper on her desk just to give her something to do. She'd continued to think that Sylvia's Douglas sounded like a bit of a prat, giving his wife no encouragement at all with her business. 'Oh dear. I'm sorry. Anything to do with—um—work?'

'Everything to do with work.' Sylvia snuffled a bit more. 'He's told me to give it up. *Told* me, mark you. He says it's imperative now it looks as though we're going to be taken over. He says everyone else's wife is happy to stay at home and watch daytime telly and do gardening and make cakes at the weekend. He says I'm too old to be dressing in shorts and thinking I'm a proper person.'

'Bastard,' Billie said, hugging Sylvia against her. 'He's just jealous, Sylv. That's all. He probably reckoned that once you both retired he'd have his days on the golf course or whatever and you'd be waiting at home ready to hang on his every word. It's just masculine pride, nothing more sinister. Tell him to get stuffed.'

Wasn't it a rather strange time, though, Billie thought, for them to have a falling-out? It wasn't as though the topic was a new one. Sylvia was still sobbing, although more gently now, shredding

176

tissues with her mittens.

Billie moved to arm's length and tried an encouraging smile. 'So? What brought this to a head, then? I mean, it's getting on for midnight and—'

Sylvia wriggled herself free, dashing away the tears with her fists and looking like a rather plump orange mouse. 'Yes, and he—the old sod—had been out for the evening with some of his Rotarian chums. I was in bed with the new Barbara Taylor Bradford, and he comes swanning in all full of brandy and says that we're off to cruise the Caribbean—for three months!'

Call me pedantic, Billie thought, but it isn't the sort of suggestion that would lead most people to running away in tears in the middle of the night. 'But, surely, that's lovely. You've always wanted to see all those places on your posters, haven't you? And you always said you'd never had the time to travel and—'

'He's only agreed to go because it's with his bloody chums! He never wanted to go just with me!' Sylvia wailed. 'He knows that if I go, then I'll have to give up the business! He just kept saying it makes sense now—especially if someone's buying up the units. He says I can probably sell my lease at a profit—and that I'll have a lovely time on the yacht with Daphne and Cicely and Margaret! And I bloody won't, Billie! I bloody damn well won't!'

Billie exhaled. 'No, I can see that you probably wouldn't, under the circumstances. So—um—what are you intending to do? I mean, short term? Tonight?'

'I don't know . . .' Sylvia grabbed at another tissue. 'I only popped in because I saw your Nova

177

outside and your lights on in here and I thought you'd understand. I thought you'd know what to do . . .'

Billie understood only too well. 'Oh, that's easy-peasy. If it was me, I'd make him sweat. I'd hole up in my shed and let him worry his guts out all night and . . .' She stopped. Shut up, Billie, she thought quickly. Just shut up. There's a lot of difference between you in your twenties, free and single, and Sylvia who's possibly well into her sixties and—

'You mean I should move into my unit? Like I was pretending to do the day we met?' Sylvia smiled damply and clapped her mittens. 'Oh, yes! Oh, you're such a diamond, Billie! Of course—it's got everything I need for survival. I could sneak home and pack a few extra bits and pieces, clothes and what-have-you, tomorrow and—'

Jesus! 'Well, no, I'm not sure . . . I wasn't saying you should leave Douglas now. I mean, I was just saying what I would do. But my circumstances are very different from yours. Look, I'm going to talk to Maynard and Pollock about the leases tomorrow. Maybe you should go home and sort things out with Douglas until we know what's happening.'

Sylvia looked horrified. 'Go home? Go back and admit defeat? Not a damned chance! No, you're right! I'm going to take your advice and leave him!'

Billie whimpered.

Sylvia was well into her stride. 'This place has been my salvation, and I'm buggered if I'm going to chuck it up just to have drinkies on board some tax-evasion yacht with the Tory ladies of Amberley Hill! I will not hurl away my independence for girlie gossips about William and Ffion and the price of

178

Harvey Nicks' knickers! I bloody won't!'

And slamming down her coffee mug, Sylvia gave Billie a swift hug and then stomped out of the office.

Strange, Billie thought, the sort of hold a few hundred feet of breeze blocks can have on a girl. She'd fight tooth and nail to keep hers too, of course—but at the cost of three months cruising the Caribbean? It would be a pretty tough choice. And now she'd aided and abetted a pensioner not only to leave her husband, abandon said Caribbean jolly, and chuck away a retirement no doubt nicely cushioned by endowments, but also to take up squatting in a sub-zero concrete shed. Nice one.

Knowing that she'd never sleep through the guilt, Billie gave up all ideas of going home, refilled the kettle, and found Radio Four. The double doors' drum roll interrupted her adding anything further to 'Custs Prospect'.

'Thank God for that,' she muttered to herself, skirting the plane again and heading for the doors. 'Sylv's seen sense. Probably pretty scary in there on her own. Especially with that plastic parrot and—' She pulled the doors open. 'Look, we'll talk about it properly tomorrow, OK? There's got to be some way round it. You go home and get a good night's sleep—'

'I'd love to,' Jonah Sullivan said wearily. 'Believe me I can't think of anything I'd like better. But insomnia rules at the moment.'

'I—er—thought you were Sylvia.' Billie stood back as he walked in. 'I—um—thought you had a key.'

She stopped and looked at him. Richard Gere at the end of *An Officer and a Gentleman* wasn't in it!

179

Old-fashioned it might be, but there was definitely something about a man in uniform . . .

'Sylvia?'

'The lady next door. With the holiday brochures.'

Jonah nodded. 'Ah, yes. I saw her light on too. Quite a little hive of industry.'

Well no, Billie thought. Just me and Sylvia. Both running away.

Jonah abruptly snatched off the peaked cap as if he'd just remembered he was wearing it. He looked completely exhausted. 'I wasn't planning on doing anything with the Stearman, to be honest. I've just got in from Manchester and I'd intended to go straight home. Then I thought that there was absolutely nothing to go home for and that the thing that means most to me is here, so—'

He stopped, and shrugged, looking as if he'd said far too much. Billie, who didn't think he'd said half enough, was a bit miffed. Surely, if he'd just got back from flying the Sullivanair thing to Manchester he'd be absolutely bursting to get home to Estelle's pneumatic charms, wouldn't he? Or maybe they'd had a falling-out too.

'If you want to work, it's fine by me.' She headed back towards the office. 'I'm just about finished. I was—er—going home anyway.'

Jonah followed her. 'Is that coffee?'

'It's only instant. And we've run out of milk.'

'Black would suit my current mood nicely.'

She made two mugsful. Jonah clutched his and perched on the edge of the desk, removed the navy jacket with the gold flashes and loosened the striped tie. Billie, trying not stare, fiddled with a few more pages of 'Custs Prospect'. Jonah seemed too preoccupied or exhausted to talk, and she simply didn't know what to say.

'You should switch those round,' he said quietly.

'What?'

'Sorry. I was being nosy. Reading the "What I Can Affords" upside down. You should try to afford the van first and then think about getting the modem second.'

She leaned back in her chair. 'Should I?'

He nodded. 'It's always a bonus to be able to offer to collect goods. You could make an extra charge for it, of course, but most people are far too lazy to try and hire something of their own or strap things to roof racks and drive out here. Apart from that it'd be great mobile advertising with Pascoe's Warehousing plastered all over it. The e-mail and stuff can come later—when you're more established.'

She wanted to tell him to mind his own business—but then he obviously did—and he owned an airline while she was the proud possessor of a shed. He might just be a few rungs further up the trade acumen ladder than she was. And he was dead right about the advertising. She shrugged. 'It makes sense. I might just do that. Always supposing that I've still got a business to run.'

Bugger. She shouldn't have said that. He was a customer. He'd probably go hot-footing off to find somewhere more secure. She smiled, trying to diffuse the situation. 'There's a silly rumour going around that someone wants to buy up the leases here. I don't think it'll make any difference to us as tenants, even if it is true—which I doubt. That's what Sylvia and I were discussing earlier.'

Jonah placed his coffee mug down beside hers and exhaled. 'Christ—you as well? I thought they'd

181

be happy with just buying up the airfield. I didn't think they'd be interested in anything outside the perimeter.'

Billie felt a squirm of foreboding in her stomach. 'Who? What—you mean you've heard the same thing? You think it's *true*?'

'Too true, I'm afraid. I think we're all in the same boat.'

'And whoever it is, is going to buy the airfield *and* the units? And do what? Not what Zia said, surely? Not turn it into a Bluewater? The bastards! The greedy bastards! If I could find out who it was then I'd—'

'Oh, I think I can help you on that one.' Jonah stood up and ran his fingers through his hair. It flopped forward again straight away. 'I think Whiteacres is being bought up by my ex-wife and her lover.'

chapter fifteen

As conversation-stoppers went, it was a killer. In the stunned silence Billie, still in the middle of 'Custs Prospect', completely forgot herself and switched off the computer. It made an angry buzzing noise and flashed a bit. She stared at the blank screen. 'Oh, sod it! I've probably wiped everything off.'

Jonah was reassuringly confident. 'You shouldn't have done. Not as long as you've used your document-save option.'

Had she? She didn't know, but she was damned if she was going to admit it. She played with the

182

pages of her notepad instead.

'Er—your ex-wife, you said? Um—is buying up an airfield the normal sort of post-marital settlement in aviation, then?' She didn't want to look at him. She didn't want to see betrayal in his eyes. He could well be on the other side, after all. A lot of people were very chummy with their exes.

'No, thank God.' He swooshed the remains of his coffee about in the bottom of the mug. 'I can't be absolutely sure, of course, but the last time Claire came to see me, she sort of hinted that there may be a takeover in the offing. I assumed she just meant the airfield, not the adjoining land, but as I hadn't heard anything on the grapevine I just put it down to her being—um—well, to her imagining things . . .'

Hell of an imagination, Billie thought, and suspiciously selective. Especially if she was the one who was intending to buy the airfield. And if she was, why did she tell Jonah first? Did she still love him? Was it a warning, or was it a vendetta, or what? And what, she wondered, did Estelle Rainbow, make of the whole affair?

It certainly put everything on a different footing, though: this was in a whole bigger league to someone coming in and taking over the leases of the sheds for a bit of extra pocket money. It could finish her and Sylvia altogether—not to mention Zi-Zi's and the Gusper boys. Fred 'n' Dick, she always felt, were a touch subversive. They may well welcome the intervention.

'But surely, no one can just *buy* an airfield, can they? Otherwise, people like Richard Branson or that guy that owns Ryanair or someone would buy up Gatwick and Heathrow and have a monopoly and—'

'Whiteacres is privately owned,' Jonah said, putting his mug down on top of 'What I Can Afford'. 'I've checked. I lease two hangars and rent my parking spaces from Whiteacres Aviation Inc. They've always just sucked money out of my bank account on a regular basis and written to me every so often on Airforce Blue Conqueror paper. I was never sure if they were *real*. After Claire's visit, I was concerned enough to ask a few questions.'

And? Billie thought. Bloody and? This is my livelihood we're discussing here. For God's sake get on with it.

Jonah took a deep breath and stared at the ceiling. '\Whiteacres Aviation Incs happen to be the rather disinterested descendants of a lot of World War Two aces who flew from here in the forties. Their fathers bought the field and premises out of sentimentality; their offspring have no such high ideals. I gather that if all the board members are in favour and the price was right, then yes, the airfield could be offered to an outside consortium, and wouldn't necessarily have to retain its identity.'

'Oh, bugger. Then that means that they could sell lock, stock and fuselage and the whole place could be turned into AeroDisney or something.' She was rather pleased with the avionics allusion. Not bad for a planephobe. 'But surely, it would still cost a fortune—and—well, forgive me if I'm straying into personal territory here, but is your ex-wife in a position to stump up that sort of cash?'

Jonah laughed. It didn't sound very good-humoured. 'If Claire's right, and Aerobatic Archie is behind it, then the price would probably make a mere dent in his small change.'

'Who the hell is Aerobatic Archie?'

Jonah grinned, but it didn't flicker across the pale blue of his eyes. 'It's what my copilot, Vinny, calls my—um—replacement in Claire's life. Antony Archibald. Aviation Ace and Arsehole.'

Whoops, Billie thought. 'Another pilot?'

'Pilot, predator and prat.' Jonah picked up her notepad and started flicking through the pages. 'Heavily decorated, Gulf War hero, mentioned in dispatches, daredevil—all that sort of gung-ho crap.'

Billie, who was totally unaware of the flyers' pecking order, pulled a face. 'Not one of your best buddies, then?'

Jonah fanned out the pages of the notepad in irritation. Billie wished he'd stop. There were all sorts of personal things in there like: 'Must buy deodorant and Tampax.' 'Remember loo cleaner.' 'Kieran Squires is a bastard—Reuben Wainwright is a—'

She reached for the pad before he realised what sort of infant he was talking to. 'And this—er—Archie? If he bought Whiteacres, would he keep it as an airfield?'

Jonah let go of the notepad with some reluctance and picked up a pen instead. 'According to Claire, yes. But not as a working one like it is now. More, as you suggested, as a sort of combined museum, theme park, and corporate hospitality jamboree.'

Just the sort of place then, Billie thought, that would be gagging to have a warehouse and a replacement window company, not to mention sheds full of old clothes and holiday brochures, on its doorstep.

'And, do they, the Aviation Incs, own the land

these units are on as well, then?'

Jonah dropped the pen and looked rather longingly once more at the notepad. 'I honestly don't know. I've got no idea whether they're part of the package. I suppose they must be though, if you're getting letters saying someone's interested in buying.'

Suddenly it dawned on her that the survival of Whiteacres was Jonah's future too. She hadn't really thought of that. She'd been so busy worrying about the sheds that she hadn't given a moment's thought to how it would affect everyone at the airfield.

How selfish could she get? She may be losing premises that she'd had for no longer than an eyelash bat, but he'd have to find somewhere else to house *planes* . . . And to be bought out by your ex-wife's lover was very much like having acid poured into your gaping wound.

Billie, tucking the notepad securely at the bottom of her bag, stood up. It was late. She was exhausted. And now she was dispirited as well. 'Maybe the Aviation Incs won't want to sell. Maybe they'll turn—er—Archie down. Maybe it's someone else altogether that wants to buy us up—someone who will keep it all going just as it is. . .'

It sounded a bit feeble when spoken out loud. She started to gather up her fleece and her scarves. 'I really ought to be making tracks. I've got to see Maynard and Pollock, the leasing agents, in the morning. They should be able to confirm who the purchaser is. Perhaps we could both do a bit more digging and—um—leave notes for each other or something?'

Jonah shrugged and slid from the desk. He was

186

much taller than she was, but then most people were. 'Yeah, we could do. I'm really sorry about all this.'

'God, it's not your fault.' Billie walked out into the shed, wondering if Jonah intended staying or if she should switch off the lights and the heating. No, if she did that he'd think he had to leave, wouldn't he? Best to check. 'Are you staying on for a while?'

'Probably. If that's OK with you. I really don't want to go home.'

He'd followed her. They were now alongside the Stearman. He must have had a major falling-out with Estelle.

'Fine by me. But don't you have to have some sleep by law? Aren't pilots supposed to have legalised breaks like lorry drivers?'

'I'm not flying tomorrow. I'd thought I'd spend all day finishing off in here. There's only a bit more left to do. Barnaby had to go home to Derbyshire tonight, but he should be back at the end of next week. I'd hoped to have her completed by then before the end of the good weather, so that we can take her up.'

Next week? That quickly? That meant he wouldn't be needing to rent her floor any longer. Bang would go a nice chunk of income. She tried not to let the disappointment show.

'That was a bit transparent of you, if you don't mind me saying. You'd make a lousy poker player.' Jonah ran his hand over the Stearman's exquisite livery and grinned at her. 'Don't worry. I'll still need the storage space. I'd like to use this as a hangar for the foreseeable future. If we've got one . . .'

That would be OK then. Short term at least. The words were so gloomy. They both, she thought, had an awful lot to lose. Everything, really. Not just tangible grown-up stuff like incomes and security, but more important things like hopes and dreams and happiness.

'Of course we've got one. There're loads of people affected by this. Everyone at the airfield, and all of us in the units. Surely, if we all get together and fight—'

'It's not a 1950s feel-good film,' Jonah said. 'It's not Cliff Richard in Happy-Clappy Land. This is real life. We're not all going to band together and say things like, "Hey, kids—let's put on a show!" are we?'

'Sod real life,' Billie muttered. 'And if you'll excuse me, I'll have to go to the loo. Having drunk enough coffee tonight to wipe out the national debt of Brazil, I'll never make it back to Amberley Hill if I don't.'

Returning five minutes later, she thought Jonah had changed his mind and left. The shed looked deserted.

'I'm over here . . .'

Billie peered into the shadows. Jonah emerged from underneath the Stearman's lower wing, standing up and pushing his hair away from his eyes. He really was breathtakingly gorgeous, Billie thought. Pity he had the baggage of Claire, the obviously not-very-ex-wife, not to mention Estelle, hanging round his neck like a ton of Louis Vuitton.

'Just another three thousand rivets to go.' He looked a lot more cheerful. 'Don't you think she's beautiful?'

Estelle? Yes, damn her eyes. Claire? Very probably. Jonah didn't seem the type of man who would marry Miss Mouse. Oh—he meant the *plane*.

188

Billie nodded. 'Yes, I do. Much as I don't like planes, I was actually thinking how lovely it was earlier. Sort of friendly and beautiful at the same time. A bit like Joanna Lumley . . . Oh—sorry, it's not an it, is it? It's a she? Has she got a name?'

'Not yet—but I think she'll have to be Joanna after that. I only hope Miss L. is flattered. I'll christen her after the maiden voyage.' He was grinning. 'Not something you'll be volunteering for, I gather?'

'I'd rather have my toenails removed with rusty pliers.'

'I'll take that as a no, then.' He leaned against the wing. 'Why don't you like flying?'

Billie paused in wrapping a scarf round her throat. 'All the usual reasons. Fear, mainly. You know, the thought of floating miles up in the air in something that weighs about the same as Luton.'

'I must say, you have a superb grasp of aerodynamics.'

'Thanks. One of my best subjects at school.' Billie smiled at him. She hadn't expected him to be funny. 'Then there's the feeling of not being in control. Entrusting my survival to someone unseen up front who could just have had a row with his wife and be on a suicide mission . . . oh. . .'

'Go on.' The grin was still there.

'Oh, right—sorry—but I can never quite get out of my mind the possibility of falling out of the sky. Not just me—the whole damn thing. Don't tell me it's the safest form of travel because I'll never believe you. It's not a fear of heights or anything wimpy like that, just fear of death.'

Jonah moved away from the wing. 'So you seriously wouldn't be interested in a jaunt in the

Stearman, then? Not even when me and Barnaby have proved she's airworthy?'

'What? In something that hasn't even got a roof? You have got to be joking. I'd have to be bound and gagged and fed two bottles of gin first.'

'Really?' Jonah's eyes gleamed as he leaned into the cockpit. 'Is that all it would take? I'm sure it could be arranged.'

Billie suddenly came over very hot and tugged the scarf off again. She wished he'd stop smiling. He was much easier to cope with when he was morose. 'Is it difficult to fly?'

'Generally or specifically?'

'This plane. Is something made of sticks and sealing wax more complicated than a jumbo jet?'

'No idea. I've never flown a jumbo. My charter plane is a twin prop Shorts—which does have the advantage of a computer and an autopilot—but everyone says that flying a Stearman is a piece of cake. It's landing them that's the bugger.' He motioned towards the cockpit. 'Come and sit in her. There's nothing to be afraid of. She can't move an inch—and at least you'll know what it feels like, won't you?'

Billie hesitated. She was scared of planes. Even rigid ones. She should be going home. She should be jumping into Tigger and Piglet and getting a few hours under the duvet before facing Maynard and Pollock in the morning. She really shouldn't be hanging around in the shed with someone as glitteringly, dangerously attractive as Jonah Sullivan and playing bloody Biggles. But then again, she'd like to bet Estelle leaped into planes at the drop of a flying helmet.

'OK. But don't shout if I touch anything vital.'

'I never shout and you won't. All the controls are in the back—and no,' he grinned and fielded her next question, 'I don't mean that the pilot sits facing the other way. I mean, the plane is flown from the rear of the two seats. Front is for passengers only. Go on, then, up you get.'

'I will when you tell me where the steps are.'

'There aren't any,' Jonah patted the Stearman's lower wing. 'You just put your foot on here—look, where the treads are—and step up—just be careful not to stand on any other part. The wings are very fragile. They're made of Irish linen bonded to the ribs, your foot could go right through.'

Another damned good reason not to be in it when it's airborne, Billie thought. And his main concern was obviously more for any potential structural damage to the Stearman than the shattering of her fibula. She blinked at the wing. 'I can't get my foot up there! It's eight feet off the ground.'

'Four at the most. Look, grab hold there, lift your leg up, and haul . . . No, both hands . . . There you go!'

Billie, sweating with exertion and embarrassment, managed to pull herself on to the wing. Jonah was nodding encouragement. 'See? Piece of cake. Now slide yourself into the cockpit. Put one foot in at a time, yes, stand on the seat and slide your feet forward—oh, but don't touch the pedals.'

'You said the controls were at the back,' Billie puffed, inelegantly clambering into the cockpit, sitting down and immediately disappearing from view. 'You said—'

'The pedals have to be at the front,' Jonah

191

athletically hauled himself into the matching compartment behind her, 'because my legs go down each side of your seat to reach them. See?'

Billie saw. In the depths of the cockpit, Jonah's long legs appeared on either side of her thighs, his feet resting just short of the pedals beneath her. It was most disconcerting.

The seat seemed to tip slightly backwards, so that Billie was treated to a view of the upper wing a further three feet above her head—a lot of crisscross struts, and the high-tension wires that seemed to hold the whole plane together. Apart from that there was a tiny glass windscreen, a prototype fuel gauge like a dangling test tube, and absolutely nothing else.

Billie, who wasn't comfortable looking at Jonah's legs, fastened her gaze on the fuel gauge with fierce concentration. 'You've got to be completely mad. This is terrifying. Just sitting here, knowing we're not going anywhere, is scary enough—but you mean, you actually sit in here—and fly?'

'Loops, rolls, stall turns . . .' Jonah's voice sounded wistful from behind her. 'It's like—well, literally like nothing on earth. With the rush of the wind and the noise and, oh, I don't know—the sense of complete irresponsible freedom, I suppose. This is real flying—not cocooned inside something air-conditioned and snug and computerised.'

Dear God, Billie thought. He probably lances his own boils for fun.

And—um—your ex-wife? Did she enjoy flying? She wasn't worried about you or anything?'

'Claire loved it. It was one of the attractions, I think. Married to an RAF pilot probably sounded impossibly glamorous.'

192

Billie could think of far more glamorous occupations but felt it wasn't polite to say so. It seemed very peculiar having a conversation with him when she couldn't see his face but his answers were practically whispers in her ear. 'And—er—this Aerobatic Archie bloke, you said he's a pilot like you?'

'God, no. Not like me at all. That was the trouble. I was a lowly Flight Lieutenant in RAF Transport Command when Claire and I married. I was flying Tristars out of Brize Norton, usually to somewhere millions of miles away like the Falklands. Just long, tedious flights as far as she was concerned, which merely meant weeks of separation to her—but I loved the flying. It was a twenty-four-hour-a-day obsession. Claire got very bored very quickly. No excitement, you see.'

'But she still left you for someone in the same profession?'

'Hardly. Aerobatic Archie is now the team leader in a shit-hot flying display team. Apart from his heroic Tornado exploits in the Gulf, he's got buckets of money, and a minor title tucked away just waiting to be inherited . . . I simply couldn't compete with his superstardom.'

There *was* a definite wistful note in his voice now, Billie thought, and for a moment she felt sorry for him. Then she remembered Estelle and withdrew her sympathy. 'Blimey. He's not in the Red Arrows, is he?'

'No, not the Red Arrows, luckily,' Jonah confirmed in her ear. 'I'd never have lived that one down. Very similar, though. It involves worldwide travelling, displays in exotic places, and all the hobnobbing that goes with it. The team and their

193

partners are treated like royalty and live in the lap of luxury, which, of course, suits Claire down to the ground. As far as she's concerned it's a zillion miles away from an oik in overalls. She used to say that me flying Tristars was just like being married to a bloody taxi-driver . . .' He stopped. 'What? What have I said?'

Billie wriggled her shoulders dismissively, still staring straight ahead through the fretwork. The big leather seat was surprisingly comfortable. 'Nothing. Nothing at all. It's just that before I became a warehouse entrepreneur, I just happened to drive a cab for a living.'

'Oh, shit. Sorry.'

She wanted to get out but didn't know how, and with Jonah obviously quite happy to sit having a fantasy-fly behind her she guessed she'd just have to stay put. She thought it might be a good idea to steer the subject away from Claire and Aerobatic Archie—especially if they were intent on destroying her future. 'Have planes always been an obsession, then?'

'Yeah, since I was a lad. I lived on the Isle of Wight. I used to watch the jets flying overhead, going everywhere but there. Nothing major in the military line ever landed at Bembridge. Aeroplanes were magical and mysterious things that symbolised freedom. I mean, we had to go everywhere by sea. Flying was just the most exciting thing I could imagine. My mum and dad were so proud when I joined the RAF. No one in the family had worked off the island before. My dad has boats. Trips round the bay, bit of shellfish trawling, that sort of thing. My mum looks after other people's kids.'

Brave of her, Billie reckoned, thinking of her

194

nephews and nieces and the two new arrivals who would probably start training in infant thuggery as soon as they could walk. She smiled in the darkness. Jonah's parents sounded nice. Ordinary. Like hers. 'And are they still happy now? Even though you're out of the RAF?'

'God, yes—now they think I'm Freddie Laker. Not a great comparison, but there you go . . . that's parents for you. What about yours?'

'They have a smallholding in Devon. They scrimp and scrape all the time to make ends meet, but they're dead happy. And I've got four brothers— all older—and two sisters-in-law, and six assorted nephews and nieces now, who all still live on the farm and—what's so funny?

'Four brothers? *Four?*' Jonah's laughter in her ear was incredibly disconcerting. 'And you ended up with a name like Billie? I'd have thought your parents would have gone for something really girlie for you, like—oh—Fleur or something.'

'Oh, after the first four they'd decided I was a boy practically at conception. William had been chosen immediately. I think when I arrived they were so shocked by my gender that it robbed them of the capability to make any other rational decision for months. Billie was an easy option. Have you got any brothers or sisters?'

'Two younger sisters. Both married. One lives in Ryde, the other in Shanklin. They're both very—'

But Billie was destined never to discover anything more about Jonah's sisters. His mobile phone picked that moment to warble into life.

'Sorry,' Jonah said, rustling as he answered it. 'Hello? Oh hi, Estelle. Yeah. I'm in the shed with the Stearman—no Barnaby's gone back. I'm on my

195

own. What? Join the club. I couldn't sleep tonight, either. Why don't you come over . . . ?'

Billie stood up, deciding that three was even more of a crowd when the third member was Estelle, and levered herself out of the cockpit. Getting out, she decided, was going to be slightly easier than getting in. Making sure she didn't step on to the delicate sheeting, she scrambled clumsily on to the wing and dropped inelegantly to the ground. Jonah was still whispering sweet nothings into the mobile and hadn't noticed, so raising her hand in farewell, she gathered up her bits and pieces and headed for the door.

She shivered as she hurried towards her car. Sylvia's Mini was parked outside her unit and the lights were on in the shed. Billie could just hear Harry Belafonte singing heartbreakingly about scarlet ribbons through the crack in the door. She hoped Douglas would have a very sleepless night.

*   *   *

Billie pushed the thought of Estelle's phone call to Jonah out of her mind as she drove the Nova home through the October murk. There were far more important things to consider. And not just Douglas and Sylvia, or Claire-the-ex and Aerobatic Archie, either. She'd actually sat in a plane. A proper plane. A plane with no lid, and no comforts, and no stewardess to hold her hand. OK, so it had been firmly on the ground, but she was very pleased with the achievement.

The buzz lasted all the way back to Amberley Hill. Mercifully, the flat was in darkness and switching on just the glow-light in the hall she

196

tiptoed towards her bedroom. The pussyfooting was a waste of time. Miranda's door was wide open. Her room and her bed were both empty.

Billie, catching sight of her pale reflection in Miranda's dressing-table mirror, registered two things. Firstly, horribly, it meant that Miranda must be staying the night with Reuben. And secondly and far more horribly, she'd spent the last couple of cosy hours trying to impress Jonah Sullivan that she was a competent, grown-up businesswoman, wearing no make-up, and with tufty hair, and a selection of her brothers' clothes which made her look about as alluring as a bag lady.

chapter sixteen

'Do we have to go out? Tonight of all nights?' Stan Pascoe stretched his feet out towards the fire, sinking into the cushiony comfort of the chair. 'I'm bloody bushed. I've had a God-awful day with the kids—they don't play anything I understand. And much as I love 'em, there were moments this afternoon when I wanted to declare myself a child-free zone. It must be the double generation gap or something. Our five never seemed to have that much energy . . .'

Faith grinned from the doorway. 'That's because when our five were growing up you were only in the house for a pre-dawn breakfast and after-midnight sleep. You worked all through their boisterous period. You never saw them at their worst. Don't be such an old grouch—you're hardly into middle age and you've spent your whole life working hard, so entertaining four grandchildren for a few hours hardly constitutes penal labour, does it?'

Stan wriggled even more comfortably into his chair and closed his eyes. 'As far as I'm concerned the lambing season's a doddle compared to that lot. They're adverts for hyperactivity. They didn't stop—not even to eat. They just overdosed on E numbers on the run.'

'All the more reason for a nice relaxing supper, wouldn't you say?'

One eye opened. 'Ah—yes. One of your mixed grills would go down a treat. On a tray. With a bottle or two . . . And just us and the telly . . .'

It sounded like heaven. Faith counted to ten under her breath. She couldn't give in. 'Just because you're sinking into an early dotage, doesn't mean that I don't occasionally feel like getting into my Jaeger glad rags and—'

'But why tonight?' Stan opened the second eye and gave an exaggerated yawn. 'I'd have thought you'd have been wanting to coo over the new arrivals.'

'I've cooed aplenty, thanks. And nights at home with new babies is definitely parental territory—definitely not the place for interfering grannies.' Faith crossed the living room, leaned across the back of the shabby wing chair, and kissed the top of his head. 'Anyway, I'm damned if I want to cook tonight. And don't suggest we send out for a takeaway . . . I fancy being pampered.'

Stan eased himself to his feet. 'I've spent the last thirty-odd years pampering you rotten! Oh, OK then—as long as it's the Spread Eagle. At least if I fall asleep in my soup there it's only a few yards to drag me home . . .'

'Er . . .' Faith stared at the threadbare rug in front of the fire. 'Actually, it's Rustique.'

'Where?'

'Rustique—that French place outside Bideford.'

'Jesus Christ—that's the other side of the county, and you know I'm a complete foodiephobe. If I'm not being allowed to stay in, why can't I have one of the Spread Eagle's steak and kidney pies and a sponge pudding and four pints of beer and—'

'Because it's a special treat.' Faith kept her eyes firmly fixed on the rug. 'A bit of pampering for both of us. To celebrate becoming grandparents again twice over.'

'But it means wearing a tie!'

'It won't hurt you—Oh, and if you're intending having a bath you'd better hurry. I've booked the table for eight.'

*   *   *

Rustique was exquisite. Nestling in one of North Devon's more secret valleys, it had obviously been a farmhouse several centuries previously. And, Faith noticed approvingly, it had been skilfully renovated while still hanging on to much of the original bucolic charm. Someone had resurrected the farmhouse with good taste and a huge amount of money.

Faith played with her menu—a solid no-nonsense eight pages bound in wine-red leather, which was another plus point: it could have been in italics scrawled on parchment, or ye olde franglais pinned to a wagon wheel, or something. And Rustique's owners hadn't gone for gingham tablecloths or guttering candles in bottles or taped

199

Piaf or anything else that could claim to be a hybrid of rural-Devon-meets-Picardy.

Faith nodded with satisfaction as she gazed round at the practically full restaurant. The plaintive piano playing was muted; the scents of onion and garlic and wine and herbs just piquant enough to tingle the taste buds; the warmth from the scented apple logs a lulling welcome from the evening chill outside. Was this how it had been when Billie had come here, she wondered, in the splendour of autumn? Or had Billie been sent to cover the opening in the full bloom of summer? She wished she could remember.

Stan, as she'd known he would, had mellowed about the excursion during the journey. Relaxing beside her as she'd belted the Land Rover through the familiar back roads from South to North Devon, alternately joking about her getting social ideas above her station, and worrying out loud about the milk yield of the goats and the cows and the mysterious laying habits of the hens, he'd completely regained his equanimity long before they reached Great Torrington.

Faith lowered her menu and watched him, his brow furrowed as he studied the closely packed lines, describing food he'd probably rather not eat. She adored him. She was the business-minded partner, definitely the family mediator, always the one whose word was law. The kids had all grown up with 'you'd better ask your mother' as the Pascoe family motto. But despite all this, her world revolved around him. Without Stan she'd be useless. Terribly old-fashioned, but there it was. She always felt it was a shame she hadn't passed on these particular genes to her only daughter.

She let her eyes roam round the fire-licked walls again, and wondered if she'd unravel Billie's secrets tonight, almost immediately laughing at the absurdity of the notion. To be honest, even if there were secrets to be discovered, how exactly did she intend doing it? Who here, two years on, would remember a reporter's visit from the *Devon Argus*? Well, she supposed, someone just might—and if she didn't ask she'd never know.

Stan leaned back in his chair having already loosened the tie he'd sworn not to wear. 'Decided?'

'What? Oh, right—the menu . . . no, not yet . . . Concentrate, she told herself, flicking through the pages. Whatever link there might be between Rustique and Billie leaving Devon, it really wouldn't do to let Stan know the real reason for their visit.

Maybe it was just a mare's-nest; maybe it was something left best uncovered; maybe it was absolutely nothing at all. But since her visit to Craigie MacGowan at Willowbridge, Faith was sure that something had happened here to send her daughter on that madcap sprint to start life afresh in London. And that brief sojourn in London had led to her ending up in Amberley Hill.

Stan spoke suddenly. 'What did Billie say when you told her about the names?'

Faith blushed. Even after all these years the telepathy between them still managed to shock her. It wouldn't do for him to read too much of what was going through her mind, would it? 'Names? Oh, her new nephew and niece? She said she can't wait to see them at Christmas—and she thought the names were perfect.'

'She would. She's as daft as the rest of them.

201

What's wrong with damned proper names like—oh, I don t know . . . like Robert and David and Elizabeth and Jane, that's what I want to know?'

Faith chuckled. Their first four grandchildren were called Lilac, Mungo, Delphi and Thad. The new arrivals were Otis and Sapphire. Stan had become practically explosive when he'd been told.

'I think they wanted them to be different.'

'There's different and there's bloody insane!' Stan closed his menu with a snap. 'Poor little buggers'll have a hell of a time when they start school. Bloody airy-fairy nonsense—and you can order for me, duck. My French stinks. I keep translating everything as rabbit stuffed with goat's cheese.'

'Actually, I think I saw that . . .'

Stan groaned. 'I'll have prawn cocktail and steak and chips and Black Forest gateau—or as near as you can get.'

'You will not!' Faith skimmed the menu. 'French onion soup with proper croutons . . . beef stew with garlic and carrot dumplings . . . and—oh, something appley with Calvados. How does that sound?'

'Expensive.' Stan grinned. 'No, that sounds fine. And I'll have to have wine, will I? No beer?'

'No beer.'

'Bugger.' He removed the tie altogether. 'So, how's Billie doing with the plane? I wish I'd been in when she phoned this afternoon. I'd like to have talked to her about it.'

'Give her a ring tomorrow. I've probably forgotten all the technical details, but she was chuffed to bits that she'd actually sat in it.'

Faith reported everything she'd been told during that afternoon's telephone call.

Only pausing to give their order to the waitress, whose accent owed more to Paignton than Paris, they discussed the development of the Boeing Stearman in some depth.

'I think she was terribly disappointed that it wasn't a jet, actually.' Faith sipped her spritzer. 'But she says it's all gone together like a three-dimensional jigsaw puzzle and is sitting in her shed like something out of the crash scene in *Reach For the Sky*. The painting is practically finished, but there was a bit of a hold-up with the letting agents over fumes, which delayed things. And someone wants to buy up their leases or something, but she didn't seem too concerned about it. Otherwise, no news . . .'

'Still no man on the scene, you mean.' Stan chuckled, eyeing his huge steaming bowl of soup with delight, and lifting his spoon.

Faith raised her eyebrows. 'W-e-l-l—there are several men involved in the project, as I understand it. Billie has mentioned various names . . . Jonah Sullivan, who owns the plane—which makes him sound very Richard Branson—pops in from time to time but mostly at night when she's not there. Apparently there's also someone called Barnaby—'

'Barnaby! Bloody Barnaby?' Stan spluttered through a mouthful of soup. 'Why the hell can't anyone in this family settle for a nice ordinary person with a nice ordinary name?'

'I don't think his name's going to be a problem, love. I hardly think he's likely to become our son-in-law. At least, that's not the impression she gives on the phone.'

Stan seemed slightly mollified. 'Well, I'm pleased that this warehousing thing is working out for her. I had my doubts, but she could do worse than getting a toe in the avionics door...'

'It's hardly British Aerospace! Boeing Stearmans were even before my time.' Faith broke open her bread roll and sniffed the steam. 'And I'd say they'd used a touch too much yeast in here...'

*   *   *

The meal over, the bill paid, and the restaurant emptying for the night, Faith stood up. 'I just need to pop to the Ladies... Yes, again—you know what my bladder's like. No, you finish your brandy. No rush...'

This was pretty stupid, she thought, picking her way through the maze of tables and chairs. She'd left it far too late. And who was she going to ask, anyway? The only member of staff they'd seen all evening was their charming but very young waitress, who'd obviously had no connection with Rustique's early beginnings. Surely there was some sort of maître d', or someone in charge?

She headed for the cloakroom, hoping that no one had spotted her taking the same trail only ten minutes before. She didn't quite make it.

'Your coat, madam?'

Faith blinked. 'Sorry?'

'Your coat?' The woman behind the well-polished walnut desk beamed. 'Was that what you wanted? Or were you making for the Ladies room? Only I thought you'd just come out of there, so—'

'No—my coat! Yes!' Faith smiled maniacally,

204

noting the name badge pinned to the neat grey and white striped blouse. 'Er—yes . . . Marion. Thank you. The black one . . . And my husband's is the tweed . . .'

Faith took the coats, fumbled in her handbag for a tip, and smiled. 'Thank you so much, we've had a lovely evening. I—um—wondered if there was anyone I could thank personally? The manager? Or the owner . . . ?'

'It's Mr Reynolds' night off—but I'll be sure to let him know. Your first visit, was it? I hope you'll be back.'

'Oh, yes—definitely, yes. Mr Reynolds? Does he own Rustique, then?'

Marion, pocketing the tip, hoisted herself back on to her stool and shook her head. 'No, he's the manager. Been here since we opened. Done a great job. I've worked in some places where they've been OK to start with and then got complacent, you know? But Mr Reynolds has kept the standards high—and we've got customers coming back every week who ate here on the opening night. That's got to say something, hasn't it?'

Faith nodded vehemently, thanking the gods of Devon for the loquacity of the locals, and cursing herself at the same time for booking a table on Mr Reynolds' night off. Now she'd have to go through the whole palaver all over again—and Stan would never swallow it twice, she was sure of it.

'Mind,' Marion leaned forward, 'it's not been all beer and skittles.'

Well, no, probably not. What was? Faith tried to lighten the gloom. 'More champagne and boules?'

'Beg pardon?' Marion obviously ranked alongside Stan in the translation stakes. 'No, what I

205

mean is, we've had some pretty dodgy publicity . . .'

Faith perked up. 'Really? So you've had reporters here, have you?'

'Dozens of the sods when we opened,' Marion looked like settling in for a gossip. 'All looking for an angle . . . all tarred with the same brush. Scum of the earth. Mr Reynolds and me—we gave 'em short shrift, I can tell you.'

Faith, who had just decided that Marion looked nice and chummy and chatty, and had been going to admit to parenting a journalist, rapidly changed direction. 'Were they—um—critical about the food then? Because if so, I can understand you being angry. It's wonderful, and—'

'No! Not the food. The ownership. They all wanted a piece of the action, like they do. Vultures.'

Faith, who had now got hopelessly lost, was beginning to wonder if it might not be advisable just to cut her losses and make a return visit when Mr Reynolds was in situ. Then the word reverberated in her brain—*ownership*. That had to be it. Billie had been sent here, along with the other journalists, because there was a story on the *ownership* . . .

'Your husband looks like he wants his coat,' Marion said.

Damn! Faith grabbed the Harris Tweed and practically vaulted the chairs and tables. 'Here!' She thrust the coat at Stan. 'No, look—finish your brandy . . . What? Oh—well, finish mine. I only took a sip because of driving. Sit down and relax. I won't be a moment . . .'

She belted back between the tables as fast as the tight Jaeger skirt would allow.

'Goodness,' Marion said admiringly. 'I like to see

206

a woman who knows how to take good care of her man. After all, you reaps what you sows, don't you? Now, where were we?'

'You were telling me about the ownership.' Faith slid her arms into her coat, spending ages tucking in her scarf and fiddling with the buttons. 'And the journalists . . .'

'Ah, right, yes. Well—oh, excuse me. . .'

Faith groaned with impatience as Marion retrieved coats for another table of leavers. Fulsome in their praise, they looked as though they too wanted to stop and chat. Faith clenched her fists to prevent herself treating them as she would Lilac, Delphi, Mungo and Thad, and shoving their arms into their sleeves, buttoning them up, and shooing them out of the door.

She was still fumbling with her own buttons when Marion came back. 'Regulars. Nice people. Big tippers. I always find it comes from being born the right side of the Tamar.' She peered anxiously at Faith. 'That is—er—you're not . . . ?'

'Good God, no. Born in Honiton.'

Marion hoisted herself back on to her stool. 'Yes, I thought so. You can always tell. Well, these sewer rats from the tabloids—they were everywhere. Wanting to know the ins and outs. We couldn't tell them anything, of course, because we didn't know much ourselves. Well loads of people do it, don't they? Add a second string to their bow? Pop singers and actors and that? You don't want to put all your eggs in one basket, do you?'

Faith said no, of course you didn't, and began to wish she'd stayed at home with one of her mixed grills on a tray in front of the telly.

'So, all we said to them was you'll have to go

207

up country and ask Mr and Mrs Squires—them being co-owners like—and of course once living in Willowbridge before they retired, that makes them like locals even if they have moved to Somerset, though God knows why, and—'

Willowbridge . . . Willowbridge expats . . . Why did that ring a huge clanging bell? Ah, yes . . . Craigie MacGowan had said Billie had moved on to the Willowbridge expats column, hadn't he? So that must be it—the connection between Rustique and Billie's exodus. Nothing at all that happened *here*— just something that happened as a result of being here? Something she'd discovered?

'Sorry?' Faith reached into her handbag for an envelope, a scrap of paper. 'Who did you say owned the restaurant? Squires? What a coincidence! I'd love to write and thank them, especially as they used to live in Willowbridge. My neck of the woods, so to speak . . . I knew them well—wondered what had happened to them . . . Good old—er—Ned and Doreen.'

'Declan and Maeve,' Marion laughed, obligingly copying a telephone number from a list on the wall onto the proffered gas bill. 'Mind you, they might well be Ned and Doreen really. They used to run the chippy in Willowbridge—as you'll know, of course—so this was a bit of a step up the catering ladder, so to speak. They might well have reinvented their names—especially after all the publicity with the boy. This is the number we always give out. I think they might monitor the calls still, but you'll be OK, being a friend. I'm sure they'd be pleased to hear from you. At least you're not a reporter trying to dig the dirt on their son, are you?'

'Perish the thought!' Faith said happily just as

208

Stan joined them. 'And thank you again for such a lovely evening. I really couldn't have wished for more . . .'

chapter seventeen

Miranda gazed round the daytime interior of Bazooka's and winced. She'd had no idea, during all those hazy tequila-spiked nights, how disgusting it really was. The walls were nicotine-soaked, the banquettes dusty, and the tables white-ringed and shabby. Even the dance floor, which had looked like spangled glass under the strobes, was scuffed and dull.

'Bloody hell, doll.' She shook her head at Reuben. 'The pits, or what?'

Reuben straightened up, a retractable tape measure in one hand, a calculator in the other. 'It's why nightclubs are nightclubs. Darkness, music, and mind-altering substances can perk up the ambience no end.'

He grinned at her before leaning across the bar again, inserting more figures and muttering. Miranda, on her Follicles lunch break, lusted over his neat bum and well-muscled legs, and grinned back even though he couldn't see her. She wasn't quite sure whether or not they were a couple. She wasn't even totally convinced that they were friends. Still, she was sure of one thing: they weren't lovers. At least—not yet.

Ever since the evening three weeks previously when she'd stayed in his bedsit, she'd been seeing a lot of Reuben. That is, she'd spent a lot of time in his company. She hadn't seen anything of him in a physical, fleshly, bodily way at all. It had all been very circumspect. They'd talked into the small hours, then she'd curled up on his unromantic single bed and he'd slept on a rather unpleasant plum-coloured armchair. And all their meetings since had taken place away from the flat, of course. She'd decided it would be politic not to mention the Reuben-developments to Billie. Billie seemed to have enough problems of her own, with all the goings-on at the warehouse.

And it had been disappointing to learn that there still weren't even any decent men involved with either the warehouses or the Boeing Stearman. Well, that wasn't quite true. There was Jonah Sullivan, who Billie had said was totally gorgeous to look at but a bit spiky, and who was also firmly attached to his secretary and his ex-wife, so he was ruled out. Also, Jonah Sullivan apparently, like Dracula, seemed to do all his best work in the dead of night so Billie rarely saw him. Then there was someone else who was stinking rich and called Barnaby. Miranda had become more interested at this point—but Billie had said Barnaby was the sort of man your mum always fancied, which knocked that one on the head.

So, what with one thing and another, Miranda had carried on seeing Reuben on the basis that what Billie didn't know about wouldn't worry her unduly. Apart from meeting during the day, usually for a lunch-time drink in Mulligan's where they'd discuss their respective businesses, she and Reuben had actually been out together on several evenings.

Much as she'd like to say differently, Miranda had decided that none of these could actually fall

210

into the category of a date. They had visited various other clubs in the area, usually to recce the fixtures and fittings. Reuben didn't dance, drank very little, and had seemed oddly pleased that she was there. Even so, she was no nearer to knowing exactly what made him tick.

Although, she admitted, still pleasurably watching him bend and stretch, he certainly seemed to have mellowed; the purchase of Bazooka's had given him a real purpose. He wasn't half so snappy, and his put-down lines were witty these days without the biting edge.

He hardly ever mentioned Billie, and when he did, it seemed his interest in her welfare was genuine. Miranda smiled to herself. He'd become really concerned when she'd told him about someone buying up the leases on the industrial estate. He'd asked her several times what she thought Billie would do if she had to leave the warehouse.

'Not come and drive a cab for you again, that's for sure!' Miranda had laughed. 'Or manage your nightclub!'

Reuben had nodded solicitously. 'No—I didn't think she would for a moment. Poor Billie—out of the frying pan, so to speak. I do hope things work out for her.'

And Miranda had said she hoped so too, and thought what a nice man Reuben was, and again, how wrong Billie had got him.

'There.' Reuben straightened up and snapped off the calculator. 'That's done. What do you fancy? A drink in Mulligan's, or what?'

Miranda nodded. 'A quick one. I've got a customer at two.'

She waited while he locked the double doors. Bazooka's had already been closed for ten days. The refurbishment would take at least six months. Caught Offside was due to open towards the end of May or the beginning of June next year at the latest. Whatever happened, Reuben had said, he wanted to be up and running for immediately alter the Cup Final, when all footie junkies would be screaming for their next fix, and to be able to capture the European matches through the summer. Miranda, who knew very little about football and cared about it even less, had merely smiled.

While Kitty, Debs, Anna and Sally had all mourned the passing of the club and grizzled about forking out for taxi fares to take them to Winchester or Southampton or Newbury for a decent night out, Miranda had been relieved. Giving up clubbing, apart from as a spectator on the fact-finding missions with Reuben, had been a damn sight easier than giving up smoking. At least now she had an excuse not to tart up and get plastered and end up with a man who was a definite also-ran, in preference to ending the night with no man at all.

They pushed their way into Mulligan's. As usual it was packed with the twelve-till-two brigade. Miranda touched Reuben's shoulder. 'Grab a seat somewhere, doll. I'll get the drinks.'

He nodded and disappeared into the throng. Miranda shoved her way to the bar, deciding that she liked this display of sexual equality—and thrusting to the back of her mind the knowledge that Billie would say it was just because Reuben was too tight to buy a drink.

While she was waiting to be served, she watched

Reuben fight his way to claim two tall stools in the corner. He was, she decided, an OK bloke. Certainly the lunching office ladies seemed to think so—it was almost like the Diet Coke ad. All the Amberley Hill business women in their sharp suits eased up their sleeves, flicked back their hair, and watched Reuben with interest from the privacy of their Pierre Cardin metal specs frames.

Miranda felt a moment of proprietary pride. Crazy. Reuben had never kissed her. They hadn't even touched in a personal way: she somehow couldn't see Reuben holding hands or snuggling up. It was, she felt, really refreshing. Like starting all over again. She was still smiling in a slightly soppy born-again-virgin way when the barman snapped at her.

'Uh? Oh, yeah—two lagers . . . Actually, better make that one lager and a gin and tonic—no, half of lager and an orange juice . . .'

Well, they both had to go back to work, didn't they?

Trying to cross Mulligan's with two drinks was like one of the more difficult games on *It's a Knockout*. Miranda, who reckoned she could do it with her eyes closed and without having to play her Joker, sidled round the walls, manoeuvred the tables with a zigzag swerve, dived between the karaoke machine (silent) and the jukebox (belting out 'Paddy McGinty's Goat'), and squeezed herself triumphantly alongside the tall stools.

'Only half a pint?' Reuben frowned. 'Skinflint.'

'Tight-wad yourself, doll,' she said companionably, hitching herself onto the stool. 'So, what excitements have you got planned for this afternoon?'

213

Reuben shrugged. 'Keeping that skiving shower working will take all my time. Cab-drivers—huh. They take the biscuit. Can't leave 'em for a minute. It'll be nice to branch out into something else. What about you?'

'A stress-buster massage. Two trims, a facial and a pedicure.'

'Swap?'

'OK,' she smiled at him. 'But mine are all men.'

Reuben frowned, glowered a bit, and concentrated on his lager.

He stopped frowning. 'Tonight? You free?'

'I might be.'

'Either you are or you aren't. Don't shillyshally.'

'Yes, then.'

'Good. I want you to come and give my shortlist the once over.'

'As invitations go, that's a pretty hard one to turn down.'

Reuben grinned at her. 'I used to think you were a real daft bat. Wrong. You're OK. For a woman, that is.'

'Thanks. You're not so bad for a moody bastard either. Which shortlist?'

'The potential managers for Caught Offside. I've whittled them down to four. I've arranged to meet them in the club tonight. I thought you might be able to—'

But whatever Reuben thought she might be able to add to the selection procedure went straight over Miranda's head. Sitting behind the plastic rubber plant was Mr Drop Dead Gorgeous Dreamboat Possible Husband Number Two.

Miranda knew her mouth was open. She snapped it shut. She knew Reuben was still talking, so she nodded like an automaton. It was pretty tricky, because she was trying to crane her neck at the same time to peer round the other side of the rubber plant. If Mr D-D-G was with a woman she'd probably scream.

'Oops, oh, bugger . . .' She toppled sideways from her stool, clutching at Reuben at the last moment.

He pushed her back into place. 'Those orange juices must have a hell of a kick.'

It vaguely registered that they'd just had a hand-meet. Typical. Their first physical contact had to come at the precise moment she could see Mr D-D-G was sitting opposite his elegant male companion of before. Miranda deliberately ignored the echo of Billie's voice dismissing the partnership as two gays out on a jolly. He'd had his hair cut, Miranda noticed with a professional eye, and not badly either. It still flopped nicely but didn't hang in his eyes this time. He looked tired. Bugger again. She could only see him from the waist up, which was fantastic, of course, but she leaned a bit more—ah, that was better . . .

He was wearing a very faded denim shirt over a white T-shirt and looked completely havoc-making. And surely if she yanked her neck round just a touch more . . . yes . . . she could see his hands. Yippee! No wedding ring! No signet ring! No—She stopped. Didn't gay men signify their allegiance by wearing rings on their little finger? She entwined her legs round the stool, clutched at Reuben's shoulder and leaned . . . Oh, joy and thank you God! Mr D-D-G's long, slender, sexy fingers were completely bare.

'Someone who owes you money?' Reuben drained his half-pint and slowly disentangled her clutching hands. 'Do you want me to go over and have a word?'

'Uh? Oh—no, doll. No . . . Just someone I thought I knew . . . Sorry.' Miranda straightened up, feeling a bit guilty. Even she had standards—and lusting after one man while being asked out by another was a bit below the belt. 'Hell, look at the time. I'll have to dash. Er—about tonight? Shall we meet at the club then?'

'Sounds sensible. I've asked all the people on the shortlist to come in for nine o'clock—and I presume you still don't want Billie to know that we're mates, so I won't offer to come and pick you up.'

Miranda alternatively shook and nodded her head. Mr D-D-G was just leaving. He'd stood up, pulling on the leather jacket he'd worn last time, leaning towards the older man who remained seated. They were laughing. Miranda shrank back again, just in case they spotted her and recognised her as the sad tart who had thrust the Follicles and Cuticles cards at them a couple of months earlier.

'At the club then?' Reuben repeated. 'Tonight? About half-eight?'

'What?' With a sinking heart Miranda watched Mr D-D-G disappear out of Mulligan's and into the Spicer Centre. 'Oh, yeah, great, doll. See you then . . .'

*   *   *

Follicles and Cuticles was just waking up and stretching after its lunch-time siesta, or at least that's how it seemed to Miranda as she opened the door. In truth, she knew that Kitty and Pixie had

216

been working flat out, but there was a sort of muted hum inside her head which went well with a more soporific and languorous mood. The marshmallow moment was embellished with rosy images of Reuben and Mr D-D-G, all sort of blurred round the edges.

'Hi, Randa,' Kitty mumbled through a mouthful of tail comb. 'Thank God you're back. Pixie's had a bit of disaster with the blackhead remover and while we were sorting it out we seem to have overbleached Mrs Higgins. We've put her in the kitchenette to cool down.'

Sod it. With the magic moments popping round her like rainbow bubbles, Miranda shed her PVC jacket, rolled up her sleeves, and trotted briskly through to the staff restroom to try to prevent a law suit.

*   *   *

She was still applying aloe vera and tea and sympathy and explaining to Mrs Higgins—who was sixty if she was a day—that lop-sided semi-shaven heads, especially with peroxide streaks, were very trendy, when her two o'clock body rub appointment arrived.

'Er—I've given him coffee and said you're sorting out an accident,' Pixie pirouetted in the archway. 'Is that OK?'

Miranda placated Mrs Higgins with a pat, and glared at Pixie. She gritted her teeth. 'The-coffee-is-fine-the-rest-isn't! Go-and-tell-him-it-is-NOT-an-accident! Tell-him-anything! Tell-him-I'm-doing-a-henna-tattoo!Tell-him-I'll-be-there-in-five-minutes!'

Scowling, Pixie stomped off on her tartan DMs, and Miranda smiled hopefully at Mrs Higgins. 'Actually, a henna tattoo might just set the new hairstyle off a treat. Become all the rage at the bingo? No? Oh, well—let's see what we can do, shall we? And let's look on the bright side. This is going to save you a fortune in perms, isn't it?'

It was a good ten minutes before Mrs Higgins, clutching a fifty-pound cash refund and a promise of free hairdos—when, of course, she had any appreciable amount of hair to do—for the rest of her life, left the salon. Miranda, feeling frazzled and desperate for a cigarette, swept into the treatment area.

'So, sorry to have kept you Mr—um—?' Oh God! What was his name? Why the hell hadn't she looked in the appointment book? She racked her brains. Posh, she'd thought . . . Sounded like a volcano . . . Etna? Vesuvius? Ah, no—she beamed and picked up an armful of towels. 'Mr Molton-Kusak . . . Oh, bugger . . .'

She managed to turn the expletive into a sort of cough. Her body rub appointment was Mr D-D-G's urbane and elegant chum.

*   *   *

'And—' she perched on the edge of the kitchen table, a Marlboro Light in one hand, a treble gin in the other, 'Potential Husband Number Two is called Joe. Joseph . . . Fantastic name, don't you think, Billie? Sort of strong and hunky—and, well, gypsyish . . .'

'Fantastic,' Billie echoed, looking up from the heap of papers on the kitchen table. 'Joseph and

218

Miranda . . . Sounds great. Like Chekhov. What's his surname?'

'No idea. Mr Molton-Kusak didn't say. It took me all my powers of ingenuity to get that far.'

'I can imagine,' Billie said, chewing the end of her pen. 'Like, what's the name of your mate—the one you were in the pub with—because I fancy the pants off him?'

'Nah! I was far less subtle than that.' Miranda waved her Marlboro Light under Billie's nose. 'Are you sure you don't want to take it up again, doll? I can't believe how good it feels after packing in.'

'You only gave up for two days!'

'Forty-eight hours,' Miranda affirmed vigorously. 'Forty-eight nicotine-free hours. Pure hell.' She slid from the table. 'Are you going out tonight or can I grab the bathroom?'

'Yes I am, and yes you can, because I'm only going back to work. So, what was this Mr Molten-Lava like, then? Did he have a nice bod, or what?'

'Pretty tasty considering he had to be at least forty. Rubbing it was no hardship, let me tell you! No, really, I mean if I wasn't madly in love with Reuben and Joseph, I'd go for him. He must work out a lot—his muscle tone was incredible—and he had this sort of golden tan and really blue eyes. And he gave me a stonking tip and made three more appointments . . .'

Billie gathered all the papers together, swigged back the last mouthful of gin, and pushed the chair away from the kitchen table. 'Great. You might be able to put in a good word for me, then. Sounds just like the sort of man I've been searching for. We could make up a foursome. You and Joseph, me and—' she looked at Miranda—'he does have a first name?'

'Suppose he does, doll. I just didn't discover it. Well, what with all the hoo-ha over Mrs Higgins, and me being really keen to find out about Joseph, I just stuck to calling him Mr Molton-Kusak. I'll find out next time he comes in, shall I?' She paused in the doorway. 'Are you serious, though? I mean about fixing up a foursome?'

chapter eighteen

Jonah hadn't been able to sleep. Insomnia was fast becoming a fact of life: but at least this latest attack hadn't been caused by red bank statements, or Claire and Aerobatic Archie trampling on his dreams, or even the thought of flying the Shorts to somewhere really tricky like Middlesbrough. The previous night's lack of sleep had been caused by fizzing anticipation; like childhood Christmas Eves, or the day before the holidays when he and his sisters couldn't wait to leave the confines of the Isle of Wight and go somewhere huge like Weymouth.

Jonah grinned to himself as he stared out of the window, watching the sky. He could cope with this sort of sleeplessness. Today he and Barnaby would be flying the Stearman for the first time. He looked at his watch. Almost six. Soon be daylight. And the balmy winds of the last few weeks had dropped away even further to give a perfect mild morning, more like April than the very end of October. The sky, as the weather forecasters had predicted, was hazy and clearing, the breeze slight, all of which augured ideal flying conditions. Whiteacres Aviation Inc. had given him a midday slot of airspace, and as the Stearman would take off and land from the Aeroclub's grass strip well away from the main airfield, no one outside the confines would be any the wiser.

At least there was no problem about whether or not the plane would fly. The Stearman was completely airworthy, and Barnaby had seen to it that it had come from Kentucky with all the right certification, so today the onus was on Jonah as a pilot to prove that he could simply get it off the ground—and keep it there.

As he watched, the identical block of flats opposite his was waking. Lights were flicking on in some windows; curtains were being drawn back in others; a few bleary-eyed people were stumbling into cars for the start of another day. Strange, he thought, he'd never considered what they did for a living. He'd lived a stone's throw away from them for almost two years and yet he'd pass them in the street without recognising them. The world he'd built around himself since Claire's departure was clinically anonymous. These people, his closest neighbours, could also be heading for some momentous challenge today, and he'd never know.

'I've made coffee . . .' Estelle, wrapped in his towelling robe and managing to look as perfect as a glossy magazine cover, wandered into the living room. 'I didn't bother with toast. I didn't think you'd manage any under the circumstances.'

'Thanks.' Jonah, who had had a bath and dressed in jeans and a rugby shirt somewhere around four thirty, took the mug. He hadn't managed anything. Estelle had slept alone in the big rumpled bed while

221

he'd alternately dozed on the sofa and paced the floor.

She drifted out of the room again without comment, sleepily pushing the landslide of silver-blonde hair away from her eyes. She understood him well. She knew he wouldn't want to talk yet. He had a feeling she'd have plenty to say later. He could hear the hiss of water as she switched on the shower. Not long to go now.

Barnaby, who was putting up in the Four Pillars at Amberley Hill, was going straight to Whiteacres. So were Vinny and Pam, which he reckoned was pretty good of them on their Sullivanair day off. He yawned and stretched, still watching from the window as the rest of the flats opposite suddenly erupted into life like someone kicking an ant hill. Time to move.

He wondered fleetingly how Billie was getting on, and whether she'd be there today to watch the Boeing take off. Probably not. Oh, he knew she'd be there; but he was still pretty sure that despite sitting in the Stearman, she wouldn't be overanxious to watch her fly. Strange, that: Billie, who was feisty and tough and had done really butch jobs like being a cabby and now running the warehouse, being scared of planes. It seemed a sort of fragile, feminine fear—but maybe not. Wasn't there some international footballer who was a total aerophobe? And a tough-guy actor? He shook his head: he simply couldn't understand anyone being terrified of flying. Flying gave him a reason to live. Still, there was no reasoning with phobias, was there? He was terrified of spiders—although he'd never admit it to anyone apart from his mother.

He'd met Billie only once in the last week,

passing on the doorstep after he'd arrived back from flying a computer software company in the Shorts to a conference in Exeter, and she'd been leaving for the evening. She'd spoken to the leasing agents, she'd said, but not got any joy. They hadn't been prepared to reveal the name of the interested party, or even whether there was any progress with the takeover of the units. He'd shrugged and said Whiteacres Aviation Inc. had told him much the same, and that his calls to Claire had gone unanswered.

They'd both agreed they had no choice but to carry on as normal and promised to let the other know if they heard anything at all that might shed light on their respective futures. Then they'd been interrupted by a large man with a David Niven moustache, wearing cavalry twills and a yellow waistcoat, who had demanded that they returned his wife this instant.

Billie had filled him in as they went along. Apparently Sylvia, the holiday brochures lady, had left Douglas, her cavalry-twilled husband, because he wanted to take her cruising in the Caribbean. At this point Jonah, who had long since given up trying to understand women, took a back seat while Billie said that if Sylvia didn't want to open her door to Douglas and put the phone down when he rang, then there was very little she could do about it. Yes, she'd said, she was quite sure that Sylvia was all right and that Douglas should perhaps try writing to his wife, apologising for the things he'd said, and offering to cancel the cruise and to back Sylvia's ambition and enterprise. If he did that, Billie had suggested gently, then Sylvia might just consider coming home.

This was when Jonah had thought his first-aid skills would be called upon. Douglas had turned puce and spluttered a lot and called Billie a meddlesome little madam, which she'd appeared to find amusing, and then had stomped off to hammer loudly on Sylvia's door.

'Prat,' Billie had said dismissively. 'I'll never understand why men can't support their wives in their business ventures. After all, it's what women have been expected to do for years, isn't it?'

Jonah had decided not to get drawn into any debates on feminism, and had murmured something about it probably being a generation thing. Billie had smiled and nodded her agreement and, twirling her car keys, had disappeared into the night. Sylvia's Mini, he'd noticed, had still been there when he'd left four hours later, and her lights were on, so presumably Douglas had again been unsuccessful.

'I'll go into the office for the first part of the morning,' Estelle now said, emerging from the beige bathroom, almost wrapped in a towel and dripping suds across the flat neutrality of the carpet. 'I've only got a couple of hours' work to do, so I should be able to be over at the warehouse in plenty of time.' She slid scented arms round his waist from behind. 'And as you owe me something for last night's nonevent, you are going to take me up, aren't you?'

Jonah looked down at the perfectly manicured hands gently kneading his waist. He felt nothing. Vinny, he knew, would have killed for this opportunity. 'I honestly doubt if there'll be time today. I've only scheduled one flight, and Barnaby obviously wants to go up.' He turned round to face

224

her. She didn't move away. 'Maybe next time.'

She pouted. 'Bugger off, Jonah! No way. How many times have I heard that? I'll just have to sweet-talk Barnaby into making his flight shorter so that there's time for me.' She stood on tiptoe and kissed the end of Jonah's nose. 'I'm sure he'll be reasonable about it. He's a complete poppet— unlike you.'

He smiled ruefully, watching her as she swirled away to dress in the second-skin leather trousers and waist- skimming jacket that usually constituted her secretarial uniform. Jonah knew that Barnaby was such a gentleman that he'd probably agree to cut short his flight time for her.

Still, Estelle deserved it really. She'd worked as hard as any of them on the Stearman. He liked, admired, and respected her. He felt guilty about turning down her advances last night. He wished to God that just once, when he made love to her, he didn't think of Claire.

*   *   *

The warehouse was in uproar. Jonah, who had hoped for a few minutes' solitude before anyone else arrived, looked at the pandemonium in horror. Everyone from all the other units seemed to have converged on Billie's shed, and were swarming around the Boeing. The replacement window fitters, whose names he could never remember and who always appeared to be on the periphery of everything, were standing side by side in their overalls, nodding with gloomy relish. Sylvia, swathed in a turquoise pashmina over her shorts and looking very spry, was handing out pieces of

225

paper, while the two hippies from the old clothes shop who Jonah knew were called Zia and Isla but was never sure which was which, were going through some sort of ritual chanting. The Guspers boys were darting about beneath the outstretched wings with hand-held cameras and microphone booms.

Jonah gazed at the mayhem and sighed heavily. The shed was crowded enough just with the plane: this lot made it look like the Wembley Way on Cup Final day. Surely they weren't all here to give the Stearman a send-off, were they? He tapped the shoulder of the bearded bloke—Isla or Zia?—who had finished chanting and appeared to be wearing a fair amount of his own stock. 'What the hell's going on er—Isla?'

'Cool it. I'm Zia, man. Union meeting, right?' He shook himself free of Jonah's hand on his shoulder in a cloud of aromatic dust of doubtful origin. 'We got problems. Big time.'

Shit. Whatever was going on, Billie could have chosen a better day for inciting a riot. Or at least a better venue. And where was she anyway?

'Jonah, I'm really sorry about this.' Billie suddenly appeared from the middle of the scrum and scrambled beneath the Stearman's wing. 'They'll all be gone before you want to fly, I promise. It's just that we've all had letters this morning. We're being taken over. Definitely. With no mention of honouring our contracts or anything. Just that the leases will be sold at the end of the year and that we will be given further information nearer the time.' She stopped, looking pretty crestfallen, and shrugged. 'What about you? Have you heard anything?'

226

He shook his head. 'Not a word. But then, it's not so immediately personal with me, is it? I suppose the Whiteacres Aviation Incs might just decide to get up off their backsides at some point and tell us that we're being evicted, too.' He looked at her and felt deeply sorry. 'I do sympathise, Billie. It's a shit, I know, but it might not be the end of all this. Look on the bright side. I—um—don't suppose the letters say who . . . ?'

'Your ex and her acrobatic lover? No. Nothing.' She gave a flickering smile. 'And I know how important today is for you—don't let our wake spoil it for you. Just give me half an hour or so to sort everyone out, and we'll all clear out of your way.'

'All of you? I thought you'd stick around for the inaugural flight.'

She grinned. 'Yeah, of course I will. With my Timberlands anchored firmly to the floor!'

He laughed. 'And changing the subject slightly, how is your marriage-breaking going?'

'*What?*'

Jesus—now what had he said? Billie's grin had frozen on her face. She looked about as petrified as if she'd just done a stall turn and the engine hadn't kicked back in. 'I mean with Sylvia and her obnoxious husband. She's looking pretty glam so I just assumed that—er—she'd taken your advice and—um—stuck to her principles . . .'

The colour flooded back into Billie's face. He could almost sense the relief. 'Oh, *Sylv*! Yeah, she's fine. Still encamped in her tropical paradise and repelling all boarders. Douglas has resorted to daily doses of red roses and billet-doux, but she just dumps them in the bin.'

'Great.' He was at a bit of a loss. Somewhere in

there he'd touched a nerve, but he was damned if he could figure out where. 'Look, I'll let you get on with organising your protest or whatever and I'll see you later.'

'Definitely.' She was smiling again. Maybe he'd imagined the fear? 'I'll have all my extremities crossed for a safe takeoff—and an even safer landing.'

He watched her marshalling her troops, getting everyone together in her office. She looked so fierce and tiny, he thought. So delicate in the jeans and boots and over-sized sweater. He grinned. About as delicate as lambswool softly concealing barbed wire! Younger than any of them, and newest to this warehousing game, and yet obviously the one they all turned to in times of trouble. And what the hell had that business with Sylvia and Douglas been about? He was sure he hadn't imagined it. Strange reaction to someone else's marital problems. Enigmatic lady, Billie Pascoe.

He wondered momentarily what her background was. Oh, he knew about the farming family and the taxi-driving, but there had to be more. Lots more. He stroked the Stearman's wing. Poor Billie. He hoped that the takeover wouldn't mean the end of her enterprise. He'd hate her to be hurt.

'OK. Jo? Up for it?' Barnaby strode into the shed at that moment, managing to look suave and elegant despite being clad in overalls. 'I can hardly bloody wait. Christ! What's going on in here?'

'The Industrial Revolution Mark Two,' Jonah grinned, delighted to see him. 'I'll tell you all about it later. Meantime, we've got more pressing things to do . . .'

Two hours later, the checks completed and with the shed devoid of everyone except himself, Barnaby, Estelle, Vinny and Pam, Jonah looked at his watch. 'I reckon by the time we've pushed her out onto the grass and done the final cockpit run-through, we'll be right on target.'

His palms were sweating; there was a thump of excitement beneath his ribs. God, he could do with a drink.

'We'll need a few more bodies to shove her out of here,' Barnaby said. 'All hands on deck so to speak.'

Vinny, who hadn't stopped ogling Estelle's sprayed-on leather outfit since he arrived, suddenly paid attention. 'Oh, we'll manage, won't we? We all look as though we've eaten more than our fair share of Weetabix this morning.'

How, Jonah wondered, Vinny could manage to make this remark sound salacious, he'd never know. Pam, wearing a pink tracksuit and still looking very businesslike even out of her stewardess's uniform, picked up the nuance and cuffed his ear in a maternal way. 'Wash your mouth out, Vincent Taylor!'

Estelle watched the exchange, then raised a perfectly plucked eyebrow. 'Some of us may have had more than one Weetabix, Vinny, sweetheart. But others of us, like the little pig who cried all the way home, sadly had none.' She threw a challenging look across the Stearman at Jonah. 'Did we, Mr Sullivan, sir?'

Jonah closed his eyes.

'Really?' Vinny grinned at her, then at Jonah.

229

'Falling down in all areas are we, Jonah? And I thought it was your sole aim in life to run a satisfied company?'

Estelle flicked back her silver-blonde hair. It slithered forward again in a silky rush. 'Oh, I'm sure it is. It even says so on the booking sheets: "Sullivanair—your satisfaction guaranteed." But then satisfaction is so relative, don t you think? And sadly in my experience, rarely mutual.'

Jonah winced.

Vinny shrugged. 'Dunno. You've lost me there, darling. I always thought one out of two being satisfied wasn't bad. Just as long as I'm the one, of course.'

'Bastard.' Estelle blew him a kiss. 'Another chauvinist pilot—and why am I not surprised?' She turned her pouting mouth to Barnaby. 'Seeing that Jonah has failed, yet again, in his—oh, let's say personal takeoff—has he also failed to mention to you that I'd like to sneak a tiny piece of your flying slot?'

'Oh, dear me. Yes, I have. It conveniently slipped my mind.' Jonah glared. 'And after that bloody emasculation I'm not going to, either. Tough tit, Estelle. You'll have to wait until next time.'

She stared at him for a moment and then laughed. 'The story of my life with you, sweetie. I've been waiting so long for "next time" I'm surprised I haven't got a preservation order slapped on me.'

Barnaby, ever the gentleman, gave Jonah a supplicating look, then held out the olive branch to Estelle. 'I'm quite happy for you take my place, my dear.'

'Over my bloody dead body,' Jonah growled, well aware of Vinny and Pam exchanging glances. 'You

230

deserve this, Barnaby. More than anyone.'

Ignoring Estelle, and still smouldering, Jonah climbed onto the wing and slid into the cockpit. Damn her. He wasn't going to let her spoil today by washing their dirty linen in public. Bugger all women to hell!

He ran his eye expertly over the dials on the dashboard and touched the sliding levers for the propeller pitch and the fuel mixture, and shook his head. It was his fault. He knew it was. If only he wasn't so bloody self-obsessed; if he could only think of other things rather than just the plane and flying; if he'd given some modicum of thought to Estelle . . . He slapped his palm flat on the dashboard. Stupid sod! He'd lost Claire the very same way, hadn't he?

'Jo . . .' Barnaby was stretching up into the Stearman. 'Everything OK?'

'Fine. Just me being an idiot—as ever. Estelle's right: even if I'd rather she'd kept it more private. I'm crap at relationships. Truly crap.'

'Aren't we all?' Barnaby said softly. 'It's such a minefield. Look at me—eligible or what—and I haven't had a lady on my arm, or anywhere else for that matter, for bloody months.'

Jonah grinned. Him, Barnaby and Vinny. All vastly different. All romantic failures to a man. And the women's mags always went on and on about female angst. Huh! They didn't know the damn half of it!

'I've found reinforcements!' Vinny shouted up from the floor. 'A bit press-ganged, but they're willing to shove the plane out. Of course, I've had to promise that you'll treat them all to a fish supper and a pint of best apiece in the Aeroclub.'

From the expressions on the faces of the warehousers it was clear that plane-pushing came into none of their job descriptions. He couldn't see Billie or Sylvia amongst the ground crew, and Estelle was hanging back looking sulky, but there was no time to ponder, and as he released the foot brakes along with much grunting and groaning from those beneath him, the Stearman started to move.

Having slid the double doors wide open and rolled back the perimeter fence's netting, the route was clear. The plane, emerging from the gloom and the artificial strip lighting of the shed into the gauzy freshness of the golden October day, was like a large and spectacular butterfly materialising from a chrysalis. Jonah felt the warmth of the sun on his face, felt every bump of the plane as it lurched across the springy grass, heard the panted curses from the manpower below him. Not long now and everything else would be forgotten. This was what he'd wanted for years; for as long as he could remember. Flying. Proper flying. Open cockpit, helmet, goggles: as close to heaven as it was possible to get this side of dying for it.

They were out on the pathway now. The hands had stopped pushing; the plane was still. There was no sound other than the gentle rustle of the breeze through the airstrip's coarse grass. Jonah savoured the silence for a second, then Barnaby hauled himself on to the wing and clasped Jonah's hand.

'Go for it, Jo. Go for your dream.'

Jonah went. As Barnaby strapped himself into his front seat harness, he pressed the starter button. The throaty chug of the 450 horsepower sparking into life was the sweetest music in the world.

Shaking with excitement, his body throbbing with the pulse of the radial engine, Jonah checked that the dials on the arched dash—the rev counter, slip indicator, altimeter, compass, and clock—were all set correctly and functioning. Air-traffic control gave their clearance. Barnaby turned round in his seat and gave a double thumbs up. Jonah, with a final muttered prayer of thanks, released the brake and turned the Stearman into the wind.

The engine roar was loud and smooth, immediately overtaken completely by the howl of the nine-foot propeller as its blades rotated ever faster; the sounds blurred with the motion as the power increased and the plane skimmed across the grass. Sixty miles an hour in fifteen seconds. Just over. Still on the ground. Still level . . . The wind rushed over the wings as Jonah pulled back on the joystick. With a punch of exhilaration he felt the wheels lift from the grass.

They were airborne.

Climbing steadily, the wind against Jonah's face, the glint of the sun on the transparent arc of the propeller far ahead, the dip of the twin wings, and all the time, the throaty roar of the engine suffusing his body.

Settling back in his seat, left hand on the throttle just above his knee to adjust the engine power, he used the stick to guide the Stearman easily upwards. Whiteacres spread out hundreds of feet beneath him as he dipped the wings first left and then right, then, pulling right back on the stick, soared into the sun. The first loop was orgasmic; firing each of his senses in turn as the ground replaced the sky and gravity disintegrated. The second was just as good. Barnaby turned round, his face split with a grin like a melon. God, they were lucky. Jonah felt the Stearman respond to his questions as they climbed even higher, rolling this time, soaring and falling. He wanted to stay there for ever. Never come down. Never.

For a further fifteen minutes, Jonah swooped and scaled, testing the amazing engineering of the Stearman to its limits. The plane, like a trusted friend, seemed to respond immediately and Jonah knew he'd die rather than give this up. He leaned forward and tapped Barnaby on the shoulder.

'Time to go back?' he mouthed against the wind.

Barnaby shook his head. 'I've just touched heaven, Jo. I'm never going back . . .'

Laughing, Jonah pulled the plane high into the sky again, made a sweeping turn, and dived towards the airstrip. The Stearman roared over the tops of the Retail Village, skimmed the roofs of the industrial unit, and swooshed in towards the grass only feet above the upturned faces of its stunned audience. Rocking from side to side in the crosswind, Jonah executed a hop and skip landing, the wheels butting and skimming, bouncing and gripping, until the tail wheel finally touched base, the plane braking smoothly. The propeller's circle shimmered and separated as the Stearman cruised to a jaunty halt.

Christ. Jonah shook from head to foot. He couldn't move. Couldn't speak.

Barnaby, removing his helmet and goggles, turned round and clapped him on the shoulder. There were tears in his eyes. 'Amazing. Absolutely astounding. Jo—I can't let you have this all to yourself. I'm on the next Concorde to Kentucky to buy one of my own.'

Unsteadily, Jonah climbed onto the wing. As he jumped down he dashed away his own tears. Whatever happened in his life, no one, nothing, could rob him of this feeling. 'Tonight we'll go out and celebrate. Just you and me. I still owe you so much—'

Barnaby clapped his arm around his shoulder in a gesture of an earth-shattering experience shared and remembered always. 'Wrong way round, Jo. Wrong way round. You gave me my freedom, remember? And yes, a night out sounds a perfect way to round off an exquisite day.'

Together they walked back towards the perimeter fence to an uproarious round of applause. Jonah couldn't switch off his beam. It was like being drunk and high and in love . . . Estelle was standing a little way apart from Vinny and Pam and the others, trying not to look impressed. And there was Billie with Sylvia, her mouth open. And there—oh, holy shit!—there, just inside the wire, was Claire and bloody Aerobatic bloody Archie.

chapter nineteen

Billie had watched the whole breathtaking flight with her heart in her mouth and her hand clasped tightly in Sylvia's. Her neck had ached from following the glinting, shimmering silver, purple and green colours as they had dived and tumbled through the sky, not missing a move. The climactic roar of the engine had been a sound felt rather than heard: she'd absorbed every ounce of it from the soles of her Timberlands until it had filled her body. Only when the plane had touched down and bounced to a halt, and the roar of the engine had died away and the transparent circle of the propeller had reconstituted itself into blades, had she finally exhaled.

She'd blinked back tears of fear and pride and terror and excitement as Jonah and Barnaby had shed their helmets and goggles, leaped from the Stearman and, with arms clasped like something out of *Top Gun*, had crossed the field to well-deserved applause. Jonah's momentous achievement had felt like hers. She'd shared so much of the Boeing, watching it grow over the weeks from scrap metal into a plane, and the inaugural flight had been more awesome than she'd ever imagined. God, but he was brave! And talented. And *so* glamorous.

'Bit of a turn-on, wasn't it, dear?' Sylvia's orange face had literally glowed. 'All that throbbing power. All that thrusting. And, my God, that boy is simply beautiful . . .'

He was, Billie had admitted to herself as he'd passed her and grinned in triumph. It had lightened the earlier gloom and uncertainty of the morning considerably. She'd watched as Jonah had ducked beneath the perimeter fence, only just containing her pleasure at the way he was ignoring Estelle. Then she'd seen him falter. Seen his head snap backwards. Watched his shoulders droop as he walked towards the crowd outside her shed. Something had gone wrong . . .

'Who's that, then?' Sylvia nudged her. 'That sexy-looking young baggage?'

'Estelle, of course.' Billie sighed. 'Probably soon to be Mrs Sullivan the second.'

'Not her. I know her. I mean the buxom brunette bursting out of that lemon thing.'

That lemon thing, Billie reckoned, was the latest creation by Ralph Lauren or someone way out of her own price bracket. The ravishing dark girl poured into it was a stranger. So was the tall tanned man beside her with cropped blond hair and a Robert Redford smile. Whoever they were, they seemed to have just rained on Jonah's parade.

'I've no idea. But Jonah doesn't look too delighted to see them, does he?'

Sylvia shook her head. 'Could be plane spotters after his autograph, I suppose. Groupies are probably the last thing he wants to bother himself with at the moment . . . Well, I guess that's our excitement over for today then. It's time I was getting back to my rotunda. What about you?'

'Oh, I'll wait for the hubbub to die down a bit, then I'll ring Maynard and Pollock and tell them that we've talked it over and we're all agreed and sticking together. The new owner will have to resort to legal action to get us out. Then I thought I'd go and blow my minimal profits on an ancient van that's for sale in Whiteacres and see if the sign writers can livery it up straight away.'

Sylvia smiled. 'You're a real little trooper, Billie. You're not going to give in, are you?'

'No I'm damned well not. I like what I'm doing—and I've still got four years and eight months left on my first lease. I can't afford to lose everything now. I'll do whatever it takes to keep us all in business.'

Sylvia draped her pashmina loosely round her T-shirted shoulders like a stole over an evening gown. 'You've given me a lot of strength you know, my dear. Not just in fighting off the vultures, but in

237

standing up to Douglas too. My generation were programmed to behave somewhat different from yours. I'm so delighted that you've given me the courage I needed.'

Billie, who still felt slightly guilty about inciting Sylvia to stand her ground and spend lonely nights on a Z-bed in the unit, eating boil-in-the-bags and drinking tequila slammers to the sound of Cy Grant, shrugged. 'I don't think I gave you anything that wasn't already there. Look how well you've done with your brochures. Douglas should just learn to appreciate your achievements and not to take you for granted.'

'Oh, he's doing that all right, my dear.' Sylvia chuckled as she turned away. 'He's cancelled the cruise and got in a daily for the housework and the cooking.'

'Sylv! You never said! That's wonderful. Why the hell haven't you gone home, then?'

'Because I don't want to. I'm much happier here. Douglas, the doyen of the Rotary Club, is a bombastic, overbearing, bigoted old fool who farts in his sleep. I'm absolutely delighted to be a latter-day bolter. See you later, my dear.'

Totally gobsmacked, Billie watched as Sylvia drifted back towards her unit, the turquoise pashmina floating in the spring sunshine.

'Billie!'

Jonah's voice made her jump. She squinted up at him. 'What? Oh, congratulations. You were amazing. Simply wonderful. How on earth do you get the plane to do all those things? Aren't you scared? How does—Hey! What are you doing?'

Jonah had gripped her arm just above the elbow. He turned her round and together they started hurrying towards the perimeter fence. He looked down at her, an angry muscle tensing in his cheek. Jesus! What the hell had she done?

'Sorry,' he muttered, still marching and stamping over to the fence, 'I'm not kidnapping you. I just need a friend.'

Christ—he'd got more friends than anyone she'd ever known—except perhaps Miranda. And how on earth did he docket her into 'friend' category, anyway? They'd only spent a few hours together and—'Why? Why me? Where are we going? What for?'

'Because I'm probably going to kill someone. Because you're the most normal, honest person I've ever met. To the plane. To talk. That enough answers?'

'Not really.' Billie wriggled away from him, still keeping in step. 'I mean, they're answers, but not any that I understand—and I'm not getting in that plane!'

'Please.' Jonah came to a halt beside the Stearman and pushed his dark hair away from his eyes. 'Please, Billie. I need you to. Barnaby has disappeared to put champagne on ice for the celebration, Vinny has discovered that the hippie girl in the clothes place isn't wearing a bra, Pam's gone to get sandwiches, and I couldn't find anyone else . . .'

'But, I don't understand—'

'Just get in the plane. Like you did in the shed. We can talk then. I just need you to sit in the plane.'

She looked at him doubtfully for a moment, completely at a loss. Then, sensing the urgency, scrambled onto the wing. What harm could it do?

The Stearman seemed somehow less stable out in the open, and Billie felt the sweat prickling her palms. Carefully, she lowered herself into the seat. It was still warm; in fact the whole cockpit was cosy from the heat of the recently roaring engine, and she wriggled herself into position. She felt Jonah pull himself into the seat behind her, and for the second time watched as his long legs snaked on either side of hers amongst the cables that ran the length of the plane to the engine.

'This is crazy.'

'It's also desperate.' Jonah's voice was again close in her ear. 'Sorry to hijack you, but I thought you'd understand.'

Billie, who understood less about what was going on than she did about the theory of relativity, snorted. 'I've already said twenty times that I don't.'

'Estelle wanted me to take her up in the plane. I said I couldn't because there wasn't time, but the air-traffic controllers have now extended my air slot because no one's flying from the Aeroclub today.'

'Oh, right—and? You don't want to take Estelle—er—up?'

She felt him shake his head. 'We've had a falling-out.'

Goody, Billie thought. 'Why?'

'Because I didn't make love to her last night.'

Christ, Billie blinked. Ten out of ten for pulling no punches. She was also irrationalally delighted to think that he *hadn't*—and annoyed to know that he *did*. 'And that's it? You don't want to fly with Estelle so you need someone to sit in the plane?' She skewed round in her seat to look at him. 'Why? It all sounds a bit iffy to me. Have I missed out on a vital ingredient?'

'Ah, yes . . .' The muscle was still twitching in Jonah's cheek. He wasn't smiling. 'Claire asked to be taken up, too.'

Claire? Claire the ex? 'God Almighty! Is she the stunning-looking woman in yellow? And the all-American dream with her—is he Aerobatic Archie?'

'Got it in one. They just *happened* to be passing today, because they'd just *happened* to hear about the Stearman on the aviation grapevine.' His voice was bitter. 'They also thought it would be an ideal opportunity to tell me that they'd just made their offer to Whiteacres Aviation Inc.—who apparently were happy to accept . . .'

Shit. Billie let all this filter through her brain. So it was Claire and her lover who were going to be the new owners of the units, then? She blew out her cheeks. This could put a whole new slant on it. They certainly wouldn't want to hang on to a shabby row of warehousing. And someone who was almost a Red Arrow was bound to have an awful lot of influential chums, wasn't he? It looked as though her campaign to hang on to her shed may need to nudge up a notch.

Billie craned her neck to peer across Jonah's shoulder towards the sheds. But God, Claire was beautiful! And simply oozing sex appeal. She could just see Estelle, all in black, and the bright yellow figure of Claire, obviously having some sort of head-to-head. They looked exactly like the prettier half of an Abba tribute band.

'Don't exactly see eye to eye, those two, then?'

'That's putting it mildly,' Jonah sighed, and slumped down in his seat.

Billie turned round to face the front again,

feeling desperately sorry for him. He should be on a high all day. No one should be allowed to rob him of this moment of triumph. And his future—like hers—was suddenly in jeopardy. Oh, sure, he could probably move Sullivanair to another airfield but at a hell of a cost—in the same way that she and Sylvia and Zi-Zi's and the rest could find other homes . . . But why should they? Why the hell should they?

'There's no chance that you and the other people on the airfield could form a consortium and outdo their offer, I suppose?'

'Not a hope in hell. There's no other airline actually based here—they just pick up and dump—and the Aeroclub is independent. I sank every penny I had left after my divorce settlement into Sullivanair. And I had to borrow as well to manage that. Any money I've accrued is set aside to buy a second Shorts to take on extra short-haul flights—and it certainly isn't enough to buy an airfield.'

'What about remortgaging?' Billie plucked at words she'd heard her parents mention when the farm was going through a shaky patch. 'Couldn't you raise some money that way?'

'Not a hope. I don't even own my own flat.'

Billie pulled a sympathetic face. They were in the same boat. Or plane. And it did seem doubly unfair that Claire should get two bites of the cherry. 'What about Barnaby, then? He looks—um—well, rich.'

Jonah laughed. 'He owns a minor stately home that's crumbling into disrepair, and a few good racehorses—both of which gobble up his inheritance with ease. Anyway, I don't think he'd be interested in buying Whiteacres, even if he could afford it.'

'Have you asked him?'

242

'No—but—'

'Ask him, then,' Billie said. 'He might be only too pleased to help. We're getting together in the units to become a co-op—and we're all broke. Sylv's even cashing in her funeral plan.'

Jonah sighed and shook his head. 'I think we'll have to admit defeat on this one.'

'Will we buggery! And don't laugh at me!'

'I'm not. Honestly. It just seems so funny hearing you curse like a navvy when you look so sweet.'

'And don't patronise me either—and oh, I think we're having a visitation.'

Claire and Estelle, both looking furious, lifting their legs high on the damp grass like liberty ponies, were each trying to outstride the other as they bore down on the Stearman.

Billie could hear Jonah muttering—something to do with airspeed and clearance . . . 'What the hell are you doing?'

'Billie, fasten those straps over your shoulders— and buckle the one between your legs—no, go on, just do it. That's right—there . . . No, I just need to move the plane. I've no intention of being a sitting target. OK?' Billie's fingers fumbled with the harness. 'Yes, yes—I think so . . . But we're not going far are we?' She'd watched the Stearman bobbling across the grass earlier. It had looked pretty uncomfortable.

'Not far at all. And can I ask you one question? What petrifies you most about flying?'

'Crashing.'

'Fine, then. I promise not to crash. Hold on . . .'

'Jonah—no!!!'

But it was too late. The engine in front of her growled into life, deafening her, vibrating through

243

every part of her body, and as Jonah's feet moved on the pedals beside her, the propeller started to bite into the air. Jesus! She was going to die!

The Stearman gathered speed, rocketing across the tufty grass, bouncing and pitching, getting ever faster, until Billie, clinging on to her seat, was unsure whether the scream in her head was from her or the engine or the wind or all three.

For a split second it seemed as though they would race straight into the fence, but suddenly the motion changed and the bouncing stopped and there was nothing but a gentle rocking from side to side as the sky grew closer and the ground fell away.

'Oh my God!' She couldn't open her mouth, so she muttered through her clenched teeth. 'Oh my God! I'm flying!'

Still only feet beneath, on the airstrip, Estelle and Claire's upturned and incandescently furious faces almost took away Billie's terror. Almost, but not quite. Flying in the Stearman was far noisier than she'd expected, but much warmer, burrowed down in the deep seat, and smoother. All she could see now was the pale blue and white speckled sky through the angle of the windscreen, and the struts and wires joining the two wings crisscrossing in front of her and all around her, and the huge nine-foot span of the propeller's translucent rainbow circle. The sky seemed to be nearer now and she guessed they were climbing. She didn't dare to look down.

'I'll just go up to four hundred feet and level out,' Jonah roared in her ear. 'We should have goggles and helmets, but I hadn't planned this. You OK?'

She jerked her head in an affirmative, still not able to move. Goggles and helmets were the least of

244

her worries. She wanted a parachute and Valium. She wanted to kill him—and she would, but later. On terra firma. Always assuming they'd ever touch terra firma again.

The Stearman, as steady now as a limousine, levelled out. Billie tentatively let go of her seat with one hand. The sun spiralled from the half-windscreen in front of her like lights on a leaded window, and the wind tugged through her hair. Summoning up her courage, she looked downwards. Whiteacres was stretched away in miniature, and she could see the bypass and the traffic and tiny dots of people. The motion was indescribable; nothing like being strapped into the confines of a 747 and waiting for the duty-frees. It was as much like dream flying as anything could ever get.

She worked some saliva into her mouth and took deep breaths to steady her pulse rate. She'd die before she'd admit it, but the gentle tip-tilting motion wasn't that scary at all. It was exciting and exhilarating and totally liberating.

'Want to try a stall-turn?' Jonah yelled in her ear. 'Or a loop?'

Billie shook her head. She was almost sure he was joking. Instinctively she trusted him not to frighten her. 'I'm all right . . .'

'What?'

'I said, I'm OK.' Still holding on with one hand, she allowed herself the luxury of turning round. Jonah grinned at her reassuringly. She grinned back.

Settling back into her seat, convinced now that even if the engine died in front of her, Jonah would somehow land the plane in one piece, Billie

245

smiled to herself. God—she couldn't wait to ring home and tell her parents about this. They'd never believe her. And Miranda would be pea-green with jealousy. She wanted to tell the world what she'd done.

Her ears were cold and her hair would never untangle and her nose was running, but these small inconveniences were wiped away by the sheer fun of it all. And, of course, the superb knowledge that both Estelle and Claire wanted to be in her place. Everything seemed so insignificant somehow up here: the future of the industrial units, and Miranda and Reuben, and all that awfulness with Kieran Squires. If only she could stay up here for ever, floating along with the birds, away from the real world.

She sighed. This must be how Jonah felt all the time. No wonder the thought of losing it all—and to his deadliest rival—was so painful. She understood now. She really understood. There had to be something they could do. All of them together. They must be able to fight off Undulating Claire and Aerobatic Archie, mustn't they?

The engine note changed. Billie was suddenly jolted out of her complacency. She'd always listened to the engines' noise on her holiday flights, and also watched the stewardesses. She reckoned that they'd know before the passengers if there was a problem, and as long as they were sashaying along the aisle on her 747, smiling sweetly and doling out miniature gins, she always felt there was no need to panic.

She had no such barometer today. She jerked her head round. 'What's happening?'

'Nothing,' Jonah smiled. 'We're going in to land,

246

that's all.'

Billie felt a thump of disappointment. She didn't want to. She didn't want this blissful experience to end. 'Already?'

'Yeah,' he shouted, beaming at her. 'And do I take it that I've just made a convert?'

She looked down at the floor. His legs were brushing hers. 'No! Yes, well, sort of . . .'

She heard him laugh above the Boeing's roar as they began to circle the airstrip. 'And perhaps you've also changed your mind about plane-fanatics all being sad old anoraks?'

Billie shook her head as the Stearman rock'n'rolled its way gently towards the ground. 'Nah. No chance. I'll never change my mind on that one.' She clutched the seat as Jonah pushed the plane into a nose dive. 'Jesus! Oh, yeah—OK, then—maybe I will . . .'

The plane resumed a more normal descent, and the landing, although bumpy, was far less daunting than anything she and Miranda had ridden on last summer at Alton Towers. She pressed her head back into the seat as the propeller blade stopped whirling, and exhaled. The roar of the engine was still drumming in her ears and she wanted to stay cocooned there for ever, but Jonah had already extricated his legs and jumped down on to the grass.

Her fingers were trembling as she undid the buckles of her harness, and as she stood up her legs wobbled. Jonah reached out to her. 'Just take it easy. You're bound to feel a bit strange. Put your foot there, and I'll catch you . . .'

No way, Billie thought. No bloody way. Then she teetered and stumbled and Jonah's arms were

247

round her waist, swinging her to the floor.

'Jonah!' Estelle's strident voice cut through the silence and the birdsong. 'Jonah! I think we need to talk!'

Jonah let Billie go. She beamed towards Estelle, who was still goose-stepping across the airstrip, followed by Claire, whose bosoms were bouncing uncomfortably. 'Please don't let me stop you. I've got work to do.' Billie smiled up at Jonah. 'Good luck—and thanks a lot. It was lovely . . .'

And skipping off across the airstrip, her feet scarcely touching the ground, she felt exactly as though she was walking on air.

winter

chapter twenty

The balminess of October had spread through much of November, and Billie had hoped that the Indian summer would last for ever. She and Sylvia, Zia and Isla, Fred 'n' Dick, and the Guspers all met up for coffee outside the units, basking in the low golden sunshine, watching the colours change on the trees, relishing the gentle warmth, and not giving voice to their fears. However, as the autumn rolled into December, Billie was aware that Whiteacres' new owners might well end these halcyon days with a vengeance.

Jonah, to give him his due, had kept her updated with the Claire and Aerobatic Archie developments. They had been, to say the least, disappointing. Claire, who seemed to have a very selective memory, had apparently been irritatingly vague about their plans– but insisted that their bid for Whiteacres wasn't going to take place until the spring,. Billie knew she was lying: all the warehousers knew from Maynard and Pollock that their leases would be under new ownership in January. Jonah had shrugged and said Claire was always unreliable, and Aerobatic bloody Archie was devious, and he wouldn't put it past them to announce their ownership of the airfield *and* the industrial estate immediately the final chimes of the year died away.

All in all, it was most frustrating, but in the meantime Billie had bought the van and had it liveried, invested in long-running adverts in the *Amberley Hill Echo* and the *Whiteacres Courier*, and followed Estelle's business plan instructions to the letter. Billie hated to admit it, but Estelle's methods worked, and the warehouse, by the beginning of December, was starting to show a small but healthy profit.

Almost on cue, as if to signify the end of the year and also the end of the warehousers' fragile peace of mind, the December weather had turned bitterly cold. Sylvia had taken to wearing black opaque tights beneath her shorts, and Zia and Isla were snuggling into twin yak-hair ponchos. Billie added a further layer beneath her fleece and wore an extra pair of socks with her Timberlands. The frosty mornings and grey, wind-chilled gloom did very little to raise the airfield's ambience.

On the fine autumnal days, Jonah had flown the Stearman at least half a dozen times since that momentous inaugural flight, but although she'd watched from the perimeter fence, Billie had never repeated her trip—despite Jonah's cajoling invitations. The first time, unplanned, had been exciting and illuminating, but Billie was sure if she knew in advance that she was going to be leaving the ground she'd have a return of the aerophobic panic attacks, and certainly didn't want to lose face.

Instead, Estelle had taken her place, and each flight had meant that Jonah and Estelle, always looking annoyingly stunning in her designer overalls, had returned to the shed, discussing technicalities, and fine-tuned some part of the engine. Billie still found it irritating to watch someone who looked like a supermodel so completely at home with the scary intricacies of the Boeing's innards. Especially as that someone was also sharing Jonah's bed.

Miranda's plans for a double blind date with her unknown Joseph and the eligible Mr Molton-Kusak had failed to materialise. In fact, Miranda spoke of Joseph very rarely these days—and Mr Molton-Kusak even less. All her conversations centred on the developments at Caught Offside and were peppered with Reuben-references, and although she swore that they weren't sleeping together, Billie was pretty sure it was only a matter of time.

Sad really, she thought, heading through the warehouse for the office early one December morning. If Miranda was pretty serious about Slimeball Wainwright, she wouldn't risk the relationship she was building with him, however distasteful, for a one-night stand with a total stranger—even if Joseph the Dreamboat was allegedly the most beautiful man ever to draw breath. So that was the end of that.

Billie turned on the hot-air blowers, clicked on the kettle for the first caffeine kick of the day, and sighed. She could really do with some male company. The partnerships of Miranda and Reuben, Estelle and Jonah, Isla and Zia—even the thought of Claire and Aerobatic Archie—merely reinforced the feelings that had been growing of late. That it was all very well to hurl everything of yourself into a business venture, and to live your career twenty-four hours a day, but there came a point when you really needed to switch off and have someone to laugh with, to share the down sides, and just talk to. If it hadn't been for Kieran bloody Squires, she thought, scrolling down the ever-growing list of 'Custs Estab', she might be brave enough to start looking.

That's why the blind-date foursome might have been a lot of fun. And Mr Molten-Lava sounded just what she could do with: someone older and decent and—she tapped furiously at the keyboard—what was the other word she was looking for? Oh, yeah—boring. No, she shouldn't prejudge. He might be her ideal man, he probably wasn't, but he just might be and now she was never likely to find out.

It was just before midday when Estelle arrived. Billie, who had pulled her jumper down over her hands, poking her fingers through the loose stitches in the cuffs so that they looked like mittens, and wrapped two scarves round her neck and was still cold, shivered as the north wind rattled into the unit.

'Goodness!' Estelle flicked back her hair. 'It's like an oven in here! You must be stifling!'

'I've been sitting still all morning,' Billie muttered, trying to extricate her fingers from the sleeve holes and wondering why she always looked like a tramp whenever Estelle put in an appearance. 'And it's sub-zero outside and I—er—feel the cold.'

Estelle, who, if her short skirt, cropped jacket and nil-denier stockings were anything to go by, obviously didn't, shrugged. 'I don't suppose you've seen Jonah?'

'Not today. Not for ages, in fact. Not since the last time you were both here.'

Estelle frowned. The last time they'd both been there, the atmosphere between them, Billie had thought, had been pretty chilly. In fact, there'd seemed to be a distinct freeze ever since the Stearman's maiden voyage.

Billie decided to stop speculating on the affair

254

and remembered her manners. Estelle's beauty and expertise still intimidated her, but she'd always be grateful to her for sorting out the business side of things. 'Would you like coffee? Tea? I was just going to break for lunch.'

'Nothing thanks. I'm not stopping.' Estelle cast a cursory glance over the computer screen and the ledgers on the desk. 'Things still going well?'

'Very,' Billie admitted. 'Thanks to your suggestions. I might even have to register for VAT in the new year—always supposing we're still here . . .'

Estelle tossed back her hair again, looking a bit peeved. 'I'm sure you'll still be here. I'm sure Sullivanair will still be here. In fact, even if Claire and Antony are behind the takeover then I honestly can't see things changing at all.'

'But surely Jonah wouldn't want to be beholden to his ex-wife and her lover, would he? He wouldn't want to stay here and be *owned* by them?'

Estelle laughed. Her eyes didn't. 'Oh, I'm sure Jonah would absolutely adore to be owned by Claire! He's still totally besotted by the woman! He'll never be able to get it together with anyone else while she's around.' She walked towards the door, then paused. 'Oh, and if you do see him, tell him I'm away for the rest of the day. I've left him a note, but as he was supposed to be back from Southampton ages ago and hasn't shown up in the office, I haven't got a clue where he's gone.'

Billie, her brain still reeling from the dual complexities of Jonah's relationship with Estelle and his feelings for Claire, tried to concentrate. 'God—he hasn't had an accident, has he?'

Estelle shook her head, holding the door open

and allowing the wind to howl into the unit and play havoc with the paperwork. 'No, of course he hasn't. The Shorts is back in its hangar and Vinny's in the Aeroclub bar. He said Jonah was coming straight over here. He's probably got sidetracked by someone selling a heap of junk.'

Billie blinked. 'But you love the Stearman, surely? You've spent so long on it, and—'

'Oh, he's not looking at another Stearman. He wants to buy a second passenger Shorts to bulk up Sullivanair—and possibly a Skyvan. Archaic, outmoded, totally prehistoric! That's why I'm—' She stopped and smiled. 'Oh, well—I suppose it all means nothing to you anyway.'

'Not a thing,' Billie said quickly, trying to catch the nuances and failing. 'So, are you going anywhere nice?'

'Luton,' Estelle said, swinging out of the door. 'And nice or not depends on the outcome.'

After she'd left, Billie made a Cup a Soup and some toast, and wished Sylvia was around so that they could mull over the Estelle–Jonah–Claire triangle together. But Sylvia had gone home for another discussion with Douglas. This time about Christmas. Billie, who was trying hard not to think about the festive season at all, was pretty sure that Douglas would be celebrating alone while Sylv holed up in the shed with copious measures of rum punch, a Marks and Spencer gourmet meal for one, and Johnny Mathis and 'Mary's Boy Child' on constant replay.

Telephoning a new customer who had written in, and arranging to collect in the van some much-fought-over carved Victorian commode— apparently a bequest from Great-aunt Edith's will, and which now wouldn't go through the front door of a one-bedroom starter home on the Badger's Fart Estate, or some such place—Billie drained the dregs of the soup and picked up her keys. She thought maybe she should leave a note for Jonah and was just searching for a Post-it when the doors slid open.

'Great,' she beamed. 'I was just going to write to you. Estelle says—Oh shit!'

Reuben, looking even more dark and dangerous than ever in a long black Crombie overcoat, raised his eyebrows. 'Still using cabby language, I'm glad to hear. And do I take it you're alone?'

'Er—yes—that is . . . no.'

Reuben laughed harshly. 'I'm not going to pounce on you, sweetheart, so don't look so frightened. I just wanted to have a little talk. Just the two of us. Without Miranda.'

Billie backed away towards the safety of the office. This was appalling. Reuben's snide remarks over the last three years, the subtle and not-so-subtle hints that he'd got a permanent hold over her—all came back to her in one great scary rush. 'Go away. I've got nothing to say to you. You've got no right to be here.'

'I've got every right,' Reuben's eyes trawled round the shed, took in the stacked shelves, and finally came to rest on the Stearman. He whistled. 'You're doing very nicely, sweetheart. Very nicely indeed. And I suppose you want it to stay that way?'

'What? Of course I do.' She stopped. 'What the hell are you threatening?'

Reuben looked pained. 'Threatening? I'm not threatening you at all. It was merely an innocent question from a concerned friend.'

257

'Crap,' Billie spat at him. 'Total crap. Don't think you can come here and threaten me with—with— well, anything! I've served my sentence for . . .'

'Being a silly tart?' Reuben chuckled. 'Yes, well that's a matter of opinion. And these nice people here in the warehouses? Do they know the truth about you?'

'What truth? That I was foolish enough to have an affair with a married man? Of course not—and neither would they be interested. Oh, I know you keep dropping hints to Miranda, but even if she did know about—er—about me and Kieran, why should she care? Why the hell would anyone be remotely bothered?'

'I've told you, that's not why I'm here.' Reuben ran his hand along the Stearman's fuselage. 'And this is a very exciting piece of kit, sweetheart. Miranda said you'd got a plane, but she made it sound like one of those models. I had no idea that it was something as spectacular as this.'

Billie, deciding that it was about time to take control, dangled her van keys in front of his nose. 'And what goes on here is no concern of yours, so if you'll excuse me, I was just leaving to see a customer.'

Reuben didn't move. Billie held herself in and edged round him. 'Come on, shift yourself. I have no idea why you're here anyway.'

'Like I said, because I wanted to have a little chat—just to satisfy myself that you were OK. I happened to be passing and I thought I'd pop in. We never seem to bump into each other these days, do we?'

Billie stood her ground, still clenching the van keys. 'Reuben, please go. You can take out a

258

full-page advert about me and Kieran Squires in every national newspaper on the planet and it won't bother me—so bugger off.'

Reuben laughed. 'I'm on my way. I've satisfied myself that you're all right—and doing nicely—and the plane is very interesting. Very interesting indeed . . .' He drew the Crombie closer to him as he headed for the door. 'And I'm so glad that you have no qualms about the Kieran thing going public, Billie, love. Extremely glad . . .'

He closed the door behind him. Billie hurled her van keys at it. 'Bastard! Bastard! Bastard!'

The door opened again and she cringed. 'Sod off! Now! Or I'll call the police and have you—Oh, hi . . .'

Jonah, in the Sullivanair uniform, scooped up her keys from the floor. 'I take it the man who's just driven away wasn't your favourite customer?'

'My ex-boss.' She took the keys, trying not to drool over Jonah in the gorgeous navy-blue jacket with the gold braid because of Estelle—oh, and Claire. It was proving difficult. 'We don't—um—exactly see eye to eye.'

'So I gathered.' He grinned at her. 'You've got quite a temper. I must remember not to get on the wrong side of you. Were you just leaving?'

'Trying to. I've got a collection to make. Oh, and Estelle—'

'I know. I've just been into the office and found her note.' He hurled his peaked cap into the Stearman's cockpit. 'Could you just hang on for a second. There's something I wanted to show you.'

Billie, still fuming from Reuben's visit, and really wanting to drive to Badger's Fart to collect the commode and mull over the implications of why

259

Reuben had been there and what he was trying to achieve, nodded. 'As long as it doesn't take very long. I'm running late as it is.'

'It won't take a moment. Barnaby's outside sorting it out. I ran into him just after I got in from Southampton . . .'

Barnaby suddenly appeared in the doorway, his knees buckling under the weight of a metal contraption. He placed it carefully on the floor and smiled at them both. 'Hello, my dear. How lovely to see you again. There—now—Jonah, what do you think?'

Jonah shook his head. 'It looks a bit Miss Whiplash to me. Straight out of the torture chamber. Are you sure it's legal? Is this what you get up to in that stately home? No wonder you keep heading off up there so often.'

'Good Lord, dear boy—I wish.' Barnaby tapped the top of the metal frame. 'This is just what we need to make our little enterprise go with a bang. You gave me the idea the other night when we were talking about Waldo Pepper, and I called in a favour or two on my way up country and asked around—and hey presto!'

Jonah walked slowly round the contraption. 'It's a frame and a sort of a harness and—'

'It's an Art Scholl rigid rig, Jo! The genuine article. Bolt it on to the top of the Stearman—and what have you got?'

Jonah gazed at Barnaby with dawning delight. 'The answer to our prayers?'

'Excuse me,' Billie shook her head, 'what the hell is it?'

Barnaby tapped the frame. 'It's an Art Scholl rig.'

260

'Of course it is! Silly me! Who the hell is Art Scholl? I think my mum wears his sandals.'

'He was a stunt pilot in the States—in the good old days. He devised this frame and harness, my dear. It's for the Stearman.'

Billie frowned at it. 'Fascinating—if a little scary. But what does it do?'

Jonah took a deep breath. 'It stops wingwalkers falling off.'

'Wingwalkers?' Billie's frown increased. 'Wingwalkers? You mean—on top of the plane? In the air? When it's moving? Bloody hell! You'd have to be completely mad to—Hey, why are you looking at me like that?'

Jonah dropped his gaze to the ground. 'Well, like Barnaby says, the Stearman and the rig go together like—um—biscuits and cheese or—er—fish and chips. But to put on a barnstorming display, of course, it would need—um—someone in it . . .'

'It sounds great,' Billie said, still looking puzzled. 'Maybe, come the summer, you could put on a show or something.'

'Just what I was thinking!' Jonah looked very animated. 'We've got the perfect opportunity here to do something completely different. Something Whiteacres and Amberley Hill has never seen before. Think of the crowds we'd pull in with a barnstorming display. The Stearman was made for it, and with Barnaby doing flips in the Slingsby, and Vinny doing something with the Shorts, and the small planes giving joyrides, it'd be sensational.'

Billie nodded. 'Sounds wonderful—and I'm sure everyone would love it. But this barnstorming thing, then? Don't you need a professional idiot—oh, sorry—wingwalker?'

261

'In an ideal world, of course that would be the answer. But we simply don't have the cash to engage someone just for a possible one-off—even if we could find one . . . ' He moved his eyes from the Stearman to the rigid rig and finally to her. 'Of course, I have no doubt that both Estelle and Claire would jump at the chance—but Estelle's too tall and Claire's too heavy . . . Come on, Billie, think about it—you could do it. You loved the flight in the Stearman, didn't you? You're game for anything, and as tough as old boots. Please say you'll at least try it—just for me?'

chapter twenty-one

This whole idea had been a big mistake. Faith, keeping the Land Rover chugging along the inside lane of the M5 at just over forty, glanced in her rear-view mirror. Thad, Mungo, Lilac and Delphi, all strapped into their kiddie seats, were demolishing packets of crisps with the studied aplomb of past masters of the art. At least, she thought, with their mouths full of monosodium glutamate they couldn't scream. Visiting Declan and Maeve Squires just before Christmas was a pretty crazy thing to be doing anyway—but to be doing it in the company of four hyperactive vandals, was, she knew, total insanity.

Oh, brilliant. The large green exit sign for the A38 and Taunton loomed ahead. Indicating thankfully and pulling onto the slip road, Faith prayed that this would be the end of her quest. She'd had to grab this opportunity as soon as it arose. Ever since the visit to Rustique she'd racked her brains for some plausible reason to be heading north into Somerset for the day, on her own, and failed to find one. It would have been easy if she was one of those gad-about women who were always 'popping up to town' or 'lunching out', but she never had been. There had always been far too much work to do on the farm. Days out were planned and discussed and savoured.

So when she'd casually mentioned during a family supper that it might be a good idea for her to take the four eldest children out for the day to enable Katy and Ann to do their Christmas shopping in peace, she'd expected the Spanish Inquisition at least. Surprisingly, everyone had greeted the news with a fervour bordering on rapture. Faith glanced again at her grandchildren in the rear seats and could now understand why.

Her daughters-in-law had been delighted to have a toddler-free shopping day and hadn't asked any questions at all, and Stan and the boys were all working flat out and were too exhausted to care. Faith knew she'd never find a better occasion.

Maeve and Declan Squires, not knowing her from Adam, had been very pleasant during the telephone conversation under the circumstances. Oh yes, they'd said—we know who you are. Of course we do . . . Oh, yes if you're going to be in Taunton on Wednesday you must pop in for a few minutes and have a cup of tea. Nice to see the old Willowbridge faces again . . . Bit cut off up here to be truthful . . . Looking forward to it . . .

Faith had replaced the receiver, scarlet with shame. She hadn't given her surname—just in case Billie had done something really dreadful and

263

Maeve and Declan had a fatwa out on all Pascoes. She'd just kept saying she was Faith, Stan's wife, Pat and Miriam's friend—you know—came in every Friday for cod and chips twice? Sometimes had a pickled egg . . . ? And eventually Maeve and Declan had seemed to twig. She went cold all over after the call, imagining the Squireses' puzzlement as they stood in their Taunton bungalow staring at the telephone and trying to remember exactly which nonexistent customer at their chippy they'd just invited into their home.

Well, she thought, heading towards the outer limits of the town, they were just about to find out.

*　　　*　　　*

The bungalow, excruciatingly called 'DunFryin', was a blaze of bad taste. And that was just outside. Maeve and Declan must have got designers in to tart up Rustique. The Squireses appeared to have slightly overdone things in every area. There was an illuminated Santa Claus hovering sinisterly on the chimney pot, and several herds of reindeer strobing across the pebbledash with dizzying effect. At least, Faith thought resignedly, it was extremely cheerful.

Unstrapping herself and instructing the children to stay put, she blinked at the pink and white chequered drive, the swathes of looped net curtains, and the army of primary—coloured gnomes doing everything imaginable amongst a dazzling perpetual shrubbery. No doubt, she thought, the garden would be neon bright with busy Lizzies during the summer. There also seemed to be a strange preponderance of black filigreed wrought iron.

264

'Stay,' she said again as Thad pinged his seat belt free with the ease of a junior Houdini and immediately started to release the others. 'Stay for a moment and Granno'll buy you some sweets later.'

'McDonald's.' Thad's fingers played with Lilac's buckle. 'McDonald's, Granno. Now.'

'Later, if you take your hands off Lilac's seat belt. Nothing if you don't.'

Four pairs of eyes looked at her, then at each other. Four tiny Machiavellian brains ticked. Thad nodded and reluctantly moved away from his sister. 'OK. But we can get out, can't we? Delphi wants a wee.'

Oh God. Faith counted to ten. She'd never had this trouble with her five. Never. They'd always seemed so placid.

'Let me just go and see if Mr and Mrs Squires are at home first. I'm sure they'll let Delphi use their loo.'

'Lavatory,' Mungo said. 'Mummy says we should use proper words. Lavatory, not loo. And urinate, not wee, stupid!'

'Yeah,' Lilac nodded fervently. ''S right. And penis, not willy. I haven't got a penis, Granno. Have you got a—'

Dear God alive! Faith slammed the door and sprinted up the dizzying checked pathway.

'DunFryin's' bell played a few notes of 'We Wish You a Merry Christmas'. Three separate wind chimes clanged discordantly above her head. A whole shelf of crinoline ladies made from seashells peered at her. Faith just knew that there'd be a lava lamp in the lounge.

The door opened. Declan—it had to be

265

Declan—wearing a joke pinny with breasts and a suspender belt, and a pair of Marigolds, looked at her enquiringly. 'If you're from Save the Children, the dog ate the envelope.'

'What? Oh dear. Is it all right?'

'Dog's fine. Envelope's buggered.'

Faith raised her voice a little above the onslaught of the wind chimes. 'I'm Faith—from Willowbridge . . . I telephoned . . . ? Your wife—um—Maeve suggested I might pop in for a cup of tea.'

This seemed to strike a chord. Declan nodded and peered closer. 'Ah, right. Mind, I don't recognise you meself, but don't let that faze you. With all that grease and steam and what have you, we never really got a proper look at the customers. Never remembered any of 'em. Not the good ones anyway—it was only the ones that caused trouble that we remembered. Come along in. Maeve's in the lounge area.'

With the lava lamp, Faith thought, and probably something in fibre optics. She indicated over her shoulder. 'I've left my grandchildren in the Land Rover. I—um—wondered . . .'

'Bless 'em! Bring 'em in as well.'

'They're actually not very good indoors.' Faith addressed the row of cross-eyed crinoline ladies. They all looked askance at this understatement. 'Maybe they could play in the garden—oh, after they've used the loo—um—lavatory . . .'

'Bit cold for 'em outside.'

'They're definitely better out of doors,' Faith reiterated. 'They're used to the fresh air.'

'Don't you worry about them,' Declan nodded. 'I'll take 'em off your hands while you and Maeve have a bit of a chat. I love kiddies. Love 'em. I've

266

got two grandchildren of my own.'

Not like these, you haven't, Faith thought, jerking her head towards the Land Rover.

Declan smiled at the four tiny faces gurning from the vehicle's window, then pointed towards a pink archway completely smothered with fat gilt cherubs and lavishly hung with tinselled garlands. 'You go through to the lounge and I'll go and sort out the little 'uns. All right?'

Grasping this lifeline, and hoping that Declan would at least remove his pinny before releasing the onslaught, Faith scuttled across an acre of mauve and tangerine floral carpet and ducked through the archway.

Maeve was relaxing on a leatherette chaise longue, her fluffy-slippered feet only just outdoing the candyfloss-pink frills of the cushions. The entire room twinkled and sparkled with festoons like Santa's grotto. A cinemasized television blared out in a riot of neon colours. Faith wanted to punch the air. A lava lamp, glooping globules of orange and indigo, sat foursquare on top of it.

Faith held out her hand. 'Your husband said it was OK for me to come through. I'm Faith. From Willowbridge. We spoke on the phone . . .'

'Lovely to see you!' Maeve slid the slippers to the floor. 'Dec's just made a pot of Earl Grey and we'll put an extra cup on the tray. You sit yourself down and tell me all about home.'

Faith sat on a chintz chair and immediately disappeared into a mass of fondant fancy cushions, while Maeve reached over to a black ash china cabinet and extracted a Royal Doulton Rosebud cup. Telling Maeve all about home was going to be pretty tricky seeing that Faith didn't actually live in

267

Willowbridge and had probably only been into the fish and chip shop twice in her entire life. Still, she wasn't a member of the Townswomen's Guild for nothing, and within seconds she'd started regaling Maeve with scurrilous second-hand stories about people probably neither of them knew.

Throughout all this, Maeve nodded enthusiastically and poured tea. Maeve, Faith thought, must have a direct line to the Royal Doulton factory. There were at least four of the black ash cabinets crammed full of Royal Doulton figurines. Or maybe, she thought, remembering the seashell ladies in the porch, it was the crinolines she was fixated on. Whatever it was, they certainly caught the eye.

'QVC,' Maeve said, following Faith's gaze. 'I buy 'em off satellite telly. Always have such lovely things, don't they? Smashing, aren't they?'

'Smashing . . .' Faith murmured in agreement. 'Absolutely smashing . . .' Her eyes travelled further round the room. There must be something that she could use here to get her on to Rustique and Billie.

'So—um—how are you enjoying your retirement?'

'Loving it,' Maeve said, munching a Thin Arrowroot. 'Although, of course, we're not out of catering altogether. We've got a share in a restaurant.'

Hallelujah! Faith slopped tea into her saucer. 'Oh? Really? What—here in Taunton?'

'No, bless you. Still in Devon. Just outside Bideford. It's more an investment, really, although we do pop down from time to time.'

'Er—a fish restaurant, is it?'

'No! Real posh! Frenchified. The boy bought

268

it, of course, to lose a bit of tax, but we're down as co-owners. You should go sometime.'

Faith nodded, staring at the lava lamp. 'I'd love to. It sounds really nice. So—er—when it opened, did you have a lot of publicity?' She winced. It was far too contrived . . .

It apparently wasn't. Maeve wriggled her polyester shoulders in indignation. 'I should say so! Reporters everywhere! And not just because of the restaurant, either! It was because of our boy. Always want to dig the dirt on him, bloody scumbags! If our boy wanted to set his old mum and dad up with a bit of a business to see them through their autumn years, then why shouldn't he, I say!'

Faith nodded again. This time she really hadn't got a clue what was going on. Fortunately an ear-shattering scream and some high-pitched yapping from the garden pre-empted her next question. Maeve was instantly on her feet. 'Sounds like Dec's having a bit of trouble with the dog and the rotovator—he's a martyr to the new technology. We got it off QVC—the rotovator, that is, not the dog—and he never reads the instructions properly.'

'I think it might be my grandchildren, actually,' Faith ventured, being brave enough to place her cup and saucer on the mirrored veneer of the mock Queen Anne coffee table without dislodging a nodding Rudolph. 'Declan said he'd entertain them.'

Maeve sank down again. 'Ah, that's all right then. Lovely with kiddies, is Declan. We've got two grandchildren of our own. Would you like to see their photos?'

'Yes,' said Faith, who wouldn't. She really needed to get back on course with 'our boy' and the

269

reporters and Rustique before Thad or Mungo had someone's eye out.

Maeve wobbled her way across the room. Faith followed, carefully negotiating an obstacle course of spindly-legged tables and fat-cushioned stools. The photographs, all in ornate golden frames, showed a rather athletically handsome young man with his arm round a top-heavy blonde with corkscrew curls, and a boy and a girl of about Lilac and Thad's age.

'Super, aren't they? That's our boy, Kieran, and Fenella, our daughter-in-law. Lovely girl. Real class. Was top of the *Sun*'s Page Three list for years. Our boy spent a fortune on the breast implants. He's got her down for her lips next. Halogen implants. And there's our little Edward and Jennifer . . .'

Edward? Jennifer? Huh! Faith thought. She wouldn't be telling Stan . . . She peered at the photographs. 'Our boy, Kieran' looked vaguely familiar. Wasn't he a pop singer?

'The kiddies are really looking forward to Christmas. Dead excited.' Maeve beamed. 'Just like yours, I suppose?'

Faith, still trying to work out why Kieran Squires looked so familiar, nodded.

Maeve was unstoppable. 'Me an' Dec have spent a fortune on the kiddies this year, but then you can't disappoint them, can you? The little 'uns?'

Faith shook her head.

'They wants these things what's on the telly and you just have to get them, don't you? They'd give you hell on Christmas morning elsewise. Opening their presents and not having what all the other kiddies have got. They'd never be able to hold their heads up at school, love 'em.'

270

Faith nodded again. She wondered if venturing the opinion that children should be given only what their parents could afford, and enquiring whether Edward and Jennifer were even aware of the true meaning of Christmas, may be a little rash. What the hell—

'Funny to think how it all started. I mean, I don't suppose baby Jesus was thrilled to ribbons with what he got, do you?'

'Bugger me, no,' Maeve said with feeling. 'Not if the poor little bleeder had been waiting for Buzz Lightyear or a Teletubby or one of them Furbies.'

Faith bit her lips. 'Er—you were saying about the—um—reporters and the restaurant . . .'

'Ah, so I was. None of them reporters wanted to talk to us at the restaurant, you know. They all wanted to talk to the boy. With him playing in the Premiership and all. They all got the notion that he was playing away from home, the bastards. Said he'd been spotted in nightclubs with someone else!'

'Shocking!' Faith whispered. 'How awful . . .'

'As if he would!' Maeve was bristling now. 'With his lovely little family at home—and with a wife like Fenella, too. I mean any man would give his right arm to be married to Fenella, now wouldn't they?'

'They would,' Faith nodded vigorously, pennies dropping like cents in a Las Vegas fruit machine. Billie had been one of the so-called scumbag reporters! Billie had discovered the identity of 'our boy's' extra-marital amour! Someone high up in the footballing hierarchy had put the frighteners on her! That's why she'd skedaddled off to the anonymity of London and ended up in Amberley Hill! Bingo!

Faith held out her hand. 'Well, I won't keep you.

Thank you so much for your hospitality. You must call in and have a cuppa with us next time you're back in Devon . . . Is it this way to the garden?'

She headed for the back door to collect the children. She wasn't looking forward to the journey home one bit—and she still had to endure the horrors of McDonald's—but at least she'd found out want she wanted to know. One more port of call and the mystery would be completely unravelled.

The Squireses' kitchen, which was a rather strange mixture of distressed lime, stainless steel, and Shaker, opened out on to yet another chequerboard area. Green and yellow this time. Faith wondered if they did paving slabs on QVC.

She looked over her shoulder at Maeve. 'Your son . . . Kieran—he plays for one of the northern clubs, doesn't he? Manchester United? Liverpool? Someone big like that?'

'No.' Maeve shook her head, trying to look modest and failing. 'He started his playing career with Chelsea—did ever so well. He stayed at Stamford Bridge until his transfer three years ago. You may have read about it—it was a record signing fee at the time. We were that proud of him. He and Fenella and the kiddies still live in Chelsea Harbour, it being so handy for Putney . . .'

Putney, of course. Faith nodded. She knew enough about football, because of Jon and Alex and Ben and Tom, to be aware that Putney were London's latest Premier League glamour club. She wondered how Stan would feel about going to a football match . . . Maybe she ought to go on her own . . . Maybe she ought to—She paused in dismay on the edge of the bilious patio.

'Delphi! Thad! You let Mr Squires and his dear

little dog out of the greenhouse this instant or Granno won't be buying you a burger!'

*   *   *

'Do you know,' Faith murmured sleepily against Stan's back, 'I really enjoyed today. Getting out and about.'

'Hrmmph . . .'

'So, I thought,' she snuggled more cosily into the feather mattress, 'that I might do it again.'

'Hmmm . . . Pharph . . .'

'Only next time,' she slid her arm across the comfort of Stan's ample waist, 'it would be without the children, of course.'

'Aahh . . . Hargh . . . Hmmm . . .'

'And next time I thought I might be really adventurous and go to London. What do you reckon?'

'Harph . . . Phrupp . . . Hmmm.'

'Oh, good.' Smiling, Faith reached over and switched off the bedside lamp. 'I'm so pleased that you agree . . .'

chapter twenty-two

Two weeks before Christmas, hurtling round the Spicer Centre's shops, Jonah didn't see the grey skies, or the pinched whey faces of the frantic shoppers. He didn't even feel the biting wind, or hear Slade belting out 'Merry Christmas Everybody' from a succession of in-store Tannoys. Jonah was, as he had been for days, lost in a dream world of derring-do and gutsy bravado. Jonah was piloting the Stearman through summer skies of improbable blue, while some shadowy figure performed death-defying acrobatics on the upper wing.

The figure had to remain shadowy, he realised as he grabbed a handful of CDs for his sisters' children in the Virgin Megastore, because Billie had refused his wingwalking offer point-blank. Not that he'd been surprised that she'd said no, but the ferocity of her refusal had really stunned him. He'd had no idea that she'd find the concept so terrifying. During the last few months he'd thought he'd got to know Billie pretty well, and he cherished their friendship. He certainly wouldn't want to alienate her by being insensitive to her fears.

Her physical fragility always seemed at odds with her fierce determination, and he admired her hugely for taking on the warehouse and making a go of it. Also, knowing how frightened she was of flying, he'd admired her even more for her enjoyment of the impromptu trip in the Stearman. After all that, he'd honestly thought that she'd be up for a simple bit of barnstorming.

He shrugged and battled his way to the checkout queue. Silly really, he should have realised that one short trip in a biplane wasn't going to cure Billie of her phobia overnight. He supposed that would be as unlikely as someone dangling a toy spider in front of his face and then expecting him to welcome a houseful of tarantulas with open arms. He shuddered at the thought.

'Ta.' The assistant whipped away the CDs and his credit card, went through the motions, and handed him his carrier bag. 'Happy Christmas.'

'Uh? Oh, yes—thanks . . . You too . . .'

Jonah fixed what he hoped was a festive grin and headed for Woolworths.

Christmas, without Claire, had ceased to have much meaning. And Estelle, because of the casualness of their relationship, always took off to Austria on Christmas Eve and returned in the New Year. Skiing, she said, with the girls she'd known since college. A rare treat for a crowd of single women who lived and worked in the mind-boggling, and male-dominated world, of engineering. Ten days of sheer enjoyment with no men, no sex, no problems.

So, again, he'd be alone. A solitary Christmas was probably one of the most miserable times of the year. But this year, Jonah thought, once he'd bought the last of the presents to be sent home to his Isle of Wight family, Christmas Day would merely be a bit of a hiccup in his plans. Christmas Day, spent with several drinks, a seasonal meal of beans on toast and some very dumbed-down television, would simply be a time to stop and take stock ready for next year. Next year, once the festive season was over, he could start bringing his future into the present.

He finally elbowed his way out of Woolworths and stood beside the fibre-optic fountain, buffeted by people, ticking off his mental shopping list. It seemed intact. A child with a runny nose suddenly appeared alongside and sang two lines of 'O Come All Ye Faithful' at him in a threatening manner.

'Bugger off.'

'That ain't festive.' The child gave a powerful sniff. 'You're supposed to give me money.'

'And you're supposed to sing the whole thing,

275

outside my front door, with a lantern, then wish me Merry Christmas.'

'Do what?' The sniffing was halted.

'It's traditional,' Jonah sighed. 'And then I give you a mince pie and—'

'I don't want a frigging mince pie!' The child looked askance. 'I want money.'

'So do I,' Jonah said cheerfully, moving away. 'Happy Christmas!'

'Tight bastard,' the child spat venomously, before turning his choral mugging to another unwary passer-by.

Jonah, still grinning, hurried towards the multistorey, his head once more in the clouds.

The second Shorts and the Skyvan could be purchased towards the autumn, and then the Sullivanair expansion could begin. In the meantime, with Barnaby's help and the Slingsby repairs underway, he could be up and running as an instructor by the summer, and now—with this amazing plan for the Stearman—when he could find a wingwalker, of course . . .

He stopped and glanced at his watch. Shit. He was late. He had a scheduled flight at five o'clock, and he still had to drive back to his flat, wrap the presents, and get them to the post office in Whiteacres. Today was the final day for posting parcels. As always, he'd left everything until the last minute.

He looked down at the collection of bulging carrier bags. He had wrapping paper, robin and holly Sellotape, and some appalling gift tags— the last on the shelves—of snowmen with squinty lascivious eyes. If the post office in Amberley Hill sold industrial-sized sheets of brown paper he supposed he could bundle everything up into one parcel, address it to his older sister, and let her play Santa's elves or whatever it was his nephews and nieces believed in. Smiling at the brilliant simplicity of his scheme, he thrust his way through the mittens and bootees of the Evergreen Lunch Club who were trying to get into Mulligan's, and headed for the post office.

Wrapping twenty presents on a shelf which was six inches wide and varnished to death was, Jonah discovered, even more difficult than executing a tail slide. Eventually he managed it, and triumphantly tottered off to join the queue. Sadly, the queue snaked three times round the barriers and out of the door. Jesus! He'd never be back at Whiteacres in time for the flight to East Midlands Airport.

'Excuse me . . .' He tapped the black PVC shoulder of the woman in front of him. 'I know this is a bit of a cheek, but I wondered—'

She swung round and looked at him, her face turning almost as pink as the candyfloss plaits clipped on top of her head. 'What? Oh—er—hi . . .'

'Um—hi . . .' Jonah frowned. Did he know her? No, he was sure he'd never seen her before. She looked like a Madonna, long-faced and soulful, and the pink plaits were strangely out of place with that sort of mournful beauty. 'Yeah—um—sorry, but I'm really pressed for time and I wondered if I gave you my parcel and twenty pounds—um—whether you'd post it for me, please?'

'What?' The large eyes widened, then she smiled, the smile softening the angular features. 'No sweat, doll. I'd be pleased to. Oh, but what about the change? It won't cost twenty quid. Where shall I send the change to?'

'Don't bother—no, really. I'm just so grateful.' Jonah paused. He seemed to have said something wrong. The smile had disappeared. 'Put it in your favourite charity box—or have a drink on me. Whatever. And thanks again. You're a life-saver . . .'

As he elbowed through the queue, he turned to smile his thanks again. The Madonna in the pink plaits was staring at him, still unsmiling, cuddling his poorly wrapped parcel against her like a child.

*　　　*　　　*

He'd filed his flight plan with the air-traffic controllers beneath a festoon of multicoloured streamers and hopeful mistletoe, and belted across the tarmac to the taxiway just as it was getting dark. He and Vinny had done the cockpit checks, exchanged the expected banter with Kev on the ground, and were teasing Pam unmercifully about today's passengers.

'Elvis impersonators—they should be all about the right age for you.' Vinny sat back in his seat. 'Mind you, the real one was dead before I was even born.'

'Oh, me too.' Jonah winked at Pam. 'I don't remember anything before the Rubettes.'

Vinny raised his eyebrows. 'Who? God, I didn't realise you were that old—even Duran Duran were before my time.'

Pam cuffed them both cheerfully round the ear. 'And none of them could hold a candle to Elvis—so there. And don't knock it. A whole planeload of beefy men in leather jackets will set me up for Christmas just nicely.'

Vinny and Jonah groaned in unison. 'Don't use the C word!'

'Oops, sorry.' Pam looked anything but contrite. 'I keep forgetting that some of us sad buggers will not be rushing into the bosom of our families for seasonal cheer. Now, are we ready for loading?'

They were. Jonah stood up, set his cap to the right angle, dusted off the navy and gold jacket, and walked into the cosily lit cabin. It was very hard to keep a straight face.

Three balding, pudgy middle-aged men were sitting in the back row, all struggling to cover their off-white flesh with dazzling rhinestone catsuits.

'Not taking off yet, are we, Captain?' One of them looked up at Jonah. 'Only me an' Ron are having a bit of trouble.'

Trouble? With what? Jonah was pretty sure he didn't want to know in case it involved lending a hand to shove a lot of corpulent male body into Lycra. He smiled in what he hoped was an authoritative manner. 'No, not yet. You've got plenty of time to get—er—ready.'

'Great.' Ron, presumably, beamed back. 'Can't do nothing with the glue you see, not at speed.'

Jesus. Jonah stared straight ahead. OK, so they were partially naked. And glue sniffing. So what? They'd paid well for Sullivanair's hospitality. They'd have to be fully dressed again by the time he disgorged them at East Midlands, wouldn't they? And anyway, where the hell were the rest of the party? Twenty-eight there were supposed to be. Could there possibly be twenty-five would-be Presleys lost in a time warp between the departure lounge and the Shorts? God—but the smell of glue was becoming increasingly strong. He'd be flying

279

himself before long.

'About twenty minutes to take off, gentlemen. And I really must advise against the adhesive. It could cause an explosion.' Well, he thought, it might. All solvents were risky. The Elvises looked suitably chastened anyway. He tried to soften the blow. 'Are the rest of your party—um—getting changed in the airport building or something?'

They nodded, obediently screwing the tops back on their glue nozzles. 'Weren't room for all of us in the Gents, see. And some people can get a bit—well—sniffy about this sort of thing.'

Jonah could well imagine. He leaned on the front seat, trying not to look at Pam, who was organising the drinks and peanuts in the tiny galley. Her shoulders were shaking. It would be fatal for Sullivanair if they caught each other's eye and fell about screaming with laughter. Jonah concentrated instead on the silver, green and purple interior. With the December darkness rushing in from outside, and all the overseat lights on, the inside of the Shorts looked welcoming and snug. It was a pity, he thought, that he couldn't spend Christmas in here. It certainly felt more homely than his flat.

Jonah risked looking again at his three struggling passengers, wondering if he should nip across to the departures lounge and round up the rest of the party. God Almighty! He blinked, realising now what the glue had been for. Two of the three balding pates had been covered with luxuriant black glossy wigs. The third was still busily gluing slinky jet sideburns on to his sagging cheeks. Mercifully the greying chests had been covered. To a man, his passengers were now sealed into their skin-tight white satin jump suits. The rhinestone dazzle nearly blinded him. He bit his lip and stared at the floor. Please God, he prayed, don't let Vinny come through now.

Ron gave an ear-splitting shriek. 'Oh, bugger! Me bloody sideboard's got stuck to me plectrum. Give us a hand, Nev.'

There was a communal back seat chuckle as Nev got to grips with the sideburns, the plectrum and the recalcitrant wig. Fascinated, Jonah watched as the unfortunate Ron was niftily turned into a third corpulent Elvis Presley.

'That's got it!' the fattest Elvis yelled merrily through a rigidly curled lip. 'I reckon we're all ready to rock'n'roll!'

'Ah,' Nev agreed, holding on to his sideburns. 'Just get the other boys on board and we'll be off for the biggest Presley night of the year. Derby here we come!'

Jonah coughed, remembering that if he gave them a good trip they may well book again and hasten the expansion of Sullivanair. 'I hope you have a good time and enjoy yourselves. Oh—and is this the rest of your party just coming across the tarmac?'

The three rhinestone cowboys turned to the tiny windows, peered into the darkness, and then whooped with glee. White satin flares flapped against chubby calves, and three heads of black oil slick nodded in ecstatic welcome. It was faintly bizarre, Jonah thought, to watch Elvis in all his stages clamber up the steps and storm down the aisle towards him. Pam, her greeting smile firmly in place, looked equally stunned as she was passed by several more white jump suits, a plethora of sprayed-on jeans and gingham shirts from the hee-haw era, three leather jackets with the collars turned up a la *Jailhouse Rock*, and a Julian Clary clone in full GI regalia.

'Clint . . .' Ron followed Jonah's startled eyes. 'Does the uniform a treat, doesn't he?'

He did, Jonah had to admit. It was a pity about the lilac eyeshadow.

Still not looking at Pam, he made his swift speech of greeting and returned to the cockpit.

'Fire her up,' he said tersely to Vinny. 'I think Pam's got more than she bargained for back there . . .'

*   *   *

They were cruising through the darkness somewhere above Oxfordshire, the dashboard lights like hundreds of multicoloured stars, and with Pam lustily joining in 'The Girl of My Best Friend' from the cabin behind them, when Jonah told Vinny about the plans for the Stearman.

'Wingwalking?' Vinny nearly spilled his coffee. 'Christ! Count me in!'

'As a wingwalker? Wouldn't have thought it was your style.'

'As a pilot!' Vinny inhaled expressively. 'Have you seen those birds that wingwalk professionally? The Utterly Butterly Barnstormers? My God—they're sensational! And so beautiful! What I wouldn't give to be the pilot in their Stearman . . .'

Jonah chuckled and checked the radio. He'd seen the Utterly Butterlys, too. He'd also been frantically jealous. 'I'm not aiming for that—at least, not yet. They're world class . . . but eventually, who knows? No, what I thought was just one plane and one wingwalker to start with—and maybe put on some sort of display at Whiteacres in the summer.'

Always supposing Claire and Aerobatic Archie hadn't bought it up by then, of course.

'What? A show? Like Biggin Hill?'

Jonah shook his head as they banked onto the East Midlands flight path. 'No—more like an air pageant. The sort of thing they did between the wars. I'll have to give it some thought over Christmas and come up with a game plan for the Whiteacres Aviation Incs.'

Vinny scratched his head. 'And who's going to be your aerobabe, then? Estelle?'

'She's too tall.' Jonah smiled in the darkness. 'No, I'm going to get Billie Pascoe to do it.'

'Billie from the warehouse?' Vinny whistled just as the songsters in the cabin started on Heartbreak Hotel. 'You lucky bastard! Can you imagine her wearing a bodysuit?'

Strangely, Jonah thought, as he picked up his headset, he could. The image was surprisingly disturbing. He twiddled with a few knobs and concentrated on the headings.

Vinny lobbed his coffee cup over his shoulder. 'Has she said yes, then? Billie Pascoe?'

'Not yet, no.' Jonah stared ahead into the black sky. 'But I know she will.'

chapter twenty-three

Christmas Eve in Amberley Hill. Granite skies and a chill wind, but no sign of snow. Tiny tots with their eyes all aglow seemed in pretty short supply too. Instead, brazen lights looped the Spicer Centre, and Woolworths was surreptitiously doing a window display for Valentine cards. Last-minute shoppers prepared to take a gamble were hovering around Waitrose, waiting for the turkey reductions.

Billie wriggled round in one of Follicles and Cuticles' lilac bucket seats and stopped staring out of the window. Everyone looked so miserable. Why did people find Christmas so bloody depressing? She felt a little glimmer of excitement snake into her stomach. This year, she was going home to be spoiled and pampered and teased. For the first time since she'd left Devon for London, she'd have a proper Christmas, and infantile or not, she was really looking forward to it.

Last Christmas she'd spent at the flat with Miranda and her then current man and about forty of her closest family. They'd all got roaring drunk and talked about dead people and played incomprehensible board games and Billie hadn't slept for two days. The Christmas before that had been even worse, of course. She'd been with Kieran Squires.

Well, she'd had enough of purdah. It was definitely the right time of the year to shake off the past and stride forward into . . . Billie sucked in her breath. Into what, exactly? Come New Year's Eve, what would she be promising herself? A new everything. She grinned to herself, then stopped as several ladies in tight rollers sitting beneath the dryers opposite peered at her in suspicion.

She turned the grin into a grimace and scratched her neck. The unfamiliar false nails raked at the skin and made her wince. Tendrils of damp hair were poking out irritatingly from beneath a violet towel. It was, of course, very kind of Miranda to give her a special makeover as a Christmas present on one of the busiest days of the year, but Billie felt that she'd rather have had a diary and a pair of gloves. Miranda's specials were notoriously risky.

'You'll look stunning, doll. Trust me.' Miranda, in her usual gothic black with newly dyed scarlet plaits, drifted past on her way to rescue a perm. 'I just wish you'd let us have a go at a colour rinse as well. Blondes are pretty passé this year. It's all drop-dead red. Reuben absolutely adores my plum and bilberry.' She gave an impatient sigh. 'Yes, all right Mrs Burgess. I heard you. No, the smell of burning isn't you. Yes, I'm just coming . . .'

Billie squirmed a bit more. She'd already had not only the nail extensions, but also a facial, and her legs waxed. Eyelash dyeing and eyebrow shaping were yet to come, but first Kitty, Miranda's ace assistant, was going to do a cut and restyle on Billie's rather tousled hair. It was all very girlie and rather intimidating. Not to mention wildly outlandish for a Christmas to be spent on a smallholding just north of Dartmoor.

Still, it all helped to lighten her mood. Reuben's visit to her warehouse, as well as Jonah's ludicrous suggestion that she should wingwalk, and the fact that Whiteacres would be under new ownership in a month's time, were things she definitely didn't want to think about until after Christmas.

Fortunately, Miranda hadn't mentioned Reuben too much recently. She had been far too downcast by the fact that she now *knew*, as a result of the post office encounter, that Joseph the Dreamboat was a married man. Miranda had apparently been shocked to her root-ends when he'd tapped her on the shoulder, turning round, recognising him, and thinking that Christmas had come early.

She and Billie had had a long fuzzy conversation into the small hours, nursing wine glasses and watching Granada Men and Motors, speculating on why Mr Drop-Dead Gorgeous should have been sending his Christmas presents home. Miranda had said, hopefully, that it may mean he was separated, because otherwise he'd simply have put them in the boot of his car when he drove home for the festivities, surely? Billie had leaned across the sofa and refilled the glasses and giggled at Miranda's optimism, pointing out that real life wasn't like a Steve Martin film where the hero arrives home on Christmas Eve to a chocolate box family waiting in an evergreen-clad hallway, his arms laden with presents all gift wrapped and bow-tied by Bloomingdale's.

Miranda had snorted and thrown a cushion at her head.

Emerging, and mopping up the worst of the Shiraz spillage, Billie continued by saying that it definitely reinforced her notion that Joseph was a fishing tackle rep, and that once he'd got flies and floats and maggot boxes from floor to ceiling there simply wouldn't be room in his Vauxhall Vectra for anything further, and that he probably wouldn't want the kiddies' gifts reeking of dried plaice anyway, would he?

Miranda had got quite sniffy and pointed out that plaice was a sea fish, and if Joseph was selling fishing tackle he'd hardly be carrying fish, would he? Billie, who had far too much Shiraz by this time, said the plaice were probably examples of what his tackle could hook and then the whole thing had got rather rude.

Still, Miranda had sighed as they'd staggered towards the bedrooms, at least she knew what his name was—the parcel had been addressed to Mrs Bellamy. Joseph Bellamy, they had both decided, sounded very *Upstairs Downstairs*, then they'd parted in the hall and Billie had remembered too late to ask where the parcel had been addressed to. Hopefully, she'd thought, pulling on her Piglet nightie, it was the Outer Hebrides: any closer and Miranda would be spending Christmas camped on his doorstep.

So, that was the end of Joseph the Gorgeous—which, sadly, only left Reuben in the frame. Billie thought she was probably even more disappointed than Miranda.

'Sorry to have kept you.' Kitty trotted up briskly and whisked off the towel. 'Changing the colour, are we?'

Billie shook her head vehemently. 'Just a trim.'

Kitty looked puzzled. 'You sure? I mean if you're going clubbing tonight, you'll want to stand out in the crowd, if you get my drift. You know what it's like on a party night. The competition is shit-hot.'

'I'm not going clubbing. I'm going home to my parents.'

'Bloody hell,' Kitty was stricken. 'How awful. You poor thing. And at Christmas too. You'll miss all the fun. All those men out on the pull. It's the best night of the year.'

'I know. So Miranda keeps telling me. I'll just have to live with it. Look, Kitty, if you're really busy it doesn't matter about cutting my hair at all. I like it as it is.'

'Do you? Crikey.' Kitty's forehead puckered. 'It's a bit outmoded, if you don't mind me saying so. Like, layered and spiky and that. Very boyish. We're all going geometric and glam this year. Still,' she shoved Billie's arms through a lavender coverall, 'you've always been a bit staid, haven't you? You didn't like last year's Ulrika flicks at all.'

Billie hadn't. They'd made her look like Mr Pickwick. But staid? Sodding hell.

'Go for it, then Kitty. Shave the lot off. Dye my scalp magenta. Tattoo heliotrope unicorns dancing on my skull. Pierce my cranium with garnet studs. Leave no trend untried.'

'Randa!' Kitty yelled across the salon. 'When you've got a mo! I think we've got a problem . . .'

Just over an hour later, Billie peered into the vaudeville mirror. She peered back at herself through swathes of tinsel and three phallic balloons. Kitty had drawn a line at the shaving and dyeing and tattooing and piercing, but the layers were now smooth, and the spiky fringe was a one-sided blonde sweep across very black brows and lashes. The nail extensions were silver, and Miranda had liberally dusted her cheekbones with glitter. Even with her jeans and bulky fleece and Timberland boots it looked pretty stunning.

'There, doll.' Miranda surveyed her handiwork with pride. 'Knock 'em dead on Widdecombe Moor, or what?'

'It's great. Really great, thanks. You've made me look female.'

'Not an easy task—not even for someone with my talents.' Miranda looked at her through the mirror. 'You OK?'

Billie nodded carefully, not wanting to mess up the hairdo. 'Fine. Just tired. I'm really looking forward to going home . . . but will you be all right? On your own?'

'On my own? At Christmas? With the size of my family? You've got to be joking!'

'I didn't actually mean—'

Miranda's eyes narrowed. 'Oh, right. You mean will I be snogging in Christmas under the mistletoe with Reuben? To be honest, doll, I haven't got a clue. But I very much doubt it. 'She sighed. 'I shouldn't think there was any danger of the flat becoming contaminated in your absence. It'll probably remain a Wainwright-free zone. Happy?'

Billie winced. 'Look, you know I don't mean to put a damper on your love life—'

Miranda exhaled heavily. 'Jesus. This is supposed to be the season of goodwill. Will you please, just for once, lay off the bloke?'

Billie unfastened the coverall. 'Okay—but he really isn't—'

'I'm a grown-up and I'll form my own conclusions!' Miranda snapped angrily. 'For God's sake, Billie, let it drop. You're going away for a week—and what I do in my flat in my time is my affair! OK?'

'OK . . .' Billie said quietly. 'But don't say you weren't warned . . .'

*   *   *

289

It had been, Billie thought, hardly the best way to part company. Miranda had clung on to the Follicles and Cuticles desk and waved away Billie's offer to pay for the makeover, wished her a very *sotto voce* happy Christmas, and swept away, her plaits jiggling angrily, to sort out a festive henna tattoo. Billie, feeling awful, had returned to the flat, loaded the Nova with her luggage and presents, and headed for the Amberley Hill bypass.

Two miles along nice open roads packed with normal motorists and she began to feel a bit better. Happy families. Broad daylight. Steel-grey skies. Cold wind. No rain. Several cars had late-purchase fir trees strapped to their roof racks. Miranda, Billie knew, would soon regain her sense of humour, and she'd ring her in the morning to wish her a Happy Christmas and apologise. It was always easier over the phone.

Slowing behind a queue of happy last-minute shoppers all returning from the Whiteacre Retail Village, she'd reduced the car's speed from sixty to forty in thirty seconds. The trail of lorries following her immediately let rip with a trumpet voluntary of air horns. She ignored them, and indicated to leave on the airport slip road. She needed to check that the warehouse was secure before she left.

Sad fairy lights twinkled in garish profusion round the entrance to the trading estate and a car radio was trilling 'Away in a Manger'. Everything was normal. The airport was again ringed by floodlights. Billie tried not to look. Why didn't the damn traffic get a move on? She switched on her own radio. Wizzard were wishing it could be Christmas every day. She switched it off again and

290

bumped the Nova across the speedhumps.

The other sheds were all securely locked. Fred 'n' Dick and Guspers had been closed all week, deciding that replacement windows and corporate videos were possibly not going to be at the top of anyone's Christmas list. Zia and Isla had high-tailed off to their parents' mock Tudors in Surrey's stockbroker belt, and Sylvia, after prolonged and angry discussions with Douglas, had vetoed returning home and had booked herself into a health farm until after the New Year.

It was all very cold and bleak and deserted. The grey of the units melted into the pewter sky, and the wind rattling through the airstrip's frost-bleached grass gave a mournful whippoorwill wail. Parking the Nova beside the shells of the burned-out hatchbacks which Sylvia had draped with holly and ivy in case they felt left out, Billie turned the key in the door of her unit.

It was already unlocked and she catapulted in across the floor.

'Christ!' Jonah's voice echoed from somewhere above her. 'You made me jump! I thought it was a burglar!'

Billie, dusting down her knees, stared up at him. 'And you scared me half to death, too. I didn't see your car. What the hell are you doing?'

'I walked over from the airport and I'm fixing the rig.' Jonah leaped down from the Stearman's wing, brushing grime from his faded Levis and rugby shirt. 'And you're just in time.'

'For what?' Billie blinked. 'And why are you here, anyway? Aren't you going anywhere for Christmas?'

'Just my flat. I've got charter flights booked all

291

next week.' Jonah pushed his hair from his eyes. 'You look nice . . .'

Billie, who'd completely forgotten the makeover, shrugged off the compliment. 'Oh—cheers—I suppose it makes a change from the bag-lady look.'

'Well, yeah—but I actually quite liked it. It seems funny, seeing you look sort of—um—well . . .'

'Sort of what?'

'Partyish, I suppose. I really like the sparkly face.' Jonah grinned. 'Is this what you look like when you go out?'

'God, no! When I go out I even wear lipstick with my dungarees.'

'Smart move,' Jonah nodded. 'You're not dashing off anywhere just yet, are you?'

'Devon. Home. For Christmas.' Billie stared suspiciously at the rig which was now bolted to the Stearman's upper wing and looking more sinister than ever. 'Why?'

'Because I need someone to test whether I've fitted this properly.'

'Ask Estelle. Or Barnaby.'

'Estelle's in Austria and Barnaby's in the stately home. It won't take a minute. All you need to do is sit in the plane, like you did before. We're not going anywhere.'

Billie sighed. 'And if I agree? You promise we won't move? And it doesn't mean I've changed my mind about the wingwalking thing, because I haven't and I never will, OK?'

'OK. Scouts' honour. You have the word of a founder member of the Ventnor Sparrowhawks that I will not let you fall, start up the plane, or expect this to be the beginning of anything that you don't want it to be.'

'Oh, well, in that case how can I refuse?' Billie hauled herself on to the Stearman's wing, praying that the nail extensions would stand the strain.

'Brilliant.' Jonah leaned into the cockpit. 'Now fasten all the straps on your harness. Like you did before—when we flew.'

'Why?' Billie fumbled with the meshed nylon webbing that stretched over her shoulders and between her legs and clipped together at the waist. 'We're only sitting in the shed—you said so. I promise I won't fall out.'

'I just want to see how easy it is for you—er—I mean someone—to get from the cockpit on to the wing and then fasten yourself—um—themselves in the harness on the rig. Don't argue with me. This is an experiment and you're the guinea pig and guinea pigs don't have a say—'

'I think you'll find they do, now, actually.' Billie tightened the straps. 'I think people like the BUAV have made it compulsory—and about time, too. Anyway—'

'Billie, shut up. And that's great—you've really got to grips with the straps. Now undo them again and pull yourself up using those handholds on the wing above you.'

'Uh?' Billie paused in unbuckling and stared upwards. The wing was about five feet above her head. 'I can't reach that!'

'Course you can.' Jonah leaned a bit closer. 'Look—stand on the seat, reach and grab . . .'

Billie did. It made every muscle shriek. It felt as though her arms were being pulled from their sockets as she stood on tiptoe on the edge of the seat. 'Now what then?' she panted. 'When do you bring me the thing to stand on so that I can get into the rig-thing?'

Jonah laughed. 'Still word perfect in the technical jargon, I hear.'

She wanted to slap him but didn't dare let go. She was also pretty sure he was getting an excellent view of her midriff as the jeans and fleece had long since parted company.

'I feel like I'm on the rack! Jonah! God—you don't mean I have to pull myself up there? You do, don't you? God—I hate you!'

Taking a deep breath she pulled and heaved and swung her legs upwards at the same time. After a lot of scrabbling, she was kneeling on the Stearman's wing. Outstretching her arms to gain equilibrium, she tentatively stood upright. It was probably the most inelegant manoeuvre ever attempted in a confined space. It was also totally disorientating. Billie swayed alarmingly, still trying to keep her balance.

'Edge towards the rig, and watch where you tread.' Jonah's voice carried up to her. 'You're doing great, Billie. Just great. Take it slowly. I'll catch you if you fall.'

Ever mindful of not putting her Timberlands anywhere near the linen-clad part of the wings, and remembering only to step on the ribs, she wobbled unsteadily towards the rig. While it had looked like an instrument of torture on the ground, it now looked wonderful and secure, bolted as it was foursquare and welcoming in the centre of the Stearman's upper wing.

'Bingo!' She reached it, and grabbed at it and hung on for dear life. If Jonah hadn't been lurking twenty feet beneath her she'd have probably kissed it. 'OK, then—I've reached it. Can I get down now, please?'

Jonah had walked to the nose end of the plane. Looking down, she could just see his head on a level with the propeller. He was grinning from ear to ear. 'You have got no idea how good this looks . . . Oh, what? No, not yet—if you don't mind. You're still OK? Not giddy or anything? Right— there's a harness on the rig. Just fasten it like you did the cockpit one—so that you're actually standing on the wing. There's a little seat bit and—'

'OK, OK,' Billie muttered, her fingers all thumbs as she fastened the straps. Bugger. Two of the nail extensions flew off into the gloomy recesses of the shed. This obviously wasn't a game for people with talons. Probably, she thought, easing herself into the rig, one of the reasons why Estelle couldn't have done this. She allowed herself a smug smile. It was really nice to know that there was something the perfect Estelle Rainbow couldn't achieve.

'Oh, wow!' She straightened up, leaning back against the framework. She'd done it! She was standing upright, steadily, on top of the Stearman. The view, however, was far from breathtaking. The steel girders of her shed crisscrossed away into cobwebby darkness. The wind rattled icily through the breeze blocks, and the unit's strange smell of decay had settled at this higher level with a vengeance.

'How does it feel?' Jonah craned his neck. 'Secure? Comfy?'

'Fine,' Billie said, wriggling a bit. 'Really safe, actually and—oh, bugger-shit!' The tiny ledge seat suddenly swivelled away from her, tossing her sideways. She grabbed frantically for the harness and pulled herself upright. 'Jesus, Jonah! What the

295

hell was that?'

'Oh, that's meant to happen. Although preferably when you want it to. The rig pivots. It's for the acrobatic displays.'

Billie, whose heart was still thundering, swallowed. 'What? What acrobatic displays?'

'You know—handstands, horizontal manoeuvres, dancing . . .'

'Get real!' She peered down. Jonah had disappeared beneath the wing and was no longer in sight. 'Hey you're not leaving me up here, are you? What happens if I suddenly need to go to the loo? Or come over all funny?'

'I'm not and you won't.'

And she didn't. Ten minutes later, Billie was actually enjoying herself. She'd practised waving to the nonexistent crowd, and had even been brave enough to try a little swivel of the rig. She'd also stood on one leg and pirouetted prettily. Piece of cake, this wingwalking. She was feeling pretty damned pleased with herself.

'Still all right?' Jonah shouted up. 'OK then— that's really wonderful. You're a complete star. You can get down now. Do you need any help?'

Billie, unbuckling herself, shook her head. Perversely, she didn't want Jonah to help her. She had to do it on her own. Holding on to the rig, casting a glance over her shoulder, she slithered from the harness, scrambled and slipped across the wing, and stepped backwards into the cockpit. She sat down with a thump. Her fleece was up round her ears and all the remaining nails had dropped off.

Jonah was grinning broadly. 'Incredible. Thanks so much. You're a natural.'

She shrugged. 'Piece of cake. Nothing to it. I could do it standing on my head as long as the plane was stationary and someone put a safety net under me. Actually, once I got over being petrified, I enjoyed it. It must be ace to do it for real.'

'Is that an offer?'

'No, it bloody isn't.' Billie stood up and hooked her leg over the side of the cockpit. 'Stardom has its limits and I think I've just reached mine. You'll have to advertise for a professional idiot in the flying mags or something if you're still determined to put on this show thing next summer.'

'Air pageant, and yes, I was thinking along the same lines.' Jonah sighed. 'Well, that's always depending on whether or not Claire and Antony Archibald are really going to take us over. I've got a meeting with the Whiteacres Aviation Incs in January. No doubt I'll know more then.'

Billie paused on the edge of the cockpit. 'Why don't you just ask Claire? You're still—er—friendly, aren't you?'

'Sort of, but asking Claire is one thing. Getting a straight answer is another.'

Billie pulled a face. She had had the same problem with Reuben. 'I know the feeling. Look, I'll ring Maynard and Pollock as soon as I get back from Devon and see what I can find out, but if I don't get a move on now I won't even get to Devon at all.'

She stepped onto the wing and jumped down, swaying a bit on the solid ground. Jonah reached out to steady her, then seemed to realise that she didn't need his help and backed away.

Billie headed for the door, then stopped and smiled at him. 'Well, it wasn't exactly what I'd planned to do on Christmas Eve, but I'm glad it helped.'

'It helped a lot. More than you'll ever know.'

'Oh, right . . . Good . . . Well, I'd better make tracks for Devon. Er—Happy Christmas . . .'

'You too. Thanks again and have a great time.' Jonah looked at her. 'See you next year, then?'

'What? Oh yes, of course.'

She thumped into the Nova, still feeling on top of the world, and switched on the radio. She held her breath, making a pact with the devil. If it was a carol or Chris Rea 'Driving Home for Christmas' or bloody Slade, then the New Year would bring only new horrors. If it was something unseasonal and inspirational then all her dreams would come true.

She thought she heard Jonah laughing from inside the warehouse. He might have been coughing. It was growing bitterly cold. She turned up the radio's volume. Oh, joy! The Young Rascals were Groovin' complete with birdsong and summer imagery. Yes! Billie punched the air in delight and found first gear. It was all going to be OK. This was going to be the best Christmas ever—she just knew it.

By the time she'd manoeuvred round all of Whiteacres' obstacles, and hit the southbound carriageway of the bypass the radio was offering 'Mistletoe and Wine'. Billie, still kite-high from her achievement, and positive that the future was going to be rosy, turned up the volume even further and sang along.

chapter twenty-four

Billie stared at her unpacked luggage, at the carrier bags full of Christmas presents from her family, and at the cool box which Faith had filled with good home cooking, and wanted to cry.

She felt desperately homesick. Miranda was out, there was nothing half decent on the television, and sleet was spitting despondently against the windows. The kitchen had disappeared under a week's worth of washing-up and the living room still bore unpleasant evidence of Miranda's New Year celebrations.

Billie had always felt a sense of anticlimax after Christmas, but this year it was a million times worse. She missed the bustle of the farmhouse and the warmth of her parents and the camaraderie of her brothers with painful intensity. She'd been back in Amberley Hill for less than an hour and she wanted to go home.

Billie had telephoned Miranda from Devon on Christmas morning, and apologised for being cross about Reuben, and said that falling out over someone as inconsequential as Slimeball Wainwright was sheer madness. Miranda had been a bit starchy to begin with, but had then giggled and said it didn't matter, and it was the season of goodwill—but as she hadn't found a good Will or a bad Will she'd have to make do with a wicked Reuben, wouldn't she? Billie had then been almost swamped by the tidal roar of Miranda's family in the background, and had strained her ears for Reuben's drawl but couldn't hear it, and had prayed that he was spending his usual solitary Christmas in his bedsit and wasn't sprawled on the flat's sofa regaling Miranda and her nearest and dearest with lurid tales of Billie and Kieran Squires.

Now, sitting on the bed, desperate to be anywhere other than back in the chaos of the flat, Billie clutched the phone and listened to the squawking voice in frustration.

'The offices of Maynard and Pollock will be closed for the holidays until January the third. If you wish to leave a message, please give your name and a contact telephone number and we will get back to you when the office reopens. Please speak slowly and clearly after the tone.'

She switched off the phone without leaving a message. Tomorrow was the third, and she'd ring them then. She'd go back to the warehouse in the morning and be brave and telephone to find out whether or not the shed had a future. On the drive back from Devon, the thought of sorting out the warehouse's ownership with Maynard and Pollock had kept her going. It was something to focus on for the future. Now the delay only made leaving home more poignant.

'Get a grip,' she told herself, deciding to do something positive by disgorging her mother's food parcel in the kitchen. This, at least, was easy. Both the fridge and the freezer were bare. 'You're just suffering from green grass syndrome. You'll feel better tomorrow.'

Tomorrow, she felt, may be a long time coming. It had been a wonderful Christmas. The farmhouse had been filled with her brothers and her sisters-in-law—and, surprise, surprise, Maria, the newest owner of the Mrs Pascoe mantle, was

300

already pregnant—and the children. Billie had enthused over the chubby gorgeousness of Otis and Sapphire, and played rumbustious games with Delphi, Thad, Mungo and Lilac, and had been very glad that they belonged to someone else. Christmas dinner had taken nearly all day, with the whole family informally lounging round the huge dining table, eating and drinking, talking and laughing.

Faith and Stan's New Year's Eve party had been a rerun of Ben and Maria's wedding do in the summer, and Billie had said the same things to the same people, had a lovely time, worn the Joseph dress, and made her New Year wishes out in the yard beneath a frosty sky.

She'd looked up into the twinkling distance, her teeth chattering, her arms wrapped tightly round herself, and extended her summer wish. Now, it wasn't just for the success of her own warehouse, but for Sylv and Zia and Isla and the others as well. She'd also added a wish for Jonah to wow the Aviation Incs and hang onto the aerodrome, for Claire and Aerobatic Archie to implode, for Miranda to fall in love with anyone other than Reuben, and for Reuben and Kieran Squires to do a Shergar.

Then, as the kitchen door had opened, and the rest of her family had poured outside to make their pledges, she'd added a hasty silent codicil. It was something she'd done in her nightly childhood prayers when she'd asked God to take care of everyone that she loved and liked—then suddenly realising at the age of ten that it might not cover all eventualities—she'd added, 'And everyone that likes or loves me that I don't know about.' It was the same sort of reasoning that led her to add, 'And

301

I wish that all the people involved with Whiteacres, now and in the future, will let us all stay and prosper.' And then she'd grinned at her parents, feeling guilty and rather selfish, as they made their New Year wishes for simple things like family health and happiness.

Stan and her brothers had been really interested and amazed at how well her warehouse was doing; she'd explained about how Estelle had helped her become more organised and how Sylvia had got the publicity started and how everyone helped each other. She'd shrugged off their questions about the takeover, saying that she honestly couldn't see it making any difference to the warehousers—not when they had five-year leases, and only uncrossed her fingers after she'd said it. They were all fascinated by the stories of Jonah and the Stearman—and shocked into silence when she told them about how she'd tested the Art Scholl rig.

No, she'd assured them, she certainly wasn't going to have a go at wingwalking—Jonah was advertising for a proper person—but it had been nice to be there at the right time to help him out. Oh, and definitely no, she wouldn't be taking any more joyrides in the Stearman—that had been a one-off, too.

Faith had asked a lot of strange questions—even more strange than usual. About gangsters and hitmen and people who put on both frighteners and squeezes and about Billie's all-round safety. Billie had reassured her that Whiteacres was certainly not in the middle of any gangland war and could only conclude that her mother had been reading the *Sun* again and watching too much late-night telly.

And now, she sighed as she unpeeled herself

302

from the bed and stumbled towards the bathroom, it was all over and she was back in Amberley Hill, and she still felt lonely and homesick.

*   *   *

She actually felt fractionally better after a bath and discovering half a bottle of Australian red in the cupboard and a rerun of *Friends* on Sky. Following this with a Stilton and chutney doorstep and a seventies sit com, life, if not immediately rosy, was at least gaining pinkish tinges.

It was nearly midnight when she heard the key turning in the lock.

'Happy New Year, doll!' Miranda crashed into the living room, wearing a leopardskin mini skirt and very little else. 'Why didn't you say you'd be home during opening hours? We've been in Mulligan's—you could have joined us!'

She enveloped Billie in a CK One and Malibu embrace just as Billie registered the 'us'. The man—joyfully not Reuben—lurking in the hall's twilight zone seemed to be dressed entirely in combat fatigues. Maybe they'd been to a fancy dress party? Somehow she doubted it.

Miranda straightened up. 'Did you have a good one, then? Who did you snog the New Year in with? Not dodgy Damon?'

'Damon—um—isn't around any more.' Billie did lightning calculations. Death or matrimony? She opted for the latter. 'He married someone from—oh—Venezuela—back in the summer—and—um—emigrated.'

'The bastard! You poor love! I know just what you're going through. You're talking to an expert here. Oh God—how do you feel?'

'Relieved,' Billie said with searing honesty. 'I'll just have to try and get over him . . . And I really would be happier if we never mentioned him again. So, how was your Christmas?'

'Up and down. You know. Hey, where are my manners? Say hello to Spike,' Miranda indicated the man who was now shuffling sheepishly in the doorway, 'while I go and raid the larder.' She beamed at Billie. 'Your mum has sent supplies, hasn't she?'

'The usual. She seems to think I haven't eaten properly for the last two years, so—'

'Mega!' Miranda had already disappeared into the kitchen. 'You two make friends, now.'

Spike hovered a bit more, and Billie reluctantly swung her legs to the floor and cleared empty crisp packets and wine bottles to make a space on the sofa. She warmed towards him. Spike had obviously ousted Reuben and survived not only Christmas but also New Year. This was pretty serious stuff. It almost constituted a steady relationship. There were little yelps of delight emanating from the kitchen as Miranda discovered Faith's delicacies.

Billie smiled and patted the seat beside her. 'Come and sit down. Make yourself at home— although you probably already have . . . that is— um—well, you know what Miranda's like! That is—'

Not saying anything, Spike sat down awkwardly on the other end of the sofa. He certainly wasn't up to Miranda's usual standards—and they were pretty low. He had very close-cropped red hair and no eyelashes. Billie wondered if Miranda may have experimented on him.

She tried again. 'Did you enjoy Christmas?

Miranda's parents are a scream, aren't they? And her Auntie Val can do a super Shirley Bassey when she's had a sherry. I bet Miranda didn't do the cooking, though. Was that why you were invited? Are you a bit of a closet Gary Rhodes?'

He shook his head. Christ, this was hard going. She changed tack and threw her arms wide to encompass the living room's debris. 'The New Year must have been a bit wild, too. Mine was very staid by comparison. I went home to Devon. Miranda might have mentioned it . . .'

'Nope.' He shook his head, his eyes now fixed firmly on the television screen. 'Is this a *Carry On*?'

'What? Oh, no. I think it's *On the Buses*. Do you like it?'

'Ah.'

Bloody hell. Spike must either be a demon in the kitchen or the bedroom or both. Miranda couldn't have hung on to him for his scintillating chat. Still, if he'd got rid of Reuben Billie thought she'd probably fall in love with him herself. She tried a few more general topics, like the weather and the holiday sporting results. Spike continued to stare at the television and say nothing. The boy was never going to go the full distance on *Brain of Britain*.

Shut up, Billie, she thought. Just shut up and let the missing link enjoy the programme in silence. Sadly, she wasn't listening to herself. 'So, work in the morning, is it? I hate the first day back, don't you?'

'Ah.'

Fortunately at that moment, Miranda staggered back into the room weighed down by a tray of goodies. She beamed at them both. 'Your mum is just so ace, doll! This is better than we had on

305

Christmas Day! I can't understand why you're not huge! Oh, are you two having a good chat?'

'No, but don't mind me!' Billie sprang up with feverish delight. 'I'm heading for bed anyway. I'm completely knackered. I mean if you and—er—Spike want to carry on watching the telly that's fine by me. Night, then, Randa . . . Spike . . .'

Miranda beamed in a maternal manner. 'We only met tonight, me and Spike. He's—'

'Staying? And we'll meet in the morning? Of course there'll be plenty of time to chat then. Night, all . . .'

Oh Jesus, Joseph and Mary, she thought, sprinting out of the room and slamming her bedroom door closed. No matter how desperate she got for a man, she couldn't—wouldn't—sink to those levels. What the hell was Miranda thinking of? Still, she reminded herself, Spike had replaced Reuben. One of the New Year wishes had come true. Only another three zillion to go . . .

She was just tugging on her new Winnie-the-Pooh pyjamas—this year's present from Alex and Katy—when Miranda opened the door.

'Can I have a quick word, doll?'

'Yeah, sure.' Billie fluffed at her hair. She hoped Miranda wasn't going to ask her the whereabouts of the nail extensions. She didn't want to think about Jonah or the Stearman. Not tonight. 'Was it really a nice Christmas?'

'All rightish, like I said. Actually, it got a bit shitty when I discovered my dad and Auntie Val in the kitchen doing things with pickled eggs on Boxing Day.'

Oh, bugger. 'Christ—what did you do?'

'Put them back in the jar and screwed the lid on

tight. Just remember not to touch the ones with lipstick stains on. Still, Mum didn't find out, so that's all right. And you're truly not too upset about Damon?'

Billie shook her head. She really didn't want to get drawn into yet another web of deceit. And Miranda surely couldn't want to exchange seasonal pleasantries now, could she? Still, maybe if the alternative was a night snuggling with Neanderthal man, maybe she could.

Miranda beamed. 'Good. Look, I just wanted to explain—'

'No need. Spike seems like fun, and you've never asked my permission about your sleepovers before . . .'

'What? Oh, yeah, but he isn't.'

'What isn't what?'

'Spike isn't a sleepover. I met him in Mulligan's tonight, like I said. He's new here. He's starting work in Amberley Hill tomorrow and I thought I'd introduce him to a few people and—'

'Oh, right . . . So, why's he in the living room?'

Miranda sat on the bed and twirled a plait. 'Because he can't move into his digs until tomorrow so he's having the sofa . . . He's starting work for Reuben as a taxi-driver in the morning.'

Billie closed her eyes. All the visions of Miranda in white, and Spike in a top hat and tails, and her wearing something lilac and flouncy and carrying orange blossom, slowly, sadly, faded. 'Does that mean that Reuben . . . ?'

'Is still on the books?' Miranda's tone was challenging. 'Yes. And he's stayed here all the time you were away. And he's staying tonight as soon as he's parked the car somewhere where it'll still have wheels in the morning.'

So much for New Year wishes, thought Billie. Things could only get better.

chapter twenty-five

Three weeks later, as the snow cascaded across the Spicer Centre outside, illuminated by the orange streetlamps, Reuben leaned across Follicles and Cuticles' desk and kissed Miranda. Miranda, in the middle of cashing up, grabbed the opportunity and kissed him back.

'Don't look so surprised.' Reuben straightened up, the businessman in him instinctively gathering the scattered notes and card receipts together on the desk top. He handed them to her. 'I said I'd see you after work.'

'Yeah, I know, but I wasn't expecting the—um—warm greeting.'

'Why not? We're a couple now, aren't we? Isn't that what couples are supposed to do?' Reuben looked genuinely puzzled. 'I know I'm out of practice, and all this has come as a bit of a shock, but—'

'No, no, it was lovely.' Miranda smiled encouragingly at him. She didn't want to offend him. She really liked him. 'Just—well—it still takes a bit of getting used to, doll, that's all.'

'And for me. I always thought you were a complete headcase.'

'And I thought you were the scum of the earth.'

'Made for each other, then,' Reuben said cheerfully. 'So? Are you ready?'

308

'Almost. Where are we going?' Miranda shoved the last few coins into the till. She hoped they were eating out. Having worked through the lunch hour, she was absolutely starving.

'The club. I want to show you the finished article. The painters cleared out half an hour ago, and I'm really chuffed with it.'

'Already? But it isn't opening for months yet, is it?'

'Not until the end of the football season, no. But the designers are the best in the business. I got them cheap because it's fairly slack during the winter. There's still tons to do—but it's really beginning to take shape now. Caught Offside will make Amberley Hill the talk of the clubbing world.'

Miranda smiled at his enthusiasm. He was so different these days. So open. She wished Billie could understand. 'Great—and then can we go and eat? On me.'

'Love to,' Reuben said, 'but I'm afraid I can't. I've got an evening session with the accountants. Would tomorrow do instead?'

Miranda's stomach rumbled. She'd have to defrost a lasagne. 'OK. Tomorrow will be fine, but you can pay for making me wait . . . Look—I'll be about another ten minutes here. You go on over to the club and I'll catch you up.'

The last customer of the day had buttoned herself into her coat only minutes before Reuben's arrival, given Miranda a five-pound tip, and disappeared into the thinning throng slipping and sliding in the Spicer Centre. Kitty, Debs and Pixie had left Follicles and Cuticles half an hour previously because the roads were treacherous, and there was just the usual last-minute sweeping up and straightening to be done.

Reuben glanced around the empty salon. 'OK. Don't be long, though. I can't wait for you to see the finished product.' He kissed her again as he left, lightly this time, and waved as he closed the door.

Miranda watched him as he crossed the Spicer Centre, the snowflakes settling on his dark hair. He still turned heads. Maybe as Billie always said, the Devil would turn heads in Amberley Hill too. But Reuben was no devil. Reuben was her lover. Which was a bit of a bugger, really. Oh, not that he wasn't lovely—he'd been a revelation in bed. Miranda had been all geared up for a laddish, one-sided, utterly forgettable wham-bang-thank-you-ma'am experience; but it hadn't been like that at all. Reuben had been a tender, sensitive and generous lover. Probably, she had to admit, the best she'd ever had. And that was the problem.

She still fancied the mysterious Drop-Dead Gorgeous Joseph Bellamy like mad. Or at least, she thought she did. Not that she'd seen him again since the meeting before Christmas in the post office; Mr Molton-Kusak hadn't been back for any further massage either as he'd cancelled the three appointments he'd made owing to pressure of business elsewhere in the country, so she hadn't been able to follow up her double-date plan. And now she never would.

Even if they did meet again, Miranda knew she simply couldn't do it. Joseph was obviously married—and anyway she was sleeping with Reuben. She had never been unfaithful to anyone—Noel's infidelity had ensured that she'd never inflict that sort of humiliation on anyone else—and each of her many subsequent men since

310

the disintegration of her marriage had been in series, not parallel.

And anyway, if she knew—*really* knew—that she and Reuben had any sort of future together, then she'd be able to relegate the delicious-but-married Joseph to her top ten fantasy lovers along with Paul Nicholls, Will Smith, Sean Bean and Jeremy Paxman. But close as she was growing to Reuben, there was still a little niggling doubt in the back of her mind. Billie must hate him for a good reason, other than just because he had been her boss and that was mandatory. She'd been asking Billie *why* for as long as she'd known her. And Billie had always given the same answer: because he's just not a nice person. Some are. Some aren't. Reuben isn't. Okay? And Miranda, as always, translated that as unrequited mutual lust. Reuben was still fixated on Billie, she was sure of it! Not that he mentioned her very often, and Billie was so wrapped up in the goings-on at Whiteacres that she'd barely got time to breathe, let alone slag off Reuben, but until Miranda found out exactly what it was that each truly felt about the other, and more importantly why, then her relationship with him would have no chance.

Billie had been speechless about Reuben spending the night in the flat when she came back from Devon, and had begged and pleaded with Miranda to keep him out of her way. Miranda, after tucking up Spike with the spare duvet and hustling Reuben through to her bedroom, had suggested that it might be better for everyone concerned if their sleeping arrangements moved to Reuben's bedsit in future. Reuben had laughed and said fine by him and he'd got no idea that Billie had become

311

so moralistic, and Billie the next day had said thank God for that because if Reuben was in the flat then she definitely wasn't going to be.

Miranda finished tidying the desk and moved on to the salon. Hard to believe that it was already well into January, Miranda thought, idly lobbing fat foam rollers and little spindly perm curlers into their appropriate baskets. Her life, she felt, was currently passing and changing just as quickly as the seasons.

She gazed out of the window. It had been lovely today. She adored the snow. She wondered how badly the weather was affecting Billie's business. Not at all, she hoped. Billie needed a boost at the moment. The snow had apparently hampered Jonah Sullivan's progress with the plane, the new owner of the warehouses hadn't materialised yet due to a fiscal glitch, and Billie looked frazzled every night.

All work and no play was turning Billie into a right miserable madam, Miranda thought. Maybe she'd tell her about the developments at Caught Offside tonight over a bottle of plonk and the lasagne. Maybe, because Reuben wasn't going to be around, they could have a girlie night in and laugh like they used to. Miranda sighed. It was no fun at all having girlie chats when the subjects of her current man and sex were taboo, and Billie had neither of either . . .

*   *   *

Reuben was waiting in the foyer of the club. As Bazooka's, the entrance hall had been black, with zigzags of red and yellow paint splashed across the

312

walls mixed with other more unpleasant stains. Now it was like perfectly mown emerald turf marked out with pristine chalk lines. Miranda, who knew very little about football, and who hadn't been allowed to see it at all during its transformation, looked around in pure pleasure.

'Wow, doll! It's magic!'

The dirty grey carpet had been replaced by Astroturf, the soft lighting came from towering silver floodlight pylons, and the cloakrooms were now called changing rooms, with Home for Ladies and Away for Gents. It was all very impressive.

'Wait until you see the rest.' Reuben held out his hand. 'Billie'll rue the day she turned down my offer to run this place. It's going to be a little goldmine.'

Miranda, taking his hand, groaned inwardly. She really wished he hadn't mentioned Billie. 'I'm sure it will. And I'm sure Billie might have had second thoughts—especially now her other business is a bit iffy . . . Still, Bugsy Malone will make a really good manager, won't he?'

'Bertie,' Reuben corrected. 'And yes, I'm convinced that he'll run the place exactly the way I want it.'

Bertie Malone had been the most anthropoid member of Reuben's managerial shortlist. Weeks ago, on the interview panel, Miranda had blinked at them, convinced that she'd seen precisely the same line-up on *Crimewatch*. Bertie Malone, fresh from running a Leeds rave palace and currently into something to do with tribal gatherings, had made Phil Mitchell look like Dale Winton.

'There!' Reuben led her into the body of the club. 'What do you think?'

313

'Amazing—even for the biggest footiephobe in the land!' Miranda swirled round. 'Oh, it's brilliant! It'll appeal to everyone. You're dead clever when it comes to business, aren't you?'

Reuben tried to look unassuming, but she could see that he was pleased by her reaction. She let her eyes trawl round the inside of the club.

The footballing theme was everywhere—from the black and white half-ball tables and chairs, to the perfectly marked-out pitch of the dance floor, with more floodlighting and tiers of terraced seats. The bar was a semicircle, and the names of the soccer-linked drinks—including, sadly, the Bobby Charlton Slammer—were constantly scrolling on a miniature scoreboard. The new eaterie, officially called The Penalty Spot now, was decked out like a goalmouth complete with giant nets, and huge glamorous photos of all the star players were light-boxed onto the walls and ceilings.

'Better than paintings, I thought,' Reuben followed her gaze. 'They go out of fashion so quickly, what with the transfer market and injuries, it would have cost a fortune to keep replacing them if they were permanent. Do you like the screens?'

Miranda nodded. She loved all of it. It was hopelessly overdone, of course, but it had to be. The Star Vision screens would show matches all the time, striped scarves were dangling from the ceilings, and even the banquettes had been reupholstered in a selection of Premiership team colours. Reuben had worked very hard to get everything right.

Miranda sighed. 'I can't wait to see everyone's faces when they get inside here! Why do we have to wait so long before you open?'

314

'Licensing laws—which means waiting for the appropriate magistrates sitting to grant me the bar licence—not to mention Health and Safety checks, about a million tons of triplicate paperwork, and various visits by the building regulators to check on every inch—and also because I want it to coincide with the end of the football season, remember—after the Cup Final,' Reuben said. 'Everyone will be desperate by then—the football fans and the dedicated clubbers. It'll be like offering iced water in the Sahara. I'll be sending out a press release to all the newspapers and the television and radio. And invitations to all the football clubs. Managers and players.'

Miranda grinned at him. 'What? You mean we're going to have people like Michael Owen and Alan Shearer? Here in Amberley Hill? Wow!'

'With any luck, most of the top names will accept. And I've already got my celebrity player booked to perform the opening ceremony.'

'God! Not David Ginola? Or David Beckham?' Miranda almost clapped her hands, then remembered that possibly Reuben wouldn't be that delighted at this show of adoration. Especially from someone who purported to hate the game.

She could hardly say that the two beautiful Davids could be shelf-stackers for all she cared. 'I—er—mean, they're absolutely *huge*!'

Reuben looked darkly enigmatic for a moment, then smiled. 'You'll just have to wait and see on the opening night, won't you? I think you'll be pleased, but until then it's my secret.'

*   *   *

'If you'd like to wait in the lounge for a moment, madam, and peruse the menu . . . Your first drinks will, of course, be on the house to compensate for the delay. I think we may be able to squeeze you in without too much trouble. Please—take a seat.'

The Dil Raj was packed. It always was. Miranda, who had phoned to reserve a table for two, had been told they were fully booked but she could come along and hope there was a cancellation.

'Thanks. That's lovely—ooh, and doubles, doll! Cheers!' Miranda smiled at the waiter, gratefully accepted two gin and tonics, and joined Billie in the dark green and golden tasselled splendour of the restaurant's waiting area.

Even though she was still ravenous, Miranda was delighted that the bottle of plonk and defrosted lasagne girlie night in had been jettisoned by Billie who'd, for once, arrived home as high as a kite.

'We'll eat out!' She'd twirled round the flat. 'To celebrate! Let's do the whole hog at the Dil Raj! You ring for a table and I'll just whizz into the shower!'

Billie had whizzed and Miranda had rung, and all the time Billie had been warbling early Madonna hits and like some village idiot. It was only when Billie in the Joseph dress and Miranda in leather and spandex were crammed in the taxi on the way to the Spicer Centre that the reason for Billie's delirium was revealed.

To be honest, Miranda thought, it didn't seem that much to get excited about. OK, so Jonah had his appointment with some people at the airport the following morning—and Maynard and Pollock had said it may be another month before the new owner took over the leases. Jonah's friend

Barnaby had apparently got some other plane fully functional, oh, and Billie had spent the afternoon testing the wingwalking rig—again.

Sure, she knew about Billie's fear of flying—but all she'd done was bumble about, strapped into something motionless a few feet above the ground. Inside the shed. The worst that could have happened to her was falling off. Still, Miranda thought, listening for the umpteenth time to Billie waxing lyrical about the planned air show, and having two planes and how Jonah was going to make everything OK for the future of Whiteacres, and that sitting in the plane—even on the ground—was like nothing anyone had ever experienced since Orville and Wilbur took to the skies, it had certainly done wonders for Billie's mood.

At least it meant Billie had talked about something other than Reuben, and for that reason alone Miranda would have listened to her reciting the A to Z of aviation history if it meant they could have a night out without arguing.

'Ladies?' The waiter appeared again. 'If you don't object to being seated in the smoking area, then we have a free table.'

'Smoking's brilliant.' Miranda leaped to her feet before Billie could mutter anything about preferring to wait for nonsmoking if nobody minded. 'I always say there's nothing like a Marlboro Light after a Raj Thali, don't you?'

Clutching their gin and tonics, and menus, they followed their immaculately dressed waiter through the throng, the chatter and clatter and the tang of a thousand spices making Miranda almost drool with anticipation.

'A nice little corner table.' The waiter pulled out

317

their chairs. 'I'll bring poppadoms and chutneys while you make your choices . . . and more drinks?'

'Oh, yes please,' Billie smiled dazzlingly at him. 'Could we have a bottle of Moet?'

'Certainly, madam. A celebration?'

'The biggest.' Billie beamed a bit more.

'There now,' Miranda said a bit doubtfully as the waiter wafted away, 'I bet he thinks we're lesbians celebrating our engagement or something.'

'Of course he doesn't. And, anyway, what if he does? I just want to celebrate feeling happy and confident about the future, and I always think—Oh my God!'

'What?' Miranda paused in lighting her cigarette. 'What's up?'

Billie nodded towards the nonsmoking area. 'Over there! The table by the banana plant! It's Jonah and Barnaby!'

'Where? Show me!' Miranda wriggled round as much as the leather and spandex would allow. 'You'll have to introduce me, doll. Didn't you know they were coming here, then?'

Billie shook her head. 'I knew they were going out to congratulate each other on the rebuilding of the Slingsby—and to give Jonah Dutch courage for tomorrow's meeting with the Incs. I had no idea where to. What a coincidence.'

'Are they on their own?'

'Yeah, as far as I can see . . .' Billie leaned recklessly from her chair. 'Yes—not a trace of Claire or Estelle! Goody!'

Miranda smiled. The bit about Claire and Estelle had rather spoiled the ending to Billie's account back in the summer when the Boeing thing had flown for the first time. Miranda had held out great hopes of a romance for Billie with this Jonah bloke—but a man with a not-so-ex-wife and a gorgeous girlfriend both very much on the scene was truly not up for grabs.

Despite following Billie's example and leaning, Miranda still couldn't see anyone. People moving to and from tables kept getting in the way, and then the waiter interrupted the craning and peering to deliver the champagne and chutneys and a tower block of poppadoms, and Billie ordered the Raj Thali, the full banquet, twice.

'Where are they?' Miranda said irritably. 'I can see about twenty tables by banana plants and oh—holy shit!'

Billie paused in mid-crunch. A lot of mango fell from the poppadom onto her side plate. 'What's the matter? Christ—it's not Reuben, is it?'

'It's Mr Molten-Lava—and Joe!'

'Bloody hell!' Billie scooped up her chutney again, washing it down with a swig of Moet. 'Heck of a night for men, then. Two each! I can't wait to see this vision of testosterone on legs. So—where are they?'

'Over there!' Miranda waved her cigarette wildly. 'The table over there. Look! By the banana pl . . .'

She trailed away. Billie pushed her plate aside. They looked at each other. Oh God—surely not?

'But Mr Molten-Lava called him *Joe*. I thought it was short for Joseph . . . And the parcel was addressed to Mrs Bellamy.'

'Barnaby calls him Jo. J. O. Short for Jonah. And where was the parcel addressed to?'

'I don't know. Some island . . .'

'Not the Isle of Wight?'

'Yeah, I think so. Why?'

'Jonah's family live there. I'll bet you a million pounds that Mrs Bellamy is one of his sisters.'

Miranda closed her eyes. That was it, then. Joseph Bellamy, Mr Dreamboat Potential Husband Number Two, was not only Jonah Sullivan, he was well and truly spoken for. Still, she supposed it solved one dilemma—the Reuben one. She opened her eyes again. Billie was waving at the table by the banana plant with a poppadom. There were spatters of chutney on the tablecloth.'

Miranda sighed. 'But I kept going on about Mr Molton-Kusak. Didn't you know it was Barnaby's surname?'

'Nope. I've only ever known him as Barnaby. Molton-Kusak! Posh, or what? Oh, great! I think they've seen us! But not so great—they've got a table for four. Do you think they are waiting for Claire and Estelle?'

'I really don't care.' Miranda dragged relentlessly on the cigarette and downed half a flute of champagne. 'And please, please, doll—if they come over or anything—don't breathe a word about me— well—um—fancying Joe—er—Jonah, will you?'

'God, no, of course not. I just think it's really funny that you've seen Barnaby without his clothes on.'

Miranda winced. Small world. Bloody coincidence. Fickle fate. Whatever you wanted to call it, it seemed to have made Billie very happy. And her? She examined her feelings briefly: she was OK. She'd never expected anything to come from Mr D-D-G anyway. He'd been a fantasy, like all the others. Reuben was the real thing. If Billie was cheerful about seeing them then maybe she'd got her eye on Mr Molten-Lava—which would be

320

lovely. Miranda sighed. She'd sort of got Reuben, and Billie might have Barnaby. Not too bad, really . . .

Billie was still munching her way through the tower block. She leaned across the table. 'Miranda? Are you all right? I mean, I'm so sorry about your Joe being Jonah. I know how much—'

Miranda crumbled a poppadom. 'I'm fine, doll. Just fine. It was only a silly game anyway.'

'Madam,' the waiter pushing a hostess trolley of immense proportions, loaded with steaming dishes and hot plates, paused beside her, 'the gentlemen over there are asking if you'd care to join them.'

Miranda exchanged glances with Billie, who was nodding. The waiter caught the nod. 'Just a word in that case, madam. The gentlemen's table—it is nonsmoking—so if you wouldn't mind extinguishing your cigarette . . . And if you do decide to go, can we do it now before I serve?'

'Yes, yes, of course.' Miranda ground out the cigarette in the ashtray. 'Yes, let's do it. Billie?'

But Billie had already gone, clutching the bottle of Moet. The waiter grinned at Miranda. 'Your friend—she's in high spirits, tonight? You ladies in love?'

'Not as far as I know,' Miranda muttered. 'And before you say anything, even if we are, it's definitely not with each other.'

It took about five minutes to get organised. By the time the double banquet was distributed amidst the dishes on Jonah and Barnaby's already loaded table, and the Moet had been decanted four times and another two bottles ordered, and Jonah was teasing Billie about being in a dress, and everyone had introduced themselves, and Jonah

321

had exclaimed twenty times about it being a bloody small world and thanks again for posting his parcel, Miranda's pulse had begun to calm down.

God, but Jonah Sullivan was to die for. Heaping prawn bhoona onto a mountain of pilau rice, Miranda, however, ignored him and smiled across at Barnaby. 'Strange coincidence, you and—um— Jonah knowing Billie, and us all meeting like this.'

'Very.' Barnaby saluted her with his glass. 'In fact I had been intending to contact you and invite you out for a meal, in any case. It was very ungallant of me to cancel my appointments with you. I must say you are excellent at your job.'

'Thank you very much. And the cancellations were no problem.' Embarrassed, Miranda swallowed a huge delicious mouthful and had to wait for ages before it went down. 'And I do understand how busy you are—especially now that I know you're the Barnaby that Billie's always talking about. And—um—we haven't interrupted anything, have we? The table for four . . . ?'

Barnaby shook his head, elegantly scooping up palak bhajee with his keema naan. 'No, Jo booked for Pam and Vinny—they work for Sullivanair—as well. But Vinny apparently had a previous hot date and Pam's got an unexpected in-law invasion.'

Jonah and Billie were hooting with laughter over something. Miranda tried to listen. It seemed to involve a lot of technical words like shit-scared and nose-dive.

Barnaby raised his eyebrows. 'It's nice to hear them laughing, considering the pressures they're under. Jo and I were just discussing ways to overcome the proposed takeover. We've come up with one or two quite bright, albeit drunken, ideas, haven't we, Jo?'

Jonah nodded, making patterns with his dal. 'Yeah, especially now that the Slingsby's airborne. Or at least, will be as soon as this bloody snow melts. We're going to emulate Waldo Pepper—' He looked at the noncomprehension on Miranda's face and grinned. 'Waldo Pepper was a stunt flyer in the 1930s and had a Stearman—in fact he was probably the world's greatest ever barnstormer. Anyway, that led to Barnaby saying that we really should be getting the Slingsby up and running—because of course he's ace at aerobatics and that's what the Slingsby's built for.'

Miranda smiled sadly. He was totally gorgeous. And completely unaware of it. And Billie, who was now obviously slightly squiffy and smiling at Barnaby, didn't seem to have noticed. And all this stunning talent was being channelled into insider talk about some stupid air display thing. Who would want to pay money just to watch a load of old planes?

They should have the sort of business brain that Reuben had. Buying into something that promised an instant return. He had the taxis, and now Caught Offside, and was talking about diversifying even further. And much to Miranda's surprise, on the first night she'd spent with him she'd discovered that Reuben lived in his tiny bedsit simply because it was the smallest in a rather grand four-storey house that was turned into seven similar apartments. Reuben didn't rent his accommodation, he owned the whole building and made a tidy income from it. It was something, that for some reason, she hadn't told Billie.

Barnaby was talking now, obviously fired by

323

the same ancient flying machine enthusiasm. 'Jo's got an appointment with the Whiteacres people tomorrow. He's going to propose that they let us put on some sort of show before they accept the takeover bid.'

'Great,' Miranda said vaguely, who'd heard it all before. 'That sounds lovely. But why don't you just raise the money and buy the airfield yourselves?'

'We can't afford it.' Jonah refilled her glass. 'And this way everyone has a lot of fun too. We're not aiming to raise enough cash to purchase the airfield from the show—however inebriated we are, we know we'd never make enough—'

Barnaby cut in. 'The idea is to make the show so good that it puts Whiteacres on the aviation display map. We want the hierarchy to see that they must keep it as an annual event—and to do that then they have to keep us.'

'We're going to call in the boys from the Aeroclub and get them on our side.' Jonah spooned up helpings from several dishes and piled them on his plate. 'Then we'll suggest to the Whiteacres Aviation Incs that we have the show in June—and, as Barnaby says, if it's a success we can become an official annual display on the air-show circuit—and be both self-supporting and prestigious—and keep Whiteacres running as it is now.'

Miranda shook her head. She'd been involved in business for long enough to know that instant money on the table was worth more to a seller than any amount of 'fun'. 'But if they want a whole wodge of money, surely they'll turn you down out of hand, won't they?'

'Don't know,' Jonah shrugged. 'That's what I intend to find out in the morning.'

Billie was topping up the glasses again and talking about her lease. Barnaby had returned to concentrating on making inroads into his tandoori murgh. Miranda shovelled up another mouthful of prawns and was suddenly aware how much outside this she was. Whiteacres involved the other three; it meant absolutely nothing to her. She was suddenly assailed by a huge wave of loneliness.

Oh God, she thought, staring down at her plate. I miss Reuben. I actually want to be with him. Oh, bugger—surely I'm not in love, am I . . . ?

Miranda, my dear,' Barnaby sliced through her revelations, 'about my previous suggestion. I wonder if we might have dinner together some time? Just the two of us? What do you say?'

chapter twenty-six

Estelle rolled away from him, burying her face in the pillow. Her voice was muffled but the accusation was loud and clear. 'And where was your mind that time, huh? Were you just bringing the Shorts into land at Manila? Or was it a triple loop with somersault and pike in the Stearman?' She snatched the pillow away and hurled it to the floor, sitting up, indignant in her nakedness, and glared at him. 'Or maybe it was something that really excites you—like an inverted roll in the Slingsby?'

She slid from the bed, pushing the cascade of hair away from her face so that it immediately tumbled in a silvery waterfall across her bare shoulders. 'Wherever your mind was, it wasn't with me, was it?'

Jonah propped himself up on his elbow. What was the point in denying it? Estelle was far too astute to be fobbed off. And saying sorry wasn't an option either. She deserved more, and Jonah couldn't give it. Not now, anyway. Maybe not ever.

He watched her as she walked to the window. The ubiquitous net curtains possibly prevented the occupants of the neighbouring flats getting the full-blown view of her stunning naked body, but he wouldn't bank on it. And he knew she didn't care. She was like some exotic lily in the dross of this functional bedroom, with its magnolia walls, faded curtains, and appalling padded pink velour bed-head.

'I was thinking about the meeting . . .'

'Christ, Jonah!' Estelle swirled round. 'I don't want to know that! I may not be naive enough to think that what we've got is love, but surely there should be at least a modicum of *interest*? I really don't need to go through the motions—but sometimes it'd be nice if you just remembered to tack an "e" on the front!'

And yanking his towelling robe from the bottom of the bed, she stormed off towards the bathroom.

Jonah groaned and levered himself from under the duvet. It was the first time for ages that Estelle had spent the night at his flat. She'd been busy—too busy to sleep with him, she'd said—ever since her New Year return from Austria. And, to be honest, ever since that day when they'd launched the Stearman and he'd taken Billie up in preference to Estelle or Claire, she'd changed towards him. He stared at the relentless cold whiteness pervading the room through the thin curtains. How long ago it all seemed now: that glorious autumn day when he and Barnaby had soared into the warm October sky without a care in the world.

He rolled over, burying his face in the pillow, remembering. And then, last night, when the taxi had dropped him off from the Dil Raj, he'd unsteadily unlocked the door and Estelle had been sitting on the hard-edged sofa waiting for him. Having wrinkled her nose at the smell of the spices and not even bothering to ask where he'd been or who with, she'd insisted he'd had a shower—which she'd shared—and then they'd gone to bed, and things seemed to be back to normal.

Now, in the last twenty minutes, he'd destroyed the relationship's fragility again. He exhaled. It was ironic that this time at least, it hadn't been thoughts of Claire that had interrupted the coitus.

In fact, since the day of the Stearman flight three months ago he'd been able to think of Claire with hardly any lustful stirrings at all. She'd behaved so abominably that afternoon, literally stamping her feet and having a tantrum because Jonah hadn't taken her up, that he'd fleetingly thought he was well rid of her. He'd known that she was high, of course; he'd made allowances for that. He always had. But even so, her display of ill temper, added to Antony's bloody gung-ho patronising attitude towards the Stearman's performance—especially as Jonah had been feeling on top of the world—had made him want to punch someone.

Unfortunately, because Estelle hadn't behaved that much better about not being included in the maiden flight, he'd taken it all out on her. Not physically, naturally, but with a flash of verbal temper which had shocked and dismayed him. He'd stormed back into Billie's shed, slamming

327

the doors, and cursed Claire, Antony and Estelle to hell for ruining the greatest achievement of his life. It was all the more galling because he'd been so maniacally happy only seconds before.

And now, after months and weeks of apologising to Estelle for being human, he'd blown it—again.

As he had no desire to share Estelle's shower this morning in case she garrotted him with the soap-on-a-rope, he decided that dressing quickly and sloping into the kitchen for solitary coffee and toast might be a good idea. He had to be at Whiteacres in an hour. The Aviation Incs had agreed to see him before they commenced their daily business. Half an hour with them to try to salvage his future, and then he, Vinny, Pam and the Shorts would be winging off to Bristol, weather permitting, with a party of quantity surveyors.

He got as far as boxer shorts, socks and his uniform trousers, and padded into the kitchen to switch on the kettle.

'Shit!'

All his white Sullivanair shirts were still in a damply crumpled ball inside the washing machine. He should have remembered to have rescued at least one and ironed it when he got home last night, but he had been so pleased that Estelle was there—for once it had felt wonderful to not be alone in the utilitarian beigeness—that the domesticity had completely slipped his mind.

There was no possibility on earth that Estelle might have salvaged a shirt and ironed it while waiting for him to come home. Even if Estelle was the sort of person who believed that ironing was a woman's right, she lived in clothes so tight that any creases warmed themselves out on her body during

328

wear. He very much doubted if Estelle had ever plugged in an iron in her life.

Irritably, he shook out the knot of shirts. Trickles of cold water sprayed over his feet. With a burst of wart-shrivelling curses, Jonah slammed them back inside the machine and kicked the door shut. Jesus! The only shirt that was ironed and half decent was the denim one he'd worn to the Dil Raj last night. Even if he hadn't spilled anything on it, it probably reeked of curry. He thundered back into the bedroom and snatched it from the end of the bed.

'What the hell are you doing?' Estelle dripped into the room, and watched in amazement.

'Seeing if it smells. It doesn't.'

'Well, whoopee-doo.' She tugged the towel from her hair. 'You're surely not going to wear that to plight your troth to the old farts, are you?'

'Do I have a choice?'

'No, I suppose you don't.' Estelle screwed the slithering mass of blonde hair on top of her head. 'And at least it's blue. They're probably so ancient and decrepit that they won't be able to see that it's not Turnbull and Asser.'

Jonah knotted his RAF tie and grabbed his uniform jacket. There was no time for coffee or toast now. He picked up his cap. 'Estelle, I'm sorry . . .'

'Yeah, sure you are.' She didn't turn from the dressing table. Didn't pause in massaging cream into her throat. 'So am I, Jonah. So am I.'

He paused in the doorway. 'I'll let you know the outcome, shall I?'

'Whatever. I just think you and Barnaby are being ridiculous. Why the hell would the old farts want the hassle of an air display when your beloved

329

ex and her rampant aviator are simply panting to hand over millions?'

Jonah shrugged. He really didn't know. In the cold and sober light of day, he was beginning to doubt the wisdom of the whole idea. Estelle was probably right. Was it sheer bloody-mindedness that made him want to fight? If the takeover had been mooted by complete strangers, would he still feel this sense of outrage? It annoyed him to find that he couldn't honestly answer his own question.

And even supposing sodding Aerobatic Archie bought the airfield, what would it really matter? He could move Sullivanair somewhere else and start again, couldn't he? He didn't want to, but he could do it, couldn't he?

Yes, he could. But what about Billie? And Sylvia? And the hippies and the film-makers and even the morose old boys with their replacement windows? What the hell would happen to them? It simply wasn't fair that someone as rich and egocentric as Antony Archibald should be allowed to destroy the small but all-important aspirations of people he didn't even know existed.

Belatedly, Jonah wondered whether he should kiss Estelle goodbye and decided against it. He made do with a sort of wave-cum-salute which she ignored. Jonah closed the bedroom door, swamped by a feeling of impending doom.

*   *   *

The Whiteacres Aviation Incs, all five of them, had listened to him for twenty minutes. They'd skim-read the proposals he and Barnaby had put together. They sat, blazered and immaculately trousered, and looked down their haughty noses at him, his suggestions, and his rather rumpled denim shirt.

'Fascinating,' the oldest Inc said, his tone implying that it was anything but. 'Leave it with us, Flight Lieutenant Sullivan, and we'll be in touch.'

Jonah stood up. He hated people using his obsolete title. He also felt it wasn't the time to say so. 'Thank you for seeing me, gentlemen, and for hearing me out. If there are any questions arising from our discussions, my telephone numbers are on the proposals, and of course the Sullivanair office is always manned.'

They nodded at him dismissively.

He walked towards the door. 'Can I tell my—er—colleagues, that you won't go any further in accepting the takeover offer until you've considered our suggestions?'

The youngest Inc, who had looked reasonably interested throughout, nodded. 'You can. And if you're intending to put on your little display in June then I can't see there being a major problem, actually. There'll be no difficulty with air space, we can see to that with ATC. Also, as we weren't looking to sell until September and—'

'Malcolm!' the oldest Inc roared. 'That's quite enough. Flight Lieutenant Sullivan has all the information we are able to give at this moment in time. That will be all, Flight Lieutenant. I can assure you that we will discuss your proposition thoroughly and that we will be in touch. In the meantime I bid you good day.'

Jonah escaped from the fuggy claustrophobia of the office and punched the ice-cold air. Yes! That was what he wanted to know. They'd give clearance

331

for the show whatever happened—because it would mean additional income even if they then decided to sell out to Aerobatic Archie in September.

His brain was racing as he skidded across the wet tarmac in the biting wind. He was sure now that they'd sanction the show; they'd be foolish not to. All he needed was a stunning list of participants, and publicity, and . . . his head reeled. First things first. He'd got the Stearman and the Slingsby; Barnaby was going home to Derbyshire next week to sell shares in three of his horses and was going to put the money into buying something else; Vinny— if pushed—could give pleasure flights in the Shorts; and the boys from the Aeroclub could put their Pipers and Cessnas to good use by offering trial flights, and staging mini fly-pasts and . . .

He galloped up the steps to the Sullivanair office. Estelle still wasn't in. He grabbed a handful of Post-it notes and proceeded to obliterate the computer screen.

'The old farts were a pushover! Should be OK. We'll go ahead the second weekend in June! Less than five months! It'll take some organising!'

'If Claire or Aerobatic Archie ring, tell them I'm dead.'

'If Barnaby rings or comes in to the office tell him to meet me at the Stearman after four o'clock.'

He hesitated, then added a final note.

'I truly am sorry. I'm a git and you're a star. Why don't you find yourself a man who deserves you? Especially one without destructive tendencies? In the meantime, please put up with me and forgive me for my crassness.' He looked at it. He could have added, 'Love Jonah.' But he didn't love Estelle any more than she did him. He just felt guilty about being so bloody cavalier.

He stuck the note on the middle of her diary. God—February next week. The year was racing away. He looked at Estelle's neat and methodical entries for the coming week. It was, as Vinny had always warned, a foolish thing to have done to have started sleeping with her. She was not only ace at keeping Sullivanair ticking over behind the scenes, but also had a double first in avionics and electrical engineering. If she left him she'd leave the company and replacing her would be impossible.

It was only when he was watching Kev, the ground handler, supervising the hauling of the Shorts from its hangar, that it occurred to him that he'd miss Estelle in his business far more than he'd ever miss her in his bed.

*   *   *

The flight to Bristol and back was uneventful. The snow had stopped falling overnight and brilliant sunshine had begun to melt away the worst of the yellowing pockmarked piles heaped on either side of the runway. Vinny and Pam had been very rude about Jonah's shirt and slightly sceptical about the enlargement of the proposed show. Neither of them seemed to share his optimism that Whiteacres Aviation Inc. would definitely give him the go-ahead, and even if they did, whether an air pageant would actually interest anyone.

'That's only because planes are old hat to you

333

two,' Jonah had said as they stared at him in the Shorts' sunlit cockpit while they cruised through pellucid blue sky three thousand feet over the M5. 'Look at the way they pull in hundreds of thousands of people each year at Fairford and Farnborough.'

'Jesus!' Vinny had grinned. 'Talk about delusions of grandeur. Going to fork out for the Red Arrows? The World War Two Memorial Flight? A fleet of Tornadoes and Harriers? Oh—and we mustn't forget the Concorde fly-past, must we? Hell, that'll make a bit of a hole in the Sullivan coffers!'

'Vinny's right.' Pam had clung on to the back of Jonah's seat as they'd banked suddenly. 'What you're intending to do is very small beer.'

'I know.' Jonah had concentrated on the altimeter. 'That's what I want. Something to make Whiteacres different. I want to involve local people and make it something that they can relate to. I want this pageant to be the aeronautical equivalent of the village fete.'

'Dear God . . .' Pam had shaken her head and returned to the cabin to dole out a double ration of the stale peanuts to the quantity surveyors.

Vinny had taken over the controls. 'I like village fetes, myself. All those buxom bucolic girls and frolicking in the foaming cow parsley after hours . . . Oh, bugger.' He listened intently to the radio. 'Golf Hotel Charlie Foxtrot received and understood. Fifteen minutes to landing. All AOK.' He glanced across at Jonah. 'Of course, this pastoral display would have absolutely nothing at all to do with cocking a snook at Aerobatic Archie and the delectable Claire, would it?'

'It's got everything to do with that,' Jonah had said fervently. 'Absolutely bloody everything.'

Leaving Whiteacres' air-traffic control tower following the Shorts' return, Jonah thought that after Billie's rather odd friend Miranda, and Estelle, and Vinny and Pam, anyone else who wanted to pour cold water on his plans would just have to join the queue. Sloshing through the rapidly melting slush, he pulled his jacket tighter around him in the keen wind, and deciding not to aggravate the situation with Estelle any further, he gave the office a wide berth and headed for the units.

The first thing he noticed outside Billie's warehouse was the rather scruffy white Transit van with 'Pascoe's Warehousing—Whiteacres' and the telephone number emblazoned on it in large red and black lettering. Jonah grinned. He always felt happy when the van was there. Like a talisman. If it was the Nova it always meant she wasn't stopping.

He slid the doors open. 'Have you sobered up yet? That was quite a night. I really enjoyed myself. We'll have to go there again. Has Barnaby—'

'No, he hasn't, sweetie,' Claire rose from the Stearman's cockpit. 'And your little chum—Billie is it?—has gone next door to mediate in some matrimonial dispute. Some awful old bag with an orange face and varicose veins and a wrinkly who looks like David Niven were screaming like banshees. It was quite nostalgic, actually. Just like we used to be.' She stepped unsteadily onto the Stearman's wing. 'But I doubt very much if they'll have the same sort of erotic making-up session that we did, don't you?'

Jonah winced. 'Claire—no! Don't do that! Mind

335

where you put your feet! Don't step on the wing, keep on the treads! And what the hell are you doing in here anyway?'

Claire tottered on the edge of the wing and then jumped heavily to the ground. 'Estelle told me where you would be and said it would be fine to come over. I just told that Billie girl that you were expecting me. She said I was very welcome to wait. Sweet child, really. Hasn't it been awful weather?'

Jonah closed his eyes and cursed. He really shouldn't have underestimated Estelle's anger. 'I've got nothing to say to you, Claire. Nothing at all.'

'Such a pretty plane . . . Claire ran her fingers seductively over the Stearman's vibrant colours. 'And watching you fly that day, darling—it was such a turn-on . . . Such a pity you had to be so bad-tempered about it afterwards. Antony was merely going to make you an offer.'

Jonah exhaled. Claire, looking sensational in a lilac wool dress that clung and moulded, beneath a long cashmere coat, pouted. Her hair fell over her eyes in a glossy curtain. Christ! What was wrong with him? Estelle and Claire—and he'd ballsed up on both of them by being in love with bloody planes! If he ever took the luxury of going into therapy, his counsellor would have a field day!

'I'm not selling the Stearman to Antony. I'm not parting with anything else, ever. So go back to bloody Archibald and tell him that he won't be getting his hands on Whiteacres either. I'll see to that.'

'Sweetheart—' Claire moved towards him. He could smell Obsession. It awoke a million memories—'you don't mean that. You know you don't.'

336

'I do. I bloody do. Just bugger off and leave me alone!'

The doors opened and they both turned round. Barnaby did a double take. 'Er—would you rather I vamoosed or something?'

Claire nodded. Jonah shook his head. Barnaby obviously tossed a mental coin and stepped inside the shed.

Jonah sighed. 'Claire's just leaving.'

'No, I'm not.' She smiled brilliantly at Barnaby, then stood on tiptoe and kissed Jonah's cheek. 'I'm not going anywhere, darling, until you've taken me up in your sexy plane.'

chapter twenty-seven

Billie pulled open the doors to the warehouse, stamping her feet to shake the worst of the slush from her boots, and stared at the tableau in amazement. When she'd left—less than fifteen minutes earlier—to sort out Sylv and Douglas, Claire had been mooching round the warehouse, carelessly trailing the hem of the cashmere coat through the dust and chattering about waiting for Jonah to carry her off to paradise.

Billie, who had thought Jonah's ex-wife was even more stunning in close-up, had none the less wondered seriously about her sanity. Now, the luscious Claire was sitting looking flushed but ecstatically happy in the Stearman's cockpit, while Jonah and Barnaby stood on the ground staring up at her.

Barnaby spotted Billie first. He shrugged

337

apologetically. It's a bit of an emotional blip, my dear. A small matrimonial crisis.'

'So I gather,' Billie said, watching Jonah's face darken as he leaned up towards the cockpit. 'It seems to be the day for them. I've just had to sort out Douglas and Sylvia next door.'

'Satisfactorily, I hope.' Barnaby gave another cool upper-class smile, 'I do hate unpleasantness.'

'I quite like it,' Billie admitted with a grin. 'As long as it isn't mine, of course. And I've no idea whether the outcome will be satisfactory or not. Douglas and Sylv have been daggers drawn ever since she sweated in a health farm sauna over Christmas in preference to sweating over Douglas's turkey. They're currently arguing over the custody of the cat.'

Barnaby laughed. It sounded like it should be accompanied by a good port and a rich fruit cake. 'Lovely evening last night, wasn't it? I thoroughly enjoyed myself. Superb food—and even better company. I—um—wondered . . . Your friend, the masseuse, Miranda? Is she unattached?'

'Oh, very. Totally. Completely uninvolved. The most unattached person I know.' Billie wondered how many more young, free and single epithets she could chuck in without overegging the pudding. 'She's been divorced for years. She's agreed to have dinner with you, hasn't she?'

Barnaby nodded. 'She has. But I thought I caught a nuance of hesitation prior to her acceptance. I must say I find her very attractive . . . very stimulating . . .'

'Yes, she's apparently excellent at her job.'

'I didn't actually mean the massage.'

'Oh, no. Well, yes—Miranda's certainly—um—

338

stimulating . . .' Billie beamed. 'And I'm sure she fancies you too.'

Barnaby seemed to wince a bit at 'fancies'. Maybe it wasn't upper crust enough for him. He smiled again. 'She's an extraordinarily attractive lady. Like a sad Modigliani.'

Billie tried to think back to her school art lessons. Weren't Modigliani's women the ones with faces like eggs? She wasn't too sure that Miranda would find that complimentary and hoped Barnaby used some other form of flattery when they next met. It was hardly the sort of thing guaranteed to wean her away from Reuben.

Miranda had spent most of the night saying that she shouldn't have agreed to go out with Barnaby and that she'd have to ring and cancel. Billie, in a post-champagne-and-curry fug, had said she couldn't possibly, and Reuben wouldn't mind. Miranda had wailed that Reuben would mind a bloody lot and it was all Billie's fault for wanting to sit with Jonah and Mr Molten-Lava in the first place, and it was also Billie's fault for ordering so much champagne, and actually it was definitely Billie's fault for giving the Stearman house room and bringing Jonah and Barnaby into their lives to complicate things, then she'd hiccuped a lot and stumbled off to bed.

Billie, now noticing that Barnaby had that distant gooey-eyed look which always signified the stirring of testosterone, thought it might be a good idea to change the subject. She looked enquiringly at him. 'Um—how did Jonah's meeting go this morning? With the Aviation Incs?'

Barnaby shrugged. 'Not a clue, my dear. That's why I was seeking him out. But this little setback—'

339

he gestured towards the plane—'was already taking place when I arrived.'

Billie nodded. Claire had arrived unannounced halfway through the afternoon, asking for Jonah. Billie had said she had no idea where he was, but decided to grasp the nettle and find out about the takeover plans. She'd skirted around the issue for a couple of minutes, then as Claire seemed incapable of understanding veiled hints, she'd asked outright.

'What takeover?' Claire had wrinkled her nose. 'Oh, Whiteacres . . . Goodness—why should it concern you?'

'Because it's my livelihood,' Billie had hissed, trying to hiss quietly because Mrs Blunt, a new attic-overspill customer for the warehouse, was just completing the paperwork in her office.

'What? The airport?'

'Not the airport! This! The warehouses! If you're buying up my lease I'd really like to know where I stand.'

Claire had giggled and swished the cashmere coat about a bit. 'Are you sleeping with Jonah?'

'What? No!'

'That's a pity. He's awfully good in bed—Oh, I think that lady in the appalling hat is waving at you.'

Mrs Blunt had been frantically indicating that she'd run out of room on the inventory form and Billie had galloped to the rescue, praying that she hadn't overheard Claire's headgear remark. Just as she was stapling the forms together and wondering why anyone would want to store thirteen plastic dustbins containing knitting wool in their attic and whether she'd get them into the van along with several boxes of Mrs Blunt's 'preshus artyfax', Sylvia and Douglas had started shouting outside.

340

Always feeling that she needed to protect Sylv, she'd dispatched Mrs Blunt, charged out of the shed, and abandoned the chance of any further discussions with Claire.

Jonah, who had now stomped away from the Stearman, yanked out his mobile phone, punched out an aggressive succession of numbers and barked into it. Barnaby and Billie exchanged raised eyebrows. Jonah snapped off the phone. 'Billie—open the doors. Barnaby—get ready to heave.'

Billie looked at Jonah's stony face and did as she was told. Barnaby, who obviously knew Jonah well enough not to argue, watched as he released the plane's brakes and then fitted his shoulder under the Stearman's rudder.

'Ooh! No, wait! Not while I'm in it!' Claire, who was laughing, scrambled out of the cockpit and clumsily tripping over the hem of her coat, jumped onto the concrete floor.

Billie looked at Jonah. 'What the hell is going on?'

Jonah's lips were set in a pale line. 'Claire wants to be a wingwalker. Claire insists on being a wingwalker. So Claire is going to be a bloody wingwalker. OK?'

Billie shook her head. 'You can't be serious? You're not going to take her up in that? Not today? Jonah—you'll kill her!'

'No I won't. But I hope I'll scare the shit out of her and put her off the idea for life. Then she might just go back to Aerobatic Archie and tell him that Whiteacres is best left to those who know what they're doing. The tower have given me a fifteen-minute clearance before the light goes.'

'I still think you shouldn't be doing . . . Oh, does

that mean that the Aviation Incs were hopeful this morning? That Claire and—er—Antony aren't taking over?'

'Not exactly.' Jonah's face softened slightly. 'But they didn't turn me down out of hand. One of them actually seemed almost human. To be honest, my air pageant will probably slot into their money-making plans nicely. It'll be up to us to make it a big enough success to stave off the September take-over bid.'

Dead easy, then, Billie thought morosely. She almost agreed with Miranda that the Incs wouldn't give two hoots about some two-bit air pageant putting Whiteacres on the annual display map if the rivals were offering stonking amounts of money—even if the new owners intended to raze it to the ground and build communal cesspits. The Incs, Billie was convinced, would be tipping their Panamas over their noses and snoozing in the Caribbean sunshine long before the first JCB trundled onto the runway.

However, looking at Jonah's face, this was obviously neither the time nor the place to mention it. He'd moved away and was pointing out the intricacies of the rig to Claire.

Billie, who was already sweating with second-hand fear, quickly joined them. 'Jonah— don't do it. Please. She's—um—that is, I don't think she's feeling very well. She doesn't know what it entails, does she? Look how hard it was for me just fastening myself into the rig. Anyway, surely you've told her that you've advertised for someone to do it professionally? She's not thinking that she's going to become your partner, is she?'

'Of course I am.' Claire, in a waft of Obsession,

pushed past Jonah and touched Billie's shoulder. 'Don't worry about me. Jo will look after me— he always has. Anyway, he's the best flyer in the world. Tons better than darling Antony even . . . She leaned closer to Billie and dropped her voice to a chummy whisper. 'I want Jo back. I miss him. I know him inside out, so who better to be his flying partner first and his life partner second, eh?'

Billie exhaled, watching Claire, her cloudy hair bouncing in the breeze, scamper happily towards the perimeter fence and start winding it back to give a clear exit to the grass strip.

Jonah had joined Barnaby in shoving the Stearman towards the cracked concrete. As it was a job for at least a dozen people they were making slow progress. Eventually, though, the biplane was out of the shed, and Jonah swung himself up into the cockpit and started the engine. The roar immediately brought the other warehousers, including Sylvia and Douglas with matching angry faces, out of their units.

Barnaby waved an all-encompassing hand. 'No problems!' he yelled. 'Just testing the engine! Sorry to have disturbed you!'

Billie, unsure whether anyone who couldn't lip-read had the slightest inkling of what was going on, was mightily relieved when everyone disappeared inside again. No doubt the humidity of the draughty warehouses was infinitely preferable to standing outside up to their ankles in slush and in the snatching teeth of a late January breeze. Snuggling deeper into her fleece and pushing her hands into her pockets, Billie watched miserably as Jonah hefted Claire inelegantly onto the Stearman's wing. At least he wasn't going to expect

343

her to go the full monty and climb out from the cockpit.

Billie shook her head. Claire was dressed all wrong. The flapping coat would probably pull her off even before the Stearman reached the end of the runway. It was a job for someone who knew what they were doing. She studied Jonah's furious face as he strapped his ex-wife none-too-gently into the rig. She'd never seen this side of him before. Angry. Irritable. Insensitive. And cruel. Oh, yes— he was definitely being cruel.

She turned to Barnaby. 'Can't you stop him? It's not right.'

'I think you'll find Jo knows what he's doing, my dear.' Barnaby pulled the collar of his Barbour up round his ears. 'I always feel it's best not to interfere. I trust Jo's judgement implicitly. He won't let anything happen to Claire.'

Billie wasn't so sure. She watched, her stomach squirming, as Claire stumbled awkwardly along the wing, her long coat catching on the struts of the rig, the wind whipping her hair about her face. Now Jonah was kneeling on the wing too, pushing Claire's curves into the rig, sliding the harness over her shoulders, fastening the straps with angry tugs. Then he slid backwards into the Stearman's cockpit, let out the brake and gave a mocking thumbs up in their direction.

Billie, who thought she was going to be sick, wondered what sort of bad publicity would be engendered by slamming one's ex into the ground at a hundred and fifty miles an hour. She had a feeling that the tabloids would have a field day.

As the Stearman started to move, Claire twisted from her perch high above them and gave a sort

344

of jerky two-handed wave. Her mouth was open, but the roar of the engine and the scream of the rotating propeller drowned out the words. Even if she was imploring them to set her free no one would ever know. Billie, casting another anxious glance towards Barnaby, was dismayed to see that even he looked worried. She exhaled and nervously rubbed her hands together, hardly daring to look as the Stearman picked up speed and bounced across the cracked concrete towards the gap in the fence.

The bouncing became a rocking motion as soon as the plane reached the airfield's grass, which had been swept clear of snow and slush, and the glorious silver, emerald and purple Sullivanair colours were an almost indecent slash of gaudiness against the slate of the sky. Claire had stopped waving. Billie crept closer to Barnaby, knowing that if she had been alone she'd have closed her eyes at the moment of takeoff and probably never opened them again.

Barnaby slid a comforting arm around her shoulder and pulled her against the waxy warmth of his jacket. He smelled of safety and security and cigar smoke, and reminded her of her father. Suddenly assailed again by homesickness, she longed to bury her face in his chest and cry.

The Stearman's engine note changed as Jonah headed for the grass strip, turning the plane towards the taxi way and into the wind. Claire was rigid now, a tiny figure on the huge wingspan, her arms outstretched, leaning forward, the cashmere coat billowing behind her. She looked, Billie thought as she peeked from beneath Barnaby's lapels, exactly like Kate Winslet on the prow of *Titanic*. Not the best of analogies under the circumstances. She really hoped that the outcome wasn't going to be the same.

'Christ!' Barnaby muttered beneath his breath. 'They haven't even reached takeoff speed and Claire's trying to get out!'

Billie whimpered, her teeth chattering, as she watched Claire snatching at the harnesses' buckles as the Stearman jolted along the grass runway. Despite it being only a few degrees above zero, beads of sweat prickled Billie's upper lip, and she looked helplessly at Barnaby. Surely there was something they could do?

The plane seemed to become a blur, the propeller sliced transparently through the January gloom and the engine's rumble indicated—even to Billie's avionically uneducated ears—that takeoff was imminent. Then just as suddenly, everything changed.

The plane lost speed and slewed sideways, chucking up dust and spray and debris from beneath its fat tyres. Its stubby little legs—Billie was far too distraught to remember the correct term—seemed to be screeching to a halt, and Claire had slumped forward, hanging by one strap of the harness, her head dangling downwards towards the wing.

Barnaby had shaken her free and was running. Billie, still trembling, ran after him.

By the time they'd slithered across the grass, the Stearman had stopped and Jonah was out of the cockpit, scrambling onto the wing, lifting Claire's head, his face ashen. Totally redundant, Billie stood beside the plane, which was radiating as much warmth as Faith's Aga, watching as Barnaby and Jonah lifted Claire from the upper wing, bypassed

346

the cockpit, and carried her to the ground.

The cashmere coat had billowed open, the clinging lilac wool dress was rucked up, and Claire's dark cloudy hair was tangled about her white face like manic corkscrews. Her eyes were still closed but at least she was breathing. Billie, who realised she herself wasn't, suddenly gasped in a lungful of cold air and gagged.

Jonah, leaning against the Stearman, cradled Claire in his arms. 'Claire? Claire, sweetheart? Come on . . . wake up . . . God—I'm so sorry. I'm so sorry . . . I wasn't going to take off, just belt along the runway. I didn't mean to frighten you . . . I promise I'll never hurt you . . . Christ . . .'

Barnaby was up in the cockpit, fiddling with things, and Billie felt about as out of place as a vegan at McDonald's. Wondering whether she should just stuff her hands in her pockets and make a sort of casual sauntering exit back towards the warehouses, she started to move away.

No one, it seemed, noticed. Jonah was still crooning his apologies, Barnaby was still fiddling, and Claire was still comatose. Billie, who knew that she was definitely going to be sick as soon as the terrifying numbness wore off, took one last despairing look. Estelle had been right. Jonah still loved Claire. No man had ever—or would ever—look at her with that sort of naked adoration. He'd pulled his ex-wife against him, brushing her hair away from her face, holding her tenderly as he whispered against her cheek.

Billie bit her lip and swallowed the lump in her throat. 'I'll—er—go back to the—um—shed, then . . . Make some tea . . . Dig out the brandy . . .'

Jonah didn't seem to have heard her. He had

his back to her and his face was now buried in Claire's abundant hair. Barnaby just raised a hand in acknowledgement. Billie, feeling totally superfluous, turned and then stopped. Claire opened her wide-awake eyes over Jonah's shoulder, looked at Billie with a smile of total triumph, and winked.

spring

chapter twenty-eight

February had passed in a squall of torrential rain and high winds, rendering anything to do with the Stearman impossible. March had been cold, with unseasonable snow flurries and biting frosts, again curtailing flying. The icy weather also seemed to bring a halt to people wanting to store anything, so the warehouse was merely ticking over. It was with some sense of relief that Billie, flipping the office calendar to April, noticed that the sun was actually shining.

It had been a strange couple of months. Ever since the Claire incident, Jonah had said very little about the wingwalking. He and Barnaby, and occasionally Estelle, had been in the shed, fine-tuning and tinkering, but more often than not, when Billie had finished for the day and was heading off for Amberley Hill, they'd be sitting around with mugs of coffee, poring over flight charts, old airshow brochures, and a rather ancient and tattered map of Whiteacres.

Everyone just seemed to be itching for milder temperatures so that the planning of the air pageant could get underway. Billie, who was far more worried about her lack of new customers, plus the fact that yet again the new owner of the warehouses had failed to appear, was beginning not to care too much whether the Whiteacres Air Show ever came to fruition.

Jonah, after he'd whisked Claire home that January afternoon, hadn't been seen for at least a week. Barnaby—who had now taken Miranda out four times but sadly not stayed overnight—had said that he thought Jonah was taking a well-earned rest with his family on the Isle of Wight as the Sullivanair flights had all been hit by the weather. Estelle had been less diplomatic.

'Probably taking advantage of the fact that Antony Archibald and his display team are in the Far East and is bonking Claire stupid in some cosy little hideaway.' Billie had felt this was probably far more likely and had tried not to look jealous. Estelle hadn't even tried.

It seemed apparent now that if Jonah had been merely intending to frighten Claire that afternoon, then she'd played him at his own game and scored a resounding victory. Estelle had said she wasn't in the slightest surprised at Claire's chicanery, and as she didn't seem to think that there had been any replies to Jonah's 'be a barnstormer' advert, they might end up with Claire tied to the Art Scholl rig on the Stearman for the air pageant after all.

'She'll look like someone's slung a duvet out to dry,' Estelle had said disparagingly, 'but if Jonah's happy with that, then none of us will make him change his mind.'

'Don't you want to volunteer your services?' Billie had paused in the middle of the latest quarterly return for Maynard and Pollock, which Estelle had been overseeing. 'You'd look just right standing on the wing, waving.'

'I haven't even been asked.' Estelle had pushed the pile of forms away, the set of her elegant shoulders beneath the denim jacket speaking volumes. 'What about you?'

'God, no! I mean, I tested the rig in here on the ground, of course, just to make sure they'd fastened it properly—but up in the air? Never on your life! I saw what it did to Claire—even before she *pretended* to be petrified, I mean—and they hadn't even taken off!'

Estelle had grinned at her then, and both relishing the mental picture again, they'd poured more coffee and started on the last bit of the returns; and within minutes wingwalking was the last thing on either of their minds.

*   *   *

Therefore, on the following Sunday morning, when Billie was up just after six, stumbling into the kitchen in her Winnie-the-Poohs and tufty hair, and feeling more than a little apprehensive, it came as quite a shock. Whatever other completely insane things she'd done in her life she reckoned that this had to take the biscuit. Jonah's phone call the previous evening had come completely out of the blue.

'We've only got eight weeks until the pageant, and this is the first decent weather we've had,' he'd said cheerfully down the phone. 'I'd really appreciate it if you could just give me a hand.'

Billie, who'd been trying hard not to watch *Match of the Day* and was eating a Madras takeout from the Dil Raj, wearing her pyjamas and stretched out in solitary and sluttish splendour on the sofa, had choked on a piece of green pepper. 'I'm not doing what Claire did, so forget it.' She'd winced, remembering that Jonah's recollections of what Claire had done were probably more likely linked to bedroom gymnastics than aerobatics.

He laughed. 'I'm not expecting you to. It's just

353

that we've got so far behind schedule, and the airfield is clear with it being Sunday morning, and I thought you might like to help.'

'What about Estelle? Why don't you ask her to do it?'

'Estelle's in Luton for the weekend.'

Billie had raised her eyebrows and chased pilau rice round her plate and switched off the television just as they were announcing the Premiership's blue-riband FA Cup semi-final match. Luton? Again? So, Estelle had found a Jonah-replacement, had she?

Then she'd scoffed at Jonah, told him to get lost, forget it, find some other mug, but he'd interrupted the negatives and said it was only a test run again— like she'd done before. 'Oh, right. Just on the ground, you mean? Motionless?'

'Absolutely,' Jonah had said. 'And then maybe— if you're OK with it—just a quick pootle across the grass strip to see how it feels. To see how the rig stands up.'

'Still on the ground?'

'Definitely.'

'And if we pootled, I'd be strapped on and you wouldn't go above twenty miles an hour?'

'Yes, of course, and no, I won't.'

'OK—' Billie had mumbled because her mouth was crammed with chicken. 'If we're all going to muck in to save Whiteacres I really shouldn't be such a wimp. After all, it won't be like it's flying or anything, will it?'

So, here she was, on her one day of rest, feeling as apprehensive as she had on the morning of her driving test, with the chicken Madras still rumbling uncomfortably somewhere in her intestines.

Miranda, who had recently reverted to type and was now back to obscure hair dyes and the full Morticia Adams eye make-up, unlocked the front door and drifted into the kitchen. Her hair was in vibrant pink corkscrews, her jeans held up by a strange belt, and her T-shirt on inside out.

'Oh, doll—you're a lifesaver! If that's coffee make mine strong and black—and what the hell are you doing up before lunchtime on a Sunday?'

'I'm going to work.' Billie poured two mugs of coffee. 'What's your excuse?'

'I've—um—just got home.'

Billie turned away, nursing her mug.

'Billie . . .' Miranda sighed. 'Billie, I just wish—'

'Don't.' Billie shook her head. 'As long as you don't say anything then I don't have to think about it. I hate the man—'

'Excuse me. Can we just get one thing straight? He may well have been your boss at one time—but right now he's my lover—and my friend. I'd rather you didn't trash him, OK?'

Billie blinked. Miranda hadn't raised her voice on the Reuben issue since Christmas. Things must be dead serious. Still, she really didn't want to fall out over someone as reptilian as Reuben. 'Yeah. Sorry . . . You must just see a totally different side to him than I ever did.'

'Oh, I do, doll.' Miranda sank her face towards the coffee steam. 'I just don't know why you think he's so cranky.'

'Because he was. At least with me. He's manipulative and scary. He's a control freak. It was just as though, because he knew . . .' She stopped. Miranda didn't know what Reuben knew. Miranda was never going to know.

355

'Knew what?'

'Oh, you know—that I was desperate for a job when I started working for him,' Billie improvised wildly. 'Still, I don't any more—and if you like him then that's your business, I suppose.'

'Yes, it is.' Miranda nodded, looking a bit more cheerful. And you really have got him all wrong. You should see what he's done to Bazooka's. It's magic. Caught Offside will be the best club for miles. You'll come to the opening night, won't you?'

'Will you ever speak to me again if I don't?'

'No.'

'Well, it's a difficult choice . . .' Billie grinned. 'No, of course I'll be there. For you though—not him. And does this regular staying over at Reuben's mean that you definitely no longer have the hots for Jonah?'

Miranda nodded. Billie noticed that she was only wearing one false eyelash. She speculated vaguely on the whereabouts of its twin. She hoped it had got lodged somewhere extremely painful in Reuben and was giving him gyp at that very moment.

'Jonah's totally gorgeous, of course.' Miranda yawned. 'But off limits—and I suppose it was just as well I found out about him before I made a complete prat of myself. Have you seen much of the women in his life lately?'

'Not Claire, thank God, not since she ballsed-up the wingwalking. Although I'm sure Jonah's seen plenty. Estelle and I spend quite a bit of time together, funnily enough. I still feel like a scruffy kid when she's around, but she's actually a really nice person. Jonah must be mad not to—'

'Jonah's a businessman,' Miranda sucked in a

356

dizzying amount of caffeine. 'And if Claire's the one involved in the takeover it'd make sense to pillow-talk her into submission, wouldn't it?'

'God knows, but I think you've spent too much time with Reuben—that sounds exactly like one of his edicts! Anyway, Claire left Jonah, and apparently Antony Archibald is a fairish replacement, so I think she's a bit of a scheming cow too,' Billie said tartly, not wanting to waste any sympathy on the woman who was hellbent on destroying her livelihood.

She moved away towards her bedroom. There was still the dilemma of what to wear. It was something Cosmo didn't touch on—the right outfit for being strapped on top of an aeroplane.

'Billie . . .'

She turned round. Miranda was busy peeling off the lone eyelash and not looking at her.

'What?'

'About Reuben . . . Ah! Got it! That's better . . .' Miranda dropped the eyelash on the draining board and blinked wildly. 'No, listen, doll—I do need to know what went on with you two. It's important. I can't, well, commit myself until I know if . . .'

Billie laughed bitterly. 'If we had a fling, you mean? Not a chance. God, how many times do you need to be told? And anyway—er—have you asked *him*?'

'Course I have. He says there was nothing between you, too. He just says he was looking out for you, that's all.'

Bloody funny way of doing it, Billie thought. Moral and emotional blackmail, threats, harassment. She'd hate to see what Reuben could do to someone he really disliked. Still, if that's all

357

he'd told Miranda and she believed him, then that was fine.

'Well, there you are. He was being kind to me and I must have completely misinterpreted his motives, mustn't I? Now I' m going to get dressed, and if you're going back to bed to sleep off the carnal excesses of Slimeball Wainwright could you remember to switch the water heater on this afternoon? Ta.' She paused in the doorway. 'Anyway, what does Reuben reckon to your dalliance with Barnaby? Have you told him?'

'Oh, yes. Me and Reuben tell each other everything—well, almost. He says that as Barnaby's a customer, and wealthy, and has contacts, I should keep seeing him and treat them as business meetings.' She managed to look slightly embarrassed. 'I even get to keep the receipts, though Barnaby pays. Reuben says I might as well make the meals tax-deductible.'

Does he indeed? Billie thought. She wondered how Barnaby would feel about it if he knew. She somehow sensed that Barnaby saw his dates with Miranda as something completely different.

*   *   *

Two hours later, Billie, fastened into the rig on top of the Stearman in the warehouse having executed the backbreaking manoeuvres to get there, heard the doors slide open, saw' the gentle wash of primrose sunlight swoop across the grey walls, felt the warmth pervade the steely chill.

'I won't be a moment,' Jonah's disembodied voice wavered towards her. 'I'm just going to dig out reinforcements. I hope your other warehouse

358

chums aren't members of the Lord's Day Observance Society. Try not to fall off while I'm gone.'

She didn't. Ten minutes later, when Jonah came back with Zia and Sylvia, and Fred 'n' Dick, and Mike and three of his Guspers cronies, she'd gone through her previous earth-bound routine of waving and dancing and swivelling, and felt pretty chipper about the whole thing.

'Still all right?' Jonah shouted up. 'OK then— now we're going to do the pootling. Hang on tight while we get out of the shed.'

Billie waved down to the rest of the helpers. Sylvia waved back. The plane moved slightly as Jonah climbed into the cockpit and strapped himself in. Remembering Claire's catastrophe, Billie felt all her earlier bravado seeping away. She checked the buckles on her harness and held on for dear life as Jonah released the brakes and the warehousers shouldered and tugged the Stearman through the double doors.

Billie blinked in the brilliant sunlight. They'd stopped moving and gradually the feeling of vertigo was ebbing away. God help anyone who had to stand up here while the plane was off the ground and travelling at 150 miles an hour! God help her too—she still had to pootle.

'Great . . .' Jonah's voice echoed from the depths of the cockpit. 'Still OK, Billie?'

'Fine. Shaken. Stirred. Scared out of my wits. I'm just fine.'

Zia peered up at her through a lot of straggly hair. His face ran with rivulets of sweat and he looked as though he was having second thoughts about his poncho. 'Come on, you had the easy part.

You should have been down here pushing, right?'

Billie leaned out of her harness. 'And if I was down there pushing, right, we wouldn't be doing this at all, right? Someone has to be up here to test the rig, right? And as I'm the smallest, right—'

She thought she heard Jonah laughing. She hoped he'd stop. She didn't want him veering off course during the pootle.

'Well, I think you've done very well, Billie dear,' Sylvia said loyally. 'I've made a special lunch for afterwards to celebrate. And, of course, we're all very much looking forward to the next bit.'

Billie wasn't. There had to be a lot of difference between standing up here stationary and standing up here and pootling—as Claire had proved.

Billie,' Jonah's voice cut through the doubts, 'I'm gonna to start her up. The prop wash might come as a bit of a shock, but don't worry. If at any time at all you feel unsafe or any of the bolts come loose or your harness unbuckles or anything, just lean back and give me the thumbs down and I'll stop immediately, understand?'

Billie nodded. Lions and Christians sprang to mind. And Jonah had just thrown up a lot of new terrors. She pulled tentatively on her straps and wriggled in the harness. It all seemed very secure. It was like being on the roof rack of a car, she told herself. Just a piece of luggage. Nothing would happen as long as she stood absolutely still. She twisted round and stuck up her thumb.

Jonah grinned and started the engine. Christ! The judder that shot through her body must have been equivalent to standing on the San Andreas Fault. With her teeth rattling together and every inch of her flesh vibrating, Billie clung on to the straps and prayed. Then suddenly someone was punching her in the face and tearing her hair out at the same time. Immediately in front of her the nine-foot diameter of the propeller was revolving into infinity with all the unpitying force of a hurricane.

Pushed backwards into the harness, and still vibrating from head to toe, Billie feebly guessed that this was the 'prop wash'. Nice to know the correct term, she thought. She'd need it for the solicitors later when she sued Jonah for assault. God! The Stearman was moving! If this was twenty miles an hour she was Claudia Schiffer!

She felt as though someone was pulling the flesh off her face and knotting it behind her neck. They bumped and skimmed across the grass, and despite the sun, the wind ripped icily through her T-shirt like a chain saw. Billie, unable to breathe normally, took little sucks of air and tried to acclimatise her body to hurtling through space towards the perimeter wire.

Once she'd got used to the motion, the experience wasn't truly unpleasant. Adrenaline pumped through her veins, and honestly, if she'd been wearing thermal underwear and mittens and someone would blow her nose, it was quite exhilarating. Like flying.

Tentatively, she let go of the rig, and tried a little wave. Her hand disappeared behind her head with the force of the wind. If you waved in the air travelling at supersonic speeds, she reckoned, you'd have to have biceps like Arnie at least. She slid one leg up the rig and tried waving again. This time she was ready for the G force and lifted her arm high into the air.

Bloody hell! Were your elbows supposed to bend backwards? This wasn't as easy as she'd first thought. Maybe she'd have a word with Estelle and advise her to cut her fingernails and have a go—oh, and Reuben! Reuben truly deserved to be tied to the top of a runaway plane! And Claire and Acrobatic Archie and oh, yes, Kieran bloody Squires! God, she could think of simply tons of people who deserved this treat far more than she did.

The Stearman was slowing down. Reluctantly, fairly sure that her neck was going to snap, she turned her head. Jonah, in the depths of the cockpit, was beaming and sticking up both his thumbs.

'For God's sake keep one hand on the steering wheel!' Her words were snatched away and thrown into the air. 'Are we stopping?'

They weren't. They were turning. Slowly. And even more slowly, they bumped back towards the units.

'Oh, well done, dear!' Sylvia bobbled along beside the plane as it stopped. 'Absolutely excellent!'

Billie, unbuckling herself with frozen fingers tried to smile. Her lips were in rictus. Oh, damn . . . she still had to get down. Perversely, she didn't want Jonah to help her. Everyone was watching. She had to do it on her own. Holding onto the rig, casting a glance over her shoulder, she slithered from the harness, scrambled and slipped across the wing, and stepped backwards into the cockpit. She sat down with a thump. Her T-shirt was up round her ears, her ears were roaring, her nose had fallen off along with her fingers, and she felt like someone had dunked what remained of her in a bucket of ice.

Jonah leaned forward. 'You OK?'

'Fine . . .' Because she was. She felt great. She simply couldn't understand why Claire had made such a meal of it. Oh, yes she could—it was to get Jonah into bed . . .

Billie stood up shakily, hooked her leg over the side of the cockpit, and stepped onto the wing. The warehousers clapped as she wobbled towards the edge. It was all heady stuff.

As soon as Billie was on the ground, Sylvia enveloped her in a huge cuddle. 'I'm so proud of you! And you don't like planes at all, do you?'

Billie shook her head, but flying in the Stearman last autumn had been exhilarating and, to be honest, now she knew what to expect with the harness, if she was wrapped up and had ear plugs and nose clips and gloves, she wouldn't mind doing it again. On the ground, of course.

'Oh, and there's someone to see you,' Sylvia said. 'Over there. I must say he's rather dashing, my dear. Like James Bond. He arrived while you were on the plane. I told him to wait. He looked pretty tense to be honest. Not your boyfriend you've been keeping secret, is it?'

'Not a chance.' Billie pulled away from Sylvia's maternal hug, laughing. Then: 'Oh my God!'

Standing, smiling snakily outside her unit, was Reuben Wainwright.

chapter twenty-nine

'What the hell do you want?'

Reuben pursed his lips, staring at her, shaking his head in utter disbelief. 'Glasses, I think. I can't believe what I've just seen. How often do you get up to this sort of caper?'

'Every second Thursday—not that it's any of your business. And I asked you what you wanted.'

'So you did,' Reuben smiled, obviously for the benefit of the warehousers out on the airstrip. It almost looked real. 'I wanted to talk to you.'

Billie stared at a tower of purple loosestrife forcing its way up through a crack in the weedy concrete. She'd been afraid of this. Really afraid. He was going to marry Miranda. He was going to tell Miranda about Kieran. He was going to tell the world about Kieran. Nine months ago it wouldn't have mattered at all. Now, it mattered a hell of a lot. He was going to destroy everything she'd built up. Sylvia and Zia and Isla and Jonah— oh especially Jonah—would find out all about her stupid, sordid past. They'd know how carefully she'd fabricated everything, and while they probably wouldn't judge her morality, they'd surely have doubts about her honesty, wouldn't they?

She glared at him. 'Talk, then. But I'm not promising to listen.'

'Can't we go somewhere more private? Your office, perhaps?' He still looked friendly. Like the reptile he was, she knew that was when he was at his most dangerous. Coiled, motionless, ready to sink in the fangs . . .

'Billie!' Zia called across as Jonah and the warehousers headed cheerfully towards the units from the airfield. 'Get a move on, right! We're having a committee meeting in Sylv's and she's done a Sunday roast for everyone.'

'OK—I won't be a sec.' Billie couldn't remember the last time she'd had a proper Sunday lunch. She pulled a face at Reuben. 'Sorry, I don't seem to be able to fit you in at the moment. And no, you're not setting foot inside my warehouse, ever, so if we've got to talk it'll be out here—but make it snappy.'

Reuben shifted his feet. 'I'd still rather it was inside.'

'Well, it isn't going to be. And if it's about you and Miranda being together, then I'm sure she's told you I'm fine about it. I think she's mad, but she's a grown-up. I'll just hang around and pick up the bits. If it's about Caught Offside, or cabbying, or—or—Kieran, then I don't want to know.'

'It's not any of those. And I'll only take five minutes of your time. Truly. Trust me.'

'God! I'd rather trust Gideon the Throat-Slitter!'

'Who?' Reuben looked puzzled.

'Gideon the Throat-Slitter. I made him up. He sounded like the sort of bloke that I'd trust far more than you.'

'Billie, are you quite sure you're all right?'

'I've never been better. But I'd be happier never to set eyes on you again. I really never want to talk to you ever again either. I want you to leave me alone. Not only am I missing the best Sunday lunch I'll have had since I left Devon, but I'm free and I'm happy and I've just spent half an hour buckled on top of an aeroplane and—'

'I was very impressed. That's a hell of a scary

365

thing to do. You're a lady of many talents.'

'Shut up!'

'What? Oh, I didn't mean Kieran Squires. That's history isn't it?'

'Ancient. And—and everyone here knows about it, so you can't blackmail me.' Billie's stomach rumbled. 'And you're still keeping me from my lunch.'

'Ah, yes.' Reuben sniffed the air. 'The full works if I'm not mistaken: beef, Yorkshire puddings, roast potatoes, cauliflower, peas, probably leeks, thick gravy . . .'

Billie turned to walk away. 'And such a shame you're not invited. Sylv's an ace cook.'

'And very daring—considering the leases say there's no cooking to be done on the premises.'

'What?' She turned round. 'Oh, yeah—I know. But Sylv's different. It's not commercial. She's actually liv—How the hell did you know that?'

Reuben smiled. 'Because I've read every minute word of the small print, Billie. That's what I came to tell you. I'm the new owner of the warehouses.'

The ground almost came up and smacked her in the face. Her instinctive reaction was to punch Reuben on the nose; her second was to run away screaming. Luckily she opted for a third. 'You've got to be joking! You? Don't be mad—this is way out of your league! Anyway, I know who's buying up the leases: Claire Sullivan!'

'Never heard of the lady.' Reuben was still smiling. 'And whoever she is, and whatever she's buying, it certainly isn't these units. I signed all the paperwork last week and have spent this morning tying up a few loose ends with Simon Maynard. It's taken far longer than I'd intended because of the

366

variations in the leases. I'd hoped to take control way back at the beginning of the year.'

Billie whimpered. It couldn't be true! It just couldn't . . .

'I haven't told Miranda yet,' Reuben continued. 'I haven't told anyone else—and I asked Maynard and Pollock not to reveal my identity until I could tell you myself. I thought I owed you that.'

'Billie!' Zia stuck his head out of the next-door unit. 'Come on! Hurry up! Sylv's dishing up, right!'

'What?' Billie looked blank. 'Oh, right . . . I'll be there in a minute.' She couldn't eat anything now. She felt too sick. Zia disappeared and Billie looked at Reuben again. 'You can't do this to me. I'll—I'll have you arrested for harassment!'

'I'm not harassing you.'

'You bloody are! I stayed with the taxis because I was grateful to you for giving me the job. I stayed longer than I should because I was ashamed and scared and thought you'd tell everyone! Then, when I'd been brave enough to leave, you still wouldn't let go. Suddenly you wanted me to manage your poxy nightclub, and when I turned that down you buy—*buy!*—the place I've found on my own! And you don't call that harassment? You're sick! Really sick! You're stalking me—'

'I've told you before that I'm not.' Reuben took a step towards her. The smile was demonic now. 'And you don't have to worry. My owning the leases here won't make a scrap of difference to you—or your friends.'

'Of course it bloody will!' Billie sniffed back tears of anger. 'You'll have control over me again! I'll never be free of you, will I? Never!'

'Billie, all you have to do is what you're told,

367

make me welcome as your landlord from time to time, and you and your little no-hope pals will be able to carry on your pathetic businesses without any problems. Simple, huh?'

'Go to hell!' She started running towards Sylvia's unit. 'Go to hell, Reuben, and never come back!'

She hurtled into the incongruity of half a dozen people having a full-blown Sunday roast amongst parrots and palm trees.

'Ah, there you are, dear,' Sylvia smiled, getting to her feet. 'I've dished yours up and put it to warm under the sun lamp.'

'Thanks . . .' Billie snuffled, forcing her way past the pretend waterfall and trampling a monkey underfoot in her haste. Its plastic head shot off into the stratosphere. 'Christ—sorry! I won't be a minute, Sylv. I just need to use the loo . . .'

She belted into Sylvia's bathroom, fought her way through the potted rainforest and slammed the door behind her. This must have been exactly how Jonah had felt being faced with Aerobatic Archie that day when he'd first flown the Stearman—high as a kite and then the person you hated most in all the world appearing and turning your dreams to dust. Oh God, it was a nightmare. She'd have to leave now. She couldn't stay here with Sylvia and Zia and Isla and the Guspers because Reuben would tell them the truth about her and, worse still, have a reason for being there. All the time. But she couldn't leave either, could she? Because she had to stay to make sure the others were all right. Without her, Reuben wouldn't give a damn about the rest of the warehousers. Zi-Zi's and Guspers and Sylvia would all be out on their ears with nowhere to go.

'Billie?' Jonah's voice echoed from the other side of the door. 'Are you all right?'

Billie snatched a tissue from the rainbow box on the windowsill, sniffed into it, and opened the door. 'I'm fine. Don't spoil your meal for me.'

'Sylvia's put mine under the sun lamp as well.' Jonah walked in and closed the door behind him. He parted a fern. 'And I'm not prying or anything, but I couldn't help noticing your visitor, and, well . . .'

'My visitor,' Billie sniffed, 'has just done to me what your ex-wife has done to you.' She watched various emotions flicker across Jonah's face and knew that maybe she should have phrased it differently. 'No, what I mean is, he's a bastard.'

Jonah nodded slowly. 'Right. Not an ex-lover, then? Or a current?'

'No, thank goodness. He's my ex-boss.'

'Oh, right. The one you were hurling things at in the shed last year?'

'The same. Oh, and there's an added bit, too. He's Miranda's man.'

Jonah was now looking even more perplexed. Billie sighed and perched on the edge of the avocado lavatory seat with her feet resting on a tub of hostas. 'It's very complicated.'

Jonah leaned against the door. 'So I gathered.'

'Look, you know you said that the Aviation Incs said you could go ahead with the air show because they weren't selling up until September?'

He nodded.

'And yet we'd all had letters saying that our warehouse leases would be sold at the end of last year and they weren't?

Another nod.

'Well,' Billie exhaled, 'that's not because Claire and Aerobatic Archie have messed up their dates. It's because the airfield and the unit leases are being bought separately. By different people.'

'Ah—right . . . No, sorry. I'm still not with you.'

Billie ran her fingers through her wind-blown hair. It was so tangled that they caught fast. She tugged them out again. Now she probably looked like Ken Dodd. 'He—my visitor—my ex-employer on the taxis and Miranda's lover—Reuben Wainwright—has just told me that he's the new owner of the units.'

'And that's a problem?' Jonah frowned. 'I'm sorry to be obtuse, and I know you don't like the man, but—'

'It's the biggest problem in the world. The man's a serial stalker. He's only doing it to keep tabs on me. He's—'

'Whoa. Slow down a bit. Let me get my head round all this. This—um—Wainwright bloke—your ex-boss—he's Miranda's boyfriend?'

Billie nodded.

'That's a bit of a bugger. Barnaby really likes her. I don't think he knows that she's spoken for.'

'Christ!' Billie yanked at another tissue. 'We're not discussing Miranda's love life! We're discussing my survival.'

'Yeah, sorry.' Jonah looked contrite. 'I just wanted to get things clear. So, Miranda's man is after you?'

'No! Yes! Well, not in the way you think. Not because he likes me, but because he doesn't.'

'Bloody hell,' Jonah shifted his position against the door. 'I think I'd rather be asked to explain the theory of relativity. So, this bloke hates you, and yet he follows you about? Right? So either you go to the police or I beat him to a pulp.'

'You can't!' Billie wailed. 'I can't! He hasn't actually done anything! I mean, employing me on the taxis, and then offering me other work when I left, and now buying up my lease here isn't illegal, is it?'

'Probably not. Definitely not. He sounds more benefactor than molester. I don't think the police would be remotely interested. But I still don't see—'

Billie sighed heavily. 'No, I know you don't. And I can't explain. It's just that he has this hold over me—I can't tell you what—and I thought I was free of him, but I don't think I ever will be.'

Jonah stared at the hostas reflectively, then rubbed his eyes. 'Yeah, I see what you mean about us being in the same position. But don't jump the gun. This guy—whatever his motives—might be on the level. He may well turn out to be a perfectly normal landlord who you'll never see as long as the rent's paid on time.'

'Crap! If he wanted to buy warehouses there are about three million industrial estates that would bring in more money than this place!'

Jonah exhaled. 'True . . . Still, if you think about it positively, at least it means that your tenure is safe here, doesn't it? Better the devil you know and all that. This Wainwright bloke is probably just going to run the units as they've always been run. He's not going to chuck you out. And that's a damn sight better than thinking Claire and Antony are aiming to turn you into a theme park.'

'Yes, I know, but . . .' She buried her head in her hands. 'God, you don't know what he's capable of.

How really nasty he can be. He fools everyone.'

Jonah moved away from the door towards her. For a moment she thought he was going to hug her but he seemed to have second thoughts and turned his attention to a rubber plant. She wasn't sure whether to be annoyed, relieved, or jealous.

'Billie, it may be grandmother and eggs, but this man would have no hold over you at all if you told everyone yourself what it is he knows that you're so scared about.'

She sorted out the convolutions and shook her head. 'Never! I couldn't! Not now—it's too late. Anyway, it's more than that. It started off with him *knowing*—and now it's got to him *controlling* . . . God, you just don't understand, do you?'

Jonah shrugged. 'I can't, can I? But now you've told me this much, the only advice I can give you is keep an eye on him and get in writing any changes he wants to make to your conditions of tenancy— anything. And we'll all keep tabs on him too. As tenants, you'll have rights, and if he steps out of line we can be down on him with the full clout of the law. Don't worry unduly. We'll tackle any problems as they arise, all right?'

Billie nodded, savouring Jonah's 'we'. It gave her a slight feeling of solidarity.

'Great. Now smile. You've been absolutely amazing this morning, helping me with the rig and everything when I know you hated every minute of it. Don't let Mr Wainwright spoil things.'

'He always does, though.' She slid from the lavatory seat. 'He's scary. And I didn't hate the testing—you know I didn't. It was a blast, actually.'

Jonah's eyes rested on her speculatively. Then he smiled. Good. Now—do you think you could

372

put Reuben out of your mind long enough to manage just a mouthful or two of Sylvia's roast— before we have to endure Zia's lefter-than-left-wing comrades-in-arms speech?'

Billie shook her head. Her stomach rumbled again in dismay. She clutched at it, blushing. 'Oh, well, maybe just a little bit, then . . .'

She ate it all, and seconds. It wasn't until everyone had finished plate-scraping, and she, prompted by Jonah, had given them the sanitised version of events about Reuben, and the warehousers had got quite perky and agreed that as he was a local businessman with several strings to his bow that he'd probably be an ideal landlord, and the whole mood had lifted considerably, and Sylvia had clapped her hands and said, 'Reuben Wainwright? Lovely name! Very theatrical! And so handsome!' that they got down to some serious business.

They lounged on deckchairs as Zia took the floor and droned on and on about brotherhood and union and fellowship and alliance and combating the oppressors, until Mike from Guspers mercifully interrupted the flow and said that as they were no longer fighting for their survival in the units, that everyone should join forces with Sullivanair to make the air pageant an incredible success and, with luck, save Whiteacres from the Claire and Antony takeover.

They all looked at Jonah. Jonah looked delighted, and then raised his eyebrows at Billie.

'Of course we will,' she said without hesitation, although inside she still felt stricken. 'We'll do whatever we can. But I don't see . . .'

Everyone else, though, it seemed, saw very

clearly indeed. While Jonah and his flying aces would organise the display in the skies, the warehousers would see to things on the ground. They'd all pool their various resources for advertising. Stalls and food and exhibitions and all manner of excitements were put forward.

'A treasure hunt!' Sylvia said. 'In here! It'll be like a castaway's island! They'll have to buy maps at the door and follow really complicated clues.'

'And a fortune teller.' Zia tugged at his straggly beard. 'Isla's a wow with the tarot . . .'

Mike said that Guspers could make instant films: a minute long—people could dress up in Zi-Zi's costumes and act out their fantasies and have a memento to take home at the end of it.

Everyone looked at Billie. Along with Fred 'n' Dick, she felt that her warehouse had very little to offer. Then she thought about Reuben and how much she hated him—and how Jonah felt exactly the same about Aerobatic Archie—and how kind Jonah had just been to her, and how, if Sullivanair survived at Whiteacres, then she'd retain him as a customer as well as a friend, even if he was reattached to Claire . . .

What was it Stan had always said to her when she was a child? That there was nothing to be proud of in offering what came easily, because that was a cheap gift? That the truly benevolent gave what they could least afford? That the truly kind-hearted donated their lives for the good of others? Christ— she wasn't going that far, although if she did what she thought she was going to do, it may come very close . . . She took a deep breath and wiped her damp palms on her jeans.

'Um—well . . .' Her voice was squeaky and she

374

swallowed and tried again. 'Er—that is—I don't think my unit has an awful lot to offer, but if it's OK with everyone, and Jonah hasn't got anyone else in mind, then I'd—um—like to volunteer my services as a proper wingwalker.'

chapter thirty

Two weeks after Billie's suggestion, Jonah was still shocked. Whatever else he'd expected Billie to offer to do for the show, it certainly hadn't been that. And, more specifically, not so soon after she'd been upset by the revelations of that Reuben Wainwright guy.

Given all that stuff with Reuben, and Billie's obvious terror of flying, he felt nothing but admiration for her. Wingwalking was definitely not for the faint-hearted, but for someone with her fear it was bravery bordering on insanity. He'd experienced a feeling of fleeting satisfaction in knowing that what he'd said to Vinny about Billie had been true. He'd always been sure that when the Stearman did its first barnstorming display, it would be Billie strapped above him.

God—but for her to ride the Stearman would be like him offering to stand in a pit full of house spiders to save someone else's skin. He shuddered involuntarily at the thought. Like most arachnophobes, the mere three-inch span of those awful, bouncing, scuttling, scaly, brown things which invaded the house every September and lurked to catch you unawares was enough to make his hair stand on end, his mouth go dry, his heart thunder . . .

He guessed that Billie's fear was the same. Simply terror on a different level. Mind you, he'd always found it didn't do to delve too deeply into the female psyche. If deciding to strap herself to the top of the Stearman was a catharsis for Billie's other problems, who was he to argue? He was just immensely grateful to her. And wildly proud. And, embarrassingly, totally amazed that she so obviously trusted him. It was a very long time since anyone had shown such faith.

He stared at the burbling television screen, seeing nothing, hearing less. Stretching, he zapped the TV into silence. This was, he reckoned, quite crazy. Nearly midnight and he was here, in the beige living room, watching crap and being introspective when Estelle was showered and scented and totally naked in his bed.

Again, almost hearing Vinny's hoot of incredulous laughter, Jonah lolled back on the couch's cushion, which, like everything else in this skimpy flat, was spare and hard and irritated more than comforted.

Tomorrow he'd be flying the Shorts to Dublin, which was quite a coup because it was a trip for a clutch of businessmen whom he'd been wooing for ages, and they could put a lot of regular charters his way. And then he had to telephone the ex-RAF mate in Glasgow who, he'd heard on the grapevine, might have dug out the whereabouts of a cheap Shorts and a Skyvan for him. And then he was meeting up with Billie in the shed to see how her practising had been going.

She'd left him a note to say she'd spent at least an hour every day in the stationary Stearman, practising undoing the harness, climbing onto the wing, fastening herself into the rig, and getting the feel of things generally. The ground-level rehearsals had apparently gone well. He couldn't wait to see the reality—and maybe talk to her about Reuben.

He still wasn't sure about Reuben's role in her life: surely if he wasn't involved with Billie in some way either past or present, he wouldn't have had such a profound effect on her. And if, as she said, he wasn't *involved* as such, but had some sort of hold over her, what the hell was it?

Jonah desperately hoped that it wasn't drugs. Recreational, or no, they'd been no fun for him when Claire had got hooked—and no fun for her when she was on her downers. He was pretty sure it wasn't anything along those lines, though. Billie seemed to have so much natural fizz that artificial stimulation would be somewhat gratuitous, wouldn't it? Anyway, he'd kept reassuring himself, even if it had been drugs at some time in the past, it certainly wasn't now. Billie showed none of the signs of addiction that he'd recognised so clearly and painfully in Claire.

So, maybe it was money? Maybe Billie still owed Reuben money on an unpaid loan—or perhaps she'd helped herself to the petty cash in a desperate moment when she'd been a taxi-driver? Or maybe she knew something sinister about Reuben and he was determined that it stayed between the two of them?

Whatever it was, she hadn't wanted to share it, had she? Jonah sighed. He would have liked to have been able to help her—but how could he when she clearly didn't want him to know? When they'd been in Sylv's bathroom he'd really wanted to cuddle Billie, she'd looked so frail and defenceless and almost defeated—even though he knew damn well she wasn't.

Instinctively he'd moved to put his arms round her and tell her there was nothing that would shock him, and if she wanted to talk, he'd be more than happy to listen. But, of course, he hadn't, and he was really afraid that all he'd done was end up spouting platitudes and sounding like some holier-than-thou Victorian paterfamilias.

He sighed again, knowing he should go to bed, and not wanting to. Unable to pour himself a drink because of flying, he used his normal delaying tactics and let his mind trawl through the other happenings of the past two weeks instead.

Barnaby was back from Derbyshire with wads of money from calling in debts and flogging horse shares and a couple of inherited paintings, and had spent the last week testing the Slingsby to its aerobatic limits, and wining and dining Miranda at the Dil Raj. This last bit Jonah thought was strange considering she was supposed to be attached to the odious Reuben, but Barnaby had said she'd told him that she was seeing someone, it was all cards on the table, and he and Miranda merely enjoyed each other's company.

Jonah, knowing Barnaby well, didn't believe a word of it. He knew that Barnaby was smitten by the zany Miranda; knew that her mournful beauty—so at odds with the pink hair and the frank speech—had knocked him for six. Jonah had a feeling it was all going to end in tears—and that they wouldn't be Miranda's.

Possibly the best recent news of all—after Billie's heroics, of course—had been that the Whiteacres

Aviation Incs had given the pageant the go-ahead for the second Sunday in June, and were busily arranging air space and flying slots and being generally bureaucratic. Claire, who had rejoined Antony Archibald on his tour and was currently in the States, hadn't been in touch with Jonah at all, so obviously she didn't know—yet.

Jonah stared at the blank television screen again and groaned. He had to stop thinking about Claire. He'd felt such a bastard when he'd scared her so badly, when all he'd been intending to do was to put her off having anything to do with him, the Stearman, wingwalking, and especially Whiteacres. It had all backfired so badly. He'd rushed her home to the flat, fed her brandy, run her a bath—and made love to her for hours.

It hadn't helped either of them. Claire had been stoned throughout so he could have been anybody, and he'd felt bloody stupidly guilty because of Antony. They'd dressed in silence and he'd driven her to Heathrow to fly out to join Antony's team, and he'd then gone to Southampton and hopped on the catamaran to the Isle of Wight and the no-questions sanity of his parents.

Still, he thought, stretching, he really should stop crucifying himself. It was all going to be all right. The warehousers had been frantically busy getting all their plans organised and—He stopped. And now he really should go to bed and he still didn't want to sleep with Estelle . . .

Not being into self-analysis, he wasn't really sure why. For some reason she'd been furious about Billie volunteering for the wingwalking thing, and they'd had several pretty heated rows, but it wasn't that. He enjoyed arguments. When he'd been

379

married to Claire, her tempers had spilled over into red-hot passion and they'd enjoyed incredible sex afterwards. No! He punched the rock-hard cushion. Stop thinking about bloody Claire! It's over. You both know it's over . . .

Jonah was dogged by the nagging feeling that if Estelle had ever said that she loved him, or if he felt any sort of reciprocal deep emotion for her, then making love would be a natural culmination of their fairly casual relationship. He was pretty sure that after loving Claire so deeply, he'd probably never be able to perform adequately again . . . Christ—was this it? The end of his sex life for ever? Simply because he was more hooked on planes than women? Because he always wanted what he couldn't have—and when he'd got it, it wasn't what he'd thought it would be?

Whatever it was, he really couldn't put bed off any longer or he'd be falling asleep over the Irish Sea. He switched off the lights and walked into the bedroom. Estelle was asleep. He felt guilty at the relief. He watched her as he undressed, so beautiful even with the blonde hair tousled and the make-up carefully creamed off. Claire had never removed her make-up before going to bed. There'd never been time . . .

He slid in beside Estelle, knowing that he'd let her down again, and that she must have fallen asleep waiting for him, far too proud to pad out to the living room and remind him of her presence. In the morning there would definitely be recriminations and she'd take her revenge by letting people know once more that he was no great shakes in the bedroom. And then, which was probably worse, she'd perform a few minor acts of sabotage in the Sullivanair office, and letters would be filed before they were answered or phone calls would be cut off, and he'd feel like a total shit because it was all his fault.

He switched off the bedside lamp, hitting the side of his face on the padded headboard and cursing silently. As he tentatively reached for her, Estelle turned in her sleep and nestled in his arms. Jonah swallowed and held her and felt no love, no arousal; the only emotions he felt were sorrow and regret because those vital things were missing.

* * *

'Sodding nice one,' Vinny said as they made the afternoon return trip from Dublin. 'Bloody diverted to bloody Southampton. Now we'll have to sit there for ages until we can get a slot back to Whiteacres. What the hell's going on?'

Jonah flipped off his headset. 'Air-traffic control say they've got a BAC One-Eleven making an emergency landing at Whiteacres and taking our slot there. It's no major disaster, just low fuel or something. We've got the option of circling till it's sorted, or going straight into Southampton.'

'I'll go and put it to the passengers.' Pam straightened her cap. 'I'll tell them landing at Southampton will be quicker. A few more free drinks, the last of the peanuts, and the offer of a couple of taxis up the A 34 to Whiteacres at Sullivanair's expense should do it.'

Jonah checked the dials in front of him and nodded. He hoped so. The outward journey had been a dream; the businessmen had been delighted and said they'd definitely fly with him again. He didn't want to foul-up now.

'But we'll be bloody late getting back and I've got a steaming date,' Vinny groaned, resting his head back in the copilot's chair. 'And it looks like being a really warm evening too. I thought I'd take her out into the country . . . You know—find a nice little pub by the river, and then . . .'

Jonah stopped listening. Vinny's delayed date was just slightly less important than him not being able to meet up with Billie for the Stearman run-through. He'd ring her from Southampton as soon as they'd touched down and he'd sorted out his passengers. He'd have to ring Estelle too. He'd promised her a drink to make up for the previous night's débâcle.

He tuned into Southampton's radio frequency, confirming that they'd be landing there in approximately ten minutes. The cheerful voice OKed and received, and reviewed air pressure and wind speed.

'Twelve S.O.B., Southampton, including crew,' Jonah said into his mike. 'Golf Hotel Charlie Foxtrot—heading received. Turning onto heading now . . .'

The rest was routine. Veering onto his allotted glide path, with Vinny calling out the speed and the height as both dwindled, Jonah reduced the engine power, set the flaps and began to nose-down for landing. He lifted his eyes momentarily from the control panel. Vinny was right: it was going to be a beautiful evening. Through the windscreen the sun was glinting off the sea, then the sea disappeared and the sun followed their course and melted across the mud flats like molten toffee.

Jonah banked sharply. They were over the oil

refinery at Fawley now, and turning on to follow the estuary. Five more minutes and they'd be in Southampton. Twenty minutes and he'd be able to ring Billie and talk about the Stearman.

Pam popped her head into the cabin. 'The bods back there are fine and dandy about the diversion. No probs. Chuffed to bits to be getting a taxi. They've asked for brochures for further flights.'

Jonah stuck up his thumb as she disappeared to strap herself in for landing. The suburbs of Southampton rushed up to meet them like welcoming dogs, and with the skill of years of practice, Jonah guided the Shorts' ten thousand kilos towards the runway.

*   *   *

It was half an hour before Jonah could get to a phone. First, he rang his ex-RAF contact in Glasgow and arranged to meet when he next flew up there, to view the Shorts and the Skyvan. Then he rang Estelle. Her mobile was switched off and the office answerphone was on. Sodding hell. She'd probably left—not just the office, but the company.

He tried Billie's mobile next. She'd had a landline connected, but he thought she was probably in the Stearman going through her routine. He could see her, with her hair dishevelled and the tip of her tongue protruding from the corner of her mouth as she concentrated. No answer. So he punched out Billie's warehouse number. Two rings and the answerphone kicked in.

'Pascoe's Warehousing. Thank you for ringing me—please don't think I'm not here and you can come over and burgle the place—I just can't get to the phone . . . Oh, and I'm not going to put you on hold or play "Greensleeves" or Vivaldi, so don't hang up. Please leave your name and number and a short message and I'll ring you as soon as— ooops—run out of answer tape time—Bye!'

He laughed over the screech of the tone. 'Great message, Billie. It's me: Jonah. We've had to divert to Southampton, so I'll be a bit later than I'd anticipated. Please wait for me if you can. If not, leave a note and we'll fix up another time. Hope all's well, and—'

There was a crackle and a clunk.

'Jonah?' Billie's voice was breathless. 'Hi. Sorry, I keep forgetting to switch the answerphone off. Are you OK? Why have you diverted? Not something wrong with the plane?'

'No, we're fine. Somebody else took our landing slot at Whiteacres and it was better for my passengers to fly in here rather than circle. We've been told we'll be cleared for takeoff in about thirty minutes so I can be there in an hour at the outside. Will that be OK?'

'Yeah, of course. I'm still working anyway.'

'No more hassles with Reuben?'

'None. We've all had letters from Maynard and Pollock this morning naming him as the new owner, but I haven't seen him or anything. I'm pretending it's not happening. If I don't see him before, then I'll corner him at the club.'

'Which club?'

'He's opening a new nightclub in Amberley Hill in a couple of weeks' time, remember—I think I

384

told you? Miranda's press-ganged me into going. I don't want to, but it'll give me a great opportunity to poke him in the eye, won't it?'

'Metaphorically or literally?'

'What do you think? Oh, I've got loads to tell you. Everyone's working their socks off here, getting ready for the show. It's great that the Incs are taking over health and safety and crowd control and all the boring bits, isn't it? Maybe I can be employed on the gate taking money?'

'What?' Jonah grinned into the receiver. 'You won't have time for that! I'm intending to give at least ten barnstorming displays during the afternoon and—'

'Yeah, I know.' Billie sounded impatient. 'But they won't involve me now, will they? Which is a pity because I've been weightlifting with baked bean tins and I've got this—'

'Why won't they involve you? Oh Christ—you haven't had second thoughts about it, have you?'

'No . . .' Billie sounded slightly indignant. 'I haven't. But you obviously have. I mean, I know Estelle's a lot more glamorous than me, but I'd have thought you might have told me that you were going to use her in place of me.'

'What?' Jonah screamed into the receiver, making Vinny gawp across from the next booth. 'What the hell are you talking about?'

'Estelle doing the wingwalking. She said you'd decided she'd be better because she's more aero-user-friendly or some such crap. She's here now. Practising in the Stearman.'

*   *   *

385

For the first time in his flying career, Jonah wished that he was on the ground. If he'd been driving he'd have broken all the speed limits to get back to Whiteacres. As it was, he was practically tearing his hair out by the time he landed at Whiteacres, disembarked, and dumped his paperwork with air-traffic control.

Shedding his cap, jacket and tie as he belted across the tarmac and onto the grass airstrip, and then flouting all the Aviation Incs laws by cross-countrying through the Aeroclub's allotted runways and praying he wouldn't be mown down by a Piper Cherokee or a stray Cessna, he practically hurdled the broken-down part of the perimeter fence.

The doors of the units were all open in deference to the gaudy May sunshine, and the burned-out hatchbacks on the concrete now had their seasonal covering of snaking pink and white convolvulus. And, thank God, Billie's liveried van was still parked outside her warehouse.

'Estelle!' Jonah panted to a halt inside the shed. 'Estelle! What the hell do you think you're doing?'

'Practising.' Estelle's voice floated lazily through the dusty darkness from the Stearman's upper wing. 'I know you'd said Billie had volunteered, but that was before I was given the option, wasn't it? Naturally, I assumed that as I'm of no use to you personally, then the least I could do, as a member of Sullivanair, was—'

'Please come down.'

Estelle laughed. 'Why? I thought you could start her up and we'd have a couple of hours' flying time before the light goes.'

'Estelle,' Jonah sucked in his breath, 'stop messing about. You know that Billie's doing the

386

wingwalking. We've already discussed it and—'

Estelle leaned down from her standing position on the wing high above him. Her blonde hair tumbled forwards. 'No, we didn't. There was no discussion. You'd made the decision—one which I frankly thought was insane given Billie's phobia—and to be honest I couldn't give a toss about who owns the airfield, but I do care about how outsiders will view it if I'm not part of your team, so now I'm offering my services.'

In the shafts of filtered sunlight, Jonah could see that she was strapped into the rig. She was wearing the skin-tight leather trousers and a very brief white top. He had to admit that she looked breathtaking. He wanted to slap her.

'Just get down. Billie is shorter and lighter and—'

'She looks like a boy!' Estelle hooted. 'Where's the glamour? Barnstorming is supposed to be pretty damned sexy, remember? Do you honestly think that that—that child, in her jeans and her tatty T-shirt, sweet as she is, would set anybody's pulses racing?' She leaned even further down and smiled directly into his eyes. 'Although, of course, knowing that your sex drive flickers somewhere just below impotence, she might appeal to you.'

'That's not very nice, is it?' Billie's voice said quietly from the back of the warehouse. 'And I'd really prefer it if you didn't scream at each other in my unit. I'm expecting a customer shortly, and I don't want to give the wrong impression. And, Estelle, I've done my barnstorming homework too.'

Billie walked out of the office. Estelle, from her high vantage point, having a better view than Jonah, exhaled loudly. Jonah turned and peered through the low-light gloom and nearly fainted.

Billie, glaring at them, was clad, head to toe, in a skintight shimmering bodysuit. It was spectacularly sexy and left absolutely nothing to the imagination. With its silver base and swirling tongues of emerald and purple, it was like an animated Sullivanair advertisement. Her climbing boots had been sprayed silver to match her gloves, and her hair was hidden beneath a tightly fitting silver, green and purple matching cap.

'God Almighty!' Eventually finding his voice, Jonah shook his head. 'You look absolutely bloody amazing! When—I mean who—I mean, why the hell didn't you tell me?'

'Because I wanted it to be a surprise.' Billie still wasn't smiling. 'It seemed to me that everyone else was doing so much, so quickly, to get this show up and running. I just thought that this . . .'

Jonah could hear Estelle snatching angrily at her harness straps. He didn't care. He simply couldn't take his eyes off Billie.

'Isla spent all week putting it together from material she'd dug out. It's the real thing: high-density Lycra. She's even made me a fleecy skin suit to wear underneath it to keep out the cold.' Billie shrugged. 'Pity, really, seeing that I won't be needing it.'

'Oh yes you will.' Jonah rushed across to her, again wanting to hug her. But instead, he just gazed at her, still shaking his head in disbelief. 'You'll be the star of the show. Christ—who's going to be looking at the Stearman with you dressed like that?'

'No one,' Estelle said, leaping to the ground. 'My apologies, Billie. You look wonderful, but my argument isn't with you—you know that, don't you?'

'I suppose so.' Billie shrugged, her silver shoulders sparkling. 'I mean, we've sort of become friends, haven't we?'

Estelle laughed. 'Strange as it may seem, we have. United in a common lost cause. So please don't take this personally.' She swivelled her face round to Jonah. 'Well, how about it, Mr Sullivan? You needed a wingwalker—and now you've got two. Which one of us is it going to be?'

chapter thirty-one

Confused by London, and not truly understanding the intricacies of professional football, Faith Pascoe hovered outside the imposing green and white wrought-iron gates of the Putney Soccer Village, and wanted to go home.

As nonstop traffic droned past, a million people pushed against her, speaking, it seemed to her, in every language under the sun except any that she understood. Her head ached in the throbbing May heat and her feet, in the shoes bought specially for the occasion, were absolute murder.

The earlier part of the journey had been quite fun. Buoyed by the unfamiliarity and a sense of adventure, Faith had purchased a newspaper and two packets of Polos and waited on a platform crammed with commuters, feeling very bold. She'd bagged a window seat, and the train journey from Exeter to Paddington had been remarkably swift and comfortable. She'd even struck up a conversation with someone in the buffet car and come away clutching her bacon burger and espresso feeling like a seasoned traveller.

Getting a taxi outside Paddington station hadn't been a problem either, and the chatty cab-driver had had no problems at all with finding Putney Football Club's hallowed ground. But then, she supposed, he wouldn't.

The problems were all hers now—and Faith was pretty sure they could only get worse. This time, at least, she'd only partially lied about her journey. She'd told Stan and the boys that she was going up to London for the day to visit her one-time student nursing roommate, Alice, who was over from Canada. This part was absolute fiction—her roommate was called Mary and she now lived in Clacton—but Stan had luckily forgotten, and the boys didn't know, and she wasn't going to enlighten them. To Kieran Squires, she'd told the absolute truth—well, almost. There were a few things, like her relationship to Billie, that she'd saved for later.

And that's what bothered her really: the almost frenzied speed with which Kieran had replied to her letter and invited her up to see him, despite the fact that she'd used the surname Pascoe. Did this really mean that he was desperate to get hold of Billie for exposing his extramarital affairs? She was very much afraid it did.

Even keeping Kieran's letter from Stan had been difficult. After all, plush vellum envelopes bearing the crest of one of the country's top football clubs didn't drop on to the farmhouse doormat every morning. Stan had thought they'd won the pools. She'd scooped it up and dismissed it as junk mail with a great deal of flippant overemphasis, she realised now, then hidden it in the hens' nesting boxes and thanked her lucky stars that she hadn't been born a generation earlier. She'd never have made a wartime agent.

Now, irritated beyond belief by the crowds and the noise and the nagging blisters on her heels, Faith, following the instructions in the letter, pushed the Putney FC bell and jumped as a disembodied voice answered somewhere to the left of her jawbone. Good heavens—now what was she supposed to do?

As the intergalactic voice whined for a second time, she leaned towards the gates and taking a deep breath, used the tor-trembling bellow she employed when calling home the dogs. 'Hello!!! I'm Faith Pascoe!!! I've got an appointment with—'

'Madam,' the voice remonstrated tinnily, 'you merely need to speak slowly and quietly into the grille. No need to raise your voice to that pitch.'

'Sorry!!!' Faith yelled again into the air, turning her back on a crowd of onlookers. 'We don't have things like this in Devon!!!'

'I can quite believe it. And you had an appointment with whom?'

'Kieran Squires!!! I'm here representing the North Devon Boys Football Apprentice Training Scheme!!!' OK, so she might not have told the whole truth . . . She straightened her shoulders. 'He is expecting me!!!'

'Very well, madam. When I open the gates you should proceed to reception and state your business. Quietly.' He opened and Faith proceeded. Once she'd explained her mission to a woman with too many teeth and not enough eyebrows, she was asked to take a seat and wait. Faith sat, and immediately eased off her shoes. Ooh! The bliss! The blood pinged round the veins in her sore heels, and the blisters sucked in fresh air, and the whole felt almost as good as a warm lavender bath.

Once her feet had stopped screaming and she could wriggle her toes, Faith took stock of her surroundings. It was all very swish and very tall. Like a modernist cathedral. Everywhere had the Putney FC motif picked out in green and white, and everything else appeared to be chrome and glass and chandeliers. Silent escalators rolled up and down from reception's green and white carpet, carrying elegant men and fashionable women to and from who knew where, to do who knew what. It was light years away from the football ground at home where two dogs and a man in a wheelchair constituted a crowd, and Siddy Clargo from the papershop took your pound on the gate, and his wife, Beryl, sold fruit pies and weak teas at half-time.

Through one of the plate-glass windows she could see the outlines of the Putney Shop, the Putney Bistro, the Riverside Restaurant, the Putney Hotel and a mass of turnstiles. The football ground itself, hidden from view behind huge striped fences, was only recognisable because of the floodlights.

The walls of reception were crammed with photographs of Putney players past and present, and Faith whiled away several happy minutes perusing the faces. Some she recognised, others not. She could see Kieran Squires, though. He looked much the same as he had on Maeve and Declan's Taunton mantelpiece, but without, of course, the accoutrements of Fenella and the kiddies.

'Mrs Pascoe? Faith?'

She looked up. The photograph had come to

392

life. Oh, but it didn't do the boy justice! He was gorgeous! God knows where he'd inherited his looks—certainly not from Dec and Maeve. The beauty must have skipped a generation.

'Mr Squires . . .' She stood up, extending her hand. Without her shoes she was about level with his chest. 'Thank you so much for seeing me.'

'Thank you for writing.' He was still pumping her hand in an energetic fashion. And smiling. His voice was soft and husky. Another throwback to his Irish forebears, Faith thought. He pumped harder. 'It was a bit of a lifesaver, your letter.'

It was? Faith, her hand going numb, tried to remember exactly what she'd written and couldn't—apart from the Apprentice Boys thingy, of course—so she muttered vaguely and hoped it sounded convincing.

It probably did, as Kieran let go of her hand and indicated that she should follow him towards one of the silently gliding up-escalators. He had nice manners, she thought, as he stood back to let her go first, and then stepped on behind her, close enough to prevent her tumbling backwards, but not close enough to be threatening.

Unused to mountainous moving staircases, as to much else in this teeming city, Faith decided not to pursue any further conversation until they were stationary. Apart from the unfamiliarity, she was still carrying her shoes, which meant that not only was she clinging on to the handrail for dear life, but that the escalator's treads were soothingly vibrating through her sore feet. She wondered whether she might be allowed to stay on several more times for the full massage.

As they reached the top, fearful of catching the

toes of her tights in the workings, she took a giant stride and nearly cannoned into a trophy cabinet. Kieran was there immediately, holding her elbow, making sure she was all right, and not looking in the least amused at her obvious lack of experience. Nice boy, she reaffirmed to herself. Just the way she'd brought up Jon, Alex, Tom and Ben to behave. Maeve and Dec had done a good job.

As they walked along a green and white corridor, Faith mentally reminded herself that this nice boy was not only playing away from home, risking losing Fenella and the kiddies, but had also obviously put the frighteners on her own daughter, and therefore was definitely not such a nice boy after all.

It was what they always said back home, when she and Pat and Miriam got together for coffee: the quiet ones truly were the worst. Many's the time they'd looked at the photograph of the latest baby-faced serial killer in the tabloids and read glowing reports of his character from his neighbours—nice boy . . . very quiet . . . kept himself to himself . . . bit of a loner . . . collected butterflies . . . Not that Kieran Squires was a serial killer, of course, nor had he obviously been very careful about keeping himself to himself, but the principle was the same.

Faith suddenly realised that they'd stopped walking and that Kieran was smiling at her again. She hoped he hadn't been talking to her. She didn't think he had. It dawned on her that Kieran's wide and warm smile hid rather slow thought processes.

'Through here—this is the PR room.' He opened a door leading into a tiny and deserted office crammed with brochures and folders and presenters and posters all in neat bundles ready for dispatch. 'We're very quiet today.'

Faith padded across the ankle-deep carpet and deposited her shoes under an ivy green leather chair with her handbag neatly beside them. She sat down without being asked because she was beginning to feel quite disorientated and to wish she'd left well alone. After all, Billie was as chirpy as anything at the moment, if her phone calls were anything to go by, and she'd certainly been the life and soul of the family party over Christmas. And all Faith's probing into whether Billie was being hounded by gangland hoodlums had brought hoots of laughter and not a flicker of fear—so whatever, or whoever, had driven her to flee in the first place was probably long forgotten.

If this gloriously handsome but not very bright man standing in front of her was truly the cause of Billie's flight, mightn't she just be raking up all sorts of nastiness, and causing more problems than she solved? It seemed that whatever reservations she had, it was far too late to back down now, as Kieran had hitched up a matching leather chair and was still beaming at her.

She beamed back. 'This is very nice. Very plush . . .' Oh God. Get it over . . . 'You said that my writing to you was a lifesaver. Can I ask why?'

'Yeah.'

Faith waited, then realised that he was merely answering her question. It was probably like being interviewed on *Match of the Day* to Kieran. Stating facts, not offering explanations. He'd probably say 'over the moon' or 'sick as a parrot' or 'at the end of the day' in a minute.

'Right,' Faith took control. 'So, why were you so pleased to get my letter?'

Kieran understood this one. 'Because it meant I could have a charity, see? And coming from Devon myself, a local one connected with football was just right.'

Faith groaned silently. Bugger. Now she'd have to explain to him that the North Devon Boys whatsit was a figment of her imagination. She wasn't sure that he'd be able to keep up.

'Great, eh? Oh,' Kieran nodded towards a juice trolley in the corner, 'I'm being rude, though. Would you like a drink?'

'Yes that would be lovely. It's so hot. Lots of ice please. Isn't that clever! All in the same machine? Well, I never!' She waited until Kieran had settled again, and she'd taken a couple of gulps of mango and guava. 'Now, so you need a charity, do you? Is that something that Putney encourages?'

Kieran grinned. He had obviously been programmed for this one. Settling back in his leather chair and crossing one well-muscled leg over the other, he launched into his explanation. Putney FC liked all its first-team players to be actively involved in Good Works. It was a bit of an early damage limitation exercise (Faith's interpretation—not Kieran's words) for any bad publicity. Kieran so far hadn't got one. A charity, that is. As it was the closed season—after the Cup Final and before the summer friendlies—Kieran had been told by his agent and Putney's coaching and managerial staff to find himself something to support sharpish.

'All the best ones were gone.' He opened wide eyes to Faith as if shocked to discover that Cancer Relief and Amnesty International should have been snatched away from him. 'Even the animal ones. It

396

would be really nice to be able to help kids like I was—you know, mad about football . . .'

Faith cursed herself silently again and continued to listen. Kieran would be really happy to make appearances at the boys' matches, and do some coaching, and even bring them up to Putney's ground on training days—things like that. Faith realised he was leaning forward waiting for her to hurl herself into paroxysms of joy.

She hurled. 'Wonderful! Just wonderful! The boys'll love it! It's so kind of you!'

'And they'll be in touch to make it official like, will they?' Kieran looked a tad anxious. 'So that my agent and the coach and the chairman and everyone here knows that it's for real, like? See, I gave my agent the slip today just so that I could set this up. All on my own. He'll be ever so pleased.'

Faith sighed. Christ, now she'd have to go home and ring round every under-eleven football team in the whole county and tell them Kieran Squires was happy to coach them—and they'd all think she was completely insane—and Stan and the boys were bound to get wind of it, and there'd be all sorts of awkward questions and—

'Oh, definitely. Definitely. Just give me a bit of time to get things sorted.'

She could do it. Of course she could. After the visits to the newspaper offices at Willowbridge, and then cross-questioning that nice Marion at Rustique, and blagging her way in Dec and Maeve's' QVC palace, and now this—suddenly developing a children's football charity should be a piece of cake.

'Of course,' she sipped some more juice, 'there

397

might be publicity.'

'Ah?'

'Local publicity.' She had to do it. Now. 'Like from the Devon newspapers. Like the *Devon Argus*.'

'Ah?'

Jesus! Faith downed the rest of her drink. The crushed ice caught on a none-too-secure filling and made her eyes water. 'My daughter used to work on the *Devon Argus*.'

'Ah?'

'Billie. Billie Pascoe . . .'

She could almost see the cogs turning. Kieran's beautiful eyes looked puzzled for a moment, then narrowed, then shot open. 'Fuck me!'

It wasn't quite the reaction she'd been expecting. She took refuge in her empty glass and wanted to be at home surrounded by the grandchildren—it was that bad.

'Billie's your daughter?' Kieran had gained his equilibrium. 'Billie? Tiny? Dead pretty? Blonde hair—like Zoe Ball? Real, real, clever?'

Faith nodded. That about summed her up.

'What a coincidence, eh?' Kieran looked stunned. 'It didn't click. The Pascoe bit. I—um— met her—um—once . . . No—er—twice I think it was . . . It might have been more . . .'

'Really? What a small world! And—er—how long ago was that, then?'

'Oooh—er—about two years ago . . . No, three now maybe. . .

'And she came to interview you, did she? Good heavens, I had no idea! What was she doing—an expose on the private lives of the soccer greats?'

'A what?'

'Expose. It means—oh, like an in-depth look at

398

your life away from the football field.'

This seemed to touch as raw a nerve in Kieran as the juice had done in her filling. Faith was concerned at how quickly the veil dropped over his eyes. 'I am very happily married to Fenella. We have two lovely children, Edward and Jennifer, and I don't wish to say any more.'

Kieran's agent had obviously worked very hard to instil the words. Slowly, with growing agony, Faith began to grasp the implications. Billie hadn't just been digging the dirt on Kieran's extramarital affair, had she? She'd gone along to interview him about buying Rustique, and about Maeve and Declan being Willowbridge expats, and she'd been confronted professionally at least twice by this gorgeous, very famous, gentle, unpretentious, rather dim man who had charmed her with beauty and good manners and . . .

Oh, Holy Mary Mother of God!

It all fell into place with a resounding thud.

'You and Billie . . . ?'

Kieran stared out of the window, then turned to look at her. 'I'm really sorry. Is she all right—I mean—Billie? I really liked her . . . I was a bit of a bastard, to be honest . . . '

Faith, whose head was reeling, didn't doubt it. At least it had answered all her questions. She knew she should slip on her shoes, pick up her handbag, go home, and forget any of this had ever happened. She knew she should, but she wasn't going to.

'You had an affair?'

Kieran took a deep breath. 'She hasn't told you about it? About me?'

'Not a word,' Faith said truthfully. The truth was becoming quite a stranger. 'So, what happened?'

'And you won't tell Fenella? Or the papers?'

'You have my word. And after all, Billie was the papers, wasn't she?' Faith said reasonably. 'And she didn't tell anyone, did she?'

Kieran looked reassured by this. 'You'll probably think I'm an arse too, but you're nice and you're helping me with my charity and you're Billie's mum . . .' He stopped, obviously suddenly realising that this last bit might not necessarily be a plus point. 'And I liked her . . . And I never meant to hurt her but—'

*   *   *

Afterwards, settled in the corner seat in a quiet carriage on the late afternoon train from Paddington, and hurtling towards all the comforts and familiarity of home, Faith reran the whole heart-breaking episode. She wasn't sure she'd heard the whole story, but she'd certainly heard enough of it for everything to make perfect sense.

It was true, she did think Kieran was an arse even though he'd apologized over and over again. He shouldn't have done what he did. He certainly shouldn't have left Billie to face the music. But it took two to tango, didn't it? The fact that there'd been an affair didn't shock her too much, to be honest. After all, it had happened to so many people. It hadn't been what she had been expecting to hear, but it certainly reassured her that Billie's flight from Devon had been genuine, and the subsequent one from London necessary, and answered all her own nagging questions. At least she needn't worry any longer about Billie's safety; there were no hit men gunning for her.

She stretched wearily. If she felt anything, it was pity. For both of them, but more for her daughter. As a mother she would have liked to have been able to protect Billie from the pain. Kieran had been weak and cowardly and Billie had been unwise— but who hadn't been? She wasn't angry really, or even disappointed. Who was she to judge? It was a relief to know the truth. It also explained a lot of things about Billie's behaviour and her determination to succeed on her own merits. Faith hoped that the ghosts of the past were being laid to rest by Billie's Whiteacres business and her new life in Amberley Hill.

Faith eased off her shoes and rested her head back and watched urban turn to rural, knowing that tonight she'd sleep soundly for the first time since Billy left Devon. She'd never tell Billie that she knew about the affair, of course. She'd never tell anyone. Ever. She and Kieran had been adamant on that point. He'd contact the Devon boys' football clubs on his own; his agent and the Putney hierarchy would approve of that, he was sure. He and Faith had agreed it was for the best. Today's meeting had simply never taken place.

Later, Faith thought, as the train trundled sleepily now through the Devon countryside towards the station at Whimple, just a few stops before Exeter, there was still one fly in the ointment. But she certainly wasn't going to be the one to fish it out. She'd done what she'd set out to do. Kieran and Billie were adults. They'd have to sort out the final problems on their own.

Anyway, Faith thought, if she rang Billie and told her, then she'd have to admit to the whole meddling and lying scheme, and involving the grandchildren too—so far, her grandchildren's stories of the visit to Maeve and Dec's had been put down to overactive childish imaginations and too many E numbers—and up until that point the chances of Billie and Kieran Squires ever meeting up again seemed very remote.

As she'd been leaving Putney FC's imposing portals, and Kieran had kissed her rather gallantly, and quite bravely, considering the circumstances, on her cheek, he'd looked very sheepish.

'Actually, I didn't know Billie still lived in Amberley Hill, otherwise I'd never have done it.'

'Done what?' Faith wanted to go. She tried to shut out the noise and bustle, easing the heels of her shoes away from her blisters and thinking longingly of watching the dusk falling across the moors.

'Said yes.' Kieran's endearing simplicity was beginning to grate on her. Billie, bright as a button, would never have been able to live with it for long. 'Agreed to do it.'

'Do what?' Faith could see a taxi for hire bearing down the road towards them and was itching to get away.

'Agreed to open that new nightclub in Amberley Hill next week. Still,' he'd smiled at her as she'd thrown herself towards the cab, 'at least it'll give me an opportunity to apologise to Billie, face to face, like, won't it?'

chapter thirty-two

Billie, sitting outside the warehouse in the drowsy May sunshine, tried to concentrate on filling in the latest quarterly return and failed miserably. The continued warmth, after the recent months of inclement weather, was glorious and, like the other warehousers, she'd moved her office outside onto the cracked concrete. It gave her a wonderful feeling of escaping from routine, of wicked unearned freedom. In fact, it was exactly like when she'd been at the mixed infants, and on warm Devon days the entire school had carried their diminutive chairs out of the classrooms and had had lessons beneath the playground trees, ignoring their books and watching the sun dapple patterns through the cherry blossom.

There was no tiny chair or highly coloured reading book this time though: a trestle table, with map-of-the-world grease stains from bits of the Stearman, did as a makeshift desk, and Billie had pulled up one of the wonky armchairs behind it in an attempt to look businesslike. To be honest, she thought, as she squinted into the sun, the cracked concrete rather resembled a disorganised car-boot sale immediately after the point of impact.

Sylvia, in a startling orange tankini, the Chloe sunshades, and the pink sombrero, was leisurely sorting brochures from a glossy mountain beside her deck chair; Zia and Isla, in tie-dye vests and baggies, were raking through black bin liners full of new old clothes; and the Gusper boys, in shorts, wraparound sunglasses, and baseball caps, were lounging in canvas directors' chairs editing scripts and discussing voice-overs. Only Fred 'n' Dick remained overalled and indoors.

Several small planes buzzed and bumbled above the bleached grass of the airstrip like summer bees fumbling against a shut window. Billie watched them take off and land, and felt no fear now. How quickly, she thought, she'd got used to them. How quickly Whiteacres had become home.

She yawned and looked down again at the sun dazzling in white-hot spirals from the top page of the quarterly return. This one still had the Maynard and Pollock logo—the next one, Billie knew, would bear the addition of far more sinister words— Reuben Wainwright Enterprises. She shivered as if a cloud had passed over the sun.

Fortunately she hadn't seen Reuben since he'd turned up here to make his announcement: he'd been mercifully absent from the flat too, as Miranda seemed to spend more and more time at the Wainwright bedsit and less and less time at home. Unfortunately, his physical absence did nothing to shift his threats and certainly not his existence from her thoughts.

Sadly, Billie reflected, scratching her arms as the heat started to prickle her skin, she was the only one of the warehousers who had any feelings of trepidation about their new landlord. Well, she supposed she would be, as she was the only one who knew what a bastard Reuben really was. But the others were cock-a-hoop that they were being taken over by a local entrepreneur, and had waxed lyrical about Reuben's Cabs and the forthcoming opening of Caught Offside, and all agreed that they couldn't have anyone better to own their leases.

Billie, wanting to play Judas, had just managed to keep her mouth shut. Not, she thought, that anyone would listen to her. She wished she could have taken Jonah's advice and told everyone about him—but that would mean being honest, wouldn't it? That would mean being truthful about her past and owning up to the fact that everything she'd told everyone about herself since arriving in Amberley Hill had been pure fiction. And then, as with all found-out liars, the warehousers would surely view anything she subsequently said with grave suspicion—and she'd risk losing some of the best friends she'd ever had. She should have come clean ages ago. It was far too late now.

She groaned. She had far more pressing things to worry about—like the quarterly return and, even more scary, the first proper wingwalking trial coming up on Sunday. Having always been aware, thanks to Granny Pascoe being of a witchy persuasion, of the power of negative thoughts, Billie decided not to think about Sunday.

It was one of things that had always bothered her about holiday flying: the realisation that probably three-quarters of the passengers strapped on board the 747 were as terrified as she was, and that surely, according to Granny Pascoe's Celtic lore, the culmination of all that fear could only be the materialisation of the thing which they all dreaded most.

She'd tried to explain this sort of self-induced chaos theory to Miranda and Kitty as they'd sat rigid in their three-abreast seats. But they'd just pinged off their headsets and torn their eyes away from *Lethal Weapon Twenty-Four* or *Die Hard Thirty-Seven*, and patted her hand, suggesting that

405

she took more tonic with her next gin, thought about all the gorgeous seducible men just waiting for them at their destination, and that it would be far more sensible to be thinking physical rather than metaphysical—oh, and wasn't Mel Gibson/Bruce Willis to die for?

So Billie had remained rigid with terror, trying to convince herself that flying was fun—and now, she was going to be flying *outside* a fifty-year-old plane, with no gin, no friendly hands to hold, and a pilot with severe emotional problems. She shook her head. Definitely best not to even think about it.

Jonah had, Billie conceded as she fanned herself with the quarterly return, handled the Solomon's baby wingwalking situation with her and Estelle pretty well, all things considered. He'd smiled from her to Estelle and back again and said that any man should be so lucky, having to make that sort of decision. Then he'd frowned for a while, then grinned, and said he saw no reason to choose between them. He'd got the perfect solution: he'd just go out and buy another Stearman and set up a barnstorming team and use them both.

Estelle had laughed, and said in his dreams, and then said that as Billie was dressed for it she might as well do the practising, but she'd always be a willing understudy. Then she and Estelle had rather childishly pulled faces at one another and she'd changed out of the bodysuit—she had felt a moment of total triumph, seeing the slack-jaw-making effect it had had on both Estelle and Jonah—and spent the next hour climbing in and out of the cockpit, up and down from the wing, and Estelle had watched and said it all looked pretty easy-peasy and she couldn't understand what all the

406

fuss was about.

Then she and Estelle had giggled and said they'd had enough of male company and they were off to the Aeroclub bar to enjoy a good girlie gossip. Jonah had said over his dead body—especially if he was going to be the main topic of conversation—and they'd said get a life, we've got far more interesting things to talk about. And then, of course, they'd belted off and ordered spritzers, and Billie had sat agog while Estelle proceeded to discuss Jonah in intimate detail.

Billie had been quite shocked at just how intimate Estelle was prepared to get. She left no detail out. Jonah, it appeared, was so fixated on the absent Claire that he'd been rendered impotent. It wasn't exactly what Billie had wanted to hear—but as Estelle was being lusted over by a lot of weekend pilots in the bar, and made no attempt to lower her voice, not only Billie, but most of Whiteacres' flying population was treated to a blow-by-blow account of Jonah Sullivan's failures beneath the duvet.

Billie reluctantly returned her thoughts to the matter in hand, and flicked through the pages of the quarterly return until she reached 'Anticipated Income'. This three-monthly chore was now, thanks to Estelle's ministrations, becoming a lot easier. It was her third return—which meant it was almost a year since she'd sailed up here in her Reuben's Cab with Sylvia as a passenger and marvelled at the freedom and ingenuity, and wondered if she could do something similar . . .

Things had gone reasonably well, considering. There had been that blip at the beginning of the year when the customers had dropped off, but with the longer days and warmer temperatures,

407

every man and his dog, it seemed, had started on rigorous chucking out, and spring-cleaning, and house-moving, and loft-converting, and the shelves of her warehouse were once again happily stacked with attic overspill.

A shadow loomed across her desk, casting a welcome spot of shade. Billie glanced up. Sylvia, looking like a neon barrage balloon, seemed to hover above her, the sun glinting round the edges of the mammoth tankini like an aura, and dancing from the diamanté corners of the Chloe shades.

'Time for a break, dear?' Sylv jerked the sombrero up and down, wafting papers from the table. 'I've been experimenting with one or two new cocktails for the show. I thought you could help me have a bit of a tester session.'

Billie peered at the tray of multicoloured drinks in Sylvia's hands. 'God, Sylv, I don't have to try all of them, do I? It's my turn to do Tesco this afternoon—and Miranda will slaughter me if I arrive home in a taxi with half the shopping forgotten because I'm inebriated. Things are strained enough as they are.'

Sylvia raised her eyebrows above the sunglasses, setting the tray down on the edge of the table. 'Really, dear? I'm so sorry. I do hate to hear of domestic rifts.'

'Come off it!' Billie sat upright and scanned the cocktail glasses searching for something innocuous. 'You and Douglas are hardly Mr and Mrs Perfect! Ooh—that purple one looks pretty, though. What is it?'

'It's a sort of kir.' Sylvia handed her the glass. 'Cassis with a touch of lambrusco—or was it Bacardi? Anyway, dear, it's very mild. Probably

408

tastes like Ribena.'

Billie took a sip and felt her head exploding. 'Jesus, Sylv! It's lethal!'

Sylvia looked concerned. 'Really? A touch too much alcohol, do you think, dear? I'll have to remember to dilute it a tad more on the day. It'd be disastrous if the kiddies mistook it for a cordial, wouldn't it?'

Billie, who was pretty sure no one would mistake it for anything other than rocket fuel, continued to splutter incoherently. She was convinced that her teeth had melted. Through watering eyes she watched Sylvia, who with no trace of self-consciousness had eased her bulk onto a corner of the trestle table. The extra large tankini strained at its tangerine seams, but Sylv seemed blissfully unaware of the rolls of fat or the dimpled expanses of cellulite as she leaned across the table and reached for one of the more lurid drinks.

Maybe, Billie thought, that's what happened when you grew up: you were perfectly at ease with yourself—imperfections and all—because you actually liked yourself as a person. The personal confidence which grew with age made physical perfection totally unimportant. Sylvia was comforting, like Faith, because she was comfortable with herself. Billie wished such confidence could be given to twenty-somethings too.

Sylvia beamed, knocked back half a glass of something green and translucent, and wiped her lips with the back of her hand. 'Yummy. I adore chartreuse with a dash of single malt, don't you? Do you think Fred 'n' Dick would like one?'

'I'm sure they'd love one,' Billie said cheerfully. 'It'll probably be the most fun they've had for years.

But don't dash off yet—it's far too nice to work. Stay and chat. How are your other plans coming along for the show? Is the treasure hunt developing nicely?'

'Swimmingly.' Sylvia had turned her attention to an amber concoction which seemed to have a sort of fume haze hanging over it. 'I've worked out my clues in two stages—one lot for adults and the others for children—just to make it fair, and—oh!' She cocked the sombrero to one side. 'Isn't that your office phone ringing, dear?'

'Probably.' Billie stretched languorously in the sunshine.

'Have you left the answerphone on, then?'

Billie shook her head.

'You should have brought your mobile out here then, dear, if you don't mind me saying so. It might be a customer.'

'That was why I didn't. I'm chock-a-block in there already, and the paperwork—' she indicated the collapsing pile in front of her—'is taking weeks to sort out, even sticking to Estelle's instructions. I just had no idea how much—Ah, there! The phone's stopped ringing!'

'And "Ah, there" to you too! Many more of those and you'll be bankrupt.' Sylvia was scandalised. 'You can't afford to ignore customers, dear. We're sole traders. We're supposed to be working flat out seven days a week without a moment to call our own. It's what we sign up for when we go it alone. Hard slog without any cushions. Now you get in there and do 1471 and tell them you'll be delighted to accommodate them.'

Pulling a face at Sylvia, Billie hauled herself from the armchair. Of course Sylv was right, Billie knew, it had all just got so chaotic lately. All the other warehousers had someone else to pass pressing tasks on to—even Sylvia got her sister Ethel to do her correspondence and VAT returns. If she could just have someone to help with the basic paperwork—a YTS child or something—which would free her up for collecting stuff in the van, doing the accounts, stacking the shelves, handling the publicity, oh, and practising the wingwalking, of course . . .

Billie shivered in the shed's gloom. Her vest and denim cut-offs gave little protection against the all-year-round dampness, and skirting the Stearman, she scuttled into the office and punched out 1471. Stung by Sylv's criticism, she was determined to ring back the customer and offer them storage space in the kitchenette, the office, even the loo, if necessary. By the time the snooty mechanical voice had barked out the digits of the code, Billie knew that her magnanimity wouldn't be needed. The number was home in Devon.

As she pushed 3 and heard the single ringing tone, she could see the telephone—black Bakelite complete with dial and plaited wire—sitting on the sunwashed hall table alongside discarded envelopes, junk mail, and several back issues of *Farmers Weekly*. There were dust motes dancing in the open doorway, the yard was just visible, baked into red clay ruts, and Stan's coat was topping the pile on the overloaded hatstand.

The pang of homesickness was swift and brutal.

'Hello?' Faith's voice suddenly echoed in her ear. 'Mountbrook Farm.'

'Mum—it's me. I did 1471. Is everything all right? I mean, you never call me at work and—'

411

'Oh, everything's fine. Really. I was just—er—being a bit silly...'

Billie was concerned. Silly and her mother simply didn't go together. 'Is it financial, then? Is the farm having problems? Have you lost your market stall?'

'Goodness me!' Faith's tone resumed its usual no-nonsense briskness. 'Billie, love, I was just being silly, as I said. I was clearing some stuff out of your room and I just thought how long it was since I'd seen you and I wondered—well—if you could have a bit of a break. Come down here for a few days' holiday? It's been so long since Christmas.'

Billie groaned. Going home, especially at this time of the year, would be wonderful. It was also, sadly, completely out of the question. 'Oh, Mum, I'd love to! But I can't. I'm so busy and I can't just close the warehouse up! It was different at Christmas, of course, because the estate shut down, but Sylvia's just reminded me how fragile self-employment is.' She sighed into the phone. 'Hey, look, if I can't get down to you why don't you come up here? You could stay at the flat because Miranda's not often there and—'

Faith cut in. 'Well, yes, I'd love to. But it won't be much of a break for you, will it?'

'It'll be lovely! We can do proper mother and daughter stuff! Oh, Mum, please try. How about coming up when the air pageant's on? I'm sure you'd enjoy it, and I'm—' Billie stopped and back-pedalled. She wasn't sure just how wise it would be to mention about the wingwalking. She'd keep it as a surprise. 'Think about it, and let me know.'

'Yes . . . of course . . . actually, I'm sure I could work something out. Look, love, I don't want to

412

keep you from your work, so I'll ring you later. Tonight? At the flat? Unless, of course, you're going out.'

'No, not tonight. I'll be at home being exhausted.'

Faith's tone changed. Billie sensed her shuffling her feet and pursing her lips, her eyes staring somewhere out across the distant tors. 'Oh, I wondered if you'd be going to that new nightclub place that you mentioned, the one that Miranda is involved with, I think you said . . .'

'Caught Offside?' Billie laughed. 'It doesn't open until Saturday. And even when it does, I don't think I'll be going.'

'Really? Oh, that is good news! I mean . . .'

Billie grinned into the phone. Faith had never approved of nightclubs. There'd been hell to pay when her parents had dragged her out of one of Torbay's finest in the early hours at the age of fifteen. 'Things are pretty iffy between me and Miranda right now, so I honestly can't see us socialising much. Anyway, I'm feeling far too knackered to dance until dawn. Must be old age.'

They talked a bit longer, briefly catching up on family gossip, then with a promise to speak again that evening about Faith's proposed visit, they said goodbye.

Billie wandered back into the searing sunshine. Sylvia had plonked herself in the wonky armchair, and with the sombrero tipped over her eyes and her head resting on the quarterly return, was snoring softly. Half the cocktail glasses were empty. Grinning, Billie backtracked into the warehouse and started clearing some shelf space for the next lot of 'Custs Prospect'.

Tesco was bliss. Air conditioning chilled the very soul and, flinging things into the trolley, Billie relished the icy blast on her bare and very grubby legs. She'd spent the afternoon clearing a whole area of shelving, had run off some new flyers on the computer, and totted up the month's takings before visiting the bank. All she needed to do now was stick to the shopping list, mollify Miranda, go home and have a long, cool bath.

She'd reached the most boring aisle—washing powder, kitchen cleaner, and bleach—and was just allowing herself a minute's Jonah-time. She did it occasionally; managing to forget all the nasty warts and all stuff that she knew to be the truth from Estelle, and dreaming about him piloting the Stearman in his faded Levis and baggy rugby shirt, or piloting the Shorts in that pulse-racing navy and gold-braided uniform. She resurfaced and sighed at the foolishness. Jonah Sullivan, gorgeous, funny, friendly, was no different to any other man.

No, she shook her head. That wasn't true. He *was* different. He was a pilot, and brave—she knew from Barnaby what he'd done in the Gulf—and beautiful . . . oh, and firmly attached to Claire and more loosely attached to Estelle.

'Bugger! Sod! Damn!'

'I beg your pardon?' The woman in front of her, reaching for the money-off Tesco washing powder, straightened up. 'That's no sort of language to be using in here. Oh hiya, Billie!'

'Vee!' Billie beamed at Veronica, Reuben's Cabs' radio operator. 'It's great to see you. Sorry

414

about the swearing. I hadn't realised I'd said it out loud.'

'Oh, don't mind me.' Veronica, looking dishevelled, put the washing powder into her basket. Billie couldn't help noticing that all the items were budget ones. 'It just reminded me of the taxi-drivers and I'd promised myself I'd have a day free of brooding, that's all. So, how are things going?'

'Brilliantly, thanks. What about you?'

Veronica shifted her discount basket to the other arm. 'Crap, to be honest.'

Billie pulled a sympathetic face. 'Yeah, I suppose they would be. I don't know how you've stuck working for Reuben all these years.'

Vee's face crumpled. 'You haven't heard, then? I'm not working for Reuben's Cabs any longer. The bastard sacked me. No warning, no notice, and, with no union, no bloody chance of fighting it. And at my age, finding another job's practically impossible.'

'God, Vee, I'm so sorry. No, I had no idea. What on earth did he do that for?'

'Christ knows.' Veronica puffed out her cheeks. 'He just stormed in one morning and said I was surplus to requirements. Said he was down-sizing. Down-sizing my arse! If you ask me, the man's gone power crazy. Buying up businesses left right and centre. Acting like bloody Hitler. He's totally off his trolley these days—even more than he was before. You're well out of it, Billie, duck. Well out of it. Reuben Wainwright is psychopathic!'

chapter thirty-three

Chumbawumba had just been sent off by Fat Les, and the DJ was warming up Oasis as half-time substitutes. With the football anthems going down an ear-splitting treat, Caught Offside was packed to the rafters.

Miranda glanced at the orbital wall clock ticking away the seconds in neon orange segments. Half-eleven. Another thirty minutes to go before Reuben hauled on his surprise guest for the official opening. Miranda still hadn't got a clue who he was: the posters advertising Caught Offside's opening had just promised a 'soccer mega-star', and no matter how much she'd pestered, Reuben had been uncharacteristically coy about the whole matter.

Still, she'd spotted half of the Liverpool team, most of Arsenal, some knock-outs from Man U and Putney, and the entire rich, glamorous and cerebral Chelsea squad, as well as various players from most of the other football clubs in the country. Flashbulbs were popping like jumping jacks on November the fifth, and gorgeous men were wall to wall. She could almost swear she'd just seen Vinnie Jones doing the salsa with Gary Lineker. It couldn't, as far as she was concerned, get much better than this.

Sashaying between the dancing, singing, waving crowd, she pushed her way to the bar for another bottle of water. The bar and waiting staff of both genders had been selected for their youthful, leggy appearance, and were clad in brief skin-tight satin shorts and skimpy football shirts. They reminded

Miranda of the photos of the pulse-racing 1980s footballers, when players like Glenn Hoddle took to the pitch wearing less material than you'd find in the average hankie.

Bertie Malone, the nightclub's manager, was dressed in referee black, and presiding over his domain with all the tender loving care of a Rottweiler. Miranda leaned on the bar and sighed happily. It was going to be a sensational success. All of Amberley Hill was out in party mode: Debs, Kitty, Sally, Anna, and even Pixie had been some of the first through the turnstiles at the ten o'clock opening. She hadn't seen Billie yet, but as she'd promised to be along—in the Joseph dress—before midnight, Miranda knew she'd be there. Billie never let anyone down.

Mind you, Billie had been acting strangely for weeks: up in the air one minute, pirouetting about and practising dancing on the sideboard, and then completely down in the dumps the next. And in the last few days she'd been muttering dark incantations against Reuben again. Miranda remained mystified.

Oh, she knew there had been some further problems with Jonah and Estelle and his ex-wife, but as there was no definite sex involved, only alleged, as far as she could see, Miranda hadn't really listened.

No, it was definitely Reuben that was causing Billie's blood pressure to rise at the moment. Miranda had been surprised that she'd even agreed to come tonight. But she'd been adamant that she'd be here.

'Too right,' Billie had said, standing on one leg beside the fruit bowl, a tin of baked beans in each hand as she waved her arms above her head, and almost toppling over the television. 'I wouldn't miss it for the world. Me and Mr Wainwright have one or two things to sort out. A couple of scores to settle . . .'

Miranda hadn't asked any further questions, and prayed again that it wasn't going to be the Mills and Boon ending she so dreaded. She really couldn't face being brave and magnanimous, and watch them fall panting into each other's arms. So, erring on the side of caution, she'd steered clear of all taboo subjects, and chatted about the wingwalking—which in her opinion was about as safe as bungee jumping without the bungee, and which she couldn't understand for the life of her why Billie was doing.

None of the reasons Billie had given made any sense, so Miranda had eventually left well alone and turned her attentions to Reuben, who hadn't seemed to need her ministrations either. He'd remained calm and confident all week. She'd honestly expected him to be like a hen on pins leading up to the opening, but he'd shown no sign of nerves, and had even been extra attentive. She'd wondered if it was because she'd had a couple of meals at the Dil Raj recently with Barnaby, but somehow doubted it. Reuben knew all about them, and had said that she should definitely encourage Barnaby as he sounded like the sort of bloke he himself might be able to use in future projects.

The meals had been fun, and she'd learned a lot that she didn't want to know about Jonah and Claire and the voluptuous Estelle. She'd also heard about the proposed airshow a million times, and Billie's brave wingwalking offer. Barnaby, like

Jonah, seemed to live and breathe aeroplanes. Still, however boring she found the subject matter, he'd put a lot of his friends her way, and the male massage and facial side of Follicles and Cuticles was doing extremely well.

And Barnaby was a real gentleman. It was wonderful to be treated as though she were fragile and girlie. He even liked her pink plaits. Miranda sighed and gulped at her water. It was always the same: men were truly like buses—you could wait for ages without a glimmer of one on the horizon and then—whoosh!—two came along at once.

'OK?' Reuben pushed in alongside Miranda at the bar.

'Brilliant, thanks,' she shouted in his ear. 'You must be so pleased, doll. It's going to be massive!'

'I'm pleasantly confident.' He smiled and touched her cheek. 'And you look gorgeous. I'm glad you've gone back to the full slap. The austere look didn't suit you. You're certainly a knockout tonight.'

Miranda could have cried with happiness. *Why couldn't Billie see this side of Reuben? Why did she always have to massacre his motives?* 'Thanks. You look pretty swish, yourself. And has your superstar arrived yet, then?'

Reuben glanced at his watch. 'He said he'd get here just before midnight. We thought it was best. We didn't want him getting mobbed early on.'

God! Miranda wriggled her shoulders with glee. It had to be one of the two Davids, then, didn't it? It just had to be!

'Just one thing—' she snuggled up to Reuben's tuxedo—'how on earth did you manage to get all these top footballers to come here tonight? Oh, I know they like a jolly—but in *Amberley Hill*?'

'Quite simple. A bit of boardroom bargaining. I agreed with all the chairmen and publicity bods to pay the clubs over-the-top rates for advertising Caught Offside in all next season's match programmes—on the understanding that they would issue free tickets for the opening to their players, plus a night's accommodation—and, of course, didn't mind one or two photographs being taken for publicity purposes. Everyone seemed delighted with the deal.'

Miranda nodded. They would. Reuben, it seemed, was turning into quite a Tiny Rowland on the quiet.

'Now,' he squeezed her hand tightly, 'I'd better go and get security organised for the opening ceremony. You'll be OK?'

'Course, doll. I'm going to get back on the dance floor with Sally and the rest, and Billie should be here soon.'

Reuben's smile faltered as he turned to walk away. She didn't imagine it. It may have been only for a nanosecond, but it definitely faltered. Some of her earlier elation faltered with it. She didn't have time to worry about it for long, though, as Debs and Kitty appeared at the bar then and dragged her into the throng on the dance floor, apparently bursting to tell her that Anna, Sally and Pixie were dancing with Queens Park Rangers.

'What all of them?'

'Most of them!' Kitty shrieked. 'Lucky cows!'

Five to twelve. No sign of Billie, but the DJ had just finished a final triumphant burst of 'Back Home' for the nostalgia brigade, and the floodlights were dimming.

'Time for the footie celeb.' Debs was cross-eyed. 'Oh, come on, Randa, you must know who it is. Tell us.'

'Honestly, I haven't got a clue.'

'Tell me it's Alan Smith and let me die happy!' Kitty clutched Miranda's arm, then started waving madly into the far distance. 'Yoo-hoo! Billie! Over here!'

Miranda extricated herself from Kitty's grip and pushed her way through the mob. Billie, pretty stunning in the Joseph dress and perfect make-up, and with her hair all chicly tousled, teetered on the edge of the terraces, looking completely bemused.

Miranda reached her, and hugged her. 'God, I'm so glad you're here, doll. It wouldn't be the same without you. Well—what do you think?'

Billie gazed round Caught Offside and shook her head. 'It's stunning. I'd never expected . . . and so many people! I've got to hand it to Reuben—this is totally unbelievable.' Her voice took on a bit of an edge. 'I just hope his other entrepreneurial dabblings are as successful.'

Miranda, not having a clue what she was talking about, nodded. 'Oh, they will be, doll. Reuben's got the touch all right. Oh, great—this is it—you're just in time.'

The lights had dimmed and the DJ slapped 'Three Lions' onto the turntable. With one voice, Caught Offside trumpeted raucously that football was coming home . . .

'Just in time for what?' Billie screeched over the chorus. 'The official opening. Reuben's got David Ginola or David Beckham—I'm sure of it.'

'Dream on!' Billie grinned.

Miranda grinned back as the music and singing

421

came to an end. 'Believe me, I am . . . Oh!'

'Football's coming home to Amberley Hill—and it's coming home right now!' Reuben swept onto the stage looking exactly like Pierce Brosnan tonight under the spotlights, even down to the lock of hair feathering over one eye. Miranda's stomach turned liquid with lust. He clutched the microphone, acknowledging the roof-raising cheers. 'Welcome, everyone, to Caught Offside!'

More cheers. Miranda squirmed ecstatically. He was totally, devastatingly gorgeous. She loved him. She knew she loved him. She sneaked a quick glance at Billie, who was staring at Reuben with complete disdain.

Reuben threw his arms open wide to include everyone in his corporate embrace. 'I hope that you've all enjoyed your two-hour taster—and that you'll stay on until daylight and enjoy the rest of the party!'

More screams of affirmation. Miranda hugged herself. 'Tonight and every night Caught Offside aims to bring you the best of everything—the best food, drink, dancing, music, and of course the best football!' Reuben was well into his stride now, pausing to let the cheers die away. 'And now, to perform the official opening ceremony, one of the country's star players! Not only is he from one of the Premiership's flagship clubs, but he's also been capped for England—'

'Rules out Ginola, then,' Billie hissed.

'—and is also very well-known for his television appearances!' Reuben stood back and looked towards the side of the stage. 'Ladies and gentlemen, let's have a big Caught Offside welcome for—'

'I can't bear it!' Miranda clutched at Billie's hand. 'Me and David Beckham breathing the same air!'

Reuben gave an impressive flourish with the microphone. 'Kieran Squires!'

The whole place erupted. Wolf whistles and screams and howls of delight drowned out everything else. Miranda sighed in ecstasy, watching the tall, knock-'em-dead beauty of Putney Football Club's biggest star appear on the stage. She'd never even thought of him . . . God, how had Reuben managed to pull this one off? Kieran Squires! Here, in Amberley Hill . . .

She jiggled at Billie's hand as the wolf whistles and foot-stamping began to fade. 'Ace or what? God—he is so glorious! Don't you reckon, Billie? I mean, even if you don't like football, you've got to admit he's totally divine! Billie? Billie . . . ?'

She frowned. Billie seemed to have gone into catatonic shock. She was standing stock-still, staring at the stage, her mouth slightly open, her eyes not blinking.

'Er—um—' Kieran coughed into the microphone. 'It's just fab to be here. This is a really great place. Great. I've never seen a club like this before.'

Everyone except Billie, Miranda noticed, applauded like crazy.

He beamed happily. 'It's my—um—great pleasure to declare this—er—club open. I hope you'll all enjoy being Caught Offside.' He grinned at his own joke. 'I've always hated it myself. Anyway, it's really—er—great to be here and to have the privilege of opening this club and—um—I hope you all have a lovely time. Thank you.'

The DJ belted into Putney's theme tune, which had topped the charts the previous summer when they'd done the Cup and League double. Miranda, clapping wildly and trilling along, looked at Billie. She was still staring blankly at the stage as Reuben and Kieran shook hands.

'Billie? What's up? Are you OK? Where are you—'

Billie shook her hand free, forged her way through the clapping, cheering crowds, and, pushing aside the screaming knot of girls all clamouring for Kieran's autograph and bits of his body, hitched up the Joseph dress and leaped onto the stage.

'Bloody hell!' Miranda said admiringly. 'She doesn't hang about.'

She watched as Billie forced herself between Reuben and Kieran, and before either of them realised she was there, slapped them each resoundingly round the face.

'Jesus!' Miranda was wide-eyed as Kitty, Sally, Debs, Anna and Pixie joined her in stunned silence. 'What the hell is all that about? I know she doesn't like football, but that's a bit OTT.'

The Caught Offside audience, well tanked up, whistled and catcalled and booed as Billie jumped back down from the stage and barged her way towards the exit. The whole club then roared into an Amberley Hill version of 'You're Not Singing Any More', complete with jabbing fingers.

Reuben and Kieran were still on the podium in front of the twin decks, exchanging sheepish looks and trying to shrug it all off. The DJ, caught cold with the barking anthem from the floor, decided to get his own back and immediately rushed into 'Blue

Is the Colour' at full volume. Miranda, not knowing whether to follow Billie, comfort Reuben, apologise to Kieran, or just get drunk, dithered on the dance floor.

Sally, Anna and the rest were relaying the whole thing over and over to each other in fairly inebriated falsetto voices. The rest of the crowd were laughing now, screaming along to 'Blue Is the Colour', and when Miranda looked, Reuben and Kieran had left the stage.

'Bugger . . .' Miranda gazed around. She really should go after Billie, but where should she start? The cloakrooms were hardly likely to be deserted, and it was far more likely that Billie had bombed out into the Spicer Centre and jumped in a cab and gone home. But why had she done it? In God's name, *why*?

Miranda pushed her way towards the exit, trampling on an Arsenal player she'd always sworn she'd never kick out of bed and not even stopping to apologise. She simply didn't understand what was going on.

'Miranda!' Barnaby, in a dinner jacket, had just emerged from the turnstiles.

She whimpered. Not now. Please not now. 'Oh, hi. I didn't know you were coming tonight. Um— please don t think I'm being rude, but I'm a bit busy and—'

'Jo's idea.' Barnaby beamed, holding out his hand. 'And of course I won't keep you, my dear. We'd just had a bit of an acrobatic blast in the Slingsby this afternoon, pulling a few Gs, and wanted to use up some of the leftover adrenaline.'

Miranda smiled weakly. 'Is Jonah here, then?'

'Yes, he's in the Gents. We've had one or two in

Mulligan's on the way here. Shame we missed the official opening, but this looks very jolly. I haven't been in a nightclub in years.'

Please, please, please, go away, you nice man, Miranda said silently. I've got to sort out my life. Billie's life. Oh God! 'Look, go and grab a seat in the bar, doll—if you can find one—and I'll be back in a minute. I just need to find—Oh, hello, Jonah!'

Jonah smiled. He looked staggeringly gorgeous, if a bit squinty-eyed. Miranda fleetingly wondered how much of it was due to the acrobatics and pulling the Gs, and how much was down to pulling Mulligan's Guinness.

'I was just explaining to Barnaby that I've got a couple of things to see to.'

Jonah nodded. 'Understood. Um—is Billie here?'

Miranda flinched. Possibly not the best bet to tell him that his prospective wingwalker had just belted Caught Offside's star turn. 'Oh, what a pity! You've just missed her! I think she—um—wanted an early night.'

Jonah looked crestfallen. 'That's a shame. I wanted to tell her something and I've kept missing her at the shed all week. Still, it'll keep. OK, then, it's my round.'

'You go on through, Jo,' Barnaby said. 'I don't want to keep Miranda hanging about, but there's something I wanted to say.'

Jonah, followed by a string of beautiful but rather squiffy women in strapless dresses who obviously thought he was Ginola with a haircut, disappeared towards the bar. Miranda hoped he wouldn't go for the Bobby Charlton Slammer. It would probably play havoc with the Gs.

426

'Could we just find somewhere a little quieter, my dear? A little more private?'

Miranda, suddenly realising that Barnaby was still there, frowned and pulled him through to the cubbyhole between the Home and Away dressing rooms. It wasn't particularly private, as several couples appeared to have it singled out for a trysting place, but at least no one was singing.

'Barnaby, I really am sorry if I sound impolite, but there are some really urgent things I need to do.'

'Yes, yes, this won't take a minute—'

'If it's about business—'

'It's about my small stately home, and my racehorses and my planes and my travelling.'

Oh God . . . Miranda gulped. He'd had the Guinness too. He was going to do *This Is Your Life*. She tried grinning, but it didn't quite come off. 'Yes, you've mentioned them before, doll, remember? They sound lovely.'

'Wrong consonant,' Barnaby sighed. 'Try substituting the v with an n . . .'

Miranda, who was totally crap at *Countdown*, tried and failed.

Barnaby helped her out. 'Lonely, my dear. Unutterably lonely. I wondered—I just wondered— and I wouldn't say this without a bit of Dutch courage, but I wondered if you would do me the honour of possibly considering sharing them with me . . . ?'

427

chapter thirty-four

Billie slammed into Reuben's office—at least, she assumed it was Reuben's office; it was the only one she could find in Caught Offside's warren of back stage broom cupboards and bottle stores—and leaned, gulping for air, against the desk.

The echoing vibration of the DJ's bass line shuddered through the floor beneath her, although the main bolt of noise from the club was oddly muted by several layers of plasterboard. She wiped her sweating hands on the Joseph dress. How many years would she get for manslaughter? No one would convict her of *murdering* Reuben, would they? Not after what he'd done?

How crass could he get? How cruel? After everything else he'd thrown at her, she'd assumed that she'd seen absolutely the worst side of his cunning, conniving, manipulative nature. But even she hadn't thought he was capable of *this*.

She took deep breaths, trying to steady her pulse rate. And Kieran? Just how stupid was he? Why the hell, after what had happened, had he accepted Reuben's offer to come back here, of all places?

She laughed derisively. They were as sick and twisted as each other. Thinking that by dragging up the past, taunting her with her mistakes, they would ruin her life and drive her away, or ruin her life and keep her biddable. Well, they were in for a huge shock either way. She'd run away once, she sure as hell wasn't intending to make it a career. Not a chance. She was more determined than ever to stay at Whiteacres and be successful.

Reuben hadn't been able to frighten her by threats or coercion—he hadn't even managed to pressurise her into line-toeing by buying the warehouses—so he certainly wasn't going to manage to control her by bloody bare-faced blackmail.

Still shaking, she reran the face-slapping, and was delighted not to feel the slightest twinge of remorse. She had absolutely no regrets about doing it in public. She was just glad that the press hadn't had their cameras focused on the stage at that moment; at least it meant Faith and Stan would never hear of the incident. They'd be absolutely livid if they knew what she'd done. It wasn't the way she'd been brought up.

She gulped a bit more, trying to stop hyperventilating, still feeling the shock of Kieran's appearance. She simply couldn't believe it. It had never occurred to her, not even when Miranda had been banging on about the footballing superstar who was going to open the club, and . . . She frowned. Why on earth hadn't Miranda *warned* her?

Oh, yes, Miranda didn't know about Kieran, did she? She only knew about mythical Damon. But surely, whatever she said, Miranda must have had an inkling about who Reuben's guest of honour was going to be? And Miranda always talked about everything, no matter how confidential, so why the hell had she suddenly turned into Miss Sacred-Confessional over *this*?

Billie could hear footsteps echoing along the corridor outside. Sod it. It was probably the Putney hit squad or, even worse, the hatchet-faced bouncers—oh, no, sorry—door people—that

429

Reuben had employed in droves to keep the undesirables out of Caught Offside. She laughed at the irony. The biggest undesirable in the world owned the bloody place!

Billie looked round quickly. Brilliant. Nowhere to run. No hiding places. One door to the office, and that was just opening . . .

'Billie?' Kieran's voice echoed above the sudden wave of an overamplified version of 'We Are the Champions'. 'Billie? Are you in here? Mr Wainwright said—'

Billie closed her eyes. She'd had nightmares about this happening. About being alone with him again. Outside, just now, in the club, didn't count. There'd been a crowd of thousands. This was different. Her pulse rate upped a few notches. She opened one eye. At least Kieran was on his own. So far.

He was smiling at her, albeit a little warily. 'Hiya. It's great to see you again. Great. You look really pretty.'

Jesus! She took a deep breath. 'What the hell do you want?'

'Er—what? Oh, I think I'm supposed to say sorry.'

Billie opened the other eye. Oh God. He was still lovely to look at. So handsome, so athletically superb, so bloody sexy—so damned thick . . . She felt absolutely nothing for him. Not even the hate that had festered for so long. Being faced with the reality somehow put everything into perspective at last. She wanted to laugh. Reuben, in his studied act of cruelty, had done her a massive favour.

'You're not supposed to apologise. I hit you, remember?'

Kieran nodded. 'Oh, yeah. I don't mean that. I deserved that and it didn't hurt much. I mean— about the other . . . before . . . when I left you. I want to say sorry.' He shuffled his feet. 'I couldn't even send your stuff on from the flat. I didn't know where to—my agent's still got it.'

'Tell him to burn it.'

Still looking over Kieran's shoulder for Reuben, Billie sighed. 'It's far too late to apologise for leaving me in the middle of nowhere—and where's your partner in crime?'

'Uh?'

'Reuben.' She remembered, too late, the footballer's hierarchy training. Anyone who didn't actually kick a ball was always given their full title. 'Mr Wainwright.'

She'd forgotten just how dim Kieran really was. They'd always had such a good time together, and it had been so refreshing, after all the clever, breathless, dizzying days on the *Devon Argus*, to spend time with someone who didn't want to discuss politics—national, international or office—or anything else that demanded more than a thirty-second attention span, that she'd always made allowances. Now, she simply couldn't understand why.

'He's organising a Miss Wet Footieshirt contest for me to judge later,' Kieran said happily. 'He won't be finished for ages.'

God, why shouldn't that surprise her? Well, at least it was something. With Reuben leeringly occupied, she'd be able to deal fully with the Kieran horrors first, then turn her attention to Slimeball.

'So? Why did you come here? What the hell did you think you were going to achieve?'

431

Kieran blinked, obviously trying to sort out the answers to two consecutive questions. Eventually, he managed it. 'I came because I was booked to open the club. I didn't think I was going to achieve anything, as such, except my fee, of course.'

Billie sighed. She'd also forgotten the footballers' programming machine. Only answer direct questions, son. Never volunteer information. That way they can't misquote you in the tabloids.

She tried a different tack. 'And as it was in Amberley Hill, didn't it occur to you that I'd be here? That Reuben might just have booked you to set me up?'

This took even longer to work out. Kieran's brow puckered. He shook his head. 'I didn't know this club was anything to do with Mr Wainwright. My agent took the booking. I do loads of public appearances.'

'Do you?'

'Yeah. Tons.' He looked a bit hurt—as if he thought Billie should realise that he was greatly in demand. Then he brightened. 'I only knew it was Amberley Hill when my agent told me a few weeks ago. It didn't mean anything to me, to tell the truth. I thought it sounded like it was near Walsall. And then, when I remembered it was where—where you and me sort of parted company, well—I was speechless.'

Billie took a deep breath. 'But you still came?'

'Well, yeah, of course. Personal appearances are important in my profession. But I didn't know you were still here, Billie, honest. Well, not until recently, of course, when your—that is, not right up until I got here tonight . . .'

'You cheated and lied and abandoned me in the

432

middle of nowhere without *ever* checking to see if I'd survived—'

'I couldn't could I? I said—I didn't know where you were.' He smiled beguilingly. 'I thought about you a lot though. We had some wild times, didn't we?'

Billie sighed. They had. The intellectual difference between them had hardly mattered—then.

Billie shrugged. He was probably telling the truth about tonight's appearance. He possibly wasn't intelligent enough to lie convincingly anyway. 'So, you've been taken for a mug too, have you? Reuben set us both up?'

Kieran smiled. 'Oh, no. I think you've got it wrong. I mean, I didn't even remember who Mr Wainwright was until I got here tonight. And then not straight away. It took me ages to remember where I'd seen him before. After all, he was just the taxi-driver that night, wasn't he?'

'Did he remind you of that? Or did you actually recognise him?'

'He told me. I was a bit shocked. I mean, most club owners aren't taxi-drivers, are they?'

Billie leaned more heavily against the desk. No, they weren't. But then Reuben wasn't just any old taxi-driver, was he? He may well have been 'just the taxi-driver' that night, but he'd been her tormentor ever since. It was fine for Kieran—he'd escaped. She'd had to live with the consequences of his adultery. Still, remembering again Granny Pascoe's negativity adage, she decided to search for pluses instead. What good, if any, had come out of the night the relationship ended?

Well, there was Miranda's friendship for one,

433

and Kitty, Debs, Sally and Anna, and Vee and the taxi-drivers had become good friends in her time at Reuben's Cabs, and she loved living in Amberley Hill. Then, more recently, but still as a direct result, there was Whiteacres and Sylv and the other warehousers, and Jonah and Estelle and the Stearman. None of those would be part of her life now if she hadn't been with Kieran that night.

Speculating on cause and effect, she began to trace everything back. If she hadn't worked on the *Devon Argus* she wouldn't have gone to Rustique in the first place—but then if she hadn't been born on the farm she wouldn't have worked on the *Devon Argus* . . . She exhaled. It was all too complicated.

'. . . so Mr Wainwright's got on ever so well, and you must have done really well for yourself too.' Kieran assessed her expectantly. 'You look smashing. Are you still working on a newspaper?'

Billie shook her head. Throughout her introspection, Kieran must have been talking. She hadn't heard a word. She doubted that he'd noticed.

'No, I run a warehousing company. It's doing very nicely, thank you.' She stopped. There was nothing left to say to him. There never had been much. She'd changed, because of him, and grown up, and she didn't need to punish herself any more.

'I'm going home now.' She pushed herself away from the desk. 'I won't say it was lovely seeing you again, because it wasn't. You were, and probably still are, a cheating, spineless bastard. And I'm glad I slapped your face. I've been waiting a long time to do that. Good night . . .'

'Oh, right . . . Good night.' Kieran beamed. 'It's been lovely to see you again, though, honest—and

434

we did have some good times, didn't we?'

She shrugged. She wished they hadn't.

He gestured towards the door, waving his hands. 'I don't suppose you'd like a drink or something before you go? Just for old times' sake?'

'No I bloody wouldn't.'

'Oh, OK. I just thought it'd show that I'm not taking offence at what you said—the cheating, spineless bit, I mean. Like I said to your, I mean, I was a total arse . . .'

'Yes, you were. You probably still are.'

He grinned suddenly, looking relieved. 'Yeah, maybe. So, changing the subject, did you watch the Cup Final?'

'No. Look, I just want to go home now, OK?'

'Oh, right. Um—do you still watch *Match of the Day*?'

'Sometimes.'

'Oh, good. I'd like to think that you hadn't gone off football because of me.'

Jesus! Billie pushed past him and headed for the door. His suit was expensive, probably Paul Smith, his cologne must have cost more than her annual takings. He was still lovely to look at, still guileless, and she'd probably now be able to watch his long muscular thighs loping across Putney's hallowed turf on telly and feel nothing.

'Bye, then, Billie.'

She looked at him for a long time. 'Goodbye, Kieran. I do hope we never meet again.'

Grabbing her coat from the cloakroom, she walked outside into the still balmy warmth of a May early morning. She felt shell-shocked, but oddly liberated. Where to go? Not home just in case Miranda came looking for her. She couldn't face

Miranda yet. So if it couldn't be the flat, then her second home seemed the best bet—the only bet . . .

Ignoring all her own advice about not walking home in the darkness, she hurried through the Centre and into Amberley Hill's deserted streets. She didn't even feel afraid, just emancipated and fizzing with energy. She'd laid Kieran's ghost—and later today she'd face Reuben and shove his spectre from her shoulder too.

Her Pascoe's Warehousing van was outside the flat and, unlocking it and kicking off her high-heeled shoes, she started the engine and headed for the bypass.

chapter thirty-five

Billie woke, feeling stiff and woolly-headed, to the sound of someone hammering on the shed's double doors. God, please, not a customer already . . . She eased herself up from the chair behind her desk and stumbled out of the office, staggered round the Stearman and the accumulated warehouse contents, and pulled open half an inch of door.

Half an inch of sunlight immediately rushed in and jabbed her in the eyes.

'Good morning! I've got something to tell—My word, dear.' Sylvia looked concerned. 'A bit "after the Lord Mayor's Show", if you don't mind me saying.'

Billie squinted down at the rumpled Joseph dress which she'd never, ever, wear again, and at her bare feet, which were dusty from the warehouse floor, and could only guess that the bits of her that she couldn't see were equally as disgusting. She pushed her hands up to her hair. Her fingers stuck fast in the residue of the previous night's gel spray. Her hairdo would probably rival Don King's now, and she knew that her eyelashes had clogged together. Her mouth tasted furry and foul.

'Er—I worked late . . .'

Sylvia nodded. 'I heard your van arrive in the early hours. I guessed it was work—or an assignation.'

'Oh God, it wasn't either. Actually, I've made a bit of a fool of myself . . .'

'Who hasn't, my dear? And I don't want to hear about it unless you want to tell me.' Sylvia squeezed through the gap and embraced Billie in a motherly hug. 'Look, you come along to mine, get yourself all washed and prettied up in the bathroom while I put on the coffee and cook you some breakfast. What do you say?'

Thank you, Mum, was top of the list. Billie bit back tears of gratitude. Oh God—she hoped she wasn't going to spend the rest of her life snivelling and becoming overemotional at every tiny act of kindness. 'That would be lovely, Sylv. You're lovely . . . Thanks—but didn't you want to tell me something?'

'It'll keep. Now, have you got any clothes to change into, or shall I have a rummage through my wardrobe?' Luckily Billie had a spare pair of jeans and a sweat shirt in the unit. Somehow, wonderful as Sylvia was, she couldn't see herself working in David Attenborough shorts and swaddled in a voluminous pashmina like a child with a degenerative chest complaint. Clean underwear, however, was a bit of a problem.

'Not to worry,' Sylvia said breezily as they erupted into the palm trees and tropical splendour. 'I've got some frillies I'll never squeeze into. Brought them from the house the last time I visited.' She sighed. 'Sadly, they never saw the light of day. Douglas didn't approve of that sort of frippery.' Billie could quite believe it. As she showered, she could hear Sylvia singing to Bob Marley, could smell coffee and bacon, and began to feel human again. Her stupidity over Kieran was a thing of the past—he'd probably forgotten most of it—and she would never make it public, so— she stopped in mid-soap—so it really, really meant that Reuben had no hold over her, didn't it?

He'd brought them together again—and neither of them cared. Both she and Kieran had pushed the past where it belonged and—she turned the shower up and let the thrumming water wash away the very last vestiges of shame—today Reuben was going to do the same . . .

She had eggs and bacon and toast and coffee, wrapped in a bath sheet and sitting beside the turquoise waterfall. The sun through the doors dappled between the branches of the palm trees, and Sylvia, in preparation for her treasure hunt, had liberally smothered the surrounding floor with silver sand. If it hadn't been for the drone of the planes, the rush of the bypass traffic, and Fred 'n' Dick loudly cursing the recalcitrant fork-lift, Billie could have believed herself to be in the Seychelles.

'That was wonderful. I feel much better.' She stretched her feet out towards the pool. 'Thank you so much.'

'The least I could do.' Sylvia bustled through with an armful of lace. 'After all, you changed my

438

life, my dear. You gave me courage when I had none. Now, is there anything here that takes your fancy?'

The underwear was exquisite. Delicate brand-new knickers and bras, slips and camisoles, made in Austrian and Swiss silk and lace, still wrapped in layers of tissue paper; every piece in fragile, soft colours—and all in a size that surely Sylvia could never have been . . .

'Oh, yes. I was slender once, dear. I bought these regularly, hoarded them away, for years . . . waiting to take a lover and leave Douglas . . . Waiting to wear them for someone who would appreciate them. Sadly, he never arrived. I'd really like you to have them.'

'But I couldn't!'

'Yes, dear, you could. And make good use of them. Please. For me. I married the wrong man. You won't.'

The tears were stinging Billie's eyes again. She leaped up and hugged Sylvia, unable to speak. Then selecting a bra and pants set in lilac silk edged with pale jade-green lace, Billie headed for the bathroom again. The underwear, beneath the workmanlike jeans and sweat shirt, completely transformed the way she felt: like the real her for the first time in ages.

'Much better,' Sylvia approved on her re-emergence. 'Now, let me pour some more coffee and tell you my bit of news. I've had a letter from your nice Mr Wainwright.'

Billie almost dropped her beaker.

Sylvia was grinning. 'Love him! What a nice man. Here—let me show you . . .'

Billie scanned the typewritten sheet. Reuben, it

seemed, was determined to be a caring landlord. Informed, as he had been, that Sylvia was—for whatever reason—living in her unit, he would, at his own expense, make sure that her accommodation was secure, comfortable, and suitable for domestic purposes. Sylvia, he added, must have no worries about her safety or long-term tenure. He would inspect her unit himself, and if anything needed to be added to make it suitable for both home and work use, she was to let him know. He signed himself off, with all best wishes.

'Wonderful, isn't it?' Sylvia beamed. 'No more worries at all. Not that I think I'll need much titivating, I've got it fairly cosy here, but what a lovely man to be so concerned!'

Billie handed back the letter. She didn't know quite what to think. Reuben was so bloody snaky— but surely even he wouldn't say this to Sylv and then evict her or anything, would he? Christ—that must mean he was genuine, then. Was the man totally schizophrenic? Last night, setting up that awful meeting with Kieran; this morning, suddenly turning into the biggest benefactor since Abel Magwitch? Something, somewhere was very wrong.

'Billie! Thank God—I thought you'd done a runner.' Jonah, in a crumpled flying suit and carrying helmet, gloves and goggles, stood in the gap between the parrots and monkeys, and Sylvia's latest acquisition—a quite unpleasant life-sized plastic crocodile. 'The whole world's gone crazy so I thought I'd come down here and grab a bit of sanity—and then I couldn't find you in your shed and—What's up?'

'Nothing,' Billie shook her head and handed the letter back to Sylvia, who started carrying the breakfast dishes away to the kitchenette. 'Sylv and I were just finishing breakfast.'

'You've eaten?'

'Yes, why?'

'Because I wanted to do a bit more pootling. I don't know if it's a good idea on a full stomach.'

Billie, who felt that pootling was going to be a piece of cake after the events of the last few hours, shrugged. 'I'm up for it. I've been practising for days, anyway: getting from the cockpit on to the rig in the shed, and I've done all my arm and leg exercises with the baked bean tins and . . . Why did you say the whole world's gone mad?'

'Barnaby's asked Miranda to marry him.'

'Wow.' Billie blinked. 'And?'

'And she's refused him. So he's spectacularly down in the dumps and is threatening to commit hara-kiri in the Slingsbury.'

'Poor Barnaby. And Miranda must be mad.' Billie exhaled. Why did she—'

'Because she's in love with your unpleasant Mr Wainwright, apparently. God help me, I'll never understand women.'

Billie wasn't sure she would either. I mean, Barnaby and Reuben? No contest . . . 'But I saw Miranda last night. She certainly didn't mention that Barnaby had proposed then.' She stopped, not wanting to go into any further details. 'At least, I only saw her for a little while. I—um—didn't go home to the flat, because I—er—wanted to get on with some work.'

'Yes, she'd said you'd left. That was just before I had a Bobby Charlton Slammer.'

Jesus! 'You were at Caught Offside? Last night?'

'We didn't make the opening because we'd had

a couple of Guinnesses in Mulligan's. They were saying in the bar there'd been some sort of Jarvis Cocker-type protest—but we missed it. Still, we got there just in time for the wet T-shirt contest. Not of course,' he added quickly, 'that it interested me in the slightest. Apparently one of Miranda's friends—Kitty?—won it, and was last seen necking with the footballer who did the judging.'

Billie's head reeled. There were far too many complexities to continue the conversation, and Jonah looked about as dodgy as she'd felt earlier. 'Guinness and the Bobby Charlton Slammer? God, are you fit to pootle?'

'I got rid of most of it practically straight away.' Jonah looked shame-faced. 'And I'm now filled to the brim with caffeine and Alka-Seltzer, so don't worry.'

She wasn't. Not about his sobriety. There were far more important things to worry about. A terrifying blast in the Stearman might just be the solution.

*   *   *

With the help of the Guspers and Fred 'n' Dick, Jonah had got the Stearman onto the grass strip. The sun was spiralling in a cloudless sky, and Billie, snuggled into the sweat shirt, felt that this time she was better prepared. For half an hour she practised getting out of the seat, hauling herself onto the wing, strapping herself into the rig, and then reversing the process while the plane was stationary.

'OK, absolutely brilliant.' Jonah pulled on his flying jacket and climbed into the cockpit behind her. 'Now let's try it on the move.'

'On the ground on the move?' Billie looked nervously at Jonah over her shoulder from the depths of the seat.

'Of course. And don't forget, if at any time you're not happy, just thumbs down. OK?'

She nodded, then clutched onto the sides of the plane as it roared into life. To be honest, she thought, as they bounded across the grass, throwing herself onto the top of a plane which was being driven by a hung-over pilot was probably quite sensible compared to her past misdemeanours.

Jonah touched her shoulder. 'OK, Billie. Go.'

She went. The whole routine that she'd practised religiously was a million times more difficult on the move; the bumpy motion of the plane and the rush of the wind made everything so much more complicated. She was concentrating so hard on getting from the seat to the wing and from the wing to the rig and fastening and unfastening the right straps, though, that there simply wasn't any time to feel nervous.

After what seemed like three hours, she'd finally made it. 'There!' She gulped in triumph, so tightly strapped that she felt like she was wearing one of Zi-Zi's whalebone corsets. Gingerly, she leaned back against the comparative safety of the rig's padded seat. 'I've done it! I've bloody done it!'

She had. She really had. The feeling of achievement, of fulfilment, was totally unbelievable. Clutching hold of the wire stays, she turned and grinned down at Jonah.

He grinned back and stuck up his thumb, mouthing the words, 'Wonderful. Now get back in and we'll try it again.'

She did. Very unsteadily. Climbing backwards down into the plane while it was bundling along the ground was actually easier than scrambling out onto the wing. Eventually, she sank down into the seat, feeling as though she'd conquered her own Everest.

'Completely brilliant!' Jonah yelled in her ear, swooping the Stearman back towards the warehouses. 'Now let's try it once more . . .'

They tried it another six times. They'd got quite an audience by this time, but Billie didn't really notice. She was just so exhilarated by her achievement, by overcoming her fear, by the fact that each time she became a little more adept, that everything paled into insignificance.

'Do you feel up to flying?' Jonah asked. 'I mean, I'll understand if you don't, but I thought if we just took it slowly—starting off with you strapped to the rig, of course, then if you feel ready, we'll try the cockpit to wing to rig transfer . . .'

She nodded. She'd come this far. She climbed back onto the wing and fastened the rig's harness.

As Jonah kept the Stearman level, Billie felt the heady adrenaline rush again as they raced across the grass, gradually accelerating. The wind punched against her, pushing her neck backwards, and her stomach was left behind on the ground, but at the moment of takeoff she felt nothing but pure excitement.

God! It was wonderful. She didn't dare look down, but she knew they were flying. She clung onto the rig, not reckless enough to move, just savouring the feeling of being, literally, on top of the world. She was amazed that she wasn't more frightened. But fear was out of place here. She had every faith in the plane and in Jonah, and, to be honest, swooping through the sky was such a blissful experience that she honestly couldn't understand why she'd dreaded it before.

There were still the earlier drawbacks, of course. Despite the sweat shirt, she was absolutely frozen. The wind stung her eyes, her fingers had turned to icicles, her ears were roaring and her nose was running. The noise was incredible. Next time, she promised herself, she'd have earplugs and nose plugs and wear Isla's fluffy undersuit and the leather-lined silver gloves . . . Oooh! She felt her stomach slip away as the Stearman banked, then realised they were going into land. Bugger . . .

'Just great! Ready to try again?' Jonah shouted as soon as the throbbing had died away. 'You still all right?'

Billie nodded stiffly. She couldn't speak. Her mouth, which she'd opened somewhere above the bypass, had been caught and frozen in time. She desperately needed to blow her nose and wipe her face. Everything hurt: her armpits, stomach, spine, and shins all felt as though they'd been pulverised. Tomorrow, she knew, she'd be black and blue. Tomorrow, she'd deal with it. Right now, other things took priority.

She took a deep breath and nodded. 'Let's go.'

They repeated the performance for an hour. Each time, the sensations were heightened. Each time, Jonah coaxed the Stearman higher and into slightly more adventurous moves: steeper climbs, sharper dives, shorter turns. Billie, feeling brave, practised smiling and discovered that once she'd started she couldn't stop. The wind solidified the rictus, and thrust all sorts of small airborne insects between her teeth. Not being able to spit, she

445

swallowed.

Waving was almost as bad. Even the muscle-building with the baked bean tins hadn't prepared her for the powerful snatch of the wind. It took all her strength to lift her arms above her head and keep them there. Billie, by now desperate to go to the loo, jiggled about on the seat and found herself slipping sideways.

Christ! The view was surprising, to say the least. Totally disorientated, with the bypass and the airport now tip-tilted, and the sky on a diagonal slant, she remembered to keep waving and point her toes, despite the wind trying to dismember her. She wanted to punch the air in triumph. She'd just—albeit by accident—executed her first acrobatic airborne manoeuvre!

After they'd landed and Jonah had hugged her and she'd hugged him back, and he'd belted off to refill the Stearman with AVGAS, and she'd wobbled dizzily off to the loo, it was time for the real test. Climbing from the cockpit, out onto the wing, and into the rig. Much as she'd have been happier to delay the process, Billie knew, as they all did, that with merely weeks to go until she did it for real, it was now or never.

Jonah hugged her again and Sylvia kissed her and everyone clapped, then she climbed into the cockpit, strapped herself in and waited for takeoff. She didn't have to wait long. After climbing quickly, Jonah levelled the Stearman out at the prescribed thousand feet, and tapped her on the shoulder. With a hastily muttered prayer, Billie gripped the sides of the cockpit and levered herself out of her seat.

It was all so different. All the practising in the

446

world could not have prepared her for the force of the wind as she clung to the handholds on the wing and lodged her feet onto the back of the seat. She was going to fall—she knew she was . . . Taking a deep breath, she repeated the procedures over and over inside her head, all the while aware of the steady drone of the engine and the roar of the propeller.

Pushing off with her feet, she launched into mid-air, scrambled, kneeled on the wing and, still fighting the wind, crawled towards the rig's supports. She wasn't aware of speed, just motion and the relentless nonstop force of the gale. Reaching upwards, grabbing the rig stanchions, she teetered upright and edged her way carefully between the wires, watching her feet all the time.

There—now her feet were in the right place and—yes!—she backed into the rig. God, it felt great. Sturdy and safe. With one hand, she buckled herself into the harness, then leaned back. She'd done it!

She raised her hands above her head and waved in triumph. Jonah and the Stearman gave the tiniest roll in salute and she laughed out loud. Then she stopped. She still had to get back in. Still, there was ages yet . . . Might as well make the most of the power-rush that was surging through her body.

Confident in the harness, she twisted the seat a little, then a little more, then completely round . . . Wow! Now she was doing a handstand, upside down in mid-air, at 150 miles an hour . . . and it was the greatest feeling in the world. She swivelled back, dancing now on the rig, practising all the moves she'd practised on the sideboard. It was truly awesome . . .

Jonah, obviously sensing her assurance, rolled the Stearman to one side. The sky looped the loop in the opposite direction to her stomach. Then the ground was where the sky should have been, and the plane was flipping over backwards and she was hanging suspended . . . She lost count of the loops and rolls, but gradually became accustomed to the motion. She had never, in her life, felt so high.

When both she and the plane were the right way up, she glanced over her shoulder, and Jonah nodded, making a T with his hands. Oh shit, time to get back in . . .

Undoing the harness with rigid fingers, she inched her feet carefully out of the rig, walking backwards, slowly—so slowly,—then, hanging onto the wire supports and kneeling down, she reached back with one foot until it touched the windscreen. That was fine . . . She slid the foot down until it touched the back of the seat . . . Then the other one . . . Then she flopped down after it, and fastened her seat belt.

Crying and laughing at the same time, she turned round to look at Jonah. He was shaking his head, smiling, biting back some sort of emotion.

They landed to tumultuous applause. Billie, totally exhausted and not quite able to get her land legs, fumbled with the buckle of her harness. Jonah, having already opened his and shed his goggles, helmet and jacket, leaned across to help her.

'You are a complete star . . .' His voice was choked. 'Christ, I can't believe what we've got. We'll take 'em by storm . . . God Almighty, Billie— how can I ever thank you?'

'Just get me out of here and buy me a gin and tonic,' she muttered, clinging onto him, her knees giving way.

He laughed and lifted her down. 'Did you mean that? About the drink?'

'Too right. But not straight away.' She dashed her hand across her face, smearing all sorts of detritus into the crevices and not caring. Still wobbling she stood on tiptoe and kissed his cheek. 'I'll catch you later. And, Jonah, thank you . . .'

summer

chapter thirty-six

With a week to go before the air pageant, Jonah drove towards Whiteacres on his one day off for ages, and tried not to panic. He was growing increasingly worried about the lack of dedication of his partners.

Barnaby, bruised and stoically silent about Miranda's rejection, had flown off to Kentucky to view more horses at the Keenland sales and was last heard muttering about four legs being more faithful than two, and that maybe he'd settle in Derbyshire on a permanent basis and forget that Whiteacres ever existed. Vinny and Pam were still sceptical about the small-scale pageant managing to attract any attention from a public already sated with festivals, and rock concerts, and huge organised outdoor events. Estelle, who had suddenly announced that wingwalking was definitely not for her and that Billie was welcome to the limelight, wasn't even pretending to have any interest—either in the air display, Sullivanair, or Jonah personally.

It was only Billie who, like him, was throwing herself wholeheartedly into the preparations.

Jonah pulled onto the airport road and bumped his car none too gently over the speed humps. The sky was the colour of flax flowers, the breeze slight, and there was not a trace of nimbus or cumulus. He hoped the perfect June weather would last for the next seven days at least. The success or failure of the air pageant, he felt, would mirror the triumph or otherwise of his further expansion. He grinned to himself as, with crossed fingers, he yanked the car into a parking space beside the Sullivanair office. It was a good job that his passengers didn't realise that they were being flown by a man who never walked under ladders, refused to look at the new moon through glass, and always chucked a few grains of spilled salt over his left shoulder.

He was still grinning, reliving for the millionth time that amazing trial run with the Stearman, as he opened the office door.

After the success of the wingwalking, Jonah had watched Billie go, swaying a little as she crossed the grass, skipping with elation as she hauled herself into her van, and had felt the urge to run after her. He hadn't wanted to let her out of his sight. He'd known exactly how she felt. The Stearman had bonded them together with ties far stronger than words; the experience they'd just shared had been so momentous that he'd felt totally incapable of even trying to explain it to anyone else.

It was only after the van had rattled away across the dusty concrete that he'd realised he hadn't told her about his breakthrough. The previous night he'd only gone along with Barnaby's suggestion to visit Caught Offside in the hope of seeing Billie. He'd wanted to tell her then about the Sullivanair expansion developments. Which, he'd thought, was pretty stupid, given that she hated all things aeronautical. It was just that he valued Billie's opinion.

He'd flown the Shorts to Renfrew on a charter, and in the two hours before returning, he'd met up with his ex RAF colleague and moved a step closer to making the fleet dream a reality. He'd viewed the second Shorts and the Skyvan at Glasgow, inspected their CAA certificates, discussed the lease-buy terms, and after a bit of haggling had agreed a price on having them liveried in the silver, emerald and purple of Sullivanair. He'd then proffered his banker's draft, signed the paperwork, and agreed on a possible September delivery.

He hadn't mentioned any of this to Barnaby or Estelle. Twitching with excitement, he'd toyed with the idea of discussing it with Vinny on the return flight, but decided that Vinny would have probably laughed and dismissed it as yet another impossible dream. Jonah really hadn't wanted to hear Vinny put his most feared thoughts into words—that what the hell was the point in spending all the company profits on two more planes to be delivered in September when the possibility of Sullivanair still running out of Whiteacres in the autumn was pretty slim indeed.

Billie, he'd felt, would at least have given it some consideration. Billie, he'd been sure, would have said great and go for it, and made him feel a bit better about the amount of money he may well have just chucked away. Anyway, he valued Billie's opinion as a businesswoman; after all, she'd been as smart as paint in getting her warehouse up and running from nothing, hadn't she?

He'd missed her at Caught Offside, and then, amidst all the euphoria of the wingwalking, he'd completely forgotten to mention it.

Sylvia had then broken loose from the cluster of onlooking warehousers that morning, and had swayed towards him, carrying a tray of cocktails complete with impaled cherries and gaily coloured umbrellas. 'Jonah! We're having a little celebration! I've never seen anything so incredible in my life! Billie couldn't stay—but you'll have a piña colada with us, won't you, dear? Just to be matey?'

Jonah had groaned, suddenly feeling the restirring of the dregs of the Mulligan's Guinness and Caught Offside's Bobby Charlton Slammer. He'd smiled bravely. 'I'll certainly try.'

'Good-oh,' Sylvia had said. 'We want to show you all the posters and flyers and press releases and things that Zia and Isla and Mike have done for the airshow before we start distributing them tomorrow.'

And he'd spent the rest of the morning admiring the amount of work the warehousers had put into their ground-level part of the pageant, and courageously—considering the parlous state of his liver—test-driving some of the most dubious cocktails he'd ever encountered in his life.

He stopped daydreaming, stepped inside the office and walked into immediate reality.

'Good morning.' Estelle didn't look up from her keyboard. 'Or at least it was. Sadly there's been a bit of a blip.'

The blip was Claire. Dressed in tight jeans and a cropped T-shirt, she was undulating round the far end of the Sullivanair office, stroking things and smiling.

'She's been here for ages and she's stoned out of her brain!' Estelle hissed. 'Stupid cow says she's jacked in Aerobatic Archie.'

'Christ!' Had she told Antony about their stupid emotionless sexual reunion? Jonah sincerely hoped not. It hadn't meant anything to either of them. 'What does she want?'

'You, of course.' Estelle concentrated on a spreadsheet. 'Like everyone else. No, sorry. I mustn't be bitchy. Yes, she wants you—but she

456

also still thinks she's going to be a wingwalker.' She looked at him for the first time. 'I've told her the position is already filled.'

Despite the atmosphere, Jonah couldn't keep the excitement out of his voice. 'Yeah, well, I somehow can't see Claire doing the full barnstorming stunt at a thousand feet.'

'Neither can I.' Estelle pushed her chair away from her desk. 'If I can't compete with Billie Pascoe, Claire hasn't got a dog's chance, has she?'

'Not really. God, I wish you could have seen Billie. She was stupendous! Out of this world! Took to it like a real trouper. You should have seen—' He stopped. 'No, sorry. Tactless of me . . .'

'Not really.' Estelle looked away. 'I do know my limitations. I was being a bit pathetic, really, earlier on, clinging onto the hope . . .'

Jonah felt terrible. He'd been unfair and selfish. Again. Was he ever anything else when it came to a choice between planes and women? 'Shit—sorry. You've been brilliant at helping with the Stearman's rebuild and everything. It's just—'

'That she's five foot nothing and made of fresh air, while I'm—' Estelle flexed her incredible body—'constructed more solidly, shall we say?'

Jonah grinned. It wasn't quite how Vinny described her. At that moment Claire clattered a pile of books from the windowsill and laughed. They both stared at her in dismay as she ignored them and started opening cupboards, singing loudly.

Jonah turned away from the travesty that he'd once sworn he loved enough to die for, and touched Estelle's shoulder. 'You've had more than enough to put up with from the Sullivans, haven't you? And why are you working, anyway? We've got a free day today—and we're fully booked until mid-July. You could have taken the day off and just left the answerphone on.'

Still singing, Claire turned round from the cupboard, beamed beatifically at them both, and swept a pile of files to the floor.

Estelle half rose, then sank back into her seat. 'Bitch. Still, she's your responsibility. You can clear up after her. And I'm not really working, I'm just tidying a few things.'

Jonah walked to the window. The Shorts was hangared, but he could see the silver, green and purple colours of the Slingsby parked alongside the Aeroclub planes. Hopefully it meant that when Barnaby returned from the States he would abandon his threatened suicide missions after his rejected proposal, and concentrate on flipping the Slingsby through the air at next week's show. That was, of course, if Barnaby came back at all.

Jonah sucked in his breath. Poor Barnaby. What the hell had inspired him to propose to Miranda? He'd only taken her out a few times, after all. He liked her and enjoyed her company, that much Jonah knew, and probably loneliness and too much Guinness had overcome the fear of a rebuff that strange night at Caught Offside. However, if—just if—his new scheme worked out, he would have not just the answer to his prayers and Sullivanair's future, but also to Barnaby s eremitic existence.

Claire was still drifting, still smiling, still touching. She was OK like this, if extremely irritating for those not in the same state. The black gloom wouldn't descend until later. Jonah decided to make the most of her good mood and ignore her.

458

He looked back at Estelle. He couldn't put it off. 'You're leaving, aren't you?'

'That obvious, is it?'

'Fairly,' he nodded, feeling sad. It could have been so very different. Estelle had put up with a lot more than most women. 'Is it irrevocable?'

'Definitely. Sorry, Jonah. It's not just us, although you'd drive a saint to sinning, but it's mainly Sullivanair being so—well—small-time. I knew when you started to fight to save Whiteacres that it was time for me to quit. I really don't want to be a glamorous front for a two-bit outfit, you know, typing and filing and making coffee . . . I've loved it—it's been a blast—but I want to use my qualifications . . . be appreciated . . .'

Jonah understood. If he'd fallen in love with her she would have probably stayed and helped him work Sullivanair up into the middle rankings. As it was he wouldn't even tell her about the new developments. 'We're doing all right now, though. The figures—'

'The figures are great. We're making a profit. Even if you do go ahead and lease the other planes we'll still be in profit. The bank manager is a happy bunny.' She smiled. 'Which helped my decision a lot. I don't feel that I'm a rat leaving the proverbial. Sullivanair is at last in the black and getting blacker. But I'm still not staying.'

'You've got somewhere else to go, then?'

'Easyjet. On the maintenance side. I won't be just a pretty face there. In fact, my looks won't come into it. They want my shit-hot brain and a pair of oily but dexterous hands.' She tossed her hair over her shoulder. 'You had very little need of those—the oily but dexterous hands—didn't you?'

459

'Personally or professionally?'

Both.' She looked down at her desk and took a deep breath. 'Now bugger off and take that sad cow with you. Easyjet want me to start in July, so I'll still be around to add a touch of corporate glamour to your air display, and work my notice—and it should give you plenty of time to find a replacement.'

Jonah crossed the office and hugged her. It was the sort of hug he would have given Pam or even Sylvia. 'Replacing you will be impossible. And I'll miss you.'

'Yeah, sure you will. Now, like I said, clear off before I cry.'

He moved awkwardly away from her, knowing that he could have persuaded her to change her mind. Knowing that he wouldn't even try.

'Jonah! Darling!' Claire crashed across the office towards him. 'When did you arrive? I've been waiting for ages. I've left Antony! I've come back to you!'

'Christ,' Estelle muttered. 'Get her out of here. You sure know how to pick 'em, Jonah, don't you? The junkie, the sad clinger-on, and the trainee dyke . . .'

He'd bundled Claire into his car and was heading for the flat before Estelle's parting shot really hit home. She'd been a bit caustic: well, Claire was only a part-time addict, Estelle would have made any normal man's dreams come true, but Billie . . . ? God! Surely Estelle didn't have some female sixth sense about Billie's sexuality, did she? Estelle and Billie had become pretty pally over the last few months. Had Billie confided in her? He'd never thought that Billie might be gay. He was pretty sure there was no man in her life, but as he rarely thought about her life away from Whiteacres, he may have got it spectacularly wrong.

'Are we going straight to bed again?' Claire snuggled up against him, practically knocking the steering wheel out of his hands. 'Antony's crap in bed.'

Jonah pushed her away. He didn't want to have this conversation. He didn't want her close to him, or fuelled up on amphetamines, or disturbing his senses with her scent.

'Pig,' she giggled, sliding down in the passenger seat and kicking her feet up onto the dashboard. 'Still, it's lovely to be back together, isn't it? We're going to have such a lovely time, Jo.'

He rushed her into the flat. Even if his neighbours were strangers, he still didn't want them watching. He'd had to take Claire there. There really wasn't anywhere else for her to go. She was still twitchy, unable to stay still. She moved restlessly round the living room, picking things up and casually dropping them again.

He made coffee and pushed a mug into her hands. It was very hot and most of the contents slopped over her fingers but she didn't seem to notice. She just laughed.

'Claire, slow down for a sec. Have you and Antony really split up?'

She nodded. 'Yesterday. I left him in Eastbourne after a display. He's becoming so boring. The season's getting underway and he's ignoring me— like you did. And anyway, once he's out of the team at the end of this year, what on earth are we going to do?'

Jonah shrugged. 'Well, as far as I knew, you were going to buy Whiteacres and put me out of

461

business.'

'Naughty!' She put the coffee mug down unsteadily and danced across the room. 'I never said that! It was his idea, and I thought it sounded great, but now . . .'

'Now you think that being grounded in Hampshire might not be quite so much fun?'

Claire entwined her arms round his neck. The cloudy curls brushed his face and Obsession filled his senses. 'Jo, sweetheart, please can we stop talking about boring business? Please can we go to bed?'

He held her because he'd loved her. He cradled her against him because he felt guilty. If he'd paid more attention to her she wouldn't be like this, would she? They would still be married. She wriggled closer. Their bodies fitted together so well. It was so familiar . . . so right . . .

'We're not going to bed.'

'Floor, then. Or the sofa. Or the bathroom. Or—'

'Nowhere. I'm not sleeping with you. I don't want to make love to you. Never, ever again. Understand?' He stopped, looking down at the disbelief on her face. 'I think we should ring Antony and get him to come and collect you and—'

'No!' The surprised expression had puckered into hurt. She looked like a child. 'He doesn't love me like you do.'

'I don't love you at all. Not any more. And I'm not bothered about what you and Antony think you can do to my business. God, you'd never understand, will you? You left me because I was obsessed with flying and couldn't give you what you wanted. Antony can give you everything that I couldn't. Antony can go on giving you that. Maybe not touring with the team, but money and excitement and—' He stopped again. He wasn't going to say speed, even if it would sway the argument.

She pulled away from him, the impending tears turning to wide smiles. 'If he buys Whiteacres, you mean? You mean he wouldn't actually have to be there running it all the time? You mean it would bring in loads of money and we could still go travelling for most of the year, and—' He stopped listening. Once she started talking, this high, she'd talk for ever. And very little of it would make sense. And shit, anyway! He hadn't meant to try to persuade her back to bloody Aerobatic Archie because buying Whiteacres would be a good idea!

He left her, still chattering animatedly, and dialled Antony's mobile.

'Antony? Jonah. Claire's here. What? No, at my flat. She's fine—yeah—buzzing . . . What? No, I haven't got a clue where she was last night . . . Can you—What? Why? Yes . . . OK, I'll tell her . . .'

Claire was dancing the salsa with one of the flat sofa cushions as he switched off the phone. 'Antony's coming to collect you. It'll take him an hour or so—will you be OK?'

She stopped dancing. 'I don't want to leave you.'

Jonah felt a punch of sadness deep in his stomach. Estelle was leaving. Claire had left. Was there ever going to be a time when he felt truly happy?

'You've already left me. Antony loves you. He's been worried sick. He's going to come and fetch you and then we're all going to talk.'

'Are we?' Claire wrinkled her nose. 'OK, that'll

be nice. Have we got time to go to bed before he gets here, then?'

'No, sweetheart, we haven't.' Jonah swallowed the lump in his throat. 'Now be a good girl and try to get some sleep before Antony arrives.'

Claire looked at him with sorrowful little-girl eyes, then obediently trotted into the bedroom. Alone.

*   *   *

Two hours later, the three of them perched on the edges of the hard oatmeal furniture and looked at each other. To give him his due, Jonah thought, Aerobatic Archie looked bloody awful. He obviously hadn't slept; he really must have been frantic about Claire.

'She wants to come back to you.' Antony Archibald's cut-glass accent rang through the flat's functional dross. 'She wants to leave me.'

'Not really, I don't,' Claire giggled. 'Oh, I don't know—it was just yesterday and the show and you talking to those foreign people and not me, and I thought being with Jo was so *uncomplicated* . . .'

'Those foreign people,' Antony said wearily, 'were canvassing me regarding forming another display team. To be based in Chantilly.'

Claire was clearly turning the word over in her head. Her eyes flicked wide. 'Chantilly? Near Paris, you mean? With horse racing and glamour? And all those shops? Ooh, Paris!' She jumped up from the sofa and plonked herself onto Jonah's lap. 'Paris, Jo? Doesn't that sound great?'

'I won't be coming with you.' He pushed her gently away, 'It'll just be you and Antony.'

464

Antony coughed. 'Not necessarily. I'll—er—be looking for flyers. And you're good, Jonah—much as I hate to say it. And, of course, you're very pally with Molton-Kusak, aren't you? And he's one of the best.'

Jesus! Jonah stared at him. Him? Flying in a stunt display team? With Barnaby? Travelling the world, being paid megabucks for doing what he loved most?

'We'll have the brand-new Hawks,' Antony said matter-of-factly. 'And a five-year deal. We'll be on the international circuit, as well as the domestic one. It'll be a lot of hard work, but the money should make up for it.'

Claire stood up again, and danced a few more salsa steps between them. 'Oh, yes! Think about it! And both of you—I'll have both of you!'

Jonah felt as though someone had just skewered out his brain. 'And—um—if you accept this Chantilly deal? Where will that leave the Whiteacres takeover?'

Antony winced as Claire landed on his lap. 'Not altogether sure, to be honest. Nice to have two strings to the bow, though. Whiteacres would be a super little pension plan . . .'

'Oooh, yes!' Claire gurgled with laughter. 'We could have both! And even if Jo didn't come and fly your Hawks, Antony darling, he could still work at Whiteacres, couldn't he? Because you'd be ever so kind and let him stay there, wouldn't you?'

The skewer ratcheted up a bit. Jonah felt that everything he'd fought for, everything he'd achieved, was being snatched away. Whichever way he jumped now, he'd merely be a marionette and Aerobatic Archie would be pulling the bloody

465

strings.

'No need to let me have your answer straight away.' Antony spoke gruffly, standing up and taking Claire's hand. 'Mull it over—and have a chat to Molton-Kusak. I know you're getting this little air pageant together, so you're probably busy like I am. I'll give you a week or so after your show to decide.' He looked down at Claire. 'Now, honey—which is it to be? Stay here with Jonah, or fly out to Chantilly for a bit of a recce with me?'

'Silly!' Claire pouted and threw her arms round Antony's neck. 'Why would I want to stay here in all this dismal gloom when I could have such a lovely time shopping in Paris?'

*   *   *

Jonah drove back to Whiteacres and the warehouses on autopilot. Estelle . . . Claire . . . Aerobatic Archie . . . In the last few hours they'd managed to kick his Glasgow expansion dreams into oblivion. Without Estelle, the behind-the-scenes running of Sullivanair would grind to a halt. He'd never find a replacement as feisty and knowledgeable. And Antony Archibald would have even more money from this new deal and be able to pick up Whiteacres like a mere frippery to play with. He'd never agree to an extended Sullivanair taking over the main slots—even if Jonah wanted to stay. And did he want to stay? Would any pilot in his right mind turn down an opportunity like the one Aerobatic Archie had just offered him?

He groaned out loud. Even Billie and the triumphal wingwalking seemed to belong to another lifetime.

466

'Hello, dear.' Sylvia waved from the crowd of warehousers crowded round a trestle table as Jonah parked the car on the weedy concrete. 'Come to check up on us, have you?'

Jonah shook his head, noticing with dismay that Billie's van wasn't there and she wasn't among the warehousers. 'No, the posters and everything were wonderful. You've all worked very hard . . . The show will be a sell-out.'

God—what else could he say to them? He couldn't tell them that they could be wasting their time, could he? That no matter how hard they worked, how wonderful their publicity for the pageant, it might not even matter, because Antony Archibald and Claire would simply blow them out of the water financially, wouldn't they? Oh sure, the warehousers would probably stay where they were, but Aerobatic Archie could close down the link road, refuse access, all manner of things to put this tiny industrial estate out of business.

'Come and see the costumes, then.' Sylvia grabbed his arm. 'Zia and Isla have been simply brilliant. We're all going to dress up—even just to sell programmes. Wonderful, aren't they? Fred 'n' Dick are going to be astronauts, and Zia's going to be Fidel Castro. Isla's got a real Romany outfit for her tarot readings and goodness, it's so exciting!' She flipped through the piles of clothes. 'Look— this is my Captain Hook suit for the treasure hunt, and these are the outfits for the Guspers' films—gangsters, and flappers, and *Star Wars* and *Star Trek*, and Wild West, and—ooh—these skimpy ones are a bit risque, don't you think? And here's—'

Jonah really wanted to cry. They'd made so much

467

effort.

Billie's van rattled across the concrete at that moment, and she slammed out of the door. God, Jonah thought, she looks pretty murderous too.

Billie pursed her lips as she walked towards him, her eyes fixed on the costumes. 'Hi. What's going on here?'

'Show preparations. Can I talk to you about ten million other things?'

'Yeah, sure. Have you heard from Barnaby?'

'Not a word. The Slingsby's just waiting for him to come back.' Jonah sighed. 'Maybe he'll take a break in his Kentucky horse-buying and get roaring drunk and decide to replace Miranda with a Stearman or something.'

'Much like you did?'

He grinned at her. She made him feel normal. Stable. OK. As though none of the other problems were anything more than minor glitches. He took a deep breath. 'Life's just become slightly more complicated . . .'

After he'd told her—all of it—she looked about as shell-shocked as he felt.

'And I thought I had problems . . . I still can't find Reuben—or Miranda. They've been missing for ages now. They've probably run off to get married. Oh, sorry, we're talking about your troubles, not mine. And you haven't got a clue what you want to do? Which way you want to jump?'

'Yes, I have. Seeing this—and you—has made me realise that Whiteacres means more to me than any bloody feted aerobatic display team. But it'll mean putting my proposals to the Aviation Incs as quickly as possible.'

Billie nodded. 'OK then, let's do it. Now. They

should be in their office, shouldn't they?'

'Yes, but you need an appointment. They don't see anyone without an appointment.'

'So, we'll pop over and wait until we get one. God, Jonah, I've had such a buzz with the Stearman. You'll never know how much you've helped me. Now it's my turn to repay the favour. Hang on for about five minutes. I've just got to do something in the shed . . .'

Three and a half minutes later, Billie re-emerged dressed in the wingwalking outfit. Everyone round the table stopped and stared, their jaws dropping. Zia, ignoring Isla's glares, even whistled.

'What the hell are you doing?' Jonah said, gazing at her. 'The old farts will have a heart attack! Are you trying to seduce them into saying yes?'

Billie looked affronted. 'Goodness, no. It's just what we in the journalistic trade used to refer to as a honey trap.'

chapter thirty-seven

They'd started to walk across the airstrip. Jonah stopped so abruptly that Billie almost cannoned into him. He peered at her in disbelief. 'You mean you were a *journalist*?'

'Before I was a taxi-driver, and a warehouse proprietor, and a wingwalker, yes.'

'Good God, I had no idea.'

Billie looked at him for a long time, then smiled. 'Why should you have? Apart from families and immediate stuff, we don't know very much about each other at all, really, do we?'

'And are there any more secrets that you're going to share with me?'

She shook her head. 'Not yet. One day—who knows? What about you?'

'A soul-bearing session at fifteen hundred feet, you mean? OK—it's a date.'

Billie started to jog towards the Whiteacres tarmac. 'I was thinking more of somewhere cosy with a gallon of gin and tonic, actually, like you promised me ages ago for being the best wingwalker you've ever had, and never delivered.' She looked over her shoulder. 'And yes, mentioning dates, there is something else you might like to know, just to cheer you up.'

'What?' Jonah lengthened his stride to keep up with her trot. 'But I'm warning you, it'll have to be bloody good to lift my sense of impending doom.'

Billie sucked in her breath. She felt no sense of betrayal. She had been frustrated and furious that neither Miranda nor Reuben had been at home, nor at work, since the opening night at Caught Offside. 'You and Barnaby, and me and Miranda, were going to have a blind date.'

'What? When? Why didn't I know about it?'

'Because you were Miranda's fantasy man, only I didn't know it was you, and—'

By the time she'd finished, Jonah was grinning from ear to ear, and they'd slowed to a crawl. 'So, that night we all met up in the Dil Raj . . .'

'Was unplanned, but the culmination of Miranda's wildest dreams, yes.'

'And you were supposed to be with Barnaby?'

'Yes.'

'Do you—um—like him, then?'

'Of course. Oh, but not as a potential partner or

470

anything. I said I didn't know it was Barnaby, you see. I was just going to be making up the numbers.' She smiled at him, trying hard not to let the smile erupt into a giveaway grin, and bounded ahead of him across the runway. 'There—so now that's cheered you up, we'd better get a move on.'

'God, I hate bossy women!' Jonah overtook her. 'And everyone is staring at you.'

'Great—as long as it's with lust not pity.'

Jonah reached back and grabbed her hand. 'Believe me, it isn't pity. Come along—try to keep up.'

Still giggling immoderately they arrived outside the Whiteacres Aviation Incs' offices.

She pulled a face. 'Are you really sure you want to do this?'

Jonah nodded, but Billie sensed his trepidation. Once he'd put the idea into words it was a reality; a black and white proposal. If the Aviation Incs turned him down what option would he have? Oh, yes—flying off to Paris to be a glamorous daredevil with Aerobatic Archie. She took a deep breath and bit her lip. She didn't want him to go . . .

Oh, great. The first man she'd felt drawn to since Kieran bloody Squires—and it had to be the one who treated her with the same sort of friendly familiarity as her brothers. Clever choice, Billie, she thought. He's just lost Estelle and Claire: the man's obviously going to declare himself a woman-free zone until he's in his dotage.

The Aviation Incs were obviously about to pack up for lunch. Their receptionist, Melanie according to the badge pinned to her navy-blue jacket, was surprisingly, Billie thought, young and zizzy. Billie had quite expected Vera Lynn. Melanie asked them to wait, casting flirty eyes at Jonah and rather more startled ones at Billie's outfit. Someone, Melanie said, might be available to see them.

'Pray it's Malcolm,' Jonah whispered. 'He was the only one with half a brain.'

They waited. The waiting area was very 'chocks away'. The planes pictured on the walls all made the Stearman look quite hi-tech. Jonah fiddled with his fingers, stared out of the window, and kept clearing his throat. Billie longed to be able to reassure him but didn't want to raise his hopes. What the hell did she know, anyway? Maybe, secretly, he'd love to wing off with Aerobatic Archie—especially now that Estelle was about to hitch her wagon to the easyjet star. Billie was still frightened of flying, she still disliked everything that wasn't earthbound, and yet, to keep Jonah at Whiteacres, she'd do handstands in mid-air . . .

Her introspection was diverted by Melanie leaning over from behind the desk and saying that Mr Bletchley could spare them five minutes, if they'd just like to pop up the stairs and take the third door on the left. 'Is Mr Bletchley, Malcolm?' Billie hissed.

Jonah shrugged. 'No idea. Like you and Miranda with Barnaby, we didn't get round to surnames.'

Crossing their fingers, they popped up the stairs and took the aforementioned door.

Mr Bletchley, plump and florid, stood up from behind his desk, extending a flaccid hand. Jonah grasped it with a sideways look of triumph at Billie. 'Malcolm! How kind of you!'

'Flight Lieutenant Sullivan.' Malcolm waggled Jonah's hand and stared unashamedly at Billie. 'The pleasure's all mine.'

472

Billie couldn't help it. 'Flight Lieutenant? That's you? You're a—well—a titled person?'

'That would be Sir Flight Lieutenant Sullivan,' Jonah sat down beside her. 'It's my RAF rank. I don't use it.'

'But it's courtesy to do so, my dear.' Malcolm leered at her. 'Don't you agree?'

'Oh, absolutely,' Billie said fervently, batting her eyelashes and leaning forward. 'I'll never call him anything else.'

Malcolm was still gazing at her. Jonah coughed. 'Malcolm, allow me to introduce Billie Pascoe. She's my partner in crime.'

Malcolm practically vaulted the desk to shake her hand. It was as warm and flabby as the rest of him. Billie remembered not to yank her hand away and to keep smiling. He squeezed her fingers. 'That's a very fetching costume, my dear. Does it have any significance?'

'No, I always dress like—'

'Actually, it does,' Jonah interrupted, intervening in the prolonged hand squeezing. 'And it's partly what we want to talk about this afternoon.'

Malcolm, to give him credit, listened attentively and also made notes. At any point where he looked like he might be about to intercept Jonah's flow, Billie leaned forward and simpered a bit to get him back on track.

'. . . and so,' Jonah concluded, 'we wondered if you could put all this to your colleagues and stave off the takeover bid? Especially now that my bank's lawyers have informed me about the CAA flying charter. That it is always to be a fully working air field.'

Malcolm nodded for a full thirty seconds in

Billie's direction before speaking. He then seemed to shake himself and nod instead at Jonah. 'Your backers have certainly researched thoroughly. Whiteacres must never be static—thank the Lord. As you know, I was always fully in favour of your little air display—and I must say preparations are coming on in leaps and bounds. It's going to be very exciting. Even my partners, who were a little sceptical at the outset, can see great things developing . . . And now this other information regarding the expansion of your company could sway things massively in your favour.'

Billie leaned forward. 'But, what if some of your other Incs—I mean the other members of the committee—really want to retire? I mean, suppose they've all had enough of Whiteacres and just want to get away and snooze in the sun? Wouldn't they just grab Aerobatic Archie's money and run?'

Malcolm nodded a bit more and mopped at his neck with a spotted handkerchief. 'A valid point, Miss Pascoe. But the other bid, while attractive, does seem to miss out on several vital aspects, as Flight Lieutenant Sullivan has pointed out. To be honest, I think two of our more senior members are ready to go. However, I'm certainly not, and nor are some of my more sprightly partners, and we outnumber the would-be retirees so it wouldn't be outside the realms of possibility for us to elect two new board members—always assuming that the information regarding Squadron Leader Archibald and Mrs—um—Sullivan decamping to France and not intending to be on-the-spot owners of the airfield is correct.'

Squadron Leader who? Billie frowned. Oh, he must mean Aerobatic Archie!

474

'It's definitely correct,' Jonah said quickly as Malcolm paused for breath. 'So, if you could just dig into your files and find out definitely whether Whiteacres must, under civil aviation law, not only be an active flying zone but also have an incumbent hands-on owner, and then canvass the other Incs to see who needs paying off—I mean, exactly how much money would be needed to buy their shares in the company and two seats on the board . . .'

Malcolm didn't take his eyes from Billie. 'I'll do it first thing after lunch. However, I'm already fairly confident that we wouldn't accept an all-out bid from anyone who didn't intend to be a resident owner of the airfield. And certainly not from someone who wanted to turn it into a static display area. After all, Whiteacres has been designated for civil flights—and emergency military usage for the next fifty years—we'd have to have someone here all the time.'

Billie cast another triumphant look across the office at Jonah, whom, she noticed, still had his fingers crossed.

Malcolm Bletchley did a spot more mopping with the handkerchief. 'And I'm also quietly confident that, if we turn down the offer from Squadron Leader Archibald and Mrs Sullivan, and the terms that you and—er—Wing Commander Molton-Kusak are able to offer us are mutually agreeable, then my colleagues and I will certainly welcome new and young blood round the boardroom table.' Malcolm stood up and shook Jonah's hand briefly, and Billie's for far longer. 'And I must say I can't wait to see you wingwalking, Miss Pascoe. You'll be the star of the show, my dear.'

'She is, believe me,' Jonah said, steering Billie away from the damp grasp. 'And I'm very grateful to you for your time. I'll look forward to hearing from you.'

Neither spoke until they got outside the building, then, grinning hugely at each other, Jonah uncrossed his fingers and they exchanged high-fives.

'Yes!' Jonah picked her up and swung her round. 'Yes! I think we've done it!'

'So do I, Flight Lieutenant Sullivan.' Billie made no attempt to be put down. Being held by Jonah was disturbingly wonderful, and it might never happen again. 'But, even if you manage to pull everything off, are you absolutely sure you can find enough money to buy out the retiring Incs?'

'Absolutely positive.' Jonah let her slither down the length of his body, but still didn't let go. 'It shouldn't be a problem for me now that the bank have OKed the lease-buy project, and I'm sure Barnaby would be delighted to chip in—especially now Miranda's turned him down. He'll need something to occupy him. I'll just have to persuade him that he'll be desperately lonely in Derbyshire and that he should consider selling out his pile to the National Trust. His horses should bring in some money too—and I'll sway it with him and Vinny by letting them choose Estelle's replacement—and all the stewardesses. I just need him to come back from America so that I can tell him.'

'And you don't feel guilty about dropping Aerobatic Archie and Claire in the mire?'

'Not at all. In fact, it was immensely liberating. They can bugger off to Chantilly for the rest of their stinking-rich lives, as far as I'm concerned. Now, shall we go and have that drink?'

Billie moved reluctantly away from him. 'I'd really love to, but it'll still have to wait. You might have almost sorted out most of your problems, but I've still got one or two of my own to resolve . . .'

*　　*　　*

Driving the van back to Amberley Hill, more respectably dressed again in jeans and T-shirt, Billie sang along to the radio. It was some sort of golden hour, and the tunes blasting from the speakers were all from the sixties and fizzed with toe-tapping intensity. Perfect for the barnstorming, she thought, leaving the bypass and heading into suburbia. They'd have really red-hot thumping tunes pumping from the Tannoy across the airfield during her wingwalking display, so that the excitement in the skies was shared by everyone watching . . . God, she couldn't wait to get back and tell Jonah.

She groaned. Telling Jonah would be great, but first she had to find Miranda. She and Reuben had to be *somewhere*. Surely, with them both being up to their eyeballs in their respective businesses, they wouldn't just abandon them, would they? She had to speak to Miranda urgently about the flat. Faith had managed to scrape a few days away from the farm and would be arriving from Devon on Wednesday, in plenty of time to see the sights of Amberley Hill before enjoying the air pageant. Billie had promised her Miranda's bedroom. She somehow couldn't see her mother making up a cosy threesome with Miranda and Reuben Wainwright . . .

She really didn't want to think about it. She'd still far rather think about Jonah . . . Flight Lieutenant Sullivan . . . She tried hard not to let her lips curl round the words. It was far too reminiscent of the way Estelle had behaved the first time they'd met— she groaned again—and probably about as sad.

If Jonah hadn't wanted Estelle, why on earth would he want her? In fact, after his disaster with Claire, why would he want any woman? Still, if his plans came off, then he and Barnaby would be on the board of Whiteacres Aviation and staying on at the airfield. At least she'd be able to see him. Still be able to be friends . . . She grinned to herself. Not only a flight lieutenant, but also an Inc. It all seemed very grown up.

Jonah's plans, apart from scuppering any chance Aerobatic Archie and Claire might have had as bidders for the airfield, apparently involved lease-buying another Shorts 330 and a Skyvan— whatever that was—from an ex-RAF contact in Glasgow. Whatever it was, it seemed to make sense to Malcolm, so it was presumably OK. Sullivanair would then have three planes in their fleet—two for passengers and one designated for cargo— and would therefore be a much bigger force to be reckoned with.

Jonah and his pal in Glasgow had been doing their homework; because so many of the big established airline companies were abandoning economy short-hauls in favour of long luxury flights, the way was currently open for charter firms like Sullivanair to nip into the breach. The mention of the revenue to be raised by publicity and the installation of check-in desks and hangarage and recruitment of air and ground crew to accommodate the huge influx of passengers had all gone over Billie's head.

However, she understood, along with Malcolm, that with Jonah, Barnaby and Vinny piloting three planes and thus having to employ more staff, and of course, the air pageant putting Whiteacres firmly on the map, that the money currently trickling into Whiteacres' coffers via Sullivanair could rapidly become a torrent.

Malcolm could probably see Whiteacres' status surging forward towards Stansted or somewhere, she thought cheerfully. And with the—what was it? Oh, yes—Slingsby being available for pilot-training and aerobatics, and the possibility of Barnaby getting his hands on another Stearman to make a barnstorming team, Malcolm had been practically orgasmic without her even needing to flutter her eyelashes or press together her breasts. Jonah and Sullivanair, she thought, as she approached Amberley Hill's winding streets, were definitely onto a winner. She only hoped she was.

*   *   *

The drivers in the taxi office said no, Reuben still hadn't been in. No one had a clue where he was. Lucky, they said, that the cabbies knew how to run the business with their eyes closed, and yeah, to be honest, things had been much better without him. Oh, and wasn't it a shit about Vee being sacked? Reuben was a bastard . . .

A very hung-over Pixie said much the same thing about Miranda at Follicles and Cuticles, and added that it was an extra shit because did Billie know that Kitty had buggered off with that lush footballer who'd declared her the winner of the wet footie-shirt competition on the opening night of the club and hadn't been seen since? Billie said yes, she'd heard the story several times in the last couple of weeks, and made Pixie promise to ring her the minute Miranda—or even Kitty—showed up.

Billie probed her feelings as she drove to the flat and found that she hadn't any. The first time she'd heard about Kieran and Kitty she'd actually laughed. She knew now that Kieran wouldn't change—and there had probably been dozens like her, like Kitty, in the intervening years. She just felt a bit sorry for Fenella and the children.

Miranda wasn't at the flat, and there was still no evidence that she'd even been in to collect her post. Billie drove back to the Spicer Centre and parked the van. Drawing a blank at Mulligan's, she mooched idly though the precinct, looking in shop windows. A road-sweeper, collecting the debris outside Caught Offside, looked up and winked. Billie, forgetting to be offended, winked back.

She watched him shovelling up broken bottles and abandoned glasses and cans . . . Yes, of course . . . Crunching the litter underfoot, she pushed her way through the double doors.

Caught Offside's entrance hall smelled strange, clean and lemony. Someone was working hard to maintain the new regime's standard, she thought. As Bazooka's it had always had a lingering aroma of stale smoke and sour alcohol.

She walked through into the club. Beneath the overhead lighting, it all looked sparkling and brand-new—and still, much as she hated to admit it, very impressive. Amazingly, Miranda,

480

heavily tanned and wearing jeans, a T-shirt and a workmanlike apron, was pushing a broom across the floor and laughing to herself. Unseen, Billie watched her for a moment. Miranda was obviously blissfully happy. Was she wearing a wedding ring? Billie couldn't see. She chewed her lips, watching Miranda's happiness. She couldn't bear it if Miranda was hurt again—and Reuben would surely hurt her, wouldn't he? And anyway, where the hell was he?

'I wonder if I could have a word?'

'Billie! Doll!' Miranda, her plaits clipped on top of her head and her eyelashes skewwhiff, dropped her broom with a clatter and leaped across the halfway line and through the terraces. 'Brill to see you! Have you missed me? Oh God, we've got so much to talk about! I haven't seen you since the opening night and—well, so many things have happened!'

'Have they?' Billie peered at Miranda's left hand. She was wearing rubber gloves and there didn't seem to be a tell-tale lump underneath the latex on the ring finger. 'I thought you might have been in touch.'

Miranda looked shamefaced. 'Yeah, I know— and I really should have been. Especially after that hoo-ha with Kieran Thingy. I was frantic about you!'

'Yeah,' Billie said. 'So frantic that you couldn't even be bothered to ring my mobile or the warehouse or—'

'To be honest, doll,' Miranda hugged her, 'we haven't long got back. We've been away, see, and we touched down at seven this morning, and Bertie Malone was on the phone straight away to say the cleaners hadn't turned up yet so Reuben went to see him to get all the griff and I came straight here—complete with jet lag and—Oh! Are you all right?'

'I'm fine, I just need to talk to you. And where the hell have you been?'

'The Maldives! Ace, or what?' Miranda led her to the seats behind the faux goalpost. 'It was Reuben's treat. Straight from the opening night to the airport. Just a minute to go back to flat, grab me passport and me slap bag—and whoosh! Away!' She looked distinctly soppy. 'He said we both needed a break, so he'd planned it all. He bought me a whole new wardrobe out there—not that I wore much of it . . . Romantic, eh, doll?'

'Oh, very. And it didn't occur to you to let anyone know where you'd gone?'

'Kitty knew, so Follicles was OK. And Bertie Malone runs things like a boot camp here, but Reuben swore him to secrecy in case anyone took advantage of him being away. I would have told you if you'd been back at the flat but you weren't.' She peered at Billie. 'Why the hell didn't Kitty tell you, then, doll?'

'Because Kitty has apparently buggered off with Kieran Squires.'

'Really? Wow! Shit—then who's been running Follicles?'

'Pixie.'

'Christ! I'll have to get down there!' Miranda started tearing off her apron. 'Oh, so much has happened. And look, your secret's safe with me, doll—Reuben's explained it all to me. He understands about what you did . . . Slapping him and that Kieran whatshisname . . . He's not angry.'

Big of him, Billie thought, under the circumstances. So, Miranda knew about Kieran now, did she? Funnily enough, Billie really didn't care.

'We talked about it on the flight out,' Miranda stretched her feet up onto the back of the seat in front, 'and decided that you must be exhausted. What with spending all the hours God sends at the warehouse and this wingwalking thing, and then, not liking football. Reuben said it was probably just an aberration. A reaction . . . With you being overtired . . . But even if you're heading for a nervous breakdown or something, I won't say anything.'

Billie snorted. So Reuben hadn't told the truth. Again. He'd merely explained away her retaliation on the grounds of nervous exhaustion. She glanced at Miranda's now ungloved hands. Oh, hallelujah! No wedding ring!

'Yes, it must have been something like that. Still, I'm feeling much better now so there's no need to worry. Look, Miranda, I know about Barnaby asking you to marry him. Are you sure you wouldn't consider him?'

'God, doll!' Miranda rocked in her chair. 'Six months ago I'd have said yes and please and been hotfooting up to Derbyshire with my tiara in my rucksack! Barnaby's such a darling, a real sweetie. But as it is . . .' she shrugged, 'I couldn't. I truly love Reuben, you see. After all this time, he really is the only person I feel comfortable with . . . the only person I want to be with. And he's asked me to move in with him permanently.'

Billie closed her eyes. She felt sick. Miranda— shacking up with Reuben in his awful bachelor

483

bedsit?

Miranda misinterpreted the silence. 'Look, I know it'll be difficult for you with the flat and everything; but I'll keep paying my part of the rent until we can find someone else for you to share with.' She hugged Billie again. 'I know how you feel about Reuben, doll, but couldn't you say you're pleased for me . . . ?'

chapter thirty-eight

Faith gazed around the flat. It certainly wasn't anything like she'd expected it to be. Arriving yesterday and anticipating urban decay, she'd been very impressed by the large airy rooms, swathes of cream voile draped at the windows to maximise the light, and huge cushiony furniture. Surfaces gleamed, there were flowers, and everywhere was neat and tidy and co-ordinated like a furniture showroom.

Having spent twenty-odd years dunging out Billie's bedroom at the farm, she was well aware that this show had been orchestrated for her benefit, and was oddly touched. They'd had a lovely time the previous evening, just her and Billie, eating in a really swish Indian restaurant, talking all the time, and then coming back to the flat to share a bottle of wine and continue the gossip. Then, both yawning, they'd eventually tottered off to bed in the early hours.

Faith, who by necessity had always been an early-to-bed, early-to-rise person, found it all wonderfully decadent. And Billie seemed happy,

484

which was great. The opening of the nightclub appeared to have passed without any glitches—which meant either Kieran hadn't turned up, or Billie hadn't gone. Faith had rather hogged this part of the conversation, trying to find out if they had actually come face to face, but Billie hadn't seemed in the least interested in discussing it. Eventually, Faith had fallen into Miranda's freshly laundered bed and slept soundly, cheerfully assured that her meddling hadn't caused any problems.

However, she thought now, washing up her breakfast things in the kitchen, there were various bits and pieces that she had managed to glean during their mother-and-daughter chat the night before, and the two days before the air show thing—which she wasn't sure she'd enjoy, but as Billie was involved in some way she'd feigned enthusiasm for it just as she had for numerous school concerts over the years—would give her ample opportunity to iron out the remaining creases in her daughter's life.

*   *   *

Amberley Hill was quite charming, Faith decided, with its mellow stone buildings and steep winding roads. Not unlike Brixham, really. The Spicer Centre, however, she thought, she could live without. Still, this was her first port of call, having, as she did, the day free while Billie was at work. Billie had kindly invited her to spend the day at Whiteacres, but Faith had refused the offer saying it would keep until tomorrow and she'd find plenty to do to amuse herself so Billie wasn't to worry about her at all.

She pushed open the door to Follicles and Cuticles and was immediately assailed by various pungent aromas. The little girls all skipping between the lilac chairs looked like school children in their black outfits, and the music blasting from the radio was a far cry from the soothing burble of BBC Devon that she was used to in Valda's, where she had her hair done at home.

In Valda's you got a shampoo and set half-price on a Wednesday, and a chance to catch up with all the gossip. Follicles and Cuticles looked more like a multicoloured operating theatre—and oh, my goodness! Faith peered through the lavender saloon door halfway along—there were men! In towels!

'Can I help you?' An elfin child with neon hair bounced up to the desk. 'Do you have a 'poinment?'

'No, I'm afraid I don't.' Faith dragged her eyes away from the men in towels being led towards a flat leather table. 'I—um—wondered if you could squeeze me in sometime today? Just a trim. Is—er—Miranda free?'

''Dunno.' The elf spun on her chequered DMs and flicked through the appointment book. 'Well, nah—not really. Mind, she might be. She's got a body rub what hasn't turned up. I'll go an' check, shall I?'

'Please.' Faith was mesmerised and watched the tartan boots stomping away across the pale mauve floor. She really must mention it to Valda when she got back. Valda's assistant, Daphne—who was sixty-five if she was a day—would look a treat in a pair of those, and the air cushioning would be a real boon for her bunions.

'Hi.' A tall skinny woman with Dusty Springfield

eyes and vivid pink plaits beamed at her. 'Pixie said you'd like a trim. I've had a cancellation, so I could squeeze you in right away. However, if you'd prefer something later in the day, I—'

'No, no. Thank you. Now would be wonderful. And—er—are you Miranda?'

The pink plaits nodded. Faith beamed. She hadn't visualised Miranda looking like this at all. She'd seen her as more blonde and, well, tarty. This woman, with her beautifully tanned sad face and her glorious bone structure, was stunning. Oh, not in the conventional sense, of course, and the false eyelashes and that strange hair colour let the side down a bit, but this was Hampshire, after all.

'I'm Faith. Faith Pascoe.'

The eyelashes batted for a second, then the pale lips split into a grin. 'No! Billie's mum? Really? Wow, doll It's brilliant to see you!'

Faith found herself being clasped to a black T-shirted and bra-less bosom. Miranda smelled of almond oil and musk. Faith extricated herself. Possibly not one to pass onto Valda. Daphne was a generous 44D and only ever used Tweed.

'Come along then, we'll have to roll out the red carpet a bit, won't we?' Miranda led the way through the crowded salon. 'Only the best'll do. Billie said you were coming.' Miranda indicated a chair at the basins and reached for a lilac coverall. 'You've got my room—or what was my room—is it OK?' She tucked towels round Faith's neck. 'Handy that I'd moved out, really. Did Billie tell you?'

My, but the girl could chatter! Faith listened, and made noncommittal noises. She'd been a bit shocked that Miranda did the hair-washing herself. At Valda's, if Daphne was busy on the

487

desk, Valda's husband Derek was always on hand to do the shampoo and conditioning. As he usually smelled of sheep-dip, Faith preferred Daphne.

'There . . .' Miranda was turbanning Faith's hair in a deep purple towel. 'Now if you'd like to come over to the mirror, doll . . . I don't usually do the washing myself, but we're a bit short-handed since Kitty buggered off. Did Billie tell you about it?'

No, Faith thought afterwards, as her damp perfumed hair was being combed through, Billie didn't. Well, well, so that's what happened at the opening night of Caught Offside, then? Kitty and Kieran . . . She wanted to smile with maternal relief, but remembered the photograph of the pneumatic Fenella and the kiddies on Maeve's mantelshelf, and didn't like to.

'You've got lovely hair.' Miranda flicked the comb through, stopping at the ends, snipping each layer exactly level. Valda tended more towards chunks. 'Thick, like Billie's. Same colour, too.' Miranda leaned across Faith's shoulder. 'Billie is OK, isn't she? About me and Reuben?'

Faith blinked. She hadn't been expecting to get on to Reuben quite so quickly. She'd hoped to insert him just after Miranda had mentioned that she'd left the flat but Miranda hadn't allowed her to get a word in edgeways. 'Oh, yes. I think so. I know that she's very glad that you've found someone and are happy—but I gather there's a little bit of bad feeling somewhere along the line.'

'God, doll! You don't know the half of it!' Miranda paused with the scissors. 'I've been so worried for ages, you know, that Reuben and Billie—well—fancied one another. I just thought that I was playing second fiddle.'

'Reuben? And Billie?' Faith met Miranda's reflected eyes. 'Oh no, dear. You've got nothing to worry about on that score. She detests the man. Ah, well, that is—'

'Yeah, I know.' The snipping resumed. 'You don't have to spare my feelings. I love Reuben to bits, and Billie's ace—and I'd really like them to like each other—but, they've both told me they don't, and now, well—' Miranda heaved her shoulders—'Reuben and I are sort of committed so I've got to believe them, haven't I?'

'Oh, yes, you must believe them,' Faith said fervently. 'Look, dear, I really wouldn't worry about it. I have no idea why Billie dislikes your Reuben so much, but you love him and he loves you, and that's all that matters, isn't it?'

Miranda beamed happily. 'You're ace, doll, do you know that? My mum wasn't half so supportive. No, you're right. I mean, it'd be perfect if everyone liked everyone else, wouldn't it—but a bit boring. Now, what about your fringe?'

After they'd sorted out the fringe, and had a very surreal conversation about an ex-boyfriend of Billie's called Damon, and Miranda had blown her dry, and the whole thing had made her look miraculously ten years younger, Faith shrugged off the coverall and hugged Miranda.

'Thank you, dear. It's lovely! I'm so glad we've had this little chat. You've been a good friend to Billie ever since she came here—and you mustn't let her dislike of Reuben come between you. So, promise me when I've gone back home, you'll pop round and see her? Go out like you used to? She really misses you, you see. It doesn't matter how much you love a man, dear, you should never give up all your girlfriends for him. You never know when you'll need them.'

Afterwards, stepping out into the Spicer Centre with her new bouncy hairdo and feeling as glamorous as a television newscaster, Faith was mightily pleased with the way her first encounter had gone. She glanced at her watch. Just time for a bit of shopping for Stan and the grandchildren, maybe a spot of lunch in that nice Irish pub, and then on to her second port of call . . .

*   *   *

It was fairly difficult, Faith felt, being in a taxi office when she didn't actually want a taxi. The man on the radio contraption didn't look the sort you could fob off with needing to see the proprietor to organise wedding cars or anything—which had been her first plan. She took a deep breath and went for her second.

'Excuse me. I'd like to see Mr Wainwright. Is he available?'

It transpired that he wasn't. Two hundred strings to his bow these days, she was told. Could be bloody anywhere, pardon my French. Try the club. Caught Offside—can't miss it. Far side of the Spicer Centre. Past Woolies.

Faith found it, after spending far longer than she would have liked being hassled by a lot of people who were protesting about the extension to the Amberley Hill bypass and eventually signing a petition to keep Hampshire rural. Rural! She'd cast an ironic look at the fibre-optic fountain and chrome and glass mall, and wondered if she and the protesters used the same dictionary.

490

Eventually pushing her way into Caught Offside's deserted lobby, she blinked in the gloom. Never having been a devotee of nightclubs, to Faith this was unfamiliar territory. Still, she thought, after the Putney Football Village, this one should really be a piece of cake. She tiptoed through the turnstiles and into the club proper.

It was very murky, but quite, she had to admit, impressive. It certainly looked like a football stadium—and a very rich one at that. Man U at least. She sucked in her breath. If Reuben Wainwright was behind this little venture, then he was no mug. Strange then, she thought, heading for the halfway line, that such an astute businessman should leave his premises wide open to the street and apparently unattended.

'Excuse me!' An imperious voice rang from the upper terraces. 'May I help you?'

'Yes, you may.' Faith shielded her eyes with her hand and peered into the tiers of seats. Three men, one looking like a thug from EastEnders, one rather weedy and innocuous, and the other— good heavens—very James Bond, were having a discussion on the top row. 'I'm looking for Reuben Wainwright.'

There was a chuckle. 'And you've found him. Excuse me a moment.'

The three men shook hands and stood up, and the James Bond one vaulted neatly to the floor. Faith raised her eyebrows. Reuben Wainwright, she'd thought—probably because Billie had said he looked like a pirate—would be old and grey and stubbly, possibly with squinty eyes and no teeth. This man, tall, dark, sun tanned, extremely handsome, and dressed in a very expensive suit, couldn't possibly be . . .

'I'm Reuben Wainwright.' He extended a hand. 'Sorry to have kept you waiting. My manager and I were just engaging a new security firm. Oh—damn.' He sneezed violently and delved into his pocket for a small white box. Beaming at Faith, he popped a couple of pills into his mouth. 'Please excuse me. Hayfever. Miranda's just put me onto this homeopathic remedy—and so far, so good. Now, how can I help?'

Faith was nonplussed. And, to tell the truth, a little overawed. Kieran Squires had been handsome—but far too young for her. This man, smiling so kindly at her, was a different matter all together. No wonder Miranda was crazy about him. 'Er—I needed to talk to you. About my daughter.'

She sensed, rather than heard, his slight intake of breath. There was an infinitesimal pause. 'Your daughter?'

'Billie Pascoe.'

Reuben's dark eyes flickered for a moment, then he smiled. Slowly. 'Billie? You're Billie's mother? Never! You don't look old enough.'

Faith was about to snort disdainfully at the ancient line, then stopped and wondered if perhaps, in this light, and with Miranda's magical hairdo, she in fact didn't. 'Thank you, but I can assure you I am. And a grandmother six times over.' Damn—why had she said that?

'So I believe from Billie. She didn't tell me you were beautiful, too. Please, come and have a drink . . .'

Faith followed him to the bar, deciding to have just a small orange juice. She'd had half a pint of Guinness with her bacon and cabbage in Mulligan's at lunchtime and was still feeling light-headed.

'I'd advise steering away from the Bobby Charlton Slammer,' Reuben slid behind the bar, 'but otherwise the choice is yours. Oh, just orange juice? Not a G and T devotee like Billie, then?'

'Well, yes. But not halfway through the afternoon. No, no ice, thank you.'

Drinks sorted, Reuben sat beside her on one of the tall stools. 'Now, how can I help you with Billie? She's not in any trouble, is she?'

For the first time since she'd embarked on her undercover investigations, Faith felt guilty. She'd expected Reuben to be a fire-breathing monster, a man who would eff and blind and be totally obnoxious.

She sipped the orange juice. 'No, no trouble. In fact, there's nothing wrong, to be honest. Oh, just put it down to a mother's natural curiosity. After all, you employed Billie for more than two years and I've heard so much about you. I just wanted to meet you in the flesh.'

She flinched. Flesh perhaps wasn't the best word to have chosen. Reuben, however, was nodding as though her maternal concern was the most natural thing in the world.

'Understandable. Now you tell me what you know about my—um—relationship with Billie, and I'll try and fill in the gaps, and then you won't have any worries, will you?'

Faith found this bit quite difficult. Everything Billie had said about Reuben had been so appalling that all her powers of imagination were going to be stretched to the limits to find any good bits. She opted for the taxi-driving—so kind of Reuben to employ Billie when she was new to the area—and then petered out.

Reuben, who was sipping an iced mineral water, nodded. 'Especially under the circumstances, of course . . .'

'Which circumstances were they?' Faith knocked back the second half of the orange juice. 'I'm not quite clear exactly how Billie did come to work for you in the first place.'

Reuben told her. It really shouldn't have come as a shock, but it did. Of course Kieran hadn't told her any of this part because Kieran, the spineless toad, had done a runner by this time in the story, hadn't he? All Reuben had done was slot the final piece of the jigsaw into place.

Reuben finished his water. 'We don't speak about it any more, Billie and I. It's over. She no longer works for my company, and she's doing very nicely for herself—as I'm sure you're aware. Oh,' he looked at her, his eyes full of contrition, 'I'm so sorry! I've just realised! I've just blurted out some of Billie's darkest secrets and, of course, I assumed you knew. How terrible for you if this is all news . . .'

Faith, having placed her empty glass on the bar, looked at him carefully. Was the remorse genuine? Did he really look like someone who had just blabbed a touch too much and instantly wished he hadn't? She decided he did.

'Don't worry yourself, Mr Wainwright. I already knew all about it.' She slid from the bar stool. 'No doubt you have things to do, and I'm sorry to have taken up so much of your time. It's been very nice to meet you.'

'And you too.' Reuben was already on his feet, shaking her hand. 'And I do so hope we'll meet again during your stay in Amberley Hill.'

Faith hurried outside, and sucked in a deep breath of hot June air. Now she was totally confused. Did Billie hate Reuben just because he knew? She hurried across the Spicer Centre, giving the eco warriors a wide berth, and decided that it was time she and Billie had a real heart-to-heart.

chapter thirty-nine

The morning of the air pageant was manic. Billie, who was feeling more nervous than she had ever done before in her life, screeched the Nova to a halt on the cracked concrete and gazed at the mayhem. She couldn't speak or let go of the steering wheel. Her mouth was too dry and her palms were too damp. She wanted to turn round and go home.

Faith, sitting beside her and scrabbling at her seat belt, had no such qualms. 'Oh, my goodness! Look at all those people queuing! And that tailback of cars! And so early! This is going to be such fun, isn't it?'

Billie viewed Faith with suspicion. She'd been up to something—Billie knew it. Ever since Thursday, when Faith had shown up at the flat with the stunning new Follicles hairdo and a 'mother knows best' expression, she'd been having little digs about Reuben. Billie, whose nerves were shot to pieces, hadn't wanted to talk about him. She guessed that her mother and Miranda had had a good old chinwag during the hair-styling, and could only surmise that Faith had come down heavily on Miranda's side.

And then yesterday, when she'd brought Faith here to Whiteacres for the day, and she'd oohed and aahed over the Stearman, and had been very impressed with Billie's enterprise—and amazed at how businesslike she'd become—she'd then immediately formed a mutual appreciation society with Sylvia. Sylv, without knowing she shouldn't, had informed Faith that Reuben now owned the warehouse leases. Furthermore, Faith seemed to have become fixated with Caught Offside and had hurled it into every other sentence.

Billie, irritated that Reuben should still be the main topic of conversation when all she could think about was wingwalking, had become quite snappy— and had then felt awful—and spent ages explaining to Faith that it was Miranda who was involved with Reuben and Caught Offside, not her, and that she'd be happy never to set eyes on the place again, OK?

Faith had visibly relaxed, and Billie assumed it was because her mother thought that nightclubs equated with drugs and men in white socks— neither of which she'd aspired to for her daughter. After biting her mother's head off, Billie had felt even more awful, and hugged her and said sorry, and begged her just not to mention Reuben again— please.

So Faith hadn't, and instead spent the day— when she wasn't with Sylv—helping with the filing and answering the phone in Billie's warehouse, and Billie had been massively relieved that no one from Sullivanair had put in an appearance to muddy the now calm waters of maternal curiosity.

Fortunately, Sylvia and the other warehousers had kept Billie's wingwalking a secret from her mother. Billie had impressed upon them that it

496

had to be a surprise. So far, no one had breathed a word. Not, she thought irritably, shrugging out of her seat belt, that she'd count on them remaining silent for much longer. Sylvia, especially, seemed to think it was Faith's right to know.

'And you're sure I won't be in the way?' Faith, looking jaunty in Lesley Caron pedal pushers and a matelot T-shirt, scrambled from the Nova. 'Everyone seems so busy.'

'Not at all. I'm sure Sylvia and the rest will more than welcome an extra pair of hands.'

'And what about you, though? All the others seem to be offering something in their—um—sheds. What exactly are you going to be doing? You didn't tell me yesterday. In fact you were very secretive.'

'Oh—er—it's no secret. I'm—um—just doing things with the Stearman.'

Faith wrinkled her nose. 'What? Showing people round it? Like a curator? Not very exciting for you, then, love. And I thought it was going to *fly*.'

Mercifully, Sylvia appeared in the door of her unit at that moment and waved towards them. 'Yoo-hoo! Faith! If you've got a minute—I'm having the devil's own job with this blasted crocodile! Can't get its bloody jaws to stay open!'

'You go and help out,' Billie said with relief. 'And I'll see you later.'

She tugged open the doors of the warehouse, feeling a mixture of guilt and relief. Hopefully the recalcitrant mandibles of the crocodile—which was one of the main clues in Sylvia's treasure hunt—would keep her mother occupied for most of the morning.

It was clear that Jonah, and possibly Estelle, and

497

maybe Barnaby—if he'd got back from America—had spent the night in the warehouse cleaning the Stearman. Every inch of the paintwork gleamed, the propeller was spotless, and the zigzagged Sullivanair logo stood out in three-dimensional glory. Billie stared at the plane, her eyes travelling up to the rig, and felt her stomach disappear. God! It was no time to be having second thoughts. She should have had those—and thirds and fourths—months ago. Too many people were depending on her today for her to bottle out now.

She turned her back on the plane, and taking deep, steadying breaths, retraced her steps to the doorway. The sun spiralled from a cloudless sky, the cropped airfield grass was bleached and golden, and the lack of wind made the morning temperature feel more like midday. Billie, who had glued herself to the weather channel all week and screamed each time a low pressure system had been mentioned, basked in the scorch of the June sun, and knew she shouldn't have worried.

Well, at least, not about the weather. That was going to be perfect. And everything else could be worried about later, when the show was over. She didn't know if Miranda was going to turn up or not today, but if it was going to be with Reuben in tow, then she'd far prefer it to be not.

She smiled sadly, watching as a dozen tiny planes shimmied overhead, looking like a dragonfly swarm as they practised their manoeuvres. Bloody Reuben. Just when she thought she'd be free of him, he'd not only bought up the warehouses, but was now living with her best friend. It was as if he was determined to worm his "ay into her life by fair means or foul—but why? After all this time she still didn't understand.

She gave herself a severe mental shaking, remembering Granny Pascoe's disaster theory. She mustn't worry. Not when everything else had gone so well. She peered across the airfield. It seemed that the entire populations of Whiteacres and Amberley Hill, and all the overspill districts in between, were turning out early. The slip road from the bypass was gridlocked, according to the radio, the car park was filling rapidly, and as Faith had pointed out, the queues were snaking back behind the airport buildings. The warehousers' advertising had certainly worked. A whole raft of market traders had been called in to provide food, and already the smell of AVGAS was only slightly overlaid by the pungent scent of spun sugar and frying onions.

'Looking good, isn't it?' Estelle drifted towards Billie from the perimeter fence, wearing cut-off denim shorts and a string bikini top, her arms full of the programmes put together by Mike and his Gusper cronies. She raised her voice over the drone of the aeroengines in the sky. 'Is Jonah pleased?'

'I've no idea.' Billie unpeeled herself from the nubbly breeze blocks. 'I haven't seen him yet. I suppose he's really busy getting Vinny and the Shorts sorted. What about Barnaby?'

'Oh, he still hasn't shown. It looks like I might take over the Slingsby slot.'

'What? You? Do aerobatics?'

Estelle eased the programmes under one arm and looked at her watch. 'Yes. Why not?'

'But surely you need a licence or something?'

Estelle laughed. 'I've had a PPL since I was eighteen. I've kept up my hours, and I've done

499

quite a bit of stunt flying. I do enjoy it, but to be honest, the real thrill of aviation for me is the hands-on stuff. The design of a plane, the actual workings that get it off the ground and keep it there. I'd far rather tinker with the engines than tug on the joystick. That's why I leaped at the easyjet offer.'

Billie blinked. She'd never even thought about Estelle being a pilot! Why on earth had Jonah decided to let her go? Again she felt the futility sweep over her. Estelle, with her beauty, her brains, her expertise, and her skill as a flyer, still wasn't enough for Jonah. What hope did she have?

'Oh yes, I'm—um—glad that you're leaving . . . No, I mean, I'm pleased about your new job.'

Estelle laughed. 'It's OK, I get your drift. And I'm mostly pleased to be leaving too. Jonah is a great boss, and a gorgeous man, but now he's decided to stay put at Whiteacres he's just reinforced my opinion of him.'

'Which is?'

'That anyone who can chuck up five years in Paris flying in a display team with Antony Archibald, even if it would have meant seeing that sad wife of his all the time, for a few thousand square metres of Hampshire turf—albeit smothered in aeroplanes—needs his head examined.'

'It was the business, though,' Billie protested. 'All his expansion plans for Sullivanair. And getting onto the Aviation Incs board. The new planes, new routes, Barnaby possibly buying another Stearman . . .'

'Pie in the sky! He'll have to work his guts out to get it to succeed. Any airline company with fewer than ten planes is courting financial disaster.'

'Yes, maybe, but with the stunt flying and the Stearman and everything, he'll be diversifying and—'

Estelle laughed. The bikini top jiggled alarmingly. A whole host of men in baggy shorts and socks and sandals stopped and stared. 'Spoken like a true anorak! Actually, I hope you're right. Of course I hope Sullivanair goes on to rival the best in the business. And I'm glad you didn't include yourself in the reasons for Jonah staying at Whiteacres.'

'Well no, I wouldn't . . .'

'Because if you did,' Estelle said, hitching up her landslide of programmes again, 'you'd only be disappointed. Jonah Sullivan's just like a meringue. Absolutely delicious to look at, but break open that lovely exterior, and there's nothing at all.'

'That's hardly fair. He's a great pilot, and good at business, and—'

'I'm talking about sex, sweetie,' Estelle said gently. 'Sexually, Jonah Sullivan has about as much oomph as a castrated amoeba.'

Billie winced. 'Well, he might not fancy either of us too much, but he seemed to manage all right with Claire.'

Estelle laughed. 'Ouch! Yeah, he did, didn't he? God, it makes you wonder how men work, doesn't it? Give me a plane any time.' She pursed her lips. 'Do you know, I'm going to miss you. We've become good mates, haven't we?'

Billie nodded. 'We have, and I'll miss you, too. And I hated you to start with.'

'I wasn't too struck on you either. I thought you were pathetically wimpy—not liking planes.'

501

Estelle grinned. 'I especially disliked you when I knew about the wingwalking. I was bloody jealous. Not only was I amazed by your bravery, but it was something I'd never tried.'

'There's probably still a vacancy the way my stomach's feeling.'

'Don't be silly. You'll be astounding. You know you're good—and I know I'm the wrong size, wrong shape, wrong everything. Anyway, I'll be too busy in the Slingsby to harbour any jealousy, won't I? We'll both be working ourselves to a frazzle and risking our lives for Jonah Sullivan—and probably for the same reason.'

They laughed together. It was true. Billie shrugged. 'Well, at least you've had a crack at him. I didn't even get off the runway.'

'Oh, that's probably because I told him you were gay.' Estelle managed to look a bit shamefaced. 'Sorry . . .'

'You did *what*?'

'Said you were gay—or might be. I was feeling totally pissed off with him at the time.' Estelle bit her lip. 'See, I'm not a nice person.'

Billie didn't speak. It had been a pretty bitchy thing to do, but honestly, would it have made any difference to the way Jonah treated her? She knew it wouldn't. He treated her like a colleague, a friend, a sister. She wrinkled her nose. 'I'll just have to let him know that I'm not, then, won't I?'

'I wouldn't bother.' Estelle shifted her programmes a bit higher against the string bikini, pushing her golden breasts under her chin. 'You'll only end up being hurt, and you're too lovely for that. Go and set your sights and someone nice and uncomplicated—and ground-based. Flyers are the pits. See you later.'

Billie watched her go, then wandered back into the unit. It was far too early to change into the wingwalking suit, and far too late to volunteer to do anything else. She felt too sick to eat, and too jittery to risk coffee. What she could really do with was a double gin and tonic and someone to take her away from this quickly. At least before one o'clock, which was—she looked at the clock and groaned—only two hours away.

The office phone was ringing merrily. Billie ignored it. Despite Sylv's dire warnings, she had no desire to canvas customers today. Anyway, she'd left the answerphone on. She listened to her own voice crackling out the message, then to the beeping tone, then—'Hello, Billie. It's Barnaby. Pick this up if you're there, please. I've tried all Jonah's numbers and can't reach him.'

Billie snatched at the handset. 'Barnaby, hello. Jonah's not here, either. Can I help? Where are you?'

'Orly Airport. Paris.'

'*Paris*? You're supposed to be here! You're flying in an hour's time!'

Barnaby groaned. 'I know, my dear. I know. I'd intended to come in a spectacular fashion, with all guns blazing, so to speak, but my journey has taken far longer than I'd anticipated.'

Billie frowned. She was pretty sure she'd lost the thread. 'So does that mean you won't be here for the pageant?'

'I'm rather afraid it does, yes. Look, please explain to Jo, and tell him I'll be there as soon as I can make it. In the meantime, I guess Estelle can throw the Slingsby through its routine, can't she?'

503

'God knows. I mean, yes she can, because she's just been telling me she can, but what about Jonah?'

'Jo will be fine, my dear. Trust me. Just tell him I'll be there before nightfall—oh, and have a super pageant, won't you? And the very best of luck with the barnstorming. You'll be wonderful.'

The phone crackled a bit and went dead. Billie, sighing heavily, replaced the handset. Jonah was going to go mad. Still, at least Barnaby sounded cheerful again. He must have got over Miranda's perfidy.

'Excuse me, duck.' A portly man in a boiler suit was leaning into the warehouse. 'We OK to shift the plane?'

'What?' Billie frowned. 'Sorry, I mean. Shift the plane where?'

'Out onto the runway, Mr Sullivan said. Ready for his display. He wanted it out before twelve and we're a bit pressed, so—'

'Yes . . . yes, of course.' Billie realised her voice was getting squeaky with agitation. She swallowed and took a couple of deep breaths. 'You're not on your own, are you? Do you want me to find someone to help?'

'Nah, we've got a full airport crew.'

The man put two fingers into his mouth and let out a shrill whistle. A small battalion of men in dung-coloured overalls scampered obediently into the shed and with obvious expertise started to move the Stearman out on to the concrete.

Billie watched, her mouth even drier now. Followed by an interested crowd, the ground crew had rolled back the perimeter fence, and the Stearman, looking sensational in the sunshine, bounced across the sun-scorched grass.

Billie clapped her hand to her mouth. Oh shit. She'd never be able to do it. Not in front of all these people. Feeling very sick, she turned back into the warehouse. How empty it looked without the plane. How huge. How lonely.

Wishing that there was someone there to talk to, and then irrationally glad that there wasn't, she decided the only way to be sure that she wouldn't run away and hide in a corner until it was all over was to get dressed. At least with the suit on, she'd look the part. Of course, there'd be the added problem of umpteen nervy visits to the loo to contend with before the first display, and each one of those would mean peeling off the layers, but still . . . Taking a deep breath, Billie strode purposefully into the office and closed the door.

Getting dressed was a nightmare. Her fingers were all thumbs and her thumbs wouldn't work. Pulling on the fleecy suit over one of Sylvia's froufrou lingerie sets, she was already sweating as she fastened the safety harness. Then she picked up the silver Lycra bodysuit, which shimmered and danced in the rays of dusty sunlight, and gradually, grunting and groaning, eased herself into it. Boots . . . Her fingers shook as she tied the silver laces. Pick up the gloves . . . pick up the helmet . . . She glanced in the mirror. No make-up . . . She'd need loads. Her hands shook even more as she reached for her slap bag.

Twenty minutes later the slender silver, green, and purple person who stared back at her looked like a serpent. It didn't look like it could ever wear Timberlands and dungarees and swear a lot.

A shadow fell across her reflection. Billie swirled

round.

'You look stunning, sweetheart.' Reuben lounged in the doorway. 'But I think the Lily Savage make-up might be a bit too much.'

chapter forty

'What the hell do you want?'

Reuben frowned. 'You always greet me in the same way, Billie. I can't think why. As I own this place I have every right to be here. With all the crowds, I merely thought it would be pertinent to be on the spot to protect my investment, and also take the opportunity to inspect my—er—assets.' His eyes trawled up and down her body. 'And I must say they're shaping up very nicely indeed.'

'Sod off!'

Reuben shook his head, sighing. 'Not nice language—and especially when you look so gorgeously feminine for once . . . And very insulting since I only came in here to wish you good luck and—'

'No you didn't.' Billie gritted her teeth. 'You've come to harass me—as always.'

Reuben smiled his slow smile. 'As with so many other things, Billie, you've got it spectacularly wrong. There's absolutely nothing left to harass you over, is there?'

'What?' Billie's nerves were jangling far too loudly for this sort of convoluted argument. 'If you've got a point to make, just bloody make it— and then bog off.'

Reuben sighed even more dramatically. 'It's true

506

what they say, you know. You might be able to take the lady out of the cab-driving, but you'll never take the cab-driving out of the lady.'

'Reuben, go away! Leave me alone!'

'One day, maybe. When I'm satisfied that . . .' He shrugged. 'Oh yes, you wanted me to get to the point, didn't you? OK then, as I said, as you've apparently made everything to do with the rich and famous Mr Squires public knowledge, then I'd be very grateful if you'd stop accusing me of this ridiculous vendetta.'

Billie's head reeled. She whimpered a bit. Why the hell didn't the Whiteacres ground crew come storming back into the shed and trample Reuben into the dusty concrete? Why didn't Faith come back and hit him with her handbag? Why wasn't there anyone else around when the whole of the airfield was teeming with about ten million people?

'I don't know what you're talking about.'

Reuben shifted his weight to his other hip. He inspected his fingernails and smoothed back his hair. Sod the cavalry coming to the rescue, Billie thought, I'll just go over and punch him myself—

'Your mother knows all about Kieran.'

'*What*?' Billie thought she'd stopped breathing. She sucked in some air. 'No one knows about Kieran except you and me and Kieran. And you've never met my mother! What the hell are you talking about?'

Reuben's smile was knife-edge sharp this time. 'She came to see me a couple of days ago. Lovely lady, Billie. You didn't tell me she was so pretty.'

'She did *what*?'

'Came to see me. She'd chatted to Miranda too, apparently. I'd say she just wanted to get a perspective on your life. You obviously keep far too many secrets . . . Anyway—'

'And you *told* her about Kieran?'

'No, I didn't. She already knew. She just seemed to want to fill in the gaps. Honestly, I didn't need to tell her anything. I merely talked about your working for me, but believe me, she knew. Names, dates, times, places . . .' Reuben shifted his position again, and flexed his shoulder muscles. Then he walked towards her. She backed away. If she screamed no one would hear her, would they? Everyone outside was screaming with excitement. One more scream would be lost in the multitudes.

'So,' he stopped a couple of feet in front of her, 'can we please stop all this crap? I'm not harassing you, I'm not stalking you, I'm not intimidating you.'

'You are! You bloody always have! What the hell is your problem?'

Reuben's eyes flickered up and down her body again. 'Oh, come on, sweetheart. You're not that dumb.'

'Bastard! You're living with Miranda! She loves you!'

'Yeah, I know.' He frowned. 'And why the hell should that make any difference?'

'You total shit!' Billie screamed.

'Billie—wow, you look totally amazing! God, I'm so sorry I haven't been here. It took ages to get the Shorts organised, and Barnaby still hasn't turned up, and then I got tied up with the remaining Incs, who wanted to discuss things, and then my—' Jonah rushed into the warehouse. He skidded to a halt and looked enquiringly at them both. 'Oh, I'm sorry. I'm obviously interrupting something.'

'No you're not.' Reuben was all smiles. 'I was

just leaving. Good luck for the little display, both of you. Now, if you'll excuse me, I must go and collect Miranda. Naturally, neither of us would want to miss a minute of your show.'

Jonah looked as though he was going to thank Reuben for his good wishes. Billie flew in first. 'Bugger off and rot in hell!'

Both men flinched slightly. Billie didn't care. She couldn't believe what was happening. 'You've been in here, telling lies, propositioning me, and all the time Miranda's *here*? Why the hell didn't she come and see me, then?'

'Oh, I'm sure she will.' Reuben headed for the stream of sunlight glaring through the rolled back double doors. 'But she had a small task to do for me first. I left her next door checking with—um—Sylvia that she's OK with her new living arrangements.' He directed the smile straight at Billie. 'You see, Billie, you really have got me all wrong. I'm nothing more than a caring landlord.'

Billie squeaked. Miranda was next door. Faith was next door. Sylvia was next door. The whole bloody world would know about Kieran Squires by now. She clenched her fists and rushed towards the doorway, but Reuben, waving jauntily, was crossing the cracked concrete and just approaching Sylv, her mother, and the still-gaping crocodile. They all, with the exception of the crocodile, waved too. Faith's wave seemed a bit rigid, and her mouth sagged open. Billie, feeling no sympathy, hoped that she felt some sort of guilt on seeing Reuben and Billie in the same air space.

It was only when she'd spun round to walk back inside the warehouse that she realised she was wearing the wingwalking costume. Faith's stunned

509

expression probably had far more to do with that than the unscheduled appearance of Reuben Wainwright.

Jonah raised a quizzical eyebrow. 'And are you going to tell me about it?'

She shook her head. She felt drained and angry and shaky all at the same time. 'Nope. I've made a complete prat of myself, and now I'm reaping the consequences.'

'I think it would be better if we got it cleared up before the show. Possibly not the best thing to be doing—wingwalking—while you're jittering with nerves and in a foul temper.'

'I'm not jittering with nerves. But I am bloody angry!'

Jonah smiled. 'Yes, your ex-boss does seem to have an amazing effect on you.'

'Jesus, Jonah! You think I fancy him, don't you? Everyone thinks I bloody fancy him!' She sucked in short, angry breaths. 'Look, years ago, I had a stupid affair with a married man, OK? Reuben knew. He's held it over me ever since. There! That's it!'

If she'd expected sympathy, then she was going to be unlucky. Jonah just wrinkled his nose. 'Is that all? God, three-quarters of the consenting adults in this country have had flings with people they shouldn't have done. Why the hell would it matter to Reuben or anyone else? No, sorry. You'll have to come up with something better than that. I'd say the man had the hots for you and—'

'Get stuffed!' Billie wrenched the helmet from her head. Her ears itched and her hair was damp with sweat. Proper hearing rushed in. 'Still, I suppose I couldn't expect anything else from you, could I? Men always stick together! And your track record is pretty abysmal, isn't it?'

Jonah's face paled. Billie felt almost triumphant. Serve him right. Bloody men! The phone rang but neither of them answered it. Her recorded voice screeched through the silence, followed by Estelle's real one.

'Excuse me! Would someone please tell me if I'm flying the Slingsby? Only if I am, there are simply a couple of minutes to go before the slot, and I'll need—'

Billie skirted Jonah and grabbed the receiver. 'Estelle? Yes, sorry. Barnaby phoned me about an hour ago, I think . . . No, he's in Paris . . . No, he won't be back! What? . . . No, Jonah's here. Hang on . . .'

He took the phone from her as if it were reptilian and snapped one-syllable staccato messages into it. Billie stood and shivered with self-righteous indignation. Jonah slammed the phone down and looked at her. 'Nice of you to tell me about Barnaby. You might run the bloody warehouse, Billie, but you're not in charge of Sullivanair!'

'Christ! There was hardly time to tell you about it, was there? Now where are you going?'

'To watch Estelle in the Slingsby, of course. As you know nothing about planes I'm sure it won't interest you in the slightest, but I happen to care.' He stopped in the doorway and glared at her. 'And as we're scheduled straight afterwards, get your hat back on, and get yourself into the right frame of mind—if that's not too much to ask!'

Frustrated beyond belief, Billie rushed after him. By the time she'd reached the doorway, Jonah was striding towards the perimeter fence. Bastard, she thought, and poked out her tongue.

'Billie!' Faith suddenly erupted from the melee round the crocodile outside Sylvia's unit. 'Billie— we need to talk!'

Sylvia, Miranda and Reuben were all staring at her. Billie closed her eyes. Great. Nothing better for calming the nerves than three blazing rows in the space of an hour. 'Mum, not now. Yes, we do need to talk, but really—'

'You're wingwalking! Sylvia said so—and Miranda —and I didn't know!'

'No, I wanted it to be a surprise.' Billie exhaled, forgetting that she wasn't going to allow herself to get sucked into any more arguments. 'No doubt like you did when you'd conveniently failed to remember to mention your visit to Reuben.'

Faith blushed. 'He shouldn't have told you. I was just being—'

'Nosy? Yes, you were. And I hope you found out all you wanted to know.'

'Not really, no. And don't take that tone with me. I'm still your mother.'

Oh God. Billie suddenly felt thoroughly deflated. Why was she yelling at Faith? After all, she was the one who'd been in the wrong first, wasn't she? If she hadn't had the affair with Kieran, then Reuben wouldn't have got involved and—oh, sod it! What the hell did any of it matter? 'OK, sorry. I shouldn't have shouted.'

'No, you shouldn't. And you shouldn't be wingwalking either!'

'Mum, the wingwalking is the least of my problems, as you probably well know.'

'Really?' Faith straightened her shoulders and didn't quite meet Billie's eyes. 'I don't think I get

512

your drift.'

Billie hesitated. Reuben might have been lying. She couldn't mention Kieran—just in case. 'I think you probably do, but don't let it worry you. No doubt you'll have dug out someone else's sordid secrets before tea time!'

'Billie! What on earth is wrong with you?'

Billie shrugged. 'To be honest, Mum, I don't really know. I think I'm probably going mad. Maybe we'll talk about it one day, but not now. Not when I'm supposed to be barnstorming in less than an hour. I hope you'll watch me and maybe feel just a little bit proud. God knows, I've given you little enough to be proud of, haven't I?'

And spinning round, she raced back into the warehouse, dashing at her eyes with her silver gloves. Bugger. Bugger. Bugger.

'If you're going to cry, I hope that mascara's waterproof, doll, otherwise you'll be doing the wingwalking looking like Alice Cooper.'

Billie raised her head and blinked at Miranda. 'Are you going to start nagging at me too?'

'Course not. Look, doll, to be honest, I haven't got a clue what's going on here, but I'm sure it can all be sorted out later.'

'Has Reuben—'

'Told me that you and he have had words? Yes.' Miranda rushed across the shed and hugged her. 'Bloody hell! I'm so sorry! I've given him a right rocket! Your nerves must be shot to pieces without him playing the heavy! What was he going on about, anyway? He said it was something to do with the warehouses, but I didn't understand.'

Billie pulled a face and sniffed. 'It's all got a bit Shakespearean, if you ask me. No one is telling anyone all of everything, only half-truths, and—'

'Sorry, doll, you've lost me again. I didn't do any Shakespeare at school, but if you mean it's all going to end in a bit of a Gwyneth Paltrow, then I'm right with you on that one. Your mum looks like she's going to bawl her head off at any minute and I'm not far off it—'

'Don't!' Billie wailed into Miranda's pink plaits. 'Now I'm really going to cry and my face'll go all blotchy even before I get off the ground!'

'You look like a dream, doll. And I'm petrified for you—and I really miss you.'

'I miss you too.' Billie blew her nose. 'The flat isn't half so scuzzy.'

Miranda giggled. 'That's better. Now, you go and be sensational and I'll keep my fingers crossed and try not to panic. You must be shitting yourself, though, surely? I mean, I know you've practised, but this is the first time in public and—'

'Please don't start me off again!' Billie groaned. 'My knees are buckling as it is. Just wish me luck.'

Miranda kissed her and hugged her some more, and then, grabbing the helmet and the silver gloves, Billie ran from the warehouse. She didn't stop running until she reached the perimeter fence. It was far enough away from the warehouses for her to feel more relaxed. God—what a fiasco! She took a deep breath, aware that people were staring at her in the body suit. Let them stare. She couldn't feel any more embarrassed than she already did.

The show was in full swing. Malcolm Bletchley had appointed himself as commentator, and was droning informatively from his Tannoy across the field. It was all absolutely perfect. Well, almost . . .

There were queues right round the fence for

rides in the Aeroclub's planes, Estelle was stunning everyone with some real daredevil stunts in the Slingsby, and Vinny was proudly piloting the Shorts on the flying equivalent of 'trips round the bay'.

The warehousers' efforts were also going down a storm, with a tailback at Isla's tarot, and children screaming with delight over Sylvia's treasure hunt. Billie couldn't see her mother or the crocodile and presumed they were together somewhere. She felt they deserved each other. Zia had attached himself to the Guspers' set and was making a promotional video of the whole event.

Billie's stomach lurched again. It was simply terrifying, the prospect of wingwalking in front of all these people. There were now going to be thousands of pairs of eyes trained on her as she attempted the manoeuvres. What if she froze? What if she slipped? What on earth would happen if she and Jonah had a row in midair and—oh my God!

Hurrying towards her, shoving his way through the crowd, and dressed in his full summer finery, was her father.

'Dad!' Billie waved like mad and started to run. She threw herself at him, trying to kiss him and hug him at the same time. 'Oh—I don't believe it! Why didn't you tell me?'

'I wasn't sure if I'd be able to get away.' Stan held her at arm's length. 'But the boys were ace, so I set off at the crack of dawn, and here I am. My goodness, you look pretty! What's all this in aid of?'

'I'm—er—being a wingwalker . . .'

'My God! You're pulling my leg? Really?'

'Really. Mum's not too happy about it.'

'She wouldn't be. We had the Waldo Pepper film

from the video van. Twice. Well, you know how she's got a bit of a pash on Robert Redford? She probably thinks you'll drop off the wing or fry in the smouldering wreckage or both. You leave her to me.' He chuckled comfortingly. 'So that's what you've been up to with the Stearman, is it? A spot of barnstorming? Well, well . . .' He hugged her again, stroking her hair. 'Goodness, I'm so proud of you.'

Billie sniffed back happy tears against his chest. 'Thanks, Dad. You've no idea how pleased I am that you're here to watch me—and look, there's the plane on the runway. The one with the crowd round it. Beautiful, isn't it?'

Stan nodded. 'Very. Do you know, on second thoughts, I probably won't watch.'

'It's going to be fine. Really. Look, you know how I feel about flying, but this is quite different. It's so safe—and we've practised for ages. Oh, and I can't wait for you to see my warehouse.' She felt the happiness oozing back into her veins. Stan couldn't have appeared at a better time. 'And can you imagine what the boys would make of this costume?'

'They'd be bloody rude about it! And proud as Punch. Um—before I go and track down your mother, would it be OK if I went and had a look at the Stearman? Just to give it a bit of once-over?'

'Of course—but it's totally safe, Dad. I promise. It's inspected and tested all the time. And we've had the CAA checks done and got all the proper certificates.'

'That's as may be,' Stan said. 'But I'd just like to reassure myself.'

'Go on then. Oh, and when you meet up with

516

Mum over by the treasure hunt, we've just had a bit of a barney.'

'Tell me something that I hadn't already guessed.' Stan patted her shoulder. 'When she told me she was coming up here I knew she'd bloody ferret. Dug a bit too deeply, has she?'

'Just a bit.'

Billie watched him go and felt lonely again. Her stomach looped the loop. Her mouth was dry. It was all getting far too close. The first of the three barnstorming displays was due in five minutes.

'Ready?' Jonah suddenly marched through the crowds towards her. 'I thought you'd done a runner. I couldn't find you in the warehouse. I found about three million other people, though.'

Billie looked at Jonah's thunderous face. 'My—er—parents are here . . . My dad was looking at the plane. He—er—thinks it's great . . .'

Jonah nodded his head curtly. 'Nice to know at least one member of your family can appreciate something to do with aviation. Did you watch Estelle?'

'No, not really . . . I was talking to Miranda and—'

'God Almighty!' Jonah sighed and strode towards the Stearman. Billie, trying to keep up, looked hopefully for Stan but he'd already gone. The Whiteacres ground crew had cleared everyone back behind the perimeter fence.

Booming over the Tannoy above their introduction selection of 'Eight Miles High' and 'Something In The Air', Malcolm Bletchley was giving the crowds a brief history of the Stearman. He moved on to building up the tension no end with graphic descriptions of what they were about

517

to see as Billie clumsily scrambled into the cockpit and strapped herself into the biplane's seat.

Jonah, seated behind her, tapped her on the shoulder. 'You OK?'

Mightily relieved that he was feeling better-tempered, she turned and smiled. 'Yeah, fine, thanks.'

'I wasn't enquiring about your health. I mean for safety purposes, are you up to this?'

'Of course I am,' she said, her teeth chattering as she pulled on her gloves and fastened her helmet. 'And I really, really hate you.'

'Good—it's so important that we have a well-balanced airborne relationship. And why the hell didn't you tell me about Barnaby?'

Oh God, why hadn't she? Who had she been fighting with at the time?

Jonah started the engine and the judder rattled her bones. The roar and the shudder should have been familiar, but Billie could hear new noises: strange knockings; little gaps in the smoothness . . . She tried hard not to listen as the propeller swirled into life, cutting through the afternoon heat.

She attempted to work some saliva into her mouth. 'Look, it's none of my business, but are you sure the engine's OK? It sounds funny . . .'

'Thank fuck something does. I could do with a laugh. The engine sounds perfect. Now just sit back and stay there . . . at least until you have to get out . . .'

Releasing the brakes, Jonah steered the plane towards the runway. They were going to go up to four hundred feet for the first aerobatic sequence, climb to a thousand, then do loops, rolls and stalls, before swooping down as close to the crowd as

518

possible. They had worked out a ten-minute routine in the shed. It had all seemed like a lot of fun. Billie wished fervently that they were in the shed now so that she could shake off her harness and run.

Malcolm had stopped talking and kick-started the display music. It blasted from the speakers, still audible above the Stearman's powerful growl. Billie wished she'd remembered to go to the loo. 'I'm Alive' thumped into the idyllic June afternoon. Billie had the feeling that she might not be for very much longer.

The plane was gathering speed, bouncing across the grass and, belatedly, Billie remembered to lean from the cockpit and smile and wave . . . smile and wave . . . She had never felt less like smiling in her life. God! There were millions of people all smiling and waving back! She turned and looked at Jonah, hoping for some sign of approval.

Shit. Jonah was rigid and ashen-faced. The plane was still careering across the grass, the music was still pumping, and Jonah had had a heart attack!

'Jonah!' She screamed and leaned backwards. 'Jonah! What's happened?'

He muttered something, his lips rigid. Christ! Billie couldn't hear, couldn't move. They'd take off at any minute—and nose-dive a minute later!

'Jonah!'

She tried to read his lips and couldn't. His head was jerking downwards. Epilepsy? Did he have epilepsy? No, of course he didn't. He couldn't be a pilot if he did.

'Jonah!!!'

God! Reuben had spiked the plane! That was it! He'd cut something—like a throttle or a brake cable or a fuel line—to ensure that she was killed in the tangled wreckage. Bastard . . . They were belting across the grass towards the airport buildings at about five hundred miles an hour and Billie knew she was going to die.

'Jonah! For God's sake! Take off!'

Just in time, the Stearman soared over the fence, above the heads of the shouting, cheering, waving crowd, who obviously thought this last-minute close call was part of the stunt. Billie, more relieved than she'd ever been in her life, laughed hysterically down at them and waved back. Christ—now what? They were airborne and Jonah was still sitting there in some sort of catatonic shock, completely out of control. Was she going to have to do a Fay Wray stunt and crawl backwards into the cockpit and save the plane? Not a hope. She didn't even know which lever was up and which was down. God, all those months that the Stearman had been in the shed and she didn't know the first thing about how it worked!

She jerked her head round again. 'Jonah!'

His mouth formed one word as his head motioned downwards again. Billie frowned. What was he trying to say? It sounded like—looked like—'Spider' . . .

Billie followed the jerking motion and almost laughed aloud. A large, brown, eight-legged monster was ignoring the pace of the plane and crawling leisurely up Jonah's dashboard. God, was that all? Did Jonah think it was an Australian springing spider, something that was going to leap and go for the throat?

Shaking her head, still horrified at the speed at which they were travelling, she wriggled round, hindered by the straps, and scooped the spider up, dropping it over the side of the plane.

Superstitiously, she hoped it would float to earth and land gently.

'OK?' She had to mouth the word. The wind flapped at her lips.

Jonah was instantly back in control, although still pale. He almost smiled and mouthed back. 'Thanks ... and it's time to go ...'

'Yummy Yummy Yummy' was punching out the rhythms as she moved from the plane to the wing and fastened herself into the rig as though she'd been doing it for ever. She was concentrating too hard to be terrified any more. She was still alive. She hadn't died. Flying wasn't scary at all. Nothing could faze her now.

As they swooped and looped and rolled at over a hundred miles an hour, Billie waved and grinned and high-kicked like crazy. Even the inverted flying, which had given her such palpitations, was like a dream. It was so different, seeing the upturned faces, knowing they were watching her and Jonah, envying them maybe, maybe thinking: Never—not even for a million pounds. It didn't matter. It was the greatest high in the world.

Ten minutes later, with the strains of 'Eloise' still roaring from the speakers, the Stearman touched down. Billie, still waving, still smiling, soared again at the roar of applause. God, this was heady stuff. Easy to get hooked ... Thank goodness she'd got at least two more stints. She really couldn't give it up. Not now. Not ever.

Jonah stood up in the cockpit beside her, and, as they'd practised, they swept rather comical theatrical bows to the grinning crowd which stretched as far as the eye could see. Then he stepped out onto the wing and, jumping down to the grass, held out his arms. Billie, who was still flying, leaped into them.

He immediately let her go. She wasn't surprised. Her face was probably snotty.

His voice was gruff. 'Er—thanks again. For the wingwalking. And for the spider. And I'd really appreciate it if you didn't tell anyone.'

'It's our secret.' She didn't smile at him. He had withdrawn from her completely. She tried not to care. As long as they could work together on a professional level, what the hell did it matter?

The crowd were bearing down on them and amongst them she saw her parents, and the warehousers, and Miranda, all with ear-to-ear grins. And there, just behind them, was Claire, looking plump but stunningly gorgeous in a floaty caramel-coloured dress, her dark curls glossy and bouncing.

Claire pushed her way to the front of the crowd, and ignoring Billie, threw her arms round Jonah. 'Jo! Darling! That was simply the sexiest thing I have ever seen! You were so amazing!'

'Thanks.' He didn't try to disentangle himself. 'Er—and you look pretty good, yourself.'

Claire simpered and preened. 'So I should, darling. I'm off the stuff—and the ciggies and booze. This is a whole new me, darling! A whole new us! Jo, sweetheart—it's so exciting! I'm pregnant!'

chapter forty-one

Jonah glanced at the date on his desk diary. July 4th. Independence Day. He gave a hollow laugh and pushed his chair back until it made solid and metallic contact with the filing cabinet. After today, he'd probably never be independent again.

He'd been in the Sullivanair office since dawn, and had watched the sun fade through the airfield mist, spreading molten gold amongst the dew prisms. Today, by an ironic twist of fate, he would be interviewing the three potential candidates for Estelle's job, had an appointment with the Whiteacres Aviation Incs at board level for their final decision, and was also meeting Antony Archibald, together with Claire, to discuss their future.

Pushing the chair back further and discovering there was nowhere to go, Jonah stood up and walked to the window. Life, which he'd thought would be so easily sorted by the success of the air pageant and the purchase of the new planes, had become spectacularly complicated. He could even pinpoint the moment when it had started to fall apart: it had been on the day of the show when he'd bounded into Billie's warehouse, full of enthusiasm, and been confronted by her and that slick Reuben Wainwright. From that minute on, everything had turned inside out.

He'd wondered a dozen times since why seeing Billie and the man she purported to hate—her alleged stalker—together had incensed him so much. Billie was nothing to do with him, was she?

They were friends and colleagues, and enjoyed each other's company, and worked surprisingly well together, but never once had that friendship strayed into even the outer fringes of anything deeper. But what Jonah had felt, seeing her and Reuben together, had been a bolt of raw and irrational jealousy.

It was ludicrous to feel like that. He knew that Billie disliked Reuben intensely; he knew Reuben was shacked up with Miranda; he was sure there was nothing between them. But he'd grown fond of Billie. The closeness had grown out of his admiration and her unconditional friendship over the months they'd known each other, but why the hell should he have felt so *jealous*? And why the hell had he behaved like such a complete git?

Maybe, he thought, it was just the fact that Billie and Reuben had been together when he'd wanted her to be alone for the build-up to the display—which was, after all, something only they shared. Maybe, too, it was because of that ridiculous explanation about Reuben knowing Billie had been seeing a married man . . . He shook his head. He didn't believe it for a moment. There had to be more to it than that, surely?

Billie had been as snappy with him as he had with her—which, with hindsight, was understandable. Billie was feisty and certainly not the sort to waffle apologies for saying what she thought. And then there'd been Barnaby not turning up in time for the Slingsby slot, and that bloody spider, and then, to ice the cake, Claire.

He sighed, leaning his forehead against the windowpane. Claire was still at his flat. She'd even gone as far as signing on at Whiteacres Health

Centre to continue her antenatal classes. She had the bedroom, while he was sleeping—or trying to—on the excruciatingly uncomfortable sofa. Sleep had been something that would have eluded him even in the most luxurious of beds these past nights.

Claire was having a baby . . . His baby . . . It didn't matter how many times he said the words, it still seemed completely impossible. Throughout the time they'd been married they'd talked of having children—one day. But it was always too soon. At that time he was enjoying his RAF long-haul flights and Claire liked her office manager's job, and she had always said she didn't want to be a part-time mother. There'd be plenty of time for babies later.

He'd wondered at first if the pregnancy was a figment of Claire's imagination, just another ploy to complicate the issues that were already tangled enough, but it definitely wasn't. Claire was a blooming, gorgeous picture of pre-motherhood; nearly seven months pregnant now. The baby, she'd told him, would be born in September. She was as sweet and placid and loving as she'd been when he'd first met her, and that had thrown his emotions into total turmoil. He'd always thought he wanted children, he probably still did. The awful thing was, he certainly knew he didn't want Claire.

He'd even clutched at the straw of it *not* being his child. Claire had looked shocked that he should think such a thing 'The *dates* darling. I didn't sleep with Antony in January. I wasn't with him. I was here. With you!'

'Then why the hell didn't you say anything before?' He'd asked it a million times. 'You must have known for ages!'

And she'd smiled and said, of course she'd

thought she *might* be, but her periods were always up and down, and sometimes she didn't eat properly, you know, which threw you out, and then there was the stuff . . . and she hadn't been sure, so she hadn't done the test until it was ever so late . . .

'And does Antony know?'

Claire had curled herself around him and said, silly—why should he? He just thinks I'm getting fat. It isn't his baby, it's ours, Jo . . . and I've come back to you so that we can be a proper family. But maybe we should tell him, just to be fair . . .'

And so there had been various frantic phone calls to Aerobatic Archie, who was, understandably, distraught about the whole situation. Claire had remained calm and smiling throughout, and now seemed to have moved her amphetamine addiction onto one for buying up Mothercare.

The phone rang in the empty office. Jonah turned away from the window and stared at it. It still seemed strange that Estelle wasn't here to answer it. Hopefully, one of the three shortlisters today would fill her shoes, if not her skin-tight denim. He'd let Estelle go to Luton early so that she could start work on the new easyjet fleet. There was no point in making things difficult for her. They'd had a tearful parting, and as she'd walked away, Jonah had wanted to run after her and beg her to change her mind. But he hadn't, and would probably wonder for the rest of his life if he'd made the right decision. Barnaby and Vinny, he was well aware, were loudly and pointedly convinced that he hadn't.

The phone still rang. Jonah snatched it up.

'Jo, it's Barnaby. You'll have to do without me on the Aviation Incs board—sorry. And I'd hoped

526

to be there to offer a helping hand on the office interviews too, but I'm afraid I'm not going to be back until late.'

Jonah groaned—but not too loudly—because Barnaby had, since arriving back from Paris on the night of the air show, shovelled vast amounts of money into the Sullivanair coffers. The National Trust had snatched greedily at the Derbyshire stately home, the horse-owning had been pared down, and Barnaby was currently resident in Amberley Hill's Four Pillars and seeking out a suitable house to purchase in the area.

Since he'd been back he'd not mentioned Miranda, had been shocked rigid to hear of Claire's pregnancy, and visibly upset by Jonah's rift with Billie. However, the success of the air pageant, and his now almost certain seat on the Incs board, seemed to have cheered him up, although Jonah was pretty sure that there was still something else on his mind.

Exactly who had kept him away from Whiteacres after Miranda's rejection, Barnaby hadn't said. But as she seemed to involve a lengthy Paris stopover, and several long and secretive phone calls to France since, Jonah hoped that she was chic and long-legged and fun, and had made Barnaby a happy man.

He shrugged. 'It's OK. The Incs should just be a formality. We've both already put everything in writing anyway. And Vinny and Pam are coming in to give the job candidates the once-over and offer me moral support, so I should cope. You're all right, though? No problems?'

Barnaby's chuckle was rich. 'Quite the opposite. I'm at Orly again— buzzed over late last night—

527

and when I come back this time, I won't be alone.'

Jonah's grin was the widest it had been for weeks. 'I knew it! That's great news! Hey—she wouldn't be wanting a job running the Sullivanair office by any chance, would she?'

Barnaby chuckled again. 'Doubtful. She's a fairly independent lady. Oh, it looks as though she's ready for me, and I can't keep her waiting. We'll see you tonight . . .'

Jonah hung up, still grinning. At least someone was cheerful. And Vinny and Pam, he was sure, would be more than adequate company for grilling the interviewees. He'd spaced the interviews half an hour apart, and all three candidates seemed equally well qualified. Choosing one wasn't a task he was relishing.

*　　　*　　　*

'Not a dog's chance,' Vinny said, pulling wheelies in his chair, as the second would-be Estelle-replacement closed the office door behind her. 'She'll have her no thank you letter in the post by lunch time. She was far too high-powered for us, anyhow. You could almost see her come over faint when you mentioned the salary.'

Pam flicked at her Sullivanair jacket. 'See? I told you not everyone is prepared to dance for thrown peanuts.'

'Don't mention bloody peanuts!' Jonah groaned, linking another paperclip into his daisy chain, and squinting at her through the loops. 'Anyway, you always say you'd fly for nothing just for the love of the company—but, yeah, it's tricky trying to interpret the CV. I thought she sounded perfect.'

Pam, who had vetted the CVs and drawn up the final shortlist, looked a bit shamefaced. 'Sorry, Jonah. I had no idea just how bloody perfect she was going to be. She scared me rigid. Maybe we should have stressed in the advert that "will be working with company directors" didn't actually equate with the boardroom of ICI.'

Vinny stopped wheelying. 'Those two were quite disappointing on a physical level too. I hope the third one will be more—'

Pam snorted. 'Don't be so sodding sexist! You can't expect every woman to look like Estelle.'

'Why not?'

Jonah laughed. They'd tried really hard for the interviews; Pam was in her stewardess best, and both he and Vinny were wearing their uniforms with the peaked and braided caps placed neatly on the desk, and Jonah had even remembered to iron a shirt. It didn't seem to have cut much ice so far. The first applicant had answered all their questions promptly, smiled sweetly, asked several quite pertinent questions of her own, and then said she would only be able to work in term time and then only after and up to the school runs. No, there was no question of overtime or weekends. Hadn't she made that clear in her application letter? She wanted ten till two thirty or nothing, sorry.

Two down, one to go. Veronica O'Dowd was certainly well qualified, according to her CV, but after the first two interviewees, Jonah wasn't holding out any hopes.

'Sounds Irish,' Vinny said wistfully. 'She should have black hair, blue eyes, perfect skin—oh, and I think we're about to find out.'

Jonah stood up and opened the door. Veronica

O'Dowd was the same age as his mother, heavily hennaed, and still wreathed in a blue haze from the cigarette she'd obviously just stubbed out. As he ushered her into the office, he heard Pam's giggle and Vinny's subsequent groan. He prayed that Veronica hadn't.

The interview went like clockwork. Veronica had worked in several similar positions, lived alone, and would be more than happy to fit in with Sullivanair's antisocial hours. She could, apparently, turn her hand to anything, and was available and quite happy to start as soon as they liked.

'This morning would be brilliant.' Jonah looked at the mountain of paperwork and unopened letters on Estelle's desk. 'Yesterday morning would have been even better.'

'Right then.' Veronica hung her jacket over the back of the chair and rolled the sleeves of her lacy blouse up to her elbows. 'If one of you gorgeous boys would like to make me a cup of coffee—plenty of milk, three sugars—I'll get down to business. Oh, and no one minds if I smoke, do they?'

*   *   *

The Aviation Incs looked down their haughty noses like Barnaby's chasers staring over their stable doors. Only Malcolm Bletchley, smiling and waggling his fingers at Jonah from beneath a vast oil painting of Douglas Bader, showed any signs of being human. Jonah fidgeted on his chair at the head of the long table and wished they'd get it over with. He'd left Veronica in the office with Pam and Vinny, going through the day-to-day running

530

of Sullivanair. Estelle, of course, had left reams of notes on everything, all the computer files in order, and a brief, but probably salacious character sketch, containing the likes, dislikes, and foibles of Jonah and Vinny. Jonah was pretty sure that Veronica would cope.

The oldest Inc made a strange herumphing noise from deep in his throat. Several heads jerked up from what Jonah could only conclude was a post-lunch and pre-prandial doze. It was a very hot afternoon. Still nothing happened. The pile of paper before each of the Incs was being turned grindingly slowly, the vellum rustle just missing the beat of the clock's second hand as it ticked through the silence.

Jonah wriggled in his uniform jacket and wished he could take it off. There were no windows open, and the temperature, which was in the eighties outside, had probably reached meltdown in the stuffy boardroom. He presumed because several of the Incs were well into retirement age, their blood was thinner. They were probably all wearing thermal long johns under their three-piece suits.

They surely couldn't find anything wrong with the proposals he and Barnaby had put together, could they? The air pageant had been a total success—far more successful than he could have ever believed possible—and the second Shorts and the Skyvan would be delivered in September. He'd already advertised low-cost no-frills air transport for passengers and freight, and had been inundated with replies from people who'd got used to similar services offered by companies like easyJet and Ryanair. Early-morning business flights to Scotland and Wales, the north, and the south-west; cargo

531

routes promising a same-day delivery; holiday flights to all the popular European destinations at off-peak times, to be run on a railway-type system of buying your ticket at the check-in desk—everything had been applied for, the regulations adhered to, and all OKed by the Civil Aviation Authority.

Surely this bunch of old farts weren't going to dash his dreams now and decide to take Aerobatic Archie's offer of a lump sum to turn Whiteacres into Flying Disney, were they?

'Flight Lieutenant Sullivan—'

Jonah jumped.

The oldest Inc was smiling at him, tapping the printed proposal. 'A very comprehensive document. Most impressive. Thank you. We have all discussed this at great lengths and are agreed that our forebears—the original owners of Whiteacres—would be more than happy to see the airfield developing and prospering in this way. Also, my two retiring colleagues would be delighted to be replaced by yourself and Wing Commander Molton-Kusak. Your service records are exemplary —and your references top-notch. And,' he cleared his throat, 'the injection of the cash sum mentioned for board level allocation is most satisfactory. '

Jonah beamed.

The Inc stopped smiling. 'However—' Jonah stopped beaming.

'However, we do have to consider the offer from Squadron Leader Archibald.'

There was a hushed silence. Jonah stared desperately at the Coulson painting of *Spitfires at Dawn* on the panelled wall.

'We have decided that we should in fact,

532

interview Squadron Leader Archibald within the next week to discover his intentions. We did actually invite him to attend today but he was unfortunately otherwise engaged.'

Jonah flinched. Aerobatic Archie was, probably at this very moment, with Claire discussing the hows, whys, and whens of the conception . . .

'Should Squadron Leader Archibald be unable to assure us—as you say—that he will be a hands-on owner, occupied as you allege he will be, with his overseas display team, and that his plans are not to keep the air field working then we—Whiteacres Aviation Incorporated—will agree to your proposals wholeheartedly, will appoint yourself and Wing Commander Molton-Kusak to the board in September, and make all the necessary CAA arrangements to enlarge Whiteacres to take in your anticipated Sullivanair fleet.'

Jonah worked some saliva into his mouth. 'Thank you. Er—I'm sure that when you have spoken to Aerobatic Ar —I mean, Squadron Leader Archibald, he'll reaffirm that he will definitely be an absent owner. So, we'll wait to hear from you, shall we?'

'You will. Oh, and may I say that whatever happens, we will definitely be keeping the Whiteacres Air Pageant as an annual event. Spectacular, my dear boy. Absolutely splendid . . .'

'Thanks.'

'Especially the barnstorming,' Malcolm Bletchley piped up. 'Stunning, Jonah. Simply stunning. Miss Pascoe was a revelation . . . and I believe you've had further enquiries regarding your wingwalking displays?'

Jonah nodded. In fact, if he'd taken up every

533

offer for himself, the Stearman and Billie to appear at fetes, shows, air displays, and galas that had poured into the Sullivanair office since the pageant, they'd be double-booked until Christmas. As it was, he'd turned them all down. What was the point when the future of Sullivanair hung in the balance? What was the point when Claire was about to have his baby? What was the point when he and Billie were hardly speaking?

He walked out of the office after shaking hands, and ripped off his tie and jacket. It had gone better than he'd hoped. Aerobatic Archie would bow out, he was sure of it, and fortunately he hadn't had to tell the Incs that Claire had swapped sides—again. He felt the net of responsibility closing in on him. Still, once the Incs kicked out Antony's proposal, and Sullivanair was expanding happily, and he was on the Whiteacres board, he and Claire and the baby could move to a house with a garden and become a proper family, couldn't they? Jonah felt suddenly sad. They could, and would, and he'd regret it for the rest of his life . . .

*   *   *

'I must say,' Antony Archibald looked at Jonah with sorrowful, bloodshot eyes, 'this has hit me very hard.'

Jonah, not knowing what to reply, nodded. He could see that Antony had been knocked sideways. Claire obviously couldn't. She was floating round the functional living room in a long, drifty sundress, every so often pausing to caress the bump of her pregnancy and smile secretively. Jonah knew that she must have seen some actress or other behave in the same simpering way on a soap, and was trying it on for effect. If she'd aimed to break Aerobatic Archie's heart, she was doing a bloody good job.

'Claire, come and sit down.' Jonah patted the hard oatmeal sofa. 'You—er—should be resting.'

Christ, this was difficult. How did you go about apologising to her lover for impregnating your ex-wife? Jonah exhaled slowly. 'Antony, I really don't know what to say. It isn't—' He stopped. How could he say it wasn't what he wanted when it was what he'd got? What he deserved for being a fool. 'I mean, I know how you feel about Claire, how hard you've tried to keep her straight . . . How much you love her. I'm just so sorry.'

Antony shrugged in a defeated way. All the golden pizzazz that usually surrounded him had disappeared; he looked shrunken and grey. 'I had no idea that you and Claire were sleeping together.' He mouthed the words as though they tasted as bad as they sounded. 'It came as a huge shock to me— as you can imagine. Especially when I assumed that Claire and I were back together in Chantilly. I presume she was already pregnant at that point?'

Claire nodded happily. 'Oh, I was. But I didn't know. It happened in January.'

Christ! Jonah closed his eyes. He heard Antony's hiss of breath. 'January? You and Jonah have been sleeping together all this year?'

'No.' Jonah snapped his eyes open. 'Just once. As Claire says, in January. She came to see me at the airfield. She said you had split up again and she was unhappy. We had um—a bit of a set-to and then I brought her back here because I felt guilty, and— er—we . . .'

535

'Ended up in bed for hours!' Claire finished gaily. 'It was lovely. Just like old times, wasn't it, Jo?'

'Claire!' He really wanted to throttle her. She was being deliberately cruel now. 'It was nothing like old times. It was simply a mistake. A huge mistake.'

Antony stood up. 'You don't sound particularly thrilled about this baby.'

Jonah wanted to laugh. How could he be thrilled? He didn't love Claire, but he couldn't say that. Claire and a baby would stifle everything he'd dreamed of. If only this had happened three or four years ago it would have been the most wonderful thing in the world, but now, it was possibly the worst . . . He didn't answer.

'Of course he is! There's just been so much to do—and it's come as a bit of a shock, that's all. We haven't even really thought about names, yet, have we, Jo?' Claire snuggled closer. 'I thought maybe—'

'Claire!' Jonah shook her off and edged to the far end of the rock-hard oatmeal. Names? He didn't want this baby to have a name—it'd be real if it had a name. He looked again at Antony. 'Are you sure you won't have a drink?'

'Positive. And will you be remarrying? For the sake of the baby? I presume that's on the cards?'

Jonah shook his head slowly. Marriage? God, a year ago he'd have given his right arm to marry Claire again. A year ago, when the memory of Claire kept him awake with the pain, he'd have given everything for the opportunity. But not now. So much had changed. He'd changed. Claire wasn't his wife any longer. The drugs and the avarice and the life with Antony had turned her

536

into someone he didn't know—and certainly didn't like.

'No, well, I mean, it's not necessary, is it? Not just for the baby . . .'

Claire moved closer again and linked her arm through his. 'Don't look so dour, Jo. Antony will be all right. He's got his display team and he'll be travelling all round the world and soon forget me. And we'll have lovely Whiteacres and Sullivanair and a baby—and we'll be happy again.'

Happy? Shit!

'I'm sure you will be.' Stony-faced, Antony headed towards the hall, then stopped and stared at them both. 'Naturally, Jonah, this means that my offer of a place on the display team will be withdrawn—for both yourself and Molton-Kusak. And I shan't be following up my bid to buy Whiteacres either. In fact, I shall only come back to this country when the team is appearing at Farnborough or the RIAT. I shan't wish you luck either, because it would stick in my craw.'

'No—um—' He followed Antony to the hall. 'Look, Antony—'

'Do you love her?'

God Almighty! Now what was he supposed to say? Jonah made a sort of noncommittal noise in his throat.

'OK, then. I'm not a fool. Just promise me you'll take care of her. You wanted her back—and now you've got her. Goodbye.'

Jonah flinched as the door slammed shut. That was it. Antony had handed it to him on a plate. He'd got Whiteacres, but he'd also got Claire. It was a hollow victory.

*   *   *

Two hours later, in the golden diffused light of a perfect summer evening, Jonah drove back to the airfield. He still felt like a complete bastard. Barnaby had telephoned the flat while he and Claire were still arguing. He'd grabbed the car keys and left without telling her where he was going. He hadn't even told her who the call was from. He hadn't told her about Veronica replacing Estelle or his meeting with the Incs.

He changed gear angrily, ramming the car over the speed humps in his temper. He told Claire very little—in fact they rarely talked—except when they discussed what she'd bought that particular day for the baby. He swallowed the lump in his throat. He'd been so bloody reckless. So stupid.

Why should he have assumed that Claire was on the pill when he'd made love to her? Why couldn't he have asked and accepted some responsibility? Made sure she didn't get pregnant? Why couldn't he have acted like a grown-up instead of an overeager schoolboy? Why the hell had this had to happen?

Still feeling sorry for himself, he belted along the lane beside the perimeter fence. Barnaby had asked him to meet him, and presumably his Parisian lady, at the warehouses. Jonah didn't have a clue why, but assumed it was because Barnaby wouldn't particularly want to introduce his new amour to Jonah in the drop-dead atmosphere of the grim flat. It would hardly make for a cosy foursome. Maybe Barnaby wanted to show her the Stearman. Maybe she was into planes. Maybe . . .

Jonah screeched to a halt. The Stearman,

538

liveried with the Sullivanair logos, still made him ache with pride. He had no idea why it wasn't in the shed—perhaps Barnaby was going to take his mademoiselle for a romantic spin and show her the sights from the open cockpit . . . The plane was parked on the concrete outside the units beside the burned-out hatchbacks and the towering purple loosestrife. Barnaby was leaning against the wing, laughing and—Jonah slammed out of the car— there was Billie, looking great in cut-off dungarees and a skimpy white vest and her Timberlands. Her hair was tied up in a tufty knot and she was laughing back at Barnaby.

He walked towards them. There didn't seem to be anyone else with them, but, of course, Barnaby's lady may well be inside.

'Hello!' Barnaby grinned hugely. 'Sorry to be so cloak and dagger, Jo, but I wanted it to be a surprise.'

'I'm sure it will be. Hi, Billie.'

'Hi.'

Jonah looked round the plane. 'Well, where is she?'

'Who?' Barnaby was grinning from ear to ear.

'The lady you brought back from Paris.'

Billie seemed to find this hysterically funny, but valiantly tried to stifle her giggles. Barnaby didn't. His guffaws rang through the thick balmy silence. 'She's here, Jo! Right in front of you!'

'*Billie*? You've been meeting *Billie* in Paris?' He couldn't help it. It was all too much. 'But you can't! I mean—'

'Well, I don't see why not.' Billie was biting her bps, trying not to laugh out loud. 'But no, he hasn't. This is his lady, dumb cluck—the big one right here . . .'

They both looked in shared amusement at the Stearman. Jonah stared as well. Then stared again . . .

'Jesus! It's not mine! It's not, is it?'

Barnaby shook his head. 'I took your advice, Jo. I bought her when I went out to Kentucky and flew her home in stages. Got as far as Paris and called in some chums to do the livery.' He sighed. 'I'd hoped to have her ready in time for the air pageant but there was a delay. Still, she's here now. The second string to the Sullivan Stearman bow.'

Jonah was totally shell-shocked. 'But where are you going to hangar her?'

'We've just been discussing that,' Billie said. 'We've decided that I should approach Reuben and ask to take out an additional lease on unit six at the end there. It's been empty for years but it's big and will take both the planes. And that way it'll leave my original warehouse with more storage space for my customers. See,' she threw him a challenging look, 'you're not the only one who wants to expand their business.'

Jonah was still speechless. He'd had absolutely no idea. And now with two Stearmans . . .

Billie smiled at him, quite gently. 'Barnaby and I have had a little talk while we were waiting for you, haven't we?'

'We have,' Barnaby affirmed. 'And we've decided that by the start of next season—May next year at the latest—we should be up and running with a wingwalking display team. Two biplanes, two pilots, two wingwalkers. Billie will have to train the new girl, of course, being such a natural—'

'Mmm,' Billie butted in, 'and we thought we'd

540

call it Sullivan's Flying Circus. Sounds good, doesn't it? What do you reckon?'

chapter forty-two

'So really,' Miranda screeched above Pixie murdering a Guns 'n' Roses number on Mulligan's karaoke, 'you're not exactly feeling on top of the world?'

Billie pulled a face over her gin and tonic. 'My mother's a liability; I've just saddled myself with promising to be a member of a wingwalking team when flying still scares me rigid; I've got to kowtow to your bloody other half to rent unit six; and Jonah's sodding ex-wife is about three and a half years pregnant! How much more not on top of the world can you get?'

'Not much,' Miranda admitted, stirring her rapidly melting ice round her glass. 'Still, it's nice to see that you've kept your sense of humour. And Reuben will be chuffed to bits that you want to rent out that other warehouse—no, really! Don't interrupt—he cares about you, Billie. And I mean cares about how you're doing with the business, not cares as in phwoar!'

'Crap!'

'No, honestly. And he said how pleased he was with the way you were running the warehouse, and how happy you seemed, and he said that all we needed to do was to find you a nice man and—'

'There's no such thing.' Billie drained her glass and pushed it across the table. 'And even if there was, I don't need Reuben's help to find one, thanks. It's your round and when you come back can we please not discuss Reuben, or Claire, or my mother?'

'Whatever. But I actually thought your mum was pretty ace.'

'My mum should have been muzzled at birth.'

Miranda laughed, and got to her feet, expertly balancing the glasses as she elbowed her way to the bar. It had been a great night, just like old times. Faith might have upset Billie in some way, but she'd been dead right about this: they'd needed a girls' night out to build a few bridges. And, of course, have a good gossip. And the gossip had certainly been good.

'Two G and Ts, please, doll.' Miranda used her height to launch the empty glasses over the heads of Amberley Hill's pre-pubescents who were drinking Archers and Coke four deep round the bar.

Secure now in her relationship with Reuben, all she needed to make things perfect was for Reuben and Billie to like each other—but not too much, naturally. Oh, and of course, she thought, watching the Aussie-Irish barman lob ice into the glasses, getting Billie someone to love. She agreed wholeheartedly with Reuben on that one. It had been for ever since Billie had had a man.

Miranda had had great hopes about Jonah, especially after the three wingwalking displays at the airshow. Billie had trusted him with her life, for heaven's sake! Miranda had been confident that if you shared something as stupendously scary as that, you could share just about anything. And then when Billie had said Estelle was leaving Sullivanair, Miranda had been pretty sure that it would be only a matter of time before Billie would be belting into

Follicles and Cuticles to get her hair done for her first date with Mr Drop-Dead Gorgeous Sullivan.

She sighed, squashing three teenagers against the bar as she thrust her money across the counter and reached for her drinks. Of course, because of Claire's pregnancy, the date had never happened. Which was typical of bloody men—no sense of timing! Miranda juggled the glasses and her purse. And now, according to Billie, she and Jonah were very icy with each other, and she was only going to do the wingwalking thing because she enjoyed it, and because it would keep Sullivanair renting two warehouses. Nothing more.

However, looking on the bright side, Miranda had noticed that Barnaby had crept into Billie's conversations quite a bit recently. It appeared to have been Barnaby who had contacted her about the second plane which he'd flown in from Paris without telling Jonah; it was Barnaby with whom that Billie had discussed the wingwalking team; Barnaby to whom she had suggested renting Sullivanair a second warehouse.

Miranda skipped through the tables. Mercifully Pixie had handed over the karaoke microphone to Sally, Debs and Anna, who were now doing something kitsch by the Beverley Sisters. Miranda winced as Sally missed top C.

That, of course, would be the perfect solution. Billie and Barnaby. She still felt rigid with guilt when she thought about his blushing and gentlemanly proposal. She'd had to turn him down because it wouldn't have been fair to string him along, not when she loved Reuben—but that hadn't made it any easier. He was a lovely man whom she had led on, albeit unwittingly, and whom she had hurt in consequence. She wouldn't have done it for the world. And now, maybe Billie could repair some of the damage and solve her own loneliness at the same time.

'I got doubles, doll.' She edged the glasses onto the table. 'Save's going back up there for the next ten minutes or so. It's like youth club night by the bar. Right, so if we can't talk about your mum or Jonah's wife or Reuben, what can we talk about?'

There appeared to be quite a lot, and most of it involved nudging and winking and giggling. Miranda thought it was wonderful. Exactly like old times. Well—almost. Of course, tonight when she and Billie eventually staggered home, it wouldn't be together. Still, with Debs, Anna and Sally having been banned from the karaoke for the rest of the evening and consoling themselves with tequila, and Pixie with her nose in a pint of Guinness, it was really getting into deja vu territory.

'Jesus!' Billie, who was facing the door, suddenly spluttered into her gin. 'I don't believe it.'

'What?' Miranda craned her neck round. She couldn't see anything apart from about twenty million people. 'Is it a what or a who?'

'Definitely a who! Mind you, I don't know whether it's a who you'll want to see or not, because of what this particular who has done to you, if you get my drift.' The sentence ended in a hiccup and a giggle and a slightly glazed look of panic.

Sally, Anna, Debs and Pixie had paused in their serious drinking and were staring, open-mouthed, in the same direction as Billie. Miranda, not wanting to miss out on a bit of scandal, leaned dangerously backwards in her chair. 'Bloody hell!'

Kitty, looking very smug and carrying a small

544

suitcase that had Prada scribbled all over it, was standing in the doorway, peering through the smoky crowd.

'Kitty! Hiya!' Pixie had scrambled onto her chair and was waving both arms above her head. 'We're over here!'

While Billie, Miranda noticed, was concentrating on her beer mat, everyone else was concentrating on the prodigal Kitty as she slooped and shimmied her way through the tables towards them. Miranda, feeling delighted to see her but also blazingly angry that she'd done a runner for so long without giving notice, tried very hard to look stern. She knew it wouldn't work. It never did. She had the wrong kind of nostrils.

'Wow! Hi!' Kitty, dressed in a short, strappy pink dress, dropped the suitcase and edged herself in between Debs and Pixie. 'Long time no see, eh?'

Miranda decided to get the business side of things out of the way immediately. After all, she was as agog as the rest of them to find out what Kitty had been up to, but first things first. 'Before you say anything, do you intend stopping? I mean, are you back, permanently?'

'What? Oh, yeah? God!' Kitty looked stricken. 'You haven't given my job away, have you?'

'Kitty, you've been missing for nearly three months, doll, and—'

'I sent postcards!'

'Two lines on the back of a couple of seaside Donald McGills with ineligible—I mean illegible—postmarks is hardly keeping in touch, is it?'

Kitty looked taken aback. 'God, where's your sense of fun? Didn't you think they were a scream? And I did ask you to hang on to my job for me. 'She

545

stretched her well-tanned legs. 'Aren't you going to ask me where I've been, then? I've been—Oh, hello, Billie. You were so quiet I didn't know you were there. I guess you won't have to ask me, will you? You'll know only too well . . .'

Billie, who'd gone pale, was standing up. Miranda, pretty sure she'd missed something, flapped her hand at Kitty. 'Hush a minute. We'll talk about work tomorrow. Billie, what's up?'

'Er—nothing. I just want to go, that's all. It's been a great night—No, honest, I'm fine . . . I'll catch you all later.'

As all eyes and ears were on Kitty, the resulting goodbyes were merely desultory as Billie crashed away from the table. Miranda, torn now between hearing about the explicit details of Kitty's away games with the totally fabulous Kieran Squires, and worried about Billie, frowned. She hesitated, but not for long. There was really no contest. She drained her glass and pushed her chair away from the table.

'Be in Follicles by ten tomorrow morning.' She spoke as bossily as she could to Kitty, hoping the non-flare of her nostrils hadn't let her down. 'We'll talk about everything then. And I mean everything, doll—OK?'

'Yeah, sure, all the sordid details.' Kitty grinned and winked and then took a deep breath, leaning across the table towards Sally, Debs, Anna and Pixie. 'Well, after the wet footie-shirt thing, Kieran asked me if I fancied a drink and . . .'

Miranda thrust her way out of Mulligan's in search of Billie.

She didn't have to search far. Billie was standing outside in the warm August darkness, leaning

546

against the dark side of the pub, with the pastel light from the fibre-optic fountain sliding across her face.

Miranda leaned beside her. 'Want to talk about it?'

Billie sort of snuffled quietly. 'Yeah, actually. But I also want to do something else as well. I want to go and see Reuben about leasing the other warehouse, while I'm still in the mood. I've been putting it off for ages because, well, you know . . .'

Miranda didn't really. She had no idea why Billie, who was getting pretty astute at running her own business, should have shillyshallied for so long over contacting Reuben and taking out a second lease.

Billie tucked her hair behind her ears. 'So, is he taxiing tonight, or clubbing, or mouldering in the bedsit?'

'He's at the club.' Miranda decided this wasn't going to be the best moment to take Billie to task about slagging off Reuben. Not if she wanted to find out what the hell was going on. 'Do you want me to come with you?'

'I don't need you to hold my hand.' Billie stared at the ground. 'But, yeah, I'd be glad of a bit of moral support, thanks.' She lifted her head and stared at Miranda. 'So, how much has he told you? How much has my mother told you?'

'Uh?' Far too many gin and tonics had blunted the sharpness. Somewhere things had shifted. Somewhere from about the moment Kitty walked into Mulligan's. 'Sorry, doll. I'm not with you.'

'You soon will be.' Billie unpeeled herself from the wall. 'Let's walk round and round the Spicer Centre until I've told you everything, then we'll go

547

into the club and I'll face your precious Reuben.'

They walked, bumping into the summer night crowds, kicking at empty cans, circling the fountain, and Billie talked, and Miranda couldn't believe any of it. Kieran Squires! Billie and Kieran Squires! It was all news to her. Neither Faith nor Reuben had breathed a word. There didn't seem to be an appropriate point in Billie's hardly-pausing-for-breath revelations to stop her and let her know. Mind you, it made an awful lot of sense now: the face-slapping in Caught Offside, Billie's aversion to televised football, and her reaction when Kitty swanned into Mulligan's looking like the cat who had just got the Premiership cream.

The strangest thing, Miranda reckoned, was why on earth Billie had felt it necessary to keep it all a secret for so long. So, she'd had an affair with a married man—so what? Oh, sure, it must have been awful finding out, but it wasn't like she'd murdered anybody or anything, was it? And Reuben had helped her when she'd been all alone that night, hadn't he? So why had Billie hated him ever since? And how the hell, if Miranda didn't know anything about it, had Faith found out?

Feeling giddy, Miranda stopped Billie on their umpteenth circuit, pulling her down beside her on the wall round the fountain. 'So, was that why you left Devon, then? To be with Kieran? Not that I blame you, doll. Kieran Squires is dead lush—and after Damon—'

'Oh shit . . . That's another lie. Damon never existed. I made him up to explain why I was here. It just sounded better than that I was a silly little tart caught in the middle of nowhere with my knickers in my handbag.'

548

'Oh, I don't know—' Miranda caught sight of Billie's face. 'I mean, well, yeah, I suppose it was.' She groaned a bit. Hadn't she spent ages, when she was doing Faith's hair, discussing bloody Damon? Christ! 'So, now it's over and out in the open, and everyone knows, and the world's still turning. Do you feel better?'

Billie shrugged. 'Yes, I think so. Oh, I wish I'd told you before because it all seems so silly now. But at the time . . .'

Miranda hugged her. 'Yeah, I know. You start believing in your own fiction—we've all done it, doll. You bottle things up, and then they fester out of all proportion and then by the time you think you've got the balls to tell the truth, everyone believes the lie and it's too late.' God—she'd have to stop before they both ended in tears. Several people who had tumbled out of Mulligan's prior to tumbling into Caught Offside were eyeing them suspiciously. Miranda glared at them. 'Bugger off! We're bonding!'

Billie sniffed. 'So, now you know the truth about how I came to Amberley Hill, and I'm really surprised that Reuben hadn't already told you, and—'

'Well, he hadn't, so I think you've underestimated his integrity a bit.' Miranda interrupted, amazed at how suddenly the emotional outpouring had sobered them both up. 'But what I don't understand is, why you hate him so much? Oh sure, he saw you at your absolute worst, and you must have felt dead embarrassed, but why do you still hate him?'

Having unleashed a lot of nasty genies from her bottle, Billie obviously wasn't going to mince her words. 'Because he scares me. That night—when I found out about Kieran—Reuben was just so weird. So intense. Like he had a personal vendetta or something. And because now—oh, I don't know—he hounds me. He's everywhere, Miranda, don't you see? Ever since the night in the taxi he's always been involved in my life. It's like he wants to control me—and no, I *know* he doesn't fancy me or anything. He's just always *there*.

Miranda stood up, hauling Billie to her feet. 'I'm sorry to disagree with you on this one, but I still think you've got him wrong. He's not like that. I know Reuben, and yes, sure, he's a bit prickly on the surface, but underneath he's a good man. Kind. Caring. Funny.'

'As in peculiar?' Billie nodded. 'Yeah, dead right.'

Miranda bit her tongue and started to walk away. She almost expected Billie to cry off, to say that she didn't think she could face Reuben now, that she'd discuss the warehouse another day. But she didn't. She wandered alongside Miranda through the Spicer Centre's throng towards Caught Offside, not speaking, almost as if she was lost in a world of her own.

The club was packed, as always. Miranda, who helped Reuben with the accounts, knew how well it was doing. As an all-night dance venue and bar, it was second to none, but the Penalty Spot had also quickly become one of the area's in eateries, and the tables were constantly prebooked. Despite his bulldog appearance, Bertie Malone was a shit-hot manager, and the security staff had no truck with Amberley Hill's boy racers, teeny yobs, or petty drug pushers. Anyone contravening the club rules was dealt with swiftly, and Reuben was determined there shouldn't be a whiff of scandal at Caught Offside. Miranda smiled in the foyer as they crashed through the turnstiles. Billie and Kieran Squires could have scuppered the no-scandal clause before the club had even opened!

The noise was, as always, overwhelming, and the dance floor packed. Miranda paused on the top of the terraces, scouring the floodlit gloom for Reuben. She felt Billie stumble to a halt behind her and felt very sorry for her. This must bring back some awful memories.

She saw Reuben then, sitting at the bar, watching his leggy staff with an eagle eye. Miranda's smile widened. No one would pocket the change while Reuben was around. Leaping down the terraces and forcing her way through the dancers on the pitch, she ducked between the goal posts. She rushed towards him and flung her arms round his neck. Loving him had freed her of all inhibitions; trusting him had freed her of even more. She adored him. She had never, ever, felt like this before.

'Did you have a good night, then?' He slid from his stool and kissed her, laughing. 'I didn't expect to see you in here so soon. I thought you'd hang on in Mulligan's until kicking-out time at least. How was Billie?'

'I'm fine, thank you.' Billie stepped out from behind Miranda, raising her voice against an ear-splitting blast of Puff Daddy. 'And, yes, we had a great night. Just like the good old days.'

Reuben, still holding Miranda's hands, raised his eyebrows. 'If I didn't expect to see Miranda in here early, I certainly didn't expect to see you in

551

here at all.'

'After last time, you mean?' Billie was instantly defensive. 'Well, no, it wasn't my first choice of venue, either, but—'

Miranda shook her hands free. 'Stop it, both of you. Reuben, Billie wants to discuss some business, that's all. We decided it would be a good opportunity as we were both in town.'

Reuben's eyebrows were stuck on quizzical. 'Business? Fine. Do you want to use the office?'

Billie shook her head. 'No, thanks. I just want to know if I can have an option on leasing unit six at Whiteacres, that's all.'

'And you couldn't pick up the phone and ask me that?'

'Of course I could,' Billie shrugged. 'I just didn't particularly want you to come out to the warehouse to discuss it with me, that's all. So, can I? Will you draw up the paperwork like Maynard and Pollock did when I leased the first one? Oh, and I trust the terms will be lower—the place is a tip.'

Reuben grinned. 'I know. I've seen it. You'll have to have a small army of cleaners in before you can start storing. What exactly are you planning on storing?'

'It's for the Sullivanair planes, actually. The original Stearman and the new one they've just bought.'

'Is it indeed?' Reuben looked interested. 'Quite a coup then, Billie. Of course I'll think it over and put together a deal that should suit all parties. I'll ring you as soon as I've fixed a figure, OK?'

'Fine. Thank you.'

'No problem. I'm just delighted that your business is taking off. And it seems as if Sullivanair is doing a nice little rescue job on my ex-employees too.'

Miranda, who had listened to the ping-pong conversation and felt slightly giddy trying to read the body language at the same time, sensed the change in atmosphere.

'I'm not sure what you mean . . .' Billie was suddenly vigilant, her eyes fastened on Reuben's face. 'Sullivanair aren't doing me any favours. They're my customers. They pay me the going rate and—'

'Exactly,' Reuben smiled his closing-the-deal smile. 'They're probably your largest customer and as such are taking care of you. Like they're also taking care of Veronica O'Dowd.'

Miranda wrinkled her nose. Who the hell was Veronica O'Dowd?

Billie looked just as mystified. Well, for a split second at least. 'Veronica? Vee—from the cabs? The one you sacked?'

'The same,' Reuben beamed. 'Sullivanair have taken her on as an office manager. Goodness, didn't you know? I had to supply references yesterday—and yes, before you ask, I did. Excellent ones. Now, would you like a drink to seal the warehouse deal? On the house, of course.'

'No, thank you.' Billie was still icily polite. 'I'm sure it would choke me. I'd better be going home.' She looked at Miranda. 'Thanks for a great evening. We'll have to do it again. And thanks for listening . . .'

'No sweat. You've done it enough times for me, doll. See you soon.'

She watched Billie duck and dive her way through the dancers, then turned to Reuben. 'Why

553

did you sack this Veronica, then?'

Reuben stroked her cheek and pulled her towards him. 'I had to, sweetheart. The woman just didn't know when to keep her mouth shut. Now, what do you fancy to drink?'

chapter forty-three

The summer was coming to an end. The last days of August were golden and blue, like a faded Indian tapestry. Billie, having received a surprisingly good rental price from Reuben for the lease of unit six, was up to her armpits in sugar soap and caustic soda.

She felt liberated and happy. Apart from her mother's implication in the Kieran Squires affair, which she still had to ferret out, the spectre of her stupid dalliance had at last been laid to rest. Not only that, but she had two warehouses, some truly good friends, was getting used to living alone in the flat, and was coming to terms with fact that Jonah was now totally out of reach.

Well, almost. She sat back on her heels, wiping a dripping Marigold across her forehead. She and Jonah were still withdrawn from each other when they met. He seemed very preoccupied these days, which she supposed was understandable, as his life had tumbled upside down. The two new Sullivanair planes were being delivered in a month's time; his forthcoming elevation to the Whiteacres Aviation Incs was now, with Antony Archibald's defection, merely a formality; and he still had the flying circus to plan. Billie supposed that all these things—not

554

to mention impending fatherhood—would make anyone twitchy. But she sadly mourned the passing of their previous easy-going friendship.

And yes, OK, she still fancied him like mad. It was impossible not to. Which now made the Sullivanair dealings so much easier when they took place with Barnaby. Barnaby, burstingly proud of his Stearman, which they had christened Lumley, in keeping with Jonah's being called Joanna, had joined Sullivanair full time and would be piloting one of the new Shorts while Vinny took charge of the Skyvan. Unlike Jonah, Barnaby still spent most of his days off at the warehouse, apparently over Miranda and growing more tanned, more scruffy, and far more relaxed as he tinkered with bits of the plane.

In the last few weeks Billie had found out more about the comings and goings at Sullivanair from Barnaby than she had from Jonah. Neither of them, however, had mentioned Vee being Estelle's replacement, which she found odd, especially with the Reuben's Cabs connection, but she'd just put this down to further evidence of the gulf that had widened between Jonah and herself since the day of the air pageant.

'Wakey-wakey . . .' Isla, who was washing years of encrusted grime from the windows, chucked a chamois at her. 'I didn't know you were into transcendental meditation.'

Billie chucked the chamois back. 'I was merely reflecting on the joys of being a warehouse owner, that's all.'

'And you'll ruin your skin if you let those suds drip, my dears.' Sylvia, lounging in a deck chair, was watching the ablutions through the pulled-back doors with the critical eye of one who went nightly to bed smothered in Nivea Visage. 'You want to get a man in.'

Billie grinned. 'No way!' A man—in or out—was the last thing she needed. She gave a sigh, chucked her Marigolds into the nearest bucket of scummy water, and stood up. 'Come on, Isla. Let's call it a day. The windows look great and I've almost finished the walls.'

Isla followed Billie out of the warehouse and pushed tendrils of her snaky hair away from her face, blinking in the sudden rush of sunlight. She smiled gently at Sylvia. 'You know, Billie's right—we don't need men. Well, at least not for things like this. Women just get on and do what has to be done; men always spend ages planning and measuring and weighing things up—especially if they're an old worry-guts like Zia.'

Sylv and Billie stared at her. This, from the devoted Isla, was like hearing the Archbishop of Canterbury say that there was nothing wrong with a bit of devil worship just so long as it was done on the quiet and in the privacy of your own home.

Billie, aware that Zia had been away for almost a week on a clothes-buying mission in the Fens, laughed. 'Don't be too hasty. Yours is only away temporarily. You'd feel differently if he'd left you for good, believe me.'

'Maybe.' Isla shrugged and continued to look defiant. 'But he's always such a wet blanket about anything innovative, isn't he? Like your first warehouse, Billie, and then the planes, and well, everything. He's supposed to be all New Age and cosmic, but he uses dental floss and reads the *Daily Star*.'

556

Sylvia adjusted the chin-strap on her sombrero and chuckled. 'Can't get much more cosmic than the *Daily Star*, dear. And at least your Zia has his uses—he's a damned hard worker and you'd never be making Zi-Zi's such a success without him, would you? There's good men and bad men, and you've got one of the former, so count your blessings. Anyway, it was more Billie I was worried about.'

'Don't be,' Billie said cheerfully, wiping her hands on her dungarees and skirting Lumley's wings. 'I've done without one for long enough. I'm not going to start panicking about the lack of male company now.'

Sylvia looked hopeful. 'But, I thought, maybe Jonah . . .'

'Jonah's probably, as we speak, at the antenatal clinic with Claire, going through the rigours of panting and pushing, and not pushing, and timing contractions, and how to staple Pampers, and—'

'God Almighty!' Sylvia leaned dramatically against the Stearman's silver, purple and emerald tail fin. 'Spare me the gruesome details. I never was the slightest maternal.'

'Weren't you? What a shame—you'd have made a lovely mum. Did Douglas not want children, either?'

'Not unless he could have putted the little bastards off a tee with a nine iron, no.' Sylvia pushed the sombrero to the back of her head. 'And by the way, did I mention that Douglas and I are getting divorced?'

It was Billie and Isla's turn to look shocked. Billie shook her head. 'No, you bloody didn't, Sylv! You kept that quiet! When did all this come about, then?'

'It hasn't yet. It's being dealt with by my solicitors.' Sylv looked stoical. 'It was bound to happen, dear, really. You see, Douglas is having intercourse with Myrtle.'

Billie blinked. 'Who the hell is Myrtle, and how do you know he's—um—?'

'Myrtle's the lady from the Inner Wheel he got in to do a bit of cooking and cleaning after I left.' Sylvia pursed her lips. 'She's obviously extended her duties. My sister Ethel caught them at it in the conservatory. Our Ethel had only popped round to water the yuccas because Douglas is a bugger when it comes to house plants—and there they were! Bold as brass. Having intercourse on my cane and rattan three-piece!'

Billie, not daring to look at Isla, wondered fleetingly if that hadn't been rather uncomfortable, and tried to make appropriate sympathetic noises. Sadly, they all sounded like derisive snorts.

Sylvia clapped her hands. 'So anyway—*c'est la vie* and all that. Now we're all manless—well, Isla isn't really, but temporarily—and we're all doing nicely, so maybe I'm wrong and you're right. When do you think you'll have the unit ready?'

'In a couple of days,' Billie said. 'Hopefully by the end of the week, anyway. Then Barnaby and Jonah can move both planes in here and I can spend the Bank Holiday weekend sorting out unit three.'

Sylvia pulled a face. 'You shouldn't spend every hour working—you should get away for a little break.'

'Yeah, I know. Actually, I'd like to go home for a couple of days in September—there are a few things I need to sort out with my mum—but I can't see it happening. I've got no one to take over here and—'

'I'm sure our Ethel would love to help.' Sylvia looked animated. 'I would have suggested her before, but I thought you'd want someone sort of younger and sparky with a string of GCSEs. I mean, she does all my tax and VAT stuff brilliantly. Of course, she's well past retirement but she's itching to have a little job. She's ex-civil service, dear, like me, and she's done computers at night school and she'd be very reliable.'

Billie grinned. 'She sounds perfect. But would she want to work out here? I mean, this isn't everyone's cup of tea, is it?'

'She'd love it, dear, believe me. She's been widowed for years and is bored to tears with the Evergreen's lunch club and daytime telly. A couple of hours a day, say, doing your paperwork and answering the phone or whatever, to free you up . . . Shall I give her a ring? Ask her to come and see you?'

'Yes, please.' Billie nodded enthusiastically. If Ethel was only half as enterprising as Sylv it would mean her warehouses would be in good hands—and she could arrive unannounced in Devon to find out exactly how her mother knew about Kieran Squires. 'Shall I put the kettle on for a celebration?'

'Shouldn't bother.' Isla squinted across the cracked concrete. 'Not unless you've got a lot of cups. We've got company.'

Billie groaned. Jonah's car had just screeched to a halt beside the burned-out hatchbacks. She really wasn't in the mood to see Claire in her immaculate maternity best. Billie's dungarees barely covered her vest and her vest scarcely covered her chest, and she knew there were streaks of water snaking up her grubby arms and down her face.

'Heavens above!' Sylv peered from beneath the sombrero. 'Has Jonah gone into the white slave trade?'

Billie frowned. None of the four beautiful, svelte women pouring from the innards of the car and teetering across the cracked concrete in Jonah's wake looked anything like Claire. Maybe, she thought, he'd gone off the mumsy look and was auditioning spares.

'Billie—just the person!' Jonah's voice was false with bonhomie and his smile only just reached his upper lip. 'Glad to catch you—or maybe I should have phoned. I've been telling Amber and Sophie and Gaynor and—um—oh yes, Nikki, all about you.'

Sylv and Isla were still staring at the posse of women. Billie smiled rather sketchily, not actually catching anyone's eye. 'Really? That must have been a brief conversation.

Jonah frowned. 'What? No—oh, right . . . Look, I wondered if you were busy?'

Billie stared down at her filthy clothes and her dirt-streaked arms. 'Busy? Me? No, of course not. God, Jonah, I'm working myself into a frazzle getting the warehouse scrubbed out so that Barnaby's Stearman doesn't have to stay outside a minute longer than necessary. Of course I'm bloody busy.'

The women all looked rather disappointed at this outburst. Isla had pulled up another deckchair beside Sylv. Jonah jerked his head towards unit six. 'Could we have a word? In private?'

560

Billie, gagging for a cup of tea, sighed heavily but walked back to the warehouse anyway. 'If you've come to complain that I'm taking too long getting the shed ready, you're not my only customer and—'

'Christ!' Jonah shook his head. 'For God's sake, don't you start. I have enough nagging from Claire at home. It's got sod-all to do with the bloody warehouse. You're doing fine—brilliantly—OK?'

'OK.' Billie was slightly mollified. 'So, if it's not to do with the warehouse, what is it—and who the hell are they?'

Jonah looked at his glamorous entourage, who were now milling round Sylv and Isla and giggling a lot. 'They're the potentials . . . for the wingwalking team, you know? I advertised in the *Pilot* and various other magazines, and that's the shortlist.'

Billie stared more interestedly this time. Possibly Vinny had done the final selection, then. They were all very buxom despite the slenderness. 'Right, and they've come to have a look at the plane, have they? Come to see exactly what they've let themselves in for? Well, don't mind me. I'll keep out of your way . . .'

'Well, actually, you won't.' Jonah looked a bit shiftly. 'You see, as we're going to be a team, and you've actually done the wingwalking routine, and you know what's expected, I sort of wondered if you could put them through their paces?'

'Me? You're joking? I don't know the first thing about it. Mine was just trial and error—and how many of them are you taking on? Not all of them, surely?'

'Just one. Whichever one you think you can work with best.'

Oh God. Billie shook her head. It was like being

asked to choose just one from a litter of gorgeous and hopeful puppies. 'We're not going to be flying, though?'

'No,' Jonah looked agitated. 'Well, not to start with. Just on the ground, and then the—um—pootle . . .'

Billie tried not to grin. Ah yes, the infamous pootle . . .

'So? Will you?' Jonah looked very tired. 'Just go through the basics with them? Please, Billie?'

She stared at him. She'd never forgive him for not believing her when she'd told him about Kieran. He was the only person she'd been honest with and he hadn't believed her! She'd even more never forgive him for deciding to create a baby with Claire.

'Yes, OK. Are you using your plane or Barnaby's?'

'Barnaby's. It's got the rig fixed and it's already out here, so shall we get started?'

Billie exhaled. This really was the most ridiculous situation in the world. Initially she'd been happy to volunteer for the air pageant wingwalking—just to save Whiteacres from the clutches of Aerobatic Archie and Claire, and to help Jonah become an Inc. Oh yes, and if she searched the secrets of her soul, because she'd fancied the pants off Jonah and would have tied herself naked to a space shuttle if it had made him happy.

She'd achieved the first two—despite her terror—and didn't have a hope in hell of ever managing the third. Why on earth should she do any more for him now?

Jonah leaned against Lumley's wing and smiled properly for the first time. 'You did get a kick out of the display, didn't you? Really enjoyed it? Found it easy?'

She glared at him. 'Yes, you know I did, but . . .' There wasn't really a but. She'd loved the buzz, yes, OK, and enjoyed the showing off. She just wished Jonah would stop smiling. It was easier to hate him when he snarled. She shrugged. 'Oh, go on then—wheel them in . . .'

*   *   *

Two hours later, with an interested knot of onlookers gathered from across Whiteacres, Billie was feeling distinctly inferior. All four women were slender, supple, fearless and very keen to be chosen; all four had managed to climb elegantly from the cockpit, walk along the wing, wriggle themselves into the harness and stand looking graceful on top of the Stearman. Amber and Nikki had even got to grips with the swivelling rig without shrieking or disturbing their lip gloss.

Billie, remembering her own fumbling and clumsy early attempts, felt very second division. True, all four contenders obviously had season tickets to the gym and never let anything other than lettuce and Evian water pass their lips, but even so, she'd have expected some trepidation.

'They're all excellent, Jonah. They've listened to everything I've said, done exactly the right things, and looked great. They can climb and slide and smile and haven't got a single nerve. Any one of them will be far better than I am.' Billie shrugged. 'Tell you what, why don't you pick two of them for the team and leave me out of it altogether?'

'They haven't pootled yet,' Jonah said cheerfully,

climbing into the cockpit. 'That's the real test—not to mention actually flying. Don't be so hard on yourself. And I'm sorry, but as a founder member of Sullivan's Flying Circus, you're not allowed to quit.'

She knew he was joking. She wished he wasn't. She also wished he'd looked more shocked when she'd mentioned not being a wingwalker any more. Surely he could have made some sort of half-hearted protest?

Sylv and Isla busily rolled back the perimeter fence as Jonah started the Stearman. It gave Billie some scant satisfaction to notice that Amber and Sophie clapped their hands over their ears and screamed at the noise.

'Good, aren't they?' Isla said, as Billie joined her and Sylvia on the edge of the airstrip and watched the Stearman rock and roll across the grass. 'And Jonah's asked me to make the costume for the new girl—just like yours—and with spares, so I'm going to be busy.'

According to Sylv, who had wasted no time in drilling the hopefuls about their pasts, Nikki was an out-of-work actress and had apparently been a stunt double in a couple of minor films, Sophie was a dancer who'd once been on the shortlist for Gladiators, Amber taught aerobics to the rich and famous in a London health club, and Gaynor was a secretary with high-ranking qualifications in various martial arts. Billie again felt a swamp of self-doubt.

'I'll go and make some refreshments for when everyone's finished,' Sylvia said. 'Just a few sarnies and maybe a cocktail or two. Come along, Isla. I could do with a hand.'

Nikki, Gaynor and Amber stood beside Billie

and watched as Sophie was strapped into the rig. There was a flurry of excited giggles as the Stearman's propeller rotated, the engine roared, and the plane hurtled across the grass.

'God, but he's gorgeous!' Amber sighed. 'I'd give my breast implants to be working with him.'

'Me, too.' Nikki rolled goo-goo eyes. She looked sideways at Billie. 'Is he spoken for?'

'Very,' Billie said shortly. 'His wife's eight months pregnant.'

'So what?'

Billie resisted the urge to slap Nikki, and watched Sophie's progress in the rig with a critical eye. She didn't look as though she was enjoying it much. 'Anyway, whichever one of you he chooses will be flying with Barnaby Molton-Kusak, not Jonah.'

'Oh, I don't think so,' Amber pouted. 'He said you were going to be wingwalking with the other guy. He's having one of us.'

Yes, he probably will be, Billie thought, grinding her teeth. Bastard. He could at least have told her she was being relegated. Did he dislike her that much, then? So much so, that he couldn't even bear to have her strapped to his plane?

Sophie returned, looking green, and said she didn't think it was for her—no one had said things would stick to her face—and would Nikki like to have a go? One down, three left. Nikki went. Billie watched the operation again, clenching her fists every time Nikki's arms snaked unnecessarily round Jonah's neck to steady herself.

Gaynor, who had been observing the whole thing without saying much, moved closer to Billie. 'They're pretty bitchy, Nikki and Amber, really.

565

I mean, I know I only met them today, but they're sure they're going to be chosen. And they're sure they're going to get Jonah, too. And you really like him, don't you?'

God—was it that obvious? Billie shrugged. 'We've been through a lot together, that's all. Like I said, he's just about to become a father, which puts him out of anyone's reach.'

'Not Amber and Nikki's, I shouldn't think,' Gaynor said, watching as Sophie, still looking green, tottered away. 'According to them, they've both been out with half of *EastEnders*, most of *Trainspotting*, and Leonardo diCaprio.'

Billie giggled. 'Haven't we all?'

Gaynor shook her head. 'I turned Leonardo down, actually.'

Nikki returned then, looking smug. Billie felt even smugger. Stunt double she might have been, but she'd looked about as elegant as a sack of potatoes when the plane was moving.

'Your turn,' Nikki said to Amber. 'With the plane that is. Jonah Sullivan is going to be all mine.'

Billie fought the urge to pummel Nikki to the ground and stamp on her face. She smiled sweetly. 'Not as easy as it looks, is it?'

'Piece of cake, actually.' Nikki wriggled her specious shoulders. 'No idea why everyone makes so much fuss.'

Billie and Gaynor exchanged covert grins. Nikki's hair was plastered unflatteringly to her head, showing a good inch of dark regrowth. One eyelash was dangling, her teeth were smeared with lipstick and gnats, and her nose was running.

'Oh no, neither can I,' Billie agreed. 'But you haven't actually got off the ground yet, have you?

That's the real test—oh, and Amber doesn't seem to be enjoying it too much, does she?'

Pootling, Amber looked even more ungainly than Nikki, despite the aerobics training.

'Any advice, then?' Gaynor whispered. 'So that I don't make a real prat of myself?'

'Listen to what Jonah says—and do it even if it sounds stupid. Relax, smile, wave, and enjoy it. Don't try to be clever, and if you hate it, say so. Jonah is very kind—he'll stop if you want to.'

'Thanks . . .' Gaynor took a deep breath as Amber practically fell off the plane and staggered drunkenly across the grass strip. 'Wish me luck . . .'

'You'll be fine,' Billie held up crossed fingers. 'If I can do it, anyone can.'

Amber and Nikki went into a screeching conspiratorial huddle as Gaynor climbed onto the wing. Billie, still with her fingers crossed, prayed that she'd be OK. She knew she could work with Gaynor; she just hoped Jonah felt the same way.

After a rather shaky start, Gaynor seemed to be doing fine. Shorter than Nikki or Amber, and as slim as Billie, she fitted into the rig easily, slid one leg up the support as Billie had said, and smiled and waved all the way along the grass strip. Nikki and Amber, who were still discussing the relative bedroom merits of someone who'd had a bit part in *The Full Monty*, took no notice.

Cows, Billie thought. She wished she could think of something derisive to say. Estelle would have been great at cutting them down to size.

The Stearman returned, and Gaynor, fizzing with excitement, bounced across the grass. 'God— that was brilliant! I mean, I don't know if I was any good, but what a whizz!'

'You were great,' Billie assured her. 'And you really looked as if you enjoyed it.'

Jonah had stepped out of the cockpit. Nikki and Amber tried to untangle their hair. He nodded toward them. 'That was wonderful. Now, we'll do the same thing again, only this time we'll take off and fly round the airfield. Who's going to be first?'

Nikki and Amber nearly garrotted each other in the rush.

'Billie!' Sylvia bustled across the concrete. 'Sorry to interrupt, dear, but there's someone hanging around your shed. I couldn't see who it was, so I don't know if it's a customer or not.'

Billie nodded and touched Gaynor's shoulder. 'It'll feel really odd when you take off. But really it's as safe as houses. Just relax and behave exactly as you did on the ground. You'll be freezing and it's probably better to keep your mouth shut else you'll end up like a Venus flytrap. The wind is a million times stronger than you'd ever dream, so be prepared for your arms to disappear. Good luck—and I'll see you later . . .'

She hurried across the grass towards the units. She couldn't do any more. If Jonah chose either Nikki or Amber she'd resign from the team even before it got started. If Jonah couldn't see that Gaynor was streets ahead of the other two then—
She stopped.

Claire was standing in the doorway of unit three.

Billie smiled warily. 'Oh, hi. Jonah's still busy with the Stearman. Do you want to wait for him?'

'Please . . .' Claire pushed her hand into the small of her back and waddled towards the office. 'I hate this hot weather.'

Billie pulled out one of the wonky armchairs.

'Would you like a drink? He'll probably be ages yet.'

Claire nodded, lowering herself into the chair and stroking her stomach. She looked beautifully pregnant; glowing, plump, and radiant. 'Thank you. I can't wait until this baby is born. Only a couple of weeks to go, thank goodness.'

Billie walked slowly through to the kitchenette, her brain turning somersaults. She was no expert, of course, but after her sisters-in-law's multiple production line, she'd been around enough expectant mothers to know something about foetal development.

And if Claire Sullivan was eight and a half months pregnant, then Billie was Amelia Earhart, Amy Johnson, and Sheila Scott all rolled into one!

autumn

chapter forty-four

Faith drove away from the hospital, dreading having to face Stan. How could she possibly tell him? She'd known it was going to be bad, but hadn't dreamed it would be anywhere near as bad as this.

She steered the Land Rover away from the humming town and its mid-morning traffic, and headed towards the Willowbridge road, only vaguely registering that there was a slight change in the air. September was already casting long dappled shadows through the hazy Devon valleys, and the chestnut leaves were just starting to lose the edge of their brilliant green to smudged tinges of orange and gold and amber. Autumn. Always her favourite time of year. A time to take stock and enjoy the mellowness; a few months in which to draw breath before the rigours of a family Christmas and the start of the new farming year.

Faith changed gear, snapped off the radio, which had just started issuing forth something morbid by Roy Orbison, and headed for home.

Driving through the village, she ducked her head down as she passed the lay-by that housed the post office and the corner shop. Wednesday morning was WI market stall day and the whole community would notice she was missing and want to know why. She couldn't bear it if Miriam or Pat or one of her other friends should emerge from the bring-and-buy fray, all agog, and flag her down to ask how things had gone at the hospital. She had to tell Stan first.

573

The farmhouse was empty. Hurling her coat and handbag onto the hall table, Faith forged a path through the dogs and cats and headed for the kitchen. Maybe if she made Stan a liver and onion casserole for tonight, with one of her apple sponges and custard to follow, then sat him down with a mug of tea and talked quietly and calmly . . . Maybe it would be OK—and then again, maybe not . . .

Yanking the kettle from the top of the Aga, she went through the coffee-making motions, then leaning against the draining board, she stared out of the window. Across the yard she could see her grandchildren playing, as they always did; climbing on the bulky hessian feed sacks, jumping from the dusty hay bales, swinging from the rope ladder which Stan and the boys had fitted to the lowest branch of the farm's last remaining oak tree, hounding any of the hens which were stupid enough to stray into their paths.

Thad and Mungo, always bossy, were bellowing orders at Delphi and Lilac, while Otis and Sapphire sat plumply on the dry red ground and made muddy patterns with stones and twigs and cups of water.

It was like watching her own children all over again, she thought, sipping the coffee, and no doubt it would be like this for generations of Pascoes to come. Practically guaranteed immortality. It was a comforting thought.

'Faith!'

She winced. Watching for Stan to arrive in the yard from the moors, he'd completely wrong-footed her by coming in through the front door.

'Er—I'm in the kitchen, love!'

He kissed her, smelling, as always, of the familiar cocktail of warmth and diesel and animals. 'Well?

574

How did it go?'

'Fine. Have you got time for coffee?'

'No, thanks. Alex and Tom are waiting for me outside. We're going over to Ottery to see those ewes. So, how are things? What is it?'

Faith clutched her coffee mug. She couldn't put it off. He had to be told.

'Aphrodite.'

'God Almighty!' Stan shook his head. 'And I thought they were going to have Arthur or Brenda, after Maria's parents.'

'They've chosen Brenda as a second name, and Faith as a third.'

'Small sodding comfort!' Stan thumped his fist on the draining board. 'Poor little bugger! I'd had such huge hopes that they'd see sense this time. Especially Ben. What's wrong with them, eh? No, don't answer that.' He kissed her briefly on the cheek. 'Well, at least I know now. The speculation's over. Oh, I'll be gone all afternoon—are you going to stock up the stall for half a day or what?'

'I don't think so. Most of the serious market buyers will have gone home by midday, and then we'll only get the last few grockles, and they're in B-and-Bs, so they don't really want eggs or cheese. I need to pop into Willowbridge to do a bit of shopping—oh, and I thought I'd do liver and onions tonight.'

'Great.' Stan grinned from the doorway. 'Then we'll go and do our maternity ward visiting, and I'll pretend I love the damn name, and then we'll have a pint or two afterwards at the Spread Eagle, shall we? To wet the baby's head? Aphrodite! Bloody Aphrodite! I'll have to tell everyone it's a Brenda. We're getting to be a laughing stock . . . !'

575

He was still muttering as he slammed out of the front door. Faith heaved a sigh. Not as bad as she'd feared, then. Aphrodite Brenda Faith Pascoe, their seventh grandchild, now twenty-four hours old, was actually quite lucky. If she'd been a boy, Ben and Maria had chosen St Lucia Arthur Stanford.

*   *   *

The casserole was glugging fragrantly in the bottom oven, the potatoes were peeled, and the cabbage and carrots chopped and sliced respectively. Even the apple sponge was already rising slowly. Faith, feeling virtuous, wondered if it would be considered too self-indulgent to run a bath before she went shopping. Having a bath in the middle of the day was on a par with reading a book in the morning as far as she was concerned: a splurge of pampering only afforded by those with far too much time on their hands.

She had just finished running the water and swooshing in a gloop of herbal Radox when she heard a car pull up in the yard, followed by screams of excitement from the children. Botheration! It was probably Pat or Miriam, or both, having been dispatched from the rank and file of the WI to find out about the baby.

She padded downstairs, fixing her welcoming smile, and almost died of shock in the hall.

'Hi, Mum,' Billie grinned. 'Surprise surprise . . .'

Faltering only slightly, Faith skittered across the tiles and hugged her daughter. 'Dear God! You're the last person on earth I expected to see! Have you come to see the baby? She's absolutely gorgeous! Nearly nine pounds! Maria's fine —only six hours

576

in labour. Ben didn't take it so well, mind you. Are you stopping? Who's looking after the warehouse? You've lost weight, haven't you? Oh, Billie, it's so good to see you!'

The bath water went cold upstairs as they caught up on the gossip over several cups of coffee and two helpings of the apple sponge. Billie looked tanned and fit and contented, Faith noticed with motherly concern. And if she hadn't mentioned any upturn in her love life, then so be it. Every other area of Billie's existence seemed to be doing very nicely.

The new warehouse was a big step forward, Faith agreed, and Ethel sounded exactly the sort of person to be a right-hand man—especially if she was anything like Sylvia—and the plans for the wingwalking team were very exciting. Faith hoped she might be able to contact someone to have Sullivan's Flying Circus added to the list of events for the Devon carnival season next year. Gaynor sounded a lovely girl, and it was great that she was going to share Billie's flat until she found somewhere of her own.

'I was just going to drive into Willowbridge for a few bits and pieces,' she said in a conversational lull. 'Are you too tired to come with me? Perhaps you'd prefer to stay here with Ann and Katy and the children?'

Billie grinned. 'I'd probably prefer to have cosmetic surgery without an anaesthetic than spend an afternoon with the junior Mafia. Anyway, I haven't been to Willowbridge for years. It'll be nice to see some of the old places again. Who's going to drive, then?'

'I will.' Faith stood up and bundled the mugs and bowls into the dishwasher, 'I can get more stuff into

577

the Land Rover than you can in the Nova. And it's wonderful that you can stay for three whole days! I can't wait to see your dad's face tonight! We're going to have a whale of a time!'

*   *   *

So far, so good, Faith thought, parking the Land Rover outside Willowbridge's only convenience store. Billie hadn't yet mentioned Jonah or Reuben or—most importantly—Kieran Squires. Faith had known she'd sailed very close to the wind with that one, especially when she'd been at the air pageant. Billie had sussed out something—she was sure of it—and it had only been the unexpected arrival of Stan and the ensuing excitement of the wingwalking displays that had probably prevented Billie tackling her on the subject.

'How's Miranda?' Faith asked as they bustled round the tiny aisles with their shopping trolley. 'I really liked her, and she certainly cut my hair better than Valda has ever done. I might have to make bimonthly visits to Follicles and Cuticles just for a trim.'

'She'd be delighted to see you.' Billie lobbed a king-size packet of chocolate biscuits into the trolley. 'I think it was a bit of a mutual admiration society. And she's doing fine. She and Reuben seem to be very happy.'

Faith glanced up. Was there just the smidgen of a hesitation over the word Reuben? Maybe not. Maybe things were getting better all round. She decided to go for double top. 'Good. Good. And—um—Jonah and his ex-wife? They're still together, are they?'

578

'Mmm . . .' Billie nodded, studying the freezer section with what seemed an undue amount of consideration. 'She says her baby's due next week.'

Faith frowned. 'That's an odd way of putting it.'

Billie shrugged. 'It's a pretty odd pregnancy— and an even odder relationship . . . Hey, when we've finished here, why don't we go to Tilly's for a cream tea?'

Faith, who was pretty stuffed with apple sponge but delighted that Billie had such a good appetite, nodded gamely. 'That's a good idea. Right? So, what's next on the list?'

The shopping completed and stashed into the Land Rover, they headed for Matilda's Genuine Devon Tea Rooms. Tilly Mathieson was originally from Glasgow, and doled out scones and jam and clotted cream like a production line to the ever-eager tourists. Faith knew it was one of Billie's favourite haunts, and that she and her brothers had always made a beeline for it ever since they were children, mainly because Tilly swore like a trooper, had a seventies Afro mop of springy overhennaed hair, the only juke box in Willowbridge, and wasn't averse to sharing her Players No. 6 with her underage clientele.

At this time of year, the place was practically empty. They selected a window table, complete with ruched pink cloth and lace doilies, and ordered two cream teas.

Billie, laboriously heaping clotted cream on top of strawberry jam and manfully trying to keep the whole lot balanced on her scone, didn't even look up. 'How did you find out about me and Kieran Squires?'

Faith, having negotiated her scone to chin level,

579

looked down at the jam and cream that had just tumbled onto her plate. Talk about sneaky! 'What? I—I mean—who?'

'Come off it, Mum.' Billie was smiling. 'I've seen Kieran. Talked to him. He was never the brightest pixie in the forest. Miranda knew nothing of course, it was bloody Reuben who eventually confirmed it. So, how did you do it? Go on, tell me. I'm fascinated.'

Faith, feeling very hot and swamped with guilt, wondered fleetingly if denial was an option. It obviously wasn't. She pleated the tablecloth. 'I—oh, I—that is . . . Is that why you've come home? To find out?'

'One of the reasons.' Billie licked her fingers. 'Not the main one, honestly. I really wanted to see you all, but I'd like to know.'

Making a big show of scraping up the fallen jam and cream, and putting off the evil deed for as long as possible, Faith eventually took a deep breath. 'Last year, when you came home for Maria and Ben's wedding party, I was really worried about you. You seemed unhappy, rootless . . . I suspected you hadn't been happy for a while and that it was all to do with why you'd left Devon as quickly as you had, so . . .'

It took a long time, with a fair bit of backtracking and convoluted explanation, but eventually it was over. Billie, to give her credit, hadn't interrupted at all—just looked alternatively amazed and astounded. Faith, now having given up all pretence of wanting a damn cream tea, wondered if her daughter would ever speak to her again.

She didn't have to wonder for long.

'Bloody hell!' Billie looked almost admiring.

'I can't believe you did all that! You involved so many people and you actually went to the *football* ground? And Kieran *believed* you when you said about the boys' football club—well, yes, maybe he would—and no one—*no one*—knew what you were up to?'

Faith shook her head and tried to look modest. 'I—um —seem to have a gift for plausibility. Maybe I just look honest, and anyway, I didn't know what I was looking for, did I? I just thought someone had threatened you in some way. I had no idea that there was a man involved.'

'And if you had, would you still have done the same thing?'

'Probably not.' Faith reached for Billie's hand across the table. 'I'm really sorry, love. I wasn't prying. I was just so worried, then intrigued, then, as everything progressed, completely sucked into it. I really enjoyed having something to do that was mine—not the farm, or the kiddies, or the market stall, or anything. And I mean, once I'd started I couldn't have left it. I'd have never slept again, not *knowing*.'

'And you weren't angry, or disgusted, or anything, when you found out?'

'Good God, no! I was merely relieved that you weren't in fear for your life. And I have been young, Billie. These things happen. I'm not prudish, for goodness' sake! And Kieran was— is—an exceptionally attractive man. Not in Jonah Sullivan's league, of course, but then few men are. No, I understood—and I'm so terribly sorry that he was married, and—'

'Billie! As I live and breathe!' The voice sliced into Faith's conversation. 'And it's Faith, isn't it?

581

Billie's mum?'

'Craigie!' Billie had leaped up and thrown her arms round Craigie MacGowan's neck. 'Oh, brilliant! Come and sit down.'

Faith pulled her chair to one side to allow Craigie's bulk to squeeze in. The editor of the *Devon Argus* looked absolutely delighted to see Billie, she had to admit, and he certainly couldn't have appeared at a better time in the confessional.

'It's just like the good old days,' Craigie beamed at Faith. 'We all used to skive off for a cup of Tilly's tea and a twenty-thousand-calorie snack, didn't we, Billie?'

Billie nodded happily, and was soon nose to nose with Craigie, discussing old friends, acquaintances, and enemies. Faith sat back in her chair, feeling totally vindicated. There may be more flak to come over the Kieran thing, but she knew it would be all right—and it was such a relief to have it all out in the open at last.

'I was saying to Billie,' Craigie leaned towards Faith, 'that I'd pack in smoking, eating and drinking if she'd come back to work on the *Argus*, but apparently what with running a string of depositories and being a wingwalker—which we're going to do a feature on—she's far too settled in her new life.'

'Yes, she is,' Faith said happily, and meaning it. 'Do you have a vacancy, then?'

'Not for a full-time journo as such. We're just looking for someone local who could write us a weekly column—"Devon Diggings" or "Willowbridge Whispers"—you know, a touch of humour, ferreting out the stories behind the stories, that sort of thing.'

Faith and Billie looked at each other and grinned. Craigie finished up Faith's scone and mumbled through the crumbs. 'Why are you two smirking? Do you know of someone who might be interested?'

'Yes,' Faith nodded, trying to ignore Billie's giggles. 'I think I do. When could I come and see you to discuss it?'

'You?' Craigie gulped on a strawberry. 'You'd really be interested?'

'Very,' Faith said briskly. 'I've always maintained that Billie inherited her writing skills from me. So—shall we make an appointment so that you can interview me properly?'

'No time like the present.' Craigie was feverishly dabbing up crumbs with a dampened forefinger. 'Billie, get another lot of teas all round and let's get down to business.' He leaned closer to Faith. 'The job's yours if you want it, but are you sure you'd be OK with scrabbling around in the murky background of people's lives?'

'Oh, believe me,' Billie said, standing up and heading for the counter, 'there's no one better qualified to do that than my mum.'

Craigie beamed, wiped his fingers on his jacket and held out his hand to Faith. 'Well, that's the best reference I've ever heard. It'll do for me. Welcome to the *Devon Argus*, Faith . . .'

chapter forty-five

Billie sat on Vee's desk in the Sullivanair office and pulled a face. 'Go on, then! You can't stop there.'

'Hold your horses.' Vee took another drag on her cigarette. 'Right, so in she swans at about nine o'clock this morning, young Claire, carrying her suitcase.'

Billie stopped playing castanets with the stapler and the hole punch and looked hopeful. 'Her suitcase? Has she left him, then?'

'No, listen.' Vee cleared her throat. 'She's in here saying that her contractions have started and she thinks she better get herself off to hospital and will I call her a cab.'

Gaynor, who was leaning against the filing cabinet, gazing at the corporate Sullivanair photograph with Jonah, Vinny and Barnaby all looking mouthwatering in their uniforms, looked askance. 'That's pretty cool, isn't it? I mean, for someone just about to give birth to their first baby? Surely, you'd panic a lot and rush around and want your mum? I know I would.'

Billie, who thought she probably would too, grinned, despite being disappointed that Claire wasn't doing a runner. 'I hope you didn't ring Reuben's for a taxi.'

'As if!' Vee inhaled joyously. 'Nah, I got that dodgy outfit from the Whiteacres estate, the ones that say they're minicabs and don't even have tax discs and won't give receipts.'

'Good.' Billie nodded her approval. 'So, what did Jonah say when you told him? Did he belt off after her, or what?'

Vee looked blasé and blew a smoke ring. 'Couldn't, could he? He's not here, is he? He's up in the air. He's probably three-quarters of the way back from Glasgow with Vinny and Barnaby and the two new planes right this minute. Anyway, Claire didn't seem too fussed about Jonah being with her or not, to be honest. She was as cool as the proverbial cucumber. She said she'd had twinges in the flat this morning, after Jonah had left, and then they'd turned into bigger twinges, and then into the real thing, so, not knowing anyone else in the area, she'd walked over here to see if that speeded things up a bit.'

'God!' Billie looked scandalised. 'Is that what you're supposed to do? I thought you were supposed to rest?'

'They never rest on the soaps,' Vee said with authority. 'They always have a bath or go down the pub. I'd've tucked her up in bed and boiled a kettle, myself. Still, what do I know, eh? I've never had a baby. Maybe your hormones kick in and you come over all calm and serene and you need to walk about.'

Billie wasn't sure. And as she and Gaynor had never been pregnant either, and she'd never been on the scene for her sisters-in-law's deliveries, they were all whistling in the dark. But it meant that she'd been wrong, and that Claire's baby was being born on time, and that probably before the day was over Jonah would be a father, and she'd really have to forget all about him, even as a friend. There were going to be no halfway measures: she'd work with him on the Flying Circus, but that was it. There was no way she'd ever fall into the Kieran trap again. Married men with families were strictly no-go areas.

'So where's she gone?' Gaynor asked. 'The local hospital?'

Vee shook her head. 'Blessed if I know. They've closed maternity at Amberley Hill General, so she's probably booked into Whiteacres. Do you think we should ring and find out what's happening?'

Billie shrugged. 'I suppose we should. I mean, Jonah will obviously want to know . . . and we could possibly get a message to him in the air over the radio, from air-traffic control, couldn't we?'

'We could give it a try,' Gaynor said. 'Shall I pop across to the control tower and find out? After all, there's not much else either of us can do until Jonah and Barnaby get back, is there?'

Gaynor had taken three days' leave from her secretarial job to practise the wingwalking routines. She and Billie had been climbing in and out of the rigs and synchronising their movements on the two grounded Stearmans in unit six since first light. They were due to try their first dual airborne manoeuvres that afternoon.

Billie sighed. That would be cancelled now, no doubt, while Jonah sat at Claire's bedside, or kneeled beside her birthing pool, or whatever it was they'd opted for, and soothed her brow and held her hand and played her taped Fairport Convention music to ease her through the contractions. She tried really hard not to mind.

'She's a nice girl, isn't she?' Vee said after Gaynor had left the office and was heading across the tarmac towards air-traffic control. 'Are you getting on well?'

'Very,' Billie said. 'Although it seems really

586

strange sharing the flat with her after Miranda. Miranda was just so scuzzy and noisy and well, we talked about everything. Gaynor is much quieter, and she's far neater and more domesticated. She even likes washing up.'

'Christ.' Vee lit another cigarette. 'Chalk and cheese, then. And the wingwalking thing's going well, too, I gather. You know, I still can't get my head round it. Life's a funny bugger. Here we are working together again, well almost, and things have changed so much. I mean, look at you—you've done so well for yourself.'

'So have you. Jonah's a much better boss than Reuben.'

'And a hell of a man.' Vee sucked wistfully on her cork tip. 'That Claire's a lucky baggage. And you know what you were saying before, about it being strange that Jonah didn't make the connection between me and you and bloody Reuben's Cabs? Well, I asked him, and he said he didn't even know that's where I'd worked. He said that Pam had all the dealings with the applications and the CVs and the references for this job. He didn't even know I'd worked for Reuben until I told him.'

'Oh, well that helps a bit.' Billie slid from the desk. At least it meant that Jonah hadn't deliberately not told her that Vee had joined the company. He just wouldn't have known there was a connection between them. Still, what the hell did it matter now? None of it mattered when right at this minute Claire was giving birth to Jonah's baby.

Billie stared out of the window. Things were moving quickly at Whiteacres. Since Aerobatic Archie had backed out of the takeover, and Jonah and Barnaby had been accepted as Incs, the promised expansion was racing ahead. The JCBs were in, digging huge swathes through the grass to produce two new runways, and the Arrivals and Departures lounge and the ramshackle airport terminal were already surrounded by red and white barricades. Towards the end of the year, when things were quieter, the demolition would begin, and by the spring a new, bigger, brighter, shinier Whiteacres Airport would surge from the debris.

By then too Sullivanair would almost be a fleet—she knew Jonah was advertising for pilots—and the flying circus would be a reality, and her warehouse ownership would be almost two years old. And now Miranda was happy with Reuben, and Reuben had left Billie herself alone for ages, and Faith was going to be the next Lynda Lee-Potter, and the Kieran thing was well and truly over.

She took a deep breath. Vee was right. Things had all changed for the better. It was just something she'd have to keep reminding herself of every time she and Jonah were together . . .

'Reuben told me he'd given you glowing references, so have you still got no idea why he sacked you?'

Vee shook her head. 'Not really. I see some of the cabbies in town sometimes, and they just say he said I yakked too much. Which is a bit of a bloody cheek, to be honest. I never spoke out of turn—well, except when it was about you.'

Billie turned round. 'What about me?'

'Well, you know, he was never off your back, was he? I always stuck up for you. Asked him what his problem was. To be honest, at first I thought—like most of the lads—it was because he fancied you, and you always gave him the cold shoulder. Then I realised that it wasn't. He was just sort of watchful . . . like he wanted to control everything you did, you know, like a whatsisname—Svengali? It didn't seem healthy to me, and I said so. I told him more than once that he was turning into a serious weirdo.'

Billie exhaled. 'Brave of you, considering. Thanks, Vee. I used to feel the same myself, actually.'

'Still,' Vee clattered the coffee cups together and switched on the computer, 'you don't have to worry about him any more, do you? That part of your life is all over.'

Billie nodded. She really hoped it was. But she had a nasty feeling it wasn't . . .

'Hey, guess what!' Gaynor threw open the door. 'I actually spoke to Jonah! In the plane!'

Billie tried not to look impressed. Aviation technology was all rocket science to her.

'And?' Vee immediately ignored her screen. 'What did he say?'

'Well, not a lot. They've got the new—er—Shorts, is it? And the Skyvan, and they're flying in convoy. They'll be landing in about half an hour, apparently. Oh, and he seems to think Claire is booked into some private nursing home for the birth.'

Billie wrinkled her nose. 'You mean he doesn't know where?'

'Nope. All he said was he'd come straight up here as soon as they'd landed, and if we heard any more before that could we let him know.'

'Did he sound excited?'

'Couldn't tell. Not really. More sort of crackly.'

The phone trilled through the speculative

silence. They all stared at it for a split second, then Billie, thinking it might be Claire, picked it up. 'Hello? Sullivanair.'

It was the organiser of the Winchester Harvest Carnival. They'd engaged a helicopter display team for their show on the last weekend of September and had just that minute been informed that it was a double booking and they'd have to cancel. Please, please, please could Sullivanair come up with an aerial alternative? They'd heard, on the grapevine, about the wingwalking at the Whiteacres air pageant, and wondered if maybe, just maybe . . .

Billie cupped her hand over the mouthpiece. 'Vee, what's Jonah got in the diary for the last weekend of September?'

Vee flicked through the pages. 'Nothing, why?'

'Good.' She raised her eyebrows at Gaynor. 'Do you reckon we'll be ready to go public in two and half weeks?'

'The flying circus, you mean? No problem.'

'Brilliant.' She uncovered the phone. 'Hello, sorry to keep you. Yes, I'm sure we can help. Sullivanair now have a wingwalking team . . . What? . . . Yes, exactly like the Utterly Butterly Barnstormers. Yes, we're free that weekend . . . What? . . . *How much*? God alive! I mean, of course, yes, that sounds fine . . . Yes, we'll get everything to you in writing,' Billie scribbled down the address. '. . . If you could do the same to the Sullivanair office? . . . Wonderful—yes, we'll see you at the show. Bye!'

She replaced the receiver and grinned. 'Jonah should be chuffed to bits. Winchester Harvest Carnival have hired the flying circus—and they're paying mega bucks! Vee, get it in the diary and send them a letter of confirmation—and while we're waiting for the new Sullivanair planes to arrive, I'll nose round and try to find out where Claire is.'

*   *   *

There was no one in the Sullivanair office when Billie got back to Whiteacres. Vee had stuck her 'gone to lunch' Post-it note on the door, and Billie presumed everyone else had disappeared to admire the new planes. Where Jonah was, was anyone's guess.

Hurrying across the airport's tarmac aprons, not even noticing the roar of the planes overhead, Billie skidded to a halt outside the Sullivanair hangar. Both Shorts and the Skyvan, fully liveried and logoed, were there, still heat-shimmering from their recent exertions, but there was no sign of human life. In spite of the turmoil, Billie looked at the row of three silver, emerald and purple planes with a sense of pride. Well, OK, second-hand pride. They were Jonah's babies, really . . .

Jonah's babies! She exhaled. She had to find him—and quickly.

She jumped into the Nova and drove recklessly along the perimeter fence towards the sheds. Both Stearmans were still outside unit six surrounded by the warehousers, and she could see Gaynor strapped into Lumley's rig, and Vinny and Barnaby on the ground, looking up at her, laughing. She screeched the car to a halt. 'Where's Jonah?'

'Oh, hello, my dear.' Barnaby waved. 'Have you seen the fleet? Watch out Virgin Atlantic, is all I can say!'

'Yes, I have, and they're lovely, but where's

591

Jonah?'

'Trying to find the Middlehurst Nursing Home.' Vinny reluctantly dragged his eyes away from Gaynor. 'Oh, and he's not best pleased with you.'

Jesus! She couldn't imagine why. She hadn't even told him yet. 'Where's the Middlehurst Nursing Home?'

'Haven't got the faintest idea,' Barnaby said. 'Jo said that was all Claire had told him. She obviously hadn't expected to go into labour quite so quickly, so he's gone to seek it out. It's all very exciting, isn't it?'

Billie slammed the Nova into reverse, then wound down the window again and leaned out. 'If he gets in touch, or turns up here or something, can you tell him to ring me on my mobile? Cheers!'

And leaving them gaping after her, she hammered the Nova back towards the airport buildings. Where to go next? Should she look up the Middlehurst Nursing Home in the Yellow Pages? Would they tell her if Jonah was there? And if he wasn't, where else would he be? Home? She knew his address. Maybe he'd gone home to change or telephone or see if Claire had left a message. Well, it was somewhere to start. Billie pushed her foot flat to the floor and tore away from Whiteacres.

Jonah's flat, in a block of symmetrically identical flats, wasn't exactly how she'd imagined it would be. Somehow, she thought that, being a pilot, he'd live in leafy luxury. She couldn't see his car outside either, but perhaps there were parking bays at the back of the building. Taking a deep breath she pressed the door bell.

When he yanked the door open she almost

stumbled inside. She really hadn't expected him to be there.

'Oh—er—I've been looking for you.'

'Really?' Jonah didn't smile. He was still wearing his uniform shirt and trousers and his hair was all spiky like he'd been running his fingers through it over and over again. 'You'd better come in. We need to talk.'

She stepped into a sea of beige. Like the outside of the flats, it didn't go with Jonah at all. 'Yes, we do. Look—'

'Why the hell did you book the flying circus for a display in two weeks' time? You and Gaynor haven't even flown together yet.'

'No, but we've flown separately loads of times, and Gaynor's brilliant, and we've practised the routines for ever on the ground and we're inch-perfect—Jesus, Jonah! Why the hell are we talking about flying? What about Claire?'

'Ah, yes—Claire . . .' Jonah shrugged. 'Well, Claire is probably being well looked after by her Middlehurst midwives as we speak. She left me a note. She says she doesn't want me to be there at the birth, but that she'll ring as soon as it's over.' He gave an ironic smile. 'Sounds about right, actually. She's even diddled me out of pacing up and down outside the delivery suite. So, seeing that I'm redundant in that area, shall we get back to discussing why you took it upon yourself to act on my behalf and book us into a show when we're nowhere near ready?'

'Stop being so bloody pompous! And stop talking about bloody flying! I took the booking because the money was astonishing, and because it'll be great publicity for when we start up properly in the spring, and because I thought you'd be pleased, and because I can't wait until next year to do it again—so there! Now, let me tell you about Claire—'

'Christ! I've told you! She's at the Middlehurst and—'

'No she isn't. She's on her way to Southampton.'

'Southampton? Why the hell does she want to go to a maternity hospital in Southampton?'

'Southampton Airport, Jonah. She's flying to Paris.'

There. She'd said it. She closed her eyes and told him what she'd been able to find out from the rest. The iffy minicab firm, which had picked up Claire at Whiteacres and taken her to Amberley Hill railway station. To catch a train to Southampton from where, she'd told the driver, she'd be flying out to Paris.

'But she's in labour! She'll have the baby on the train—or the plane!'

'I don't think she will,' Billie said gently. 'I'm no expert, but I honestly don't think she'll be having the baby today.'

Jonah ran his fingers through his hair again. 'But why? What's going on? I don't understand.'

Neither did Billie. She'd given him the facts, but she was as confused as he on the abstracts. Jonah shook his head. 'We'll have to get down there—to Southampton—try to stop her. I knew she was acting strangely, but I thought it was just because of the baby.'

Billie didn't like the sound of the 'we'. 'But surely, her flight will have gone by now, won't it?'

'Doubtful. They're not scheduled to fly direct to Paris from there. It's probably a special. I'll ring and find out. Here—' he threw a bunch of keys at

594

her while he was punching out numbers on his mobile—'go and get my car—it's round the back— it'll be quicker than yours.'

Yes, sir! she thought, but decided not to say it. Anyway, she reckoned, even if he intended to do a Schumacher down the M27 he'd never make it to Southampton in time.

By the time she'd driven Jonah's Vauxhall round to the front of the flats, Billie found that he was already waiting on the pavement, impatiently shifting from foot to foot. Yanking the door open, he slid into the passenger seat. 'You drive. We've got three-quarters of an hour.'

'Christ, Jonah, we'll never do it. Not with the traffic and—'

'We'll do it in tons of time. Drive to Whiteacres and we'll grab the Slingsby. We can fly there in fifteen minutes.'

*   *   *

There was only one moment of total terror. It came somewhere between her insisting to Jonah that there was absolutely no need for her to go with him, and the moment that the Slingsby belted along the runway. For the rest of the time she was merely petrified.

Jonah, clamped into his headset and snapping indecipherable messages into his microphone, had strapped her into her tiny seat, said he'd be glad of the company and the Slingsby was a piece of cake after the Stearman, and didn't seem to notice that her teeth were rattling. Apart from knowing that she was going to die, Billie really didn't want to be in on the scene where Jonah begged Claire to come back. There were only so many horrors a girl could cope with in one day.

As the air-traffic controllers gave their clearance, and the lighter-than-air plane skimmed across the tarmac, Billie gripped her seat and stared at the floor. The seat kept slipping away from her and she hoped it was simply because her hands were sweating profusely and not an aviation design fault.

This was nothing like the Stearman. It was nothing like flying in a jumbo to foreign shores, and it was sure as hell nothing like wingwalking. This was appallingly scary.

Billie closed her eyes, clamped her teeth together in case she screamed, felt the ground rush past them, heard the change in power, and knew they were airborne.

'I'll have to keep tuned into Southampton's ATC,' Jonah said tersely as Billie opened one eye and watched as Whiteacres dipped and swayed into miniature beneath them, 'just to let them know that we're coming into land.'

'Already?' Billie felt her spirits rise slightly and opened the other eye. 'Goodness, that was quick.'

'We've only just taken off . . . I mean when we get there.' Jonah fiddled with something unseen on the dashboard. 'But they're going to give us a slot. They owe me a favour or three from way back. You OK?'

No, of course not, you insensitive sod, didn't seem to be the best answer. 'Yes, I think so—oooh!'

They'd banked sharply to the south-west and straightened up just as quickly. Billie felt that her stomach was left somewhere behind just over the A34.

'Fine. We're on the correct heading,' Jonah

596

seemed to relax a bit. 'There—it's great, isn't it?'

Great it certainly wasn't. But once they stayed level, Billie could appreciate that someone without the required amount of brain cells might find it relatively amusing. One advantage was that the Slingsby had a transparent roof which meant she could see the sky and the ground at the same time without the wind ripping her head off and her mouth being filled with insects. Another was that the seat was surprisingly comfortable. And Jonah looked relaxed. He'd surely start to twitch if there was a problem, wouldn't he?

Trying not to even think about Granny Pascoe's negative disaster theory, Billie stared up at the scudding clouds, then down at the shrunken landscape. It wasn't too bad, really. In fact, if someone could just convince her that they weren't going to plummet from the sky, she might actually enjoy it.

'Flying is dead simple,' Jonah shouted some minutes later during a lull in the crackling of the air-traffic controller's instructions. 'Maybe if you understood a bit more about Isaac Newton's third law of motion and Bernoulli's Principle . . . No seriously, that's what makes flight possible. It's just a question of aerodynamics and drag and airflow and the angle of attack. It's like most things— they're never so frightening once you understand how they work.'

'Like spiders, you mean?'

Jonah glanced at her and poked out his tongue. Billie suddenly wanted to grab him and kiss him, and probably would have done if they hadn't been breaking the sound barrier at about twenty million feet.

She stared out of the window instead. 'Yeah, great. Maybe we should have another meal at the Dil Raj and talk about it. The analysis of our phobias and a dissertation on advanced physics. I'm sure Claire wouldn't mind—or maybe she'd like to come along too. I'm positive they could provide a highchair for the baby and mash his tikka masala.'

'Don't, Billie.' Jonah looked at her. 'Don't even joke about it. Oh shit—here we go. Hold tight . . .'

As she hadn't been holding loose, Billie clung onto her seat even more, irrationally annoyed that Southampton had loomed up so quickly—and especially at that enigmatic moment.

Once they'd landed and parked between two KLM giants, and Jonah had pulled all number of avionic-old-pals strings, they hurtled into Southampton's departure lounge. Claire, still visibly pregnant and definitely not in labour, was sitting gazing out of the huge plate glass windows surrounded by a plethora of hand luggage. Billie, unsure whether she should be in on this most intimate of moments, hung back.

Jonah stopped and smiled at her. 'Please come with me. I still need the company, if you don't mind.'

She shrugged and followed him, feeling very *de trop*. Claire looked up. If she was surprised to see them, she certainly didn't show it. She merely gave a resigned smile and patted the seat beside her.

'Sit down, Jo. I was taking the coward's way out, as usual, but I almost hoped you'd come. Oh, hello, Billie. And I thought I'd covered my tracks so well.'

Not well enough for the Pascoe sniffer dogs, Billie thought, and inconsequentially wondered whether this was another talent she'd inherited

598

from her mother.

'You're not having the baby,' Jonah said. 'Well, I mean, not today . . .'

'Not for another two months, Jo, no.' Claire still smiled. 'Which means, of course, that it's not yours. I've been talking to Antony for some time now, and naturally he's delighted that the baby is his. I'm going to join him . . . We're going to be married in Paris.'

Billie couldn't have been more shocked if Claire had stood up and delivered a swift uppercut to the windpipe. Jonah looked equally astounded. There didn't seem to be anything to say.

Claire fluffed up her cloudy hair. 'I know we're finished, Jo. I might have spent a lot of time stoned but I'm not totally stupid. I know you'd fallen out of love with me—at last. When I found out I was pregnant it just seemed ideal . . .'

'Ideal for what?' Jonah sounded as though he'd got a mouth full of gobstoppers. 'Messing up everyone's lives?'

'No!' She shook her head. 'Quite the opposite. I'll always love you, Jo, but you were right: Antony can give me more. So, being selfish, I thought I'd go for it all. You wanted Whiteacres and Antony stood in your way—so, don't you see? Telling both of you that the baby was yours meant that he cleared off to start up his display team—which means I get the travel and the glamour and the excitement—while the way was then clear for you to firm up everything at boring old Whiteacres. So now—' she stood up, easing the small of her back—'we've all got what we wanted, haven't we?'

Billie was speechless, watching as Claire wandered away towards the window, seemingly oblivious to the maelstrom of emotion she'd left behind her.

Claire stared out at the busy runways, watching the takeoffs and landings, then she turned round again, and looked sorrowfully at Jonah. 'It was a risk, of course. But it's paid off. It's amazing, isn't it, Jo? The lengths we'll go to—the horrors we'll put ourselves through—for the people we love?'

chapter forty-six

'And ladies and gentlemen, in half an hour's time, we at Winchester Harvest Carnival are proud to present the one and only–Sullivan's Flying Circus!!!' The Tannoy was loud enough to be heard thirty miles away. 'Yes, Sullivan's Flying Circus—never seen before in this country—with a daring aerial display!!! Death-defying stunts of wingwalking and barnstorming, ladies and gentlemen! Every hour on the hour! First show immediately after the West Minton Brownies' country dance troupe!'

The crowds packing the field cheered and applauded. Billie and Gaynor, who were easing themselves into their costumes in the relative privacy of the cricket pavilion, pulled nervous faces at one another and grinned foolishly.

It had been a very strange couple of weeks.

Billie and Jonah had flown back to Whiteacres from Southampton without speaking. They'd waited with Claire until she'd climbed into her Aurigny Special, bound for Paris and Aerobatic Archie and glamour and motherhood, then retraced their steps to the Slingsby. Billie had wondered whether Jonah would be fit to fly, but she was too rattled to ask him. He'd sighed a lot, but kept a steady course, and Billie had been too wrecked to feel frightened. Neither of them had mentioned Claire or the baby when they'd landed, and Billie had collected the Nova from outside Jonah's flat and driven home and cried.

They hadn't seen much of each other since. She'd gathered from everyone else that Jonah had said Claire had had a false alarm, that the baby wasn't due yet and wasn't his, that she'd returned to Antony, and also gathered that his expression when delivering this bulletin had done away with the need for any further questions. There'd been a fair amount of gossip and speculation privately, of course, and Jonah had been sympathised with while Claire had been regularly and soundly vilified, but now the scandal seemed to have run its course. Only Billie knew the sacrifice Claire had made, and why, and understood. But then, she thought, she was bound too, wasn't she? She'd have done the same thing. She loved Jonah even more than Claire did.

The realisation had come as something of a shock. Great timing, Billie, she'd thought, as always, and wondered if she should volunteer her services to Jerry Springer.

They'd had three flying circus dress rehearsals over the airfield at Whiteacres, and each time, she'd been with Barnaby, and Gaynor had been with Jonah, and everything had gone swimmingly. Jonah seemed resigned, at least, to putting on today's display, even though he'd said on more than one occasion that he still didn't think they were ready to go public.

Billie, who was sure they were, hoped she'd fly with Jonah for the display—like the first time—but secretly wondered what it was going to be like carrying out the precise manoeuvres when they were in a state of such emotional disharmony.

'Stand still.' Isla, who had miraculously produced Gaynor's Sullivanair serpent costume as an exact replica of Billie's, was trying to fasten them into the fluffy undersuits. 'It's like trying to stuff a pair of mushrooms.'

They giggled, but obediently stood still. Ethel and Sylv, Pam and Vee, watched the proceedings with surrogate-motherly eyes, while the rest of the warehousers and Vinny had been relegated to the pavilion's veranda—even though Zia and the Guspers had insisted that filming the dressing wouldn't be voyeurism at all, but an important and integral part of the whole flying circus ethos. Isla had told them they were just smutty and shooed them outside.

'Billie? Can I have a word?' Jonah stuck his head round the door. 'And I've got my eyes shut.'

'Liar,' Billie said. 'Not that it matters, we're both dressed.'

She suddenly wanted to slither out of the skin-tight bodysuit and prance about before Jonah in the scarlet and black underwear that she'd selected for today from Sylvia's collection. Fortunately, it was only a temporary aberration.

She picked up her helmet and the silver gloves and walked outside. Jonah closed the door. He almost smiled. 'You look great.'

'So do you. Very Waldo Pepper.'

Both Jonah and Barnaby had rigged themselves up in genuine Irvin World War Two leather flying

602

jackets for the display. Jonah, Billie felt, looked even more gorgeous than ever—if that was humanly possible.

He scuffed at the scrubby grass where a zillion cricket bats had been hurled down in frustrated disgust outside the pavilion. 'Look, I just wanted to say that I want you to do the first show with Barnaby. It makes more sense for Gaynor to be with me, with this being her inauguration. I've suggested to Barnaby that he flies slightly ahead, so that if Gaynor gets lost on the routines she can follow you.'

'Fine,' Billie nodded, as the West Minton Brownies did a hatchet job on Sir Roger de Coverley in the roped-off arena. 'Jonah, are you OK? You look—well—pretty knackered.'

'I didn't sleep much. But I'm fit to fly if that's what's bothering you. Claire and Antony got married yesterday.'

'Oh God . . .' She moved towards him, then stepped back. 'I mean—I'm really sorry . . .'

'Thanks. And I'd be grateful if you didn't mention it again.'

'Well, no, of course not . . .'

'Good. Oh, and for the first display I want you and Gaynor to be already strapped into the rigs when we take off. We're going to do a low-level flight round the field so that everyone can see you, OK? After that, we'll come in with you both in the cockpits, still low, so that the crowd can watch you get out onto the wing before we climb for the stunts—OK? And we'll leave out the mirror formation on the first stint until I'm sure Gaynor's all right. OK?'

'OK once, twice, thrice.' She smiled to herself. It

sounded quite pilotish. 'We're almost ready to go then, aren't we?'

Jonah nodded. 'About ten minutes. Are you nervous?'

'Petrified.'

'Great.'

He walked away.

*   *   *

Ten minutes later, with 'Something in the Air' blasting from the speakers, strapped into the rigs, Billie and Gaynor looked across at each other, grinned, and gave the thumbs up. Then they braced themselves against the struts as side by side, the Stearmans' propellers swirled and roared, the engines joined in, and the planes bumped towards takeoff.

Again, as soon as they were airborne, Billie felt the rush of adrenaline, the pure pleasure, as practically wing tip to wing tip, the two planes bellowed their cavalry charge across the carnival field. They were low enough for her to see the astonishment on the upturned faces, see the waving hands, feel the whoosh of excitement as they zoomed, still low, swooped, and then started to climb.

As if joined by an invisible thread, she and Gaynor waved, kicked and pirouetted at exactly the same time. 'Eight Miles High' was just audible above the engine noise, as Barnaby and Jonah split apart, circled through the sky and came together again.

Billie, her mouth stretched into the obligatory smile, her arms aching, fought the wind and the

604

prop wash, heard the music change to 'I'm Alive' and went through the routine. She loved it. She damn well loved it. She glanced across at Gaynor . . . Gaynor looked back and gave a thumbs up . . . Barnaby waggled Lumley's wings slightly in a gesture of pleasure. Only Jonah remained impassive.

Sod him, Billie thought. He's not the only one with a broken heart.

It was all over far too quickly. Once again, as soon as they'd landed to tumultuous applause, to be surrounded by running children and excited dogs, Billie couldn't wait to get up there and do it again. Jonah leaped from his cockpit and hugged Gaynor. He didn't hug Billie but gave a double thumbs up. Barnaby hugged Billie a lot—but it wasn't the same.

Gaynor wiped her nose and her eyes and flung her arms round Billie's neck. 'Oh, my God! It's incredible! And we've got another four displays to do this afternoon! Wowee! Oh God—how long does the euphoria last?'

'About ten years,' Billie said, watching Jonah stride away.

As everyone else seemed to want drinks and loos and something to eat, and Billie didn't, she hung around the field for a while trying to come down to earth by watching the tractor-pulling, but got embarrassed by people staring at her in the costume. It was one thing to be an aerobabe high up in the sky, but quite another to be just her and feeling shy at ground level. She decided to cut her losses and go back to the cricket pavilion.

It was very quiet and stuffy and cluttered. She sank down on one of the benches.

'Hello, Billie . . .'

'Jesus Christ!'

She leaped to her feet. If she'd thought her pulse was racing before, it was doing a marathon now. Reuben, looking very serious, emerged from the shadows.

She swallowed. 'I wish to God you'd stop doing this! You lurk everywhere and then creep up on me and—Hell! There's nothing wrong with Miranda, is there?'

'Nothing at all. She's mooching round the bonnie baby competition and getting broody. She'll be over in a minute. I just wanted to talk to you. Alone.'

'Well—as always—I don't want to talk to you. Go away. Please. We've got nothing left to say to each other—except if you ever hurt Miranda, I'll kill you.'

Reuben nodded. 'Yes, I believe you would. And I won't.'

'Good.' She sucked in her breath. 'Did you ask Kieran to open the club just to bug me—because if so, it didn't work.'

'I didn't think it would—I just needed to know—' Reuben's eyes slid away from her.

'I'm very proud of you, Billie.'

'I don't want you to be proud of me! I don't want you to have anything to do with me! Understand?'

'Yes, I do—but I really need to talk to you. No, please, Billie, listen this time. It's important.'

'Crap! You're just here so that you can—'

'Can what? Make my move? Like I've done ever since I first met you? Harass you? Stalk you?'

Reuben shook his head. 'You're way off beam, Billie. Way off. And I do love Miranda. Very much. Surprisingly, as I was never going to allow myself the pleasure of that emotion again, I want her to

606

marry me. We've talked things over and she says I've got to explain everything to you.'

Billie groaned. 'OK, then—but just for Miranda. Go on then—why?'

Reuben yanked his wallet from his back pocket and took out a photograph. 'Look at it. Tell me what you see?'

Billie looked. The girl, tiny, blonde, laughing and about sixteen, looked very familiar. It was like looking at one of her own teenage photographs. She suddenly started to understand . . .

'This is some picture of your ex, isn't it? Someone who had the sense to kick you into touch, and you've held a candle for ever since? You thought I looked like her, so you lived out some sort of substitute relationship through me—just because I have the misfortune to look the same?'

'She's my daughter.'

Billie's mouth, open to hurl more invective, dropped. 'Your *daughter*? You were *married*?'

Reuben shook his head. 'Jessamy was born when I was eighteen. I was still at school, so was her mother, who I loved very much. So much so, in fact, that I swore I'd never allow myself to love anyone else. They moved away before Jessamy was born, but I kept in touch. Oh, not with her mother— that was banned. But I did my bit . . . paying maintenance—even when I was at university— sending cards and presents for her birthday and Christmas. I didn't see Jessamy again until she was ten. Her mother had married, had other children, Jess was asking questions about me. We started meeting for days out, then she'd stay with me for weekends . . . We became very close . . .'

Billie watched the emotions in his face, still not

607

moved. So? She looked like his daughter—so what? Didn't that make the whole harassment thing even more disturbing?

'How much of this does Miranda know?'

'All of it. I told you. I'm going to marry her. I didn't want there to be any secrets.'

Billie shook her head. So, a hefty chunk of Reuben's money was being whisked away by the CSA? So, he'd become bitter and twisted over the years because his teenage lover and his child had been snatched away from him? Well, it was sad, but it was a long time ago. It must have happened to a lot of men. It certainly didn't excuse his behaviour.

'I still don't see why you had to treat me so bloody awfully?'

'Because I wanted to protect you. I recognised Kieran Squires that night. I thought you were younger than you were. You looked so much like Jess . . .' He cleared his throat. 'I couldn't do it for her, so I did it for you instead. Only, I was afraid to be nice, you see? Being nice had lost me Jessamy.'

Billie closed her eyes. A psychiatrist would have a bonanza here. 'I'm glad you're not my father! You can't control your children by power. Not any more. You have to let them go their own way! God, Reuben, is this really what it's about? You wanting to employ me, watch over me, be everywhere I am, so that you could *protect* me?'

Reuben shrugged. 'It was. It's not any more. I'm sorry if I frightened you. I never meant to. I just needed to make sure you were safe, but you don't need me. I know that now. You're strong and independent and successful. You've put the Kieran Squires thing behind you and got on with your life—but I couldn't. It was just that . . . because of

608

the way I felt, I thought I'd been given a second chance . . .' He sighed. 'Sorry, Billie. My intentions were good—my methods were shit. You'll always be OK . . .'

She felt as though a weight had been lifted. She wasn't scared of him any more. She just felt sorry for him. Poor man . . . Still, he'd have babies with Miranda—Jessamy would have little brothers and sisters. Reuben would probably never be the Victorian father with them—and she understood and was free . . . She was really free!

'If I could just add one thing which might make you fully understand.' Reuben reached to take back the photograph. 'Jess was just sixteen when I took this. She'd stopped coming down to see me every weekend because she had a boyfriend at home. He was older . . . and married . . . but I didn't find that out until later.'

He stared at the photo for a long time. 'He went back to his wife. Jessamy was dumped. She pinched her mother's car and tried to find him. She was too young to have a licence, had never driven before. There was an accident—and—and she—she was killed a month after this photo was taken . . .'

Billie froze. Tears welled in her eyes. Jesus . . .

'Oh, Reuben.' She ran across the pavilion and hugged him. 'You poor thing . . . I'm so sorry . . .'

'So am I. I was pretty confused. It all happened only a couple of months before I picked you and Kieran up and I was mad with grief.' Reuben disentangled himself. 'I know now that I must have terrified you. I should have explained . . .'

'Yes, you should. But you'll be happy now, with Miranda.'

'Very. Jess would have adored her. And you

don't hate me?'

Billie smiled gently. 'I've hated you for more than three years. It'll be a hard habit to break, but I'll have a go.'

'Thanks . . . Oh, hello, sweetheart . . .'

'Hiya, dolls!' Miranda breezed through the door and kissed them both. 'Have you finished talking?'

Reuben nodded, swallowed, and with a curt nod, walked out of the pavilion.

Miranda watched him go. 'Did Reuben—I mean, has he—'

'Told me about Jessamy? Yes.'

Miranda stared at Billie. 'I'm sorry I gave you such a hard time about him. I know now what he put you through, but you do understand, don't you? Poor, poor Reuben. We've had so many tears . . .'

'Don't.' Billie sniffed. 'He must have suffered agonies. But you've helped him so much—and now I think congratulations are in order, aren't they?'

'Oooh—yes!' Miranda pulled away and waved a ruby engagement ring under Billie's nose. 'We're getting married on Christmas Eve. You will be bridesmaid, won't you, doll?'

'Try and stop me,' Billie grinned. 'But I still don't promise not to bash Reuben with my holly bouquet.'

*   *   *

Everything was still tumbling round Billie's brain as she scrambled into the cockpit in front of Jonah for the second show of the afternoon. She felt totally drained. She could really do with a lie down in a darkened room and an aromatherapy candle; hurling herself upside down tied to the top of a plane was possibly not the best antidote.

'OK?' Jonah tapped her on the shoulder.

'Fine. Oh, do you want me to check the plane for spiders before we take off?'

'Glad to see you've regained your sense of humour. Er—wasn't that Reuben I saw just now? He wasn't hassling you, was he?'

'Yes it was, and no he wasn't.'

'Good. Let's get on with this then.'

Billie sighed, then fixed her smile as the propeller turned, thumbs-upped to Gaynor, and prepared for takeoff.

She and Gaynor went through the whole routine again, getting from the cockpits to the wings and into the rigs like identical shadows. Barnaby's plane was always just visible from the corner of her eye, mimicking Jonah's moves. With the sun glinting on the silver paintwork, they performed firework patterns through the sky.

The engine note changed as Jonah pushed the Stearman into a climb. Billie leaned back against the rig, flattened by the pressure of the wind. They were going to attempt the mirror formation—and she'd probably die . . .

The sky swooped up in front of her, disappeared over her shoulder, and reappeared beneath her head. Dangling, upside down, she waved both arms as Jonah manoeuvred the Stearman above Barnaby's. They inched downwards, getting closer, until Jonah's inverted plane was hanging in the air, exactly above Lumley. With the blood rushing to her head, Billie could see Gaynor inches below her looking up, as Barnaby moved ever closer beneath them.

She took a deep breath, knowing she only had

a fraction of time, and stretched her hands down towards Gaynor's uplifted ones. And yes—oh, no, not quite. She stretched her aching arms again until she thought they'd be wrenched from their sockets—only a bit more—she had to do it . . . There! They'd made it! They'd touched fingertips!

With a triumphant roar, Jonah swept the Stearman away, righting it, and climbing. Billie, feeling the full effects of the G force, thought her head was about to explode, but it had been worth it. That was the most difficult manoeuvre to perform and they'd done it—together; she and Jonah had achieved what they'd all thought was impossible.

Within seconds they were flying at low level again, as she and Gaynor swivelled into headstands on the rigs and waved to the crowd. Then they were climbing again to 'Yummy Yummy Yummy' and high-kicking and it was almost time to unfasten the harness and climb back into the cockpit, and she didn't want to stop . . .

Billie unbuckled the straps, and felt her way backwards along the wing, swaying with the wind and the prop wash, as high as a kite. It was as addictive as any drug. She lowered herself down into her seat and turned and grinned hugely at Jonah as she fastened her safety belt. She didn't care if her face was all gloopy or if he was sitting there wishing she was Claire. To her surprise, he smiled back at her as he landed the Stearman just behind Barnaby's on the edge of the field, his eyes crinkling.

As the engine died away and the propeller solidified, his voice was warm for the first time in weeks. 'Ace, Billie. You were just ace.'

'Thanks. You weren't too bad yourself.'

They all stood up then, rather shakily, and took their bows. The crowd were still roaring their approval and chanting for more. Billie didn't blame them. She knew exactly how they felt.

Jonah scrambled from the plane first and dropped to the ground. For a second Billie wondered if she might risk a leap into his arms like she had at the pageant, but thought better of it and climbed out, stepping demurely beside him, taking her bow. Beside Lumley, Barnaby and Gaynor, she noticed with amusement, were showing no such restraint.

'Um, Jonah, about Reuben—' she said quietly. 'There's something perhaps you ought to know.'

'Is there?'

'Yeah—it's not what you think . . .'

'No, it probably isn't. Anyway, there's something I should have told you about Claire too.'

They were still bowing. The crowds were still cheering.

Billie cleared her throat. 'Maybe the whole Reuben and Claire issue is a bit too complex to discuss now . . . um, maybe we could add it to the list to discuss at the Dil Raj, along with the advanced physics and the phobias?'

Jonah stopped in mid-triumphal wave and looked down at her. 'Are you asking me out?'

'Yes, well, no—sort of . . . Only if you want to, which you probably don't, of course . . .'

He grinned. 'And to think Estelle said you weren't interested.'

Billie bridled. 'Yes, she told me. And don't get too smug. She had a snide dig at your sexuality too. She said you weren't capable . . .'

'I think we might have to prove her wrong, don't

you?' Jonah suddenly picked her up and swung her round, much to the crowds' delight. 'Like now?'

'My Granny Pascoe always said there was no time like the present.'

'Good for Granny Pascoe,' Jonah nodded. 'A woman after my own heart.'

He kissed her lightly, then not so lightly, and then very thoroughly indeed. Billie's legs buckled more than they ever had from the G force.

'Thanks . . .' he muttered, 'for everything.'

'My pleasure.' She didn't really want to stop the kissing. It was ages since she'd been kissed and never in her life by an expert like Jonah. 'An aerophobe and an arachnophobe . . . it's a hell of a combination—not to mention a bit of a tongue twister . . .'

They repeated the kissing manoeuvre again. It simply got better and better.

The crowd were bearing down on them and she pulled away from him a little. 'Can I just ask you something? Estelle got it dead wrong about me, but was she right about you . . . you know?'

Jonah kissed her again. 'Right at this moment I can assure you that Estelle has never been more wrong about anything in her life.'

'Oh, goody . . .' Billie hurled herself back into his arms, knowing now that her feet would never touch the ground again.